THE GAYNOR WOMEN

Set against the background of Civil
THE GAYNOR WOMEN tells the story of three generations of
tempestuous women, each competing for family power, social
recognition and love.

Varina, the grandmother — a grand lady in the southern
tradition, a proud matriarch lost in memories of grandeur and
guilt.

Maggilee, the mother — whose charm and practised beauty masked
her driving passion.

Ellen, the daughter — struggling to free herself from the
shadow of a dazzling mother, sharing with her an ardent love
for the same man.

All come together in this vivid, passionate tale of family
jealousy, love, and ambition.

Also by Virginia Coffman
MARSANNE
and published by Corgi Books

THE GAYNOR WOMEN

Virginia Coffman

CORGI BOOKS

All of the characters in this book are fictitious, and any resemblance to actual persons, living or dead, is purely coincidental.

THE GAYNOR WOMEN

A CORGI BOOK 0 552 99172 4

Originally published in Great Britain by Souvenir Press Ltd.

PRINTING HISTORY
Souvenir Press edition published 1981
Corgi edition published 1985

Copyright © 1978 by Virginia Coffman

Conditions of sale
1. This book is sold subject to the condition that it shall not, by way of trade *or otherwise*, be lent, re-sold, hired out or otherwise *circulated* in any form of binding or cover other than that in which it is published *and without a similar condition including this condition being imposed on the subsequent purchaser.*
2. This book is sold subject to the Standard Conditions of Sale of Net Books and may not be re-sold in the UK below the net price fixed by the publishers for the book.

This book is set in 12/13 pt Caledonian

Corgi Books are published by Transworld Publishers Ltd., Century House, 61-63 Uxbridge Road, Ealing, London W5 5SA, in Australia by Transworld Publishers (Aust.) Pty. Ltd., 26 Harley Crescent, Condell Park, NSW 2200, and in New Zealand by Transworld Publishers (N.Z.) Ltd., Cnr. Moselle and Waipareira Avenues, Henderson, Auckland.

Made and printed in Great Britain by
The Guernsey Press Co. Ltd., Guernsey, Channel Islands.

PART ONE

CHAPTER

1
* * *

*E*LLEN GAYNOR carefully avoided her reflection in the long pier glass as she carried fifteen yards of Coming-Out finery from her mother's "French Salon" to the shabby alteration room under the roof.

During these late summer days, when the slightest breeze never stirred from Virginia's Eastern Shore to the wooded country around the town of Gaynorville, Ellen always had an irresistible urge to scratch her nose. It was a very nice nose, the only thing about her that she considered artistic, but it did itch in a most annoying way when admirers of her mother brought bouquets of red and gold autumn foliage to decorate the shop at this time of year. Ellen longed to raise the ruffled satin and the tie-back bundle of silk and lining that was the latest descendant of the bustle and simply brush it lightly over the tip of her nose.

Very early in life Ellen had become aware that her mother, petite, red-haired Maggilee Gaynor, was considered the most beautiful female in Tidewater Virginia. At the age of twenty Ellen had learned to live with this fact, including the inevitable comparisons, by developing her own code of conduct:

"Don't try to challenge the unbeatable. Be dignified. What else could a tall girl with straight blonde hair be? Cool and intellectual. (She had tried that, too.) . . . But never let anyone suspect you would have given your soul to look and act like Maggilee Gaynor."

As she started toward the attic stairs, which were carefully camouflaged with elegant gray carpet up to the first landing, she knew she was being watched by two of her mother's customers, Richmond ladies, currently guests at the nearby Wychfield plantation on the Ooscanoto River. They were waiting to enter the fitting room and meanwhile busy mourning the reported demise of the bustle, which had to be removed from several of their still serviceable five-year-old gowns. They stopped talking in order to look Ellen up and down from the shining crown of her hair, severely knotted at the nape of her neck, to the hem of her dress of striped navy-and-white zephyr cloth which followed the lines of her figure in the latest fashion. The style, with its long, tight sleeves and tight basque, was too hot for the day and Ellen knew the two ladies considered her a part of the establishment, like the woodwork, no more. So it was necessary to walk proudly, ignore her itching nose, and behave in a way that would not change their mutually questioning eyebrows from, "Who is that?" to "Some poor relation or other, my dear."

Though Appomattox had taken place twenty years before, even now in 1885 many Virginia households still possessed their share of war widows and orphans taken in through benevolence plus family pride. But Ellen had her own pride and couldn't bear to be mistaken—as she often was—for an orphan taken in by the two Gaynor women. An understandable error, since Ellen was so unlike her mother. Above all, she had grown to the astonishing age of twenty years, still unmarried.

This was not an event Virginians associated with Ellen's grandmother, the elegant Varina Dunmore Gaynor, who had chosen an adoring husband from among a dozen suitors, or her beautiful, widowed daughter-in-law, Maggilee, who had, long ago, won the fickle heart of the Gaynor Plantation heir in spite of her poor-white family. Such women, being widowed, had proved to the world that they *could* catch a man, even if he was now long buried in the Confederate Cemetery outside Gaynorville.

Ellen escaped up the stairs into the attic alterations room where a wizened, peppery black woman, Biddie, once the property of Varina Dunmore Gaynor's family, worked with Ellen, trying to stretch tall, slender gowns to fit short, stout customers.

Biddie's sharp eyes studied Ellen over her steel-rimmed spectacles. "You looking awful, Miss Ellen. What you got there? Another fool ready to come out and sell herself south for a wedding ring?"

Ellen laughed. "Looks like it's still the custom, in spite of you and me." She added, on a sardonic note,

"They just haven't found how single-blessedness can pleasure a woman."

"Truer than you think, Miss Ellen. You make jokes like that, but you're young. You reckon everybody got to do like everybody else. Long time ago, they tried to bed me to that big buck used to hunt with Miss Varina's husband. No, ma'm, says I! I had my eye on the valet at Wychfield. Don't recollect him, do you, honey?"

"No, but I heard about him and how handsome he was. He died with old Mr. Wychfield and my grandfather in the Peninsula campaign."

After twenty years Biddie could take a philosophical view of the tragedy. "At least that no-good Sephora at Wychfield didn't get him. She had her claws out and don't you think she didn't!"

Ellen now finally took time to scratch her nose, then held the coming-out dress up to her figure and posed before the cracked, full-length mirror with its mahogany frame, which had been relegated in disgrace from Maggilee's salon to the attic. The white parchment satin of the gown was heavily trimmed with French lace, in an inverted triangle outlining the square neck, which formed the base of the triangle, descending to a point below the abdomen. The hem and tied-back train were weighted down by ruffles crusted with seed pearls.

Considering the gown enviously, Ellen thought it might be flattering on a girl with a small waist, but it merely called attention to all the worst features of plump, big-boned Bertha-Winn, one of the Wychfield Plantation heiresses. Even Bertha-Winn's mother had tried to talk the girl out of at least the seed pearls, but since poor Bertha-Winn had never gotten a word in edgeways with her mother for eighteen years, she was determined to have her way for once. And Ellen couldn't blame her.

Biddie stopped threading a needle long enough to eye Ellen critically. "You know what you put me in mind of? One of them tall, skinny German Christmas trees loaded down with strung popcorn, like they had at Fairevale Plantation last Christmas. I never saw the like!"

"Thanks," Ellen said stiffly, lowering the gown, the illusion gone.

"And don't you drag it in the dust neither, miss. Nobody's seen that worthless nephew of mine put broom to this floor since Monday."

"Oh, I guess he forgot to tell you. Nahum got a job loading fruit for Cousin Jonathan out at Gaynor Ferry. He'll be there until the strawberry season's over, about another week, I reckon. And maybe longer." The thought of Gaynor Ferry and Second-Cousin Jonathan, a quiet recluse, was always somehow restful to Ellen. It had been the home place of the first Jonathan Gaynor to arrive on Virginia shores in 1680. An old, two-story frame building especially comfortable on hot days, the Ferry house was perched on the bank of a stream so overgrown with greenery at certain times of the year that it was popularly referred to as a swamp. The original "Ferry" which gave it the name had probably been a rowboat. But from this tiny dock area Cousin Jonathan sent downstream most of the fruits and vegetables grown on Gaynor land reclaimed by him since the war.

Ellen took a deep breath, fanned herself with the yards of Bertha-Winn's train and discovered a way to cheer herself up.

"I'll walk out to the Ferry this evening when I'm through here." She felt better. She could already feel the cool water of the stream washing over her toes and hear in her imagination the stuttering call of one particular quail: "Bobwhite! Bobwhite! Bobwhite-white!" and the deep, mournful question of the owls: "Who? Who?" and see the ubiquitous, beautiful red cardinals.

During her childhood, with her mother hard at work making Gaynor's "Salon" pay off, and her grandmother lacking interest in the childish mind, Ellen had turned to Cousin Jonathan when she wanted quiet comfort.

There was one other person she could count on as well, the Gaynors' rich and powerful neighbor across the Ooscanoto River, Colonel Faire. Rowdon Faire had a gift with children. He could keep Ellen enraptured by the hour with his tales of romantic cavaliers and their daring exploits during the late War between the States.

Thanks to such adult companions in her formative years, she had never quite fitted into the mold of other girls her age. She knew that old Biddie disapproved of her upbringing and thought her romantic taste in males highly unrealistic. True to her habit, Biddie scoffed now at the mention of the solitary Jonathan Gaynor.

"Hmph. You tell that Nahum of mine he best hustle back here quick as ever Mister Jonathan finishes with him. Enough to do now, what with this fine sewing, and my eyes giving me no peace. No point him getting all them hermit ideas like you got from Mister Jonathan."

Ellen nodded, though she knew Biddie was proud enough to bust when she thought of how thirteen-year-old Nahum had supported his mother and three small sisters for two years.

With a sharp look at Ellen, Biddie said casually, "Your ma been a-flirtin' with them bank men from Norfolk when they was here about the lend of more money for the fancy goods she's buying from New York. Now she got a letter from one of 'em. Miss Finch at the post office told me. Reckon they took her funnin' for real."

"Biddie, you're a regular old gossip. You'd think

Mama made eyes at every male in Tudor County. It's them that go all silly over her."

"True enough," Biddie grumbled, "but at least your Ma knows a man when she sees one, which is more'n some I know."

Ellen ignored the implication, suspecting Biddie was off on her usual hobbyhorse. Sure enough, the old woman pursued her subject with sly looks at Ellen.

"There's one mighty handsome young buck all the gals in Tudor County make eyes at 'ceptin' you . . . I'm speakin' of the colonel's nephew he brought here to run Fairevale—"

"I don't want to talk about Jem Faire, if you don't mind."

Biddie chuckled. "Kissed you, did he? And about time. He's been here more'n a year. Made a real good thing of all them Fairevale fields. You too high and mighty for a fellow with Injun blood?"

"Too high and mighty for his Irish ways."

"You usually got better manners. I like to of seen just what come between you two."

"I'm glad you didn't see. You'd probably have encouraged him," Ellen told her, coloring slightly at the memory.

Since the day of his arrival from far-off Arizona Territory to oversee the Fairevale Plantation for Colonel Faire, Jem Faire had been a young man impossible to overlook. He was sincerely devoted to his uncle. He paid little attention to the silly, giggling young ladies of the county who found him "so lean and dark and virile," but he had a way of looking at Ellen that wasn't in the least like indifference. He was also the last man in the world to fit the heroes of his uncle's romantic and often humorous stories, which had formed Ellen's picture of the kind of man she would love. He made Ellen think of naked bodies when she wanted to think of soft kisses in the moonlight and cavaliers on noble steeds, like most carefully brought up Southern girls.

He had walked her home from Fairevale several times with perfect propriety, but she was ill-at-ease when he accidentally touched her, and that was hardly his fault, though he brought back all her uneasiness. But she was so accustomed to him by now that when he rode past the shop one hot afternoon a week ago and volunteered to take her home in his wagon full of farm supplies, she was pleased.

Almost immediately, however, they had quarreled over his uncle's convivial drinking, a matter that was strictly the colonel's business, as Ellen informed him. All her life she had seen the gallant veterans of the war drinking as they relived old memories, and it was not for a teetotalling newcomer like Jem Faire to tell him how he should enjoy himself.

Then, in the midst of their heated argument Jem had suddenly taken her chin in his hard thumb and forefinger and announced that he liked to see her fire up.

"You're a female now, and not a plaster saint."

Even while she indignantly demanded in the fashion of all her novel heroines that he let her go, she had been terribly conscious of his glittering almond eyes and his mouth. Thinking of his mouth had disturbed many emotions in her. What would it be like to have her flesh crushed by those full, generous lips? And then it had happened.

Her senses seemed to whirl in darkness. Dignity and common sense were lost under that power he exerted like a devilish spell.

It was not the soft, smooth, romantic encounter a kiss

should be. Women didn't care to feel like this until even after they were married. Otherwise, they would be whispered about like Maggilee Gaynor, of whose reputation she was very much aware.

"He's a savage," she said aloud to Biddie. "What about that knife fight he had with the Corrigan boys last year?"

Biddie bit off a thread from the hem she was working on. "I've heard that was the doing of the Corrigan boys. What with them and Mister Jem all having Irish blood."

But Ellen still resented being made a fool of with that kiss. He only wanted to see if he could arouse her, and he had. It didn't keep him from laughing at her and twisting her wrist till it hurt when she tried to slap him. She suspected that tenderness and gentleness were unknown to him. Dreams of savages were best left dreams.

"Anyway," she remarked in an apparent non sequitur, "there is a passel of difference between that and real, romantic love."

Biddie agreed without conviction. "So they say. I allow he's got an Irish temper like his ma. You never knew Hester Faire, the colonel's sister. Went off to keep house for the colonel down in Arizony-land before the war. That's how she come to mate with that Injun scout. It was a scandal to heaven. But they're both dead now and the boy turned out real well, I will say."

"Like I told you, it's not the Indian in him I object to, it's the Irish."

"I dunno," Biddie said. "There's worse things than wild Irish ways. Take your daddy, a fine Virginia gentleman, but he had a mighty rovin' eye for the ladies. While he was camped before that place where General Lee met the Bluebelly general—"

"Appomattox."

"Yes'm. That place. He went and made a young lady in a farm nearby think he was free to marry her. 'Course, he was awful well-favored, was Mister Beau. You don't favor either of your folks, excepting your pa's height. When you're old, you'll have the spittin' look of your grandma Miss Varina. That's why she so fond of you."

It was the remark Ellen had heard all her life: "You don't favor your parents. A beautiful pair they were."

She pretended not to notice this hurtful truth. She did wonder about her mother's past. There were secrets somewhere. They had always intrigued her.

At quitting time, with the sun low in the sky but the heat still descending on the dusty main street in long, flat layers, Biddie carefully wrapped the unfinished garments in old-fashioned silver paper and laid them on the wide shelves of a mahogany clothespress which had once graced the bedroom of an eighteenth-century Gaynor. Ellen brought out a broom, wrapped the straws in wet flannel, and swept up.

She was finished, except for the dark area under the carved legs of the clothespress, when her mother ran lightly up the attic stairs and caught her bending over to get the broom into the far corners.

Maggilee's young laugh startled her and she straightened up quickly. She never liked to appear awkward in her mother's eyes, but Maggilee only remarked with amusement and envy, "If I had hips like yours, Ellie, I wouldn't have to count the soft-shell crabs I eat, or all those dishes of Cook's strawberry cream."

Ellen's fair complexion, flushed by the heat, turned a little redder at the compliment. As for Biddie, she snorted the truth at all costs.

"Miss Maggilee, you don't need worry. You just let

well enough be. Poor Miss Ellen'll need all the help she can get to look like you and Miss Varina."

Which managed to take the wind out of Ellen's sails.

Maggilee's husky laugh only made her daughter's silence the more noticeable, and Ellen knew it. She managed a wavering smile. She didn't even object when petite, exquisitely curved Maggilee pushed tendrils of curly red hair back from her forehead and, rolling up the tight sleeves of her green batiste dress, took the broom from her as she poked hard into corners, making furious cracks and knocks.

"Honey, you're too thorough. Be a little careless. Don't put your whole life into it."

Biddie said, "Nobody but you can laugh when they sweep floors, Miss Maggilee."

Maggilee brushed this aside. "Never mind. Here's something more important. The pattern books have come and Irene Wychfield and some of the other mothers will be in tomorrow. They'll help us choose the dresses for the young ladies at Bertha's Coming-Out. And Ellie, honey, you're going to be the loveliest creature there. I'll see to it if it kills me. I want you to sweep into Wychfield Hall like all the Gaynors rolled into one. The place will be full and I'm right certain there'll be unattached males, cousins and what-nots from just about all over the South."

Ellen shivered. It was like being put on the slave block, knowing all the time she was mighty poor merchandise in a period when every "beauty" was short and well padded. She often wished she had been born earlier in the century—say, 1812. How she would have worn those high-waisted, straight-skirted Empire styles!

Maggilee gave Ellen's corn-silk hair a brisk, tender stroke.

"We must do something about that. It makes you look years older, Ellie. So severe. Maybe—if we frizzed it up —" She patted the crown of Ellen's head, though Ellen was several inches taller than she and felt like a St. Bernard being patted for good behavior. "Well—" Maggilee gave up the challenge of Ellen's hair temporarily—"we'll think of something . . . Biddie, how is Florine and how are the children? Cousin Jonathan says Nahum is getting to be a right good help."

While Maggilee gave Biddie messages for her sister and four children, Ellen studied her mother. The woman looked scarcely over her daughter's age, with a heart-shaped face and bright blue eyes, which Ellen had inherited in a cooler shade, an enchanting, girlish nose, and as for her mouth, Ellen had heard men describe it often enough. "Kissable" was the unimaginative word they used. She had kept her tiny waist, and the curves above and below were never allowed to get out of control.

"The worst of it is," Ellen had once confessed to Cousin Jonathan, "I do care for her so. I know what she must have gone through after the War, when she was so terribly young and Papa was dead. I was an infant, and she had to support Grandmama as well. It's envy I feel. I wish I could *be* Mama."

And Jonathan had replied in that quiet way of his, "She was taking care of me, too. That'll be Maggilee all over. No wonder Aunt Varina—" He broke off then because he seldom gossiped. Ellen had read in his silence the obvious end of the sentence: ". . . no wonder Aunt Varina hates her."

But was that reason enough for Grandmama Varina to resent so bitterly the very presence of the daughter-in-law who had saved Gaynor House and supported Varina herself for years?

It was a question that lingered as Ellen kissed her mother lightly on the cheek and said, "I'm going out to Cousin Jonathan's for the walk. Tell Cook I won't be home to supper." And her mother stopped gossiping with Biddie just long enough to say distractedly, "Be right careful, honey."

CHAPTER 2

* * *

SUCH WARNINGS as Maggilee's were issued almost unconsciously nowadays, and they always made Ellen think of her childhood. The warning had referred equally to Yankee carpetbaggers, or wandering ex-slaves and Confederate soldiers whose former standards in life no longer existed.

Before leaving Gaynor's shop Ellen stopped to change her shoes in the now deserted Salon, where a single fly buzzed hopelessly among heavy velvet portieres, the lacquered Japanese folding screens, and the red-plush circular banquette in the middle of the room. Ellen took out a picnic basket from the bottom drawer of an elaborate sideboard where the latest in wildly decorated millinery was on display. She changed her elegant shoes for the comfortable black morocco pumps in the picnic basket and pinned a useful wide-brimmed sailor hat on her head to shield her eyes from the blinding light of sunset. The navy straw hat was a far cry from the tiny, beribboned and befeathered bonnets displayed on the sideboard, but there was one thing to be said for an unfashionable woman. She could wear whatever she chose. Ellen walked out of Gaynor's feeling much more cheerful.

The building itself was very like all the other postcolonial frame and brick houses lining the unpaved main street of a town that had seen little change since the Virginia Greys marched off to war in 1861. Gaynor's was a two-and-a-half-story building with a high-pitched roof, weathered and long unpainted like other houses along the street, but if the wood were carefully examined the original oyster-white color might be made out. The front windows and shutters had been removed to make way for elegant show windows in which only one gown, or one (usually heavy) tailored suit was displayed at a time. Sometimes even that was missing. The passerby saw merely long, white kid gloves, a parasol, and perhaps the latest little chapeau that claimed to be from Paris.

There had been, she noticed, an accident in the dusty street. A wagon loaded with produce from the Corrigan farm along East Creek had lost a wheel and was precariously propped, half against the corner of a carriage block and half against the wide shoulder of the Corrigans' old enemy, Jem Faire. While the older Corrigan son gave orders, the younger rolled the wheel back onto its axle.

Ellen stopped with others on the street to watch. It

seemed strange to see this new comradeship between Jem Faire and the Corrigans. If Biddie had seen it, she would be sure to find this a sign of good nature in Colonel Faire's nephew. She *might* be right.

Ellen passed the busy Irish threesome loading fallen corn onto the wagon. She waved to them and the Corrigans grinned and shook corn tassels at her. She was aware that Jem Faire looked up and stopped moving until she passed.

On an impulse she turned and flipped her hand in salute to him. He had a look on his dark, finely chiseled face that made her think he was secretly amused. Or maybe it was only that his eyes smiled while his lips were somber. Impossible to know *what* he was thinking.

Swinging her picnic basket in which she carried odds and ends, including the shoes she wasn't wearing at the moment, Ellen started briskly along Beauford Street, passing several horse-and-buggy rigs bound out of town for home and supper.

Since most of these were tooled by neighbors who would be heading south past the Gaynor house turnoff, she was offered a half-dozen rides, but waved, smiled, and refused all of them with thanks. Gaynor Ferry was off the beaten track, at the end of a narrow old Indian trail. Then, too, Ellen genuinely enjoyed walking. Another eccentricity to the townspeople, but the country folk understood it very well.

As Ellen Gaynor was known to be an independent young thing, capable of giving a rebuff to "fresh" males, the buggies and carriages went rattling off, losing her in a cloud of autumn dust. She coughed, covered her face briefly with a linen handkerchief, and stepped ahead stubbornly beside the wagon ruts.

It was a relief to be wearing skirts three inches above

the grosgrain bows on her pumps. Everyone at Gaynor's had insisted that she would look "common," but Ellen was tired of catching her heels in her skirt hems, and it was easier to be unfashionable than to give up her pleasant, solitary walks.

It was now, at this hour, and alone, that she could picture herself accompanied by one of the young men who had been a part of her growing up but not, unfortunately, a part of her past. Albert Dimster from upcountry beyond the Wychfield place had seemed to her fourteen-year-old heart the handsomest man in Virginia. He was eighteen when he escorted her home from the Ferry one summer evening and reached daringly to the bodice of her white summer dress, arousing an excitement in Ellen as he touched one of her young breasts before gently kissing her trembling mouth. She felt herself respond to his touch but she had enough sense and upbringing to pull away from him as if burned.

And on that night six years ago, who should be standing on the porch, fanning herself with a lacy French fan, but Maggilee? She wore her red hair loosely confined in its old-fashioned but becoming net snood, and she must have appeared to Albert Dimster like a true belle of the Old South waiting for him.

She hadn't scolded Ellen. It was Grandmama Varina, with her rigid sense of decorum, who served as Ellen's disciplinarian, and often her confidante. But all the same, a smiling, amused Maggie had sent Ellen up to bed and told Albert Dimster he must run along home.

An hour later, hearing Maggilee's teasing laughter, Ellen got out of bed and went to the window of her room. She could see the starlight twinkling on the dark waters of the river at the bottom of the lawn, and silhouetted against the silver light were two figures—her dainty mother laughingly repulsing Albert Dimster. Her hair had tumbled out of its confining net and around her shoulders—that was no accident!—but whenever he leaned to kiss her, there was her fan, open between his mouth and hers.

She had sent him away along the river path, still hungry for that kiss. And more . . . ?

It was the first time Ellen wished there were some terrible vengeance she could bring down on her own mother. It wasn't the last time.

For weeks afterward, in great secrecy, Ellen practiced warding off a kiss with a fan. The trouble was, she seemed to succeed all too well, even in front of her own mirror. She couldn't get the knack of fending off while still inviting.

After Albert Dimster went away to William and Mary College and returned three years later with a full beard, Ellen marveled that she could ever have cared two pins whether he cared for Maggilee or not. Besides, when she was nineteen and met a young Yankee law student visiting his mother's school friend Irene Wychfield, she knew this was True Love. The symptoms were all the way the novels described them . . . the nervous pulsebeat in her throat, a tight excitement in her very vitals . . . the actual hunger for his touch . . .

Day after day Gavin would meet her and Maggilee outside Gaynor House in the morning, insist on driving them to town in his own rented buggy with the top down. He was either shy or quiet, but it was obvious he couldn't stay away from the Salon. At six o'clock he often tethered his horse and just waited until the mother and daughter came out after the long work day.

He talked almost as much to her mother as he did to Ellen, but the girl couldn't forget the sweet, intellectual manner that made him different from the coltish young men of Tudor County growing up spoiled by mothers who had lost all their well-loved males in the War.

He started taking Ellen's hand when he met her alone, though he seemed shy with her and often talked about other subjects, like the War, her father, of whom she knew nothing but legend and gossip, and Maggilee, a subject which never was exhausted, since Maggilee was an inexhaustible person.

Ellen began to feel more than a physical attraction. He read so much. He was going to be a real lawyer in the city. Richmond. Or even Washington. How *smart* he must be!

Then he talked about marriage. Curiously enough, he harped on his age, assuring Ellen he was very old for his years. Then he would sit silent, staring into space, as if he expected Ellen to disagree with him, which was nonsense. After all, he was her senior by several years. While she was thinking this, he would say to her suddenly, "You understand me so well, dear Miss Ellen. Your silent encouragement . . . it tells me how much you understand."

What a thrill that was! This intelligent man considered her not only desirable but "understanding."

And so it came close to an engagement in the minds of many. The Gaynor women daily expected his proposal. So much so that Varina Dunmore Gaynor invited him to a formal dinner at Gaynor House.

The awful thing about the dinner was that Ellen never knew exactly what happened. After being given the invitation and impressed by Irene Wychfield on the honor of dining with the Gaynor ladies, he had confided to Ellen, squeezing her hands and looking soulfully into her eyes, "I've been longing to speak to your dear mother. You may imagine why."

If he had demanded that she shock all her ancestors and herself by giving her body to him that very night, she would have done so with only a little hesitation—and that last for modesty's sake only. She hungered for romantic love, and he was, in every way, a gentleman. Right out of her grandmother's old novels.

The dinner had seemed to be a success. Grandmama was her most elegant and fascinating self, praising Ellen tactfully, but relating funny incidents in the life of the family, and providing the kind of awesome entertainment Queen Victoria might provide if the Queen used her sense of humor and were not so eternally "widowed." Everyone said that when she put her mind to it, Varina Dunmore Gaynor could be the most delightful hostess in the county. She had put her mind to it that night.

And then, afterward, Gavin had left the house without even a goodbye to Ellen.

"I reckon I scared him off," Ellen had surmised as she blinked back the burning tears, for she allowed no one but Grandmama Varina to see her cry.

Varina's delicate-boned fingers tightened over Ellen's wrist. Ellen looked up, startled out of her misery, never having seen her so coldly furious. "No, child. *You* had nothing to do with it. The Yankee trash wanted to marry your precious *mother.*"

The shock of this silenced Ellen briefly. Too late, she saw that all the signs had pointed to the truth and she had been blinded by her own conceit.

But no more. Never again.

"I hate Mama! I hate her more than the devil!" she had muttered, hammering with her fists on Varina's little hundred-year-old candlestand . . .

Gradually, this hatred had tended to burn itself out,

and she had set the blame where, she decided, it belonged —with her own lack of petite charm.

If I never love again, I can never be hurt again, she reasoned when she was feeling depressed. By the time she was twenty there were no more hurts. She didn't count the impulsive kiss Jem Faire had forced on her. Nor did she forget her body's betrayal of her by its desire during that kiss.

But time had made it impossible for men like Gavin McCrae to hurt her again ... Last year at White Sulphur Springs the elder Wychfield girl, now grown up, had met Gavin, and from the stories that came back he fell in love with the very child whose pigtails he had formerly pulled. After a whirlwind courtship of four months, Gavin McCrae and Daisy Wychfield were married. He hadn't won Maggilee, so he had taken second best. As for Ellen herself, apparently she hadn't even been in the running! She could afford to laugh now. She considered herself immune, beyond hurt ...

Just as Ellen reached the low wooden fence of the local Confederate Cemetery, full of her thoughts, a soldier on horseback approached from behind her, rode past and looked down at her. His cavalry hat concealed his eyes and his blue uniform was still unwelcome in most of Virginia, but she wondered what he had noticed about her that made him look back, even after he had gone twenty feet ahead. She saw his mouth curve into an easy grin. She also saw that he had good teeth, and sat a horse well. Not like a Virginian, of course, but undeniably with the ease of a man very sure of himself.

She pretended an interest in the cemetery. The rider was soon out of sight. Immediately, she lost interest in the cemetery whose stones with their lofty sentiments were decorated all year with whatever blooms or leaves or jars of ivy could be obtained. Though the sight was touching, it sometimes seemed to her that the ladies of Gaynorville had personally fought the War only yesterday.

The cemetery was bordered on the south by a heavy stand of maples, now in all their scarlet glory. Along the road further south, browned and dead tobacco fields sweltered in the heat, but where the maples thinned out in a westerly direction they gradually became choked with elms, willows, dogwood and heavy undergrowth. One branch of Dunmore Creek ran through this swampy area, twisting and turning until it started north through the still fallow fields of the old Gaynor Plantation, to empty into the distant James River.

The cavalry officer must, she thought, be headed south toward the tobacco farms... What was he doing in this quiet section of the state, and what difference did it make anyway, except that soldiers usually visited these little "rebel pockets" in civilian dress? It was considered good manners. The sight of a Bluecoat still gave many old ladies the palpitations. Only those men who had fought the Bluecoats seemed to take them for granted...

The minute Ellen stepped off the road and onto the Indian trail leading to the Ferry, moist, cool air began to play around her body. The unpleasant moments of the day vanished. She almost forgot that very soon she would be expected to "descend" the Wychfield great staircase and out-bloom the young bride.

Ahead of her, dust rose from the path and seemed to linger in the sunset's afterglow, floating in midair. Someone else was on the Ferry path. She had very little fear of personal danger in this quiet county off the main highways between Richmond, Norfolk and the Carolinas. When she saw the clear, recent print of a horseshoe in the dust, she raised the brim of her hat and tried to see far ahead through the foliage which now enclosed the trail, tendrils of ivy and other parasites even twining to form a green roof overhead.

Something of the emotions she had deliberately killed by starving them, stirred now. Wouldn't it be an amusing coincidence if the cavalry officer who had smiled at her on the road should be riding ahead of her now to visit Gaynor Ferry?

Better not let him see Mother, she thought with wry amusement, and was startled at how the thought rankled like a sharp needle.

After all, it was only a joke.

CHAPTER 3

***

*F*ROM A side window Maggilee watched Biddie bustling down Church Street with the help of a gnarled cane that had been left to her in his will by Varina Gaynor's husband, who claimed that Biddie had made him the man he was. Maggilee straightened her shoulders. The ache between her shoulder-blades eased a little. Another day done. At least she had shown those Richmond ladies that Gaynorville too could create Paris fashions.

Another night alone at home in that big, half-empty monument to Dunmore and Gaynor pride.

"Alone," she corrected herself with the laugh that habit had made easy, "unless you count darling Varina. What's life without at least one mortal enemy? Damn her arrogant pride . . . What a cold, heartless bitch . . ."

I shouldn't have said that, she thought . . . more of my common background. How she would love to hear me say it to her face!

The thought of such an unlikely event was so funny it made her forget the long day. She knew very well that with people like Varina, male or female, you must never reveal enough of your true self to put you in their power.

She took her usual last-minute inspection tour of the street floor, the main salon, the fitting room, the rich, heavy, overwhelming furniture, touching each piece with gentle fingers. All these possessions, accumulated by her own hard work, were talismans when she remembered she had to go home to Gaynor House and an empty bed.

Sometimes in the night she would struggle awake after dreaming of the days and nights of love so long ago. She thought of them as her nightmares. To dream of those painful joys made the present less endurable. A year or so ago a new bolt of broadcloth arrived at the shop and Ellen and the salesladies called it "Navy Blue." But the sight of it was like a knife-sharp pain. Maggilee pretended to admire it and let the others decide what was to be done with it, while Maggilee went to the outhouse in the little back yard and sobbed.

Why? she asked herself later.

It was all so long ago . . .

"Will I really be forty in a year or two? Poor Ellen. She seems to grow more like Varina every year. When I was twenty I had a daughter three years old, a great house complete with a mother-in-law, and I was saving bits of my salary from Hofer's Emporium to help buy this place. I must do something about Ellen. If she only had more confidence and fixed herself up, I know she could 'take' with men. A flirtation might do wonders for her . . ."

She bolted the front door, turned down the gas jet in the inside fitting room, and sent the general clean-up man home to his family in the "colored" district at the north end of town. Then she left by the back door. The stableboy connected with Gaynorville's Hay, Grain and Feed Store had her buggy and the tranquil mare ready.

She had just pulled out into narrow Church Street when a cavalry horse, apparently tearing along from nowhere, was reined in so suddenly by his rider that the horse reared briefly on hind legs above the buggy.

The horse had startled Maggilee but she recognized the skill of the rider. It was not until she caught a glimpse of his cavalry uniform that she abruptly had a sense of times long dead, of history repeating itself. But the man was a stranger, good-looking in a road-weary way, and from his grin and easy apology, a man who instinctively knew his way about women.

"Sorry, ma'm. I hope I didn't scare you."

His grin was contagious but she was still shaken by that first sight of his uniform, the fleeting resemblance, the tall, muscular build . . . She blamed an innocent stranger for the memory he evoked . . .

"Captain, unless you mean to ride through the Cemetery path you won't get anywhere in this direction. Go back upstreet and you'll see the spire of the Community Church. That wide street is the one you want. It will take you south beyond town. Without more damage, I hope."

He put two fingers to his hat in salute, thanked her, and signaling his horse, followed her directions. His grin had faded.

Calming her patient mare with soft words and sounds, Maggilee looked around the side of the buggy. She saw a flash of the blue uniform, the tilt of the cavalry hat before he and his nervous mount disappeared into Church Street.

Belatedly, she smiled. The stableboy, crossing the street with his long day's work ended, caught her smile and blinked, his ruddy, sunburned face turning even redder with pleasure. He stammered something she took to be a "good evening" and she rode away, past the second of Gaynorville's two churches and over the cemetery path which was a shortcut to the Gaynor estate road.

The mare jogged along the dusty road Maggilee had traveled for twenty years. Almost a quarter of a century? She wondered at the way the years had piled up. It seemed like yesterday since she had been driven here for the first time as a bride and the mistress of Gaynor. (Was Varina expected to be the Old Mistress? If so, the men of her family knew her very little.)

The Favrols were the lower-middle-class product of a French trapper who sold off his furs in New Orleans and remained there to marry a dashing madam in the French Quarter. The Favrols, like their ancestors, were people on the move. Maggilee's father had come to a halt in Portsmouth, Virginia, where he had married a despised female abolitionist who happened to be red-haired and pretty. Maggilee was the product of this reasonably happy union.

It was wartime. The Union Army was nearby on the Peninsula. It had seemed highly romantic to a fifteen-year-old girl whose family had eked a meager living from a small notions store. With her mother long dead and her father dead of dysentery after the Second Battle of Manassas, Maggilee Favrol had found the imminence of danger added to the excitement of the wedding, and its consummation.

Her handsome husband of little more than eighteen months, Beauford Dunmore Gaynor, whom everyone called "Beau," died on Appomattox Ridge five days before the Armistice.

Adored and desired by every girl he met, he had been teased and tantalized into marrying the one beauty he couldn't have without marriage. But once he had won Maggilee and seen her in his stately old home, she somehow ceased to be so valuable to him. She became, in fact, just another trophy in his endless series of conquests. Worst of all, five months after the marriage, on one of his infrequent leaves, she became pregnant with Ellen. He didn't see himself, the dashing Beau Gaynor, as a father. It was the end of any passion he might have felt for his bride.

Four months before the War's end, Ellen was born, but the father, Beau Gaynor, was busy seducing a young lady of good family in northern Virginia. Then, five days before peace came, he was killed on Appomattox Ridge, and buried near McLean, Virginia, by his new love, who, as it turned out, was not aware of his not quite seventeen-year-old wife, and Ellen, his four-month-old daughter. His funeral had been a most uncomfortable meeting for both Maggilee and the broken-hearted young lady in question . . .

Riding home through the warm dusk with its scent of late roses in the air, Maggilee tried hard to remember Beau Gaynor's good qualities, at least his dash and appeal, but they were a blur. Ellen, though, had inherited his height, a certain elegance, and his corn-silk blond hair

... Sometimes Maggilee found herself trying to forget that resemblance to an unfaithful and not very endearing husband. It did seem a shame though that Ellen couldn't develop a little of Beau Gaynor's *charm* with the opposite sex. It would certainly help the girl. Unfortunately, she seemed determined to avoid the slightest hint of a flirtation, and most southern boys still liked nothing better than that happy combination of a flirt and a lady ...

Much of the old Gaynor plantation had lain fallow ever since the War, and the land along East Dunmore Creek was now permanently settled in small parcels by hard-working families who had either lost their properties since the War, or come down from the North looking for farmland. There were some failures but most of them had done well enough to join Cousin Jonathan's fruit and vegetable shipping, as his flat-boats wended down through the swampy waters and then northward along East Creek to the powerful James River.

Mrs. Corrigan, wife of one of the most successful small-farm growers from out of state, bustled off her porch to the road, holding up her apron with its lapful of half-shelled butter beans.

"Evenin', Miss Maggilee. Reckon all the folks at Wychfield pretty excited about Bertha's entry into society, as the saying is. I hear tell all the young ladies bein' dressed by Gaynor's Salon. That true?"

"It certainly is. My, what nice beans you've grown this year!"

Mrs. Corrigan agreed, running her free hand through them. "They'd ought to fetch up a fair price. I guess you heard my Amabel's been invited to the ball. That's quite an honor. But then, Bertha-Winn and Amabel was practically raised together, playing all over the lawns at Wychfield. They even went to socials and Daisy Wychfield's cotillion together, I rec'lect, though Bertha wasn't out yet. We're pretty anxious to see what color dress Amabel's to wear. And the price, and all. Nothin' but the best for our Amabel, Mr. Corrigan says."

Maggilee assured her more happily than she felt, "All the dresses are to be coordinated. The girls who have already come out will wear pastels. Anything Amabel wears will be lovely, she's so pretty . . ."

"Prettiest blonde in the county. Ever'one agrees," Mrs. Corrigan said complacently. It was obvious she didn't consider Maggilee's own blonde daughter Ellen any competition. "Amabel is mighty partial to pink. Always was her color. Real bright pink, you know."

"I'm sure Mrs. Wychfield will take that into consideration. She is coming in tomorrow to choose the styles and materials. The young ladies will be asked to come soon after, for fittings and so forth."

"Well, my Amabel will be there on the dot . . . Think this heat's going to hold up?"

"I certainly hope not. But then—" Maggie laughed. "Think of these roads when the wet weather comes. Good day, Mrs. Corrigan."

"'Day, ma'm. My best respects to Miss Varina."

Maggilee nodded, waved goodbye with the reins and drove on, wondering how her own slim, blonde daughter could outshine the plump and beauteous Amabel with her deluge of curls framing her round, so self-satisfied face . . .

Riding up to Gaynor House would never be like the approach to Mount Vernon or Carter's Grove, or other distinguished river-view plantation houses. The three-story frame house had pillars added much later to give it the required Greek Revival look. These were much too narrow, and from the long side facing the road one always got the feeling that they would never hold up the porch roof.

On the river side, with the beautiful green view of the swift-flowing Ooscanoto River, no one paid any attention to the pillars except Maggilee, who had found them an excellent theatrical prop when she wanted to look the picturesque Southern Lady. For instance, when she wanted to take out a second mortgage on Gaynor's Salon in order to redecorate the fitting rooms, and import a delightful light "zephyr" cloth for the New Women who took up tennis, croquet and the bicycle, Maggilee invited her favorite Richmond banker down to visit Gaynor House and managed to greet him beside those pillars, looking as nearly antebellum as the styles of the mid-1880's would permit.

What bankers and casual visitors need not know was that half of the house was a mere collection of broken furniture, trunks and oddments that normally would have been found in attics. The servants had their rooms on the third floor, and Edward Hone, the butler, paid for and furnished his own quarters so elegantly they put to shame Maggilee's and Ellen's rooms. There never was enough ready money to outfit the entire house or even some of the rooms on the second floor . . . As Ellen remarked perceptively on her fourteenth birthday, "Our house has empty holes, like the place in my mouth where my baby tooth was."

Grandmother Varina always saw to it that the best furniture was displayed in those rooms open to visitors. It was a little fiction accepted and practiced by most of the great ladies in this small, select area of the world.

Edward Hone, who ran the Gaynor household, overseeing the cook, maids and stablehands, met Maggilee now as she came in from the stable. He was one of the few in the house whose loyalty went to Maggilee rather than to her mother-in-law, Varina. The butler had been born free and in spite of his position at Gaynor House he, along with Maggilee, was considered a social inferior by the Gaynor ex-slaves who remained.

"Colonel Faire's come calling on Miss Varina. So he says. But he winked at me when he came. Wanted to know when you and Miss Ellen'd be along, Miss Maggi."

"Oh, Lord!" She had hungered for a man, but not jolly, hard-drinking Colonel Rowdon Faire. Lately he had been using all his Irish charm in pathetic attempts to get Varina and Ellen to accept his wild, halfbreed nephew, Jem Faire. Unfortunately, Colonel Faire tried too hard with them. As for Maggilee, she had found the young man civil and almost polite. But Maggilee made no deliberate and obvious effort to like anyone. She said to Edward Hone, "I don't know what I can do about it. The trouble is, the colonel's a well-meaning fellow, and he tells wonderful Irish stories. I'll try and listen to them"—she yawned and added with a smile—"but I'm afraid I'm likely to fall asleep in the middle of his best one."

"Not you, Miss Maggilee. Not you."

She saw the tall, stately figure of Varina and bulky Colonel Faire on the river-front porch admiring the sunset as it fell behind the great Faire acres across the river, and tried to sneak up the white staircase in the entrance hall to her bedroom. But Varina, who was quite capable of hearing a cat stalk a mouse, called through the open porch doors without looking around,

"Maggilee, you are late. We have company. I told Cook to delay supper until you arrived."

Maggilee thanked her, hailed the colonel with a friendly wave and her best smile before going up to change.

Twenty minutes later, running down the stairs as lightly as she had when she was a girl, Maggilee was challenged by her mother-in-law at the fan-shaped foot of the stairs.

"Where is my granddaughter? Isn't Ellen coming down to supper?"

Maggilee stopped abruptly. It occurred to her with the force of a slap that it was remarkably easy to forget she had a daughter.

CHAPTER 4

***

SEEING THE little frame house around a bend in the creek, Ellen thought at first that she had been mistaken about the man on horseback. There were several side-paths meandering out of the area into open fields and the farms of what used to be called "poor whites." Probably he never intended to visit Cousin Jonathan and simply took the Ferry trail by mistake. She was surprised at her own disappointment. His unexpected appearance had been intriguing.

Jonathan's simple, two-story house was entirely surrounded by screened porches, one of which had been built over the stream. The recluse often let down a line from a hole in the screen and managed to catch his fish dinner while he worked further upriver, loading fresh produce. Much of his own food remained refrigerated in the cool stream until he waded in and took it up; occasionally he hauled in a catfish. He was fond of all non-talking creatures . . . Ellen had long since noted that he never caught a fish, shot a squirrel or brought down a duck unless he needed it for a meal.

Reaching the south side of the house, she heard a horse whinny. With a disturbing sense of excitement she realized the horseman was with Jonathan and had apparently stabled his horse on the far side of the house, near the root cellar. She stopped to brush dust off her pumps and her skirts, wishing she had worn something a little prettier, more frilly, but in spite of the tight, form-fitting basque which she knew was too high in the neck, all of the skirt's fullness was gathered in the back, outlining her abdomen and torso rather daringly in front.

She remembered her mother's plaintive remarks about her hair. The swift walk had already loosened tendrils of hair over her smooth, broad forehead and she tried vainly to push them up out of sight.

"I *never* looked more sloppy," she thought, and then in a gesture very like her mother's, she straightened her shoulders and walked up to open the screen door which was never locked, calling out in the silence of early evening, "Cousin Jonathan? It's Ellen. May I come in?"

She heard a sound in the dark, comfortable little parlor beyond the never-used dining room. A crack, like a rocking chair. Or a glass—yes. A glass set down sharply on a wooden surface. The two men must be enjoying a drink of bourbon together. They would hardly welcome her if they were. She turned uncertainly, thinking of the long, hungry walk home, even by the river path. Before she could open the screen door again the cavalry officer strolled into the dining room, which was full of crates, barrels and boxes, all of which Jonathan used for shipping his produce.

"Good evening, ma'm." He was bareheaded. His coppery brown hair with a sprinkling of gray softened the hard, wind-and-sunburned face. His accent was different. From the West somewhere . . .?

"Well, this is nice. Come in, come in."

He held out his hand, a good host welcoming a guest. Bewildered, she accepted the handclasp, but began to think in spite of his attractions that he had considerable nerve.

"Where on earth is Cousin Jonathan?"

"The tenant? I'm damned if I—sorry. I haven't found him yet, but from the look of things here in the house he's due back any time. He left a lot of green spinach or something on the sink in the kitchen. It's still fresh."

"Collards," she explained automatically, withdrawing her hand, still astounded by his use of the world "tenant" to describe the last male descendant of the land's original white owner. In spite of her indignation she was amused as he repeated vaguely, "Collards? I thought the fellow's name was Gaynor."

She suppressed a quick smile. "The *greens* in the kitchen are collards. Now then, sir, suppose you tell me why you are making yourself at home in my cousin's house. And I give you my word it *is* Jonathan's house." She was beginning to feel nervous, wondering what she would do if this extraordinarily insolent intruder became angry, or violent . . .

He laughed too easily. "Ever hear of a royal flush?

Happened in Deadwood. Out in the Dakotas. It won me this place. But come on in. I've an idea your precious Cousin Jonathan has been kidding you. I don't like to spoil his little joke, but I won this place fair and square from the real owner. So, you see?"

"The—real—owner." She repeated it in a daze and let him lead her into the parlor where he evidently thought she might be faint and offered her two fingers of bourbon. She brushed it aside. "Is this Jonathan's bourbon too?"

He looked at the rejected drink, poured it into his own glass and grinned. "My own liquor, ma'm. You have my word on it."

"Whose word may that be?" He couldn't miss the acid in her voice, though it didn't seem to bother him. He kept looking her over almost as if he liked what he saw. His unsubtle interest embarrassed her and she hardly knew where to look to avoid his bold-eyed survey. He took a drink without glancing at his glass and motioned her to sit down on the old sofa where Jonathan often slept. Straddling a chair and leaning on its back, he continued to observe her.

"Suppose we make a deal. I'll tell you my name and you tell me yours. Here I am having drinks with a pretty girl and I don't even know who she is, except that she has a Cousin Jonathan who's been filling her with tall stories, I'm afraid."

Her cheeks flamed. "He has not—I'm not—who *cares* who you are? You've got a passel of nerve, but I expect you come by it honestly, you being a Yankee and all—"

He put back his head and laughed. He was watching her mouth. He seemed to like it. Self-consciously, she raised her hand, put a finger over her lips.

Finally he said, "Until my time was up I was Captain

William Sholto. Seventh Cavalry. Ever hear of it?"

"They fight Indians," she ventured, thinking that such a dangerous occupation might explain his insanity about Jonathan's house.

"They *fought* Indians," he said dryly. "We lost most of the outfit with Custer at the Little Big Horn about a dozen years ago. Luckily, I was with Major Reno's outfit at the time. Anyway, it's all over now. I've come home to my very own house to settle down and grow watermelons and strawberry jam, and—"

"You don't grow strawberry jam. You put it up."

"Put it up where?" He looked around as if he expected to see jars hanging from the rafters overhead among the cobwebs, and now she was the one to laugh.

He really was a rather likeable rogue, but nothing could be more absurd than his claims on this house and ground. Burnt and rebuilt twice in the last two hundred years, it had escaped the ravages at the end of the War when Gaynor House, upriver in what had been rich farm country, was used by the Occupation forces, and the Gaynor women moved into the Ferry house for safety and privacy.

This was the house a perfect stranger from the wild West calmly walked in and claimed.

"You haven't told me your name, ma'm. You're obviously going to be my nearest neighbor and I can't go around saying, 'Hello there, Jonathan's Cousin.' "

"He is my mother's cousin, my second cousin, actually." Now why did she start this small talk? As though it mattered! If he kept on like this, he'd find himself in the county jail where—she was reasonably sure—his nearest neighbor would not be a Gaynor. However, she reminded herself that she really should keep the good manners expected of a lady.

"I'm Ellen Gaynor. Now, Captain, as I understand it, you played a card game—"

"Poker."

"Yes. Well. And someone gave you a deed to Cousin Jonathan's property. It was a fraud." She doubted very much that he had anything in the way of legal papers. Where would he get them? Except how had he found out about Gaynor Ferry?

"Do you know, you have the prettiest complexion I've seen in years. Like china. Porcelain. That thin, fragile kind you can see the light through."

She tried not to let him see that she was rapidly being disarmed. "Don't be silly. This is a very serious matter. A total stranger moving in with us as if—"

"I wouldn't mind moving in with you. Not a bit."

She caught her breath. "Of all the impudence!"

Just the same, she didn't know whether to be relieved or disappointed when she heard the screen door screech open and close as Jonathan Gaynor came into his house.

She tried to raise her voice, started to say, "It's Ellen. I'm in the parlor," but for some reason, her voice went off-key and she had to clear her throat while this stranger, who called himself Captain Sholto, grinned at her. She had a horrid feeling that he guessed why her voice behaved so oddly.

Meanwhile, Jonathan came into the parlor from the kitchen. Anxious, hoping it wouldn't come to blows, Ellen stood up. Captain Sholto got to his feet more slowly, swinging one booted foot over the worn petit-point cushion of the chair. Ellen noted that he didn't offer his hand. He must have recognized that the man who entered the room now was his real antagonist, and he was unquestionably surprised by the sight of him.

Ellen's Cousin Jonathan was a man slightly above six-feet-two, lean, hard-boned, with a face that did bear a resemblance to a clean-shaven Abe Lincoln, with curiously sad eyes, a tender, melancholy mouth, and a bony, prominent nose. He was thirty-eight but looked older. He had one of those faces that would look thirty-eight ten years from now. He sometimes put Ellen in mind of a granite cliff. That cliff never looked young. It would never look old.

" 'Evening, Ellen." He smiled, held out a hand to her and motioned her to sit down again. Then he glanced at Captain Sholto. " 'Evening, sir. I take it you're a friend of Cousin Ellen. Staying to supper, of course."

Frigidly, Ellen contradicted. "He's no friend of mine." She was amused to see how impressed the cavalry man was by the look of the man he had thought was a tenant farmer and a liar to boot. Jonathan had the look of a farmer, possibly a tenant, but no one could look into his gray eyes and believe him a liar.

"Beg pardon?" Jonathan looked from Ellen to the captain with eyebrows raised. Few, except Ellen, who knew him well, would have guessed that he was now very much on guard. His long arms still seemed to dangle from his slightly hunched shoulders but his fingers had curled inward, into the palms of his powerful hands.

Captain Sholto had looked him over and was frowning, though not at Jonathan to whom he offered his hand. "Captain William Sholto, sir."

"Jonathan Gaynor. Cavalry?"

"Free man now. I had a piece of good luck—" He hesitated, gave Ellen a twisted little smile, amended, "—what I thought was good luck—over a poker table in Deadwood in the Dakotas; so I thought I'd just mosey on down here, take possession and become a respectable farmer—"

"Jonathan, he seems to think he owns Gaynor Ferry," Ellen put in, wondering at her own childish hurry to put down the captain's game.

While the captain unbuttoned his tunic and reached in to take out a couple of folded papers which looked water- or whiskey-stained, Jonathan considered this startling idea. He said slowly, without any sign of humor, "No, sir. Gaynor Ferry's rightly ours."

Ellen thought it both insulting to her and a tribute to Jonathan that Captain Sholto seemed much less sure of his rights now that Jonathan had arrived.

"Well, here is the deed. Made over to me by the Reverend himself. Here's where it was certified in Deadwood. If you'll look it over . . ." As Jonathan took the paper between forefinger and middle finger, the captain, obviously suspecting he was illiterate, started to explain, "You'll notice the Reverend gives all the dimensions and specifically names the Ferry House on Dunmore Creek as well as the survey of farmlands south of the creek."

"So I see," Jonathan agreed mildly.

Ellen interrupted with indignation. "He can read, you know. Jonathan reads a whole book every night."

"Nigh every night," Jonathan corrected her, for the first time showing signs of amusement. He gave the stained papers back to the captain, who accepted them with what amounted to reluctance. He had clearly hoped for a stronger reaction.

"The judge in Deadwood told me it was legal."

Jonathan nodded. "You know this minister, this Reverend?"

"Everybody in Deadwood seemed to." But for the first time the captain began to look a little nonplussed. "Called himself a circuit rider. He rode about on a mule spreading the Good Word. Of course, he didn't get far out of town. He wouldn't have had much luck converting the Oglalas or the Lakotas. Nice, meek sort of fellow. Didn't look as if he'd dare to renege on a bet." He took a deep breath, studied the deed in his hand and added one last effort. "As you can see, the turnover of Gaynor Ferry was recorded with a local judge in Deadwood."

"Who is this Reverend?" Ellen asked finally, beginning to see the ridiculous aspects of the affair, though they were hardly ridiculous to a man who had traveled two thousand miles in search of what he thought was his new home.

Jonathan said, "Dabney Finch Bavier." He looked as if he wanted to smile, but didn't out of respect for the cheated man.

Ellen laughed outright. "The Finches used to own the land bordering Jonathan's on the south. They've let it go something awful during the last five years or so, since Mr. Finch died. Dabney married his cousin, one of the Finch girls, and ran through all the money he could lay hand to. He sold off parcels to some of the Negroes from the town. They do their loading and shipping with Jonathan. They do right well. But the Finches were foreclosed more than two years ago and Dabney went west. Deserted poor Calla."

"Lot of that going around," Jonathan remarked with a straight face.

"Well, I'll be damned!" The captain brought his fist down so hard on the table that it jumped.

Jonathan remained unruffled but understanding. "Dabney always claimed his pa was a circuit-riding preacher. I never rightly believed it, though. Must be where he got the idea."

The captain gathered himself together, shrugged and said, with a quick grin, "I guess I owe your cousin, Miss

Ellen, an apology. And you, too, sir. Strutting in here like I owned the place."

"No offense meant and none taken," said Jonathan, and the two men shook hands.

After a moment's hesitation, Ellen held out her own hand. Captain Sholto took it in his, gently squeezing her fingers. His thumb moved slowly over the flesh of her hand, almost massaging it. She felt uneasy, not frightened as she had been with the startling and assertive Jem Faire, but aware of his touch and his pressure deep inside her. She was, she reminded herself, through with all that, and then considered the rueful truth: she had never really known enough of it to be through with it . . . Life, and Maggilee, always interfered.

Well, they were *not* going to interfere this time . . .

"You'll stay to supper," Jonathan went on hospitably. "Nahum, my new foreman, left me some mighty choice soft-shell crabs. There's a-plenty. Ellen's staying. You are, aren't you, honey? I'll walk you home."

Ellen held her breath. If the captain left now there would be no reason for him ever to return. This terrible thought gave her courage to say quickly, "Maybe tomorrow Captain Sholto would like to go in to the county seat and check his deed. Satisfy himself about your ownership."

The captain had taken up his hat and was looking around for his knapsack. "That's not necessary. I know a gentleman when I see one. It all fits together. I remember some of the boys said he had mighty sneaky eyes for a preacher."

Jonathan surprised Ellen by insisting quietly, "I'd be much obliged if you would stay. Ease your mind. Tomorrow, I'll go in to the county seat with you . . . You were in the War, I expect."

"God knows I had big ideas about getting in, but I couldn't make it till '62. Didn't see much action though until long after when I joined the Seventh, some years later." The captain glanced at his hat, then at the two cousins. "I'd enjoy a good talk with an old comrade-in-arms." He added, before the obvious could be spoken, "I've found a funny thing. When you talk about the campaign days, Blue or Grey don't seem to matter. It's talking to civilians about it—begging your pardon, Miss Ellen, that's the very devil."

Jonathan nodded. "I know what you mean. You'll bed down here tonight. Tomorrow, we'll go in to Ashby.'

The captain took off his hat again and sent it sailing into a corner. It landed neatly on top of his knapsack. His ruddy, sunburned face was smiling as he said, "This is what I call *real* southern hospitality. And as for walking Miss Ellen home, I'd be proud to do it, if you'd trust me, after all the trouble I've caused you."

. . . It isn't you I mistrust, Ellen thought to herself *. . . But at all costs, I'm going to keep you away from my dear mother . . . at least, until you know me better . . . .*

CHAPTER 5

* * *

*T*HE DELICATE, feminine "supper" of tea, sweet cakes, slices of buttered bread and, possibly, sliced hard-boiled egg, never satisfied Maggilee and she doubted if it satisfied Colonel Faire's hunger either. Since she wasn't home at the dinner hour, somewhat after noon, Maggilee felt that she never did get a truly full, comfortable meal. But few people had the courage to argue the matter with Varina Gaynor, and the custom continued at Gaynor House as it did in so many other great houses of Tidewater and southern Virginia.

The only comfort was a dish of fresh strawberries for each guest, sent over from Cousin Jonathan's farm. The strawberries were eaten off their tiny stems, one by one, dipped in sugar or cordial and popped into the mouth. Colonel Faire managed to put away the contents of two of Varina's exquisite crystal dishes. Maggilee, smiling automatically whenever the colonel looked her way, stared at the river waters that appeared almost mauve in the evening light, wishing she might get rid of her dress, petticoats, drawers, and the stays which compressed her small waist even smaller, and dive into that delicious cool water. He back ached, her head ached, and she knew her conversation was far from sparkling.

But damn it! Why couldn't these two old relics talk about something interesting? Ledgers and figures interested Maggilee, a trait inherited from her father's French ancestors. When she was nine years old and her mother was dying of consumption, she went into her father's notions store, taking to it immediately. It was just before the War and her mother, who had been a schoolteacher, advised her father to put in all kinds of goods that might grow scarce. Maggilee got her guile and her brains from her mother. It had turned out just the way her mother predicted and later, with her mother dead and her father called to defend Virginia from the invaders, Maggilee had run the store with the help of *freeborn* Negroes—her mother had been that sinful creation, a Virginia abolitionist. It was a year after her father's death, and Maggilee was running the store as best she could with half her merchandise in blockade-run goods, when tall, blond, handsome Beau Gaynor strolled in looking for hard-to-find needles for his mother . . . Maggilee stared at the river and wished for the thousandth time that she had never married him. She was fairly sure Beau also must have regretted his hasty courtship, else why should he fall in love with the young lady from McLean a year later? Or was the McLean girl just one more in a long list of unimportant loves, including Maggilee Favrol . . .?

Maggilee yawned, shifting her position in the stiff porch chair. Varina and the colonel were back on the tiresome, boring, depressing subject of Virginia-before-the-War. It was one of those subjects that often provided a tie between Rowdon Faire and Maggilee's own daughter Ellen. The Irish landowner whose own daughter was a vinegary woman almost Maggilee's age had always been able to entertain the rather sober, lovely Ellen as a child by acting out the great events of his past: service on the Texas frontier early in the War, and then injury, and the Virginia defense in '64 and '65.

Secretly, Maggilee found him lacking in every quality that attracted her in a man. She couldn't forget his florid face that seemed to go with his consumption of good Kentucky liquor, or his curly thatch of white hair that reminded Maggilee of that great enemy—age. Her romantic dreams were quite different from those of her daughter Ellen, she told herself. Maggilee enjoyed reality, flesh, sensual pleasures. Pleasures of the mind were lost on her.

On the other hand, Maggilee knew that Ellen was another dreamer like her grandmother. Romantic, imagining the past wore a dazzling halo. No wonder she couldn't catch a man. She was probably repulsed by the whole idea of being bedded. But, of course, she couldn't know what she was missing.

Maggilee thought of her own bed upstairs. How much more companionable to share it with a man who matched her own lust, her own craving to be part of that man, to join him and share with him whatever experiences of flesh and emotions each had learned in half a lifetime. A man of *experience*. No such luck around Gaynorville where she was known so well, and in the ways of the Old South had to behave as an extention of regal Queen Varina.

Every spring Maggilee went to New York to do her shopping and buying. There had been adventures in the past, with suitable, respectable gentlemen who were likewise traveling to New York or New Orleans on business. But she was fastidious in spite of her normal craving for a few nights of pleasure, and she liked men who could talk intelligently about their business, the figures, profit and loss, bargains . . . She was still a bookkeeper at heart.

She smiled to herself, and Colonel Faire leaned toward her, resting his toughened, liver-spotted hand on her knee. She felt the heat of it through her green challis skirt, her petticoat and white stockings. There was still very much of the active male about Rowdon Faire.

"And what might you be thinking of, Miss Maggilee, looking so pensive and lovely?"

She forced herself not to wrinkle her nose at his brogue. It was stock-in-trade. He had been born in Virginia, to the wife of an Irish sea captain who made his fortune as a blackbirder, dealing in the triangular slave trade: West Africa, West Indies, and the Carolinas. But everyone in Tudor County associated Rowdon Faire with his friendly brogue and only Maggilee found it annoying.

Maggilee now assumed the gaiety that people were accustomed to from her. It was generally supposed that the Young Mrs. Gaynor had two moods, a bad, red-haired temper, and a great charm and general cheerfulness. Maggilee cared very little what anyone thought of her, she said over and over; yet she helped to keep up the pretense. It made her so different from her aloof mother-in-law, the only—the one—person in the world whom she genuinely hated.

"I was thinking all sorts of things, though nothing it would be proper to tell you, Colonel."

While the colonel teased her to reveal her "secret thoughts," assuming from her smile that they were about him, she became aware of Varina's elegant head turned and her cold blue eyes observing her. Out of sheer deviltry, Maggilee went on flirting, while the colonel outdid himself in his response, though he asked several times when they thought Ellen would be home.

"Sure, I'd be right proud to have my little friend Ellie give my nephew a bit of her time. They had a quarrel, Jem says. But lordy, I've had words with Ellie off and on since she was that high, and it never stopped us being friends. There's nobody like her . . . present company excepted, of course."

Varina, who had been interrupted in the midst of a pleasant conversation with the colonel and strongly disapproved of his Indian-blooded nephew, could only sit there examining her fingernails with great attention while her lips tightened. She interrupted him finally to remark, "But Colonel, we haven't even asked after your dear daughter. How is Eliza? Such a sweet child."

This was a palpable hit at Maggilee, since Miss Eliza Faire, a spinster in her late thirties, had two virulent dislikes in the world. She hated Maggilee, who had stolen Beau Gaynor, the one love of her life, and to a lesser degree, her cousin Jem Faire, who failed to discern her hidden charms. Miss Eliza had worn funeral black for twenty years as a woman eternally bereaved by the War, and for Varina to refer to her in such devoted terms could only be for Maggilee's benefit. Maggilee tried to ignore her mother-in-law and began to add up in her head her various accounts payable the first of the month, while the colonel complained that he did wish "dear Eliza" would learn to get along "sociably" with his nephew.

"Of course, the lad's no better. Jem ignores my girl when he can. But that's just his way."

Maggilee thought, she made a fool of herself fluttering around him when he first came. Small wonder he ignores her. Men seldom ignored Maggilee.

By the time darkness covered the river, and its willow borders at the lower end of the Gaynor lawn, Colonel Faire sensed Maggilee's barely disguised boredom, coughed, and said, "Wouldn't want to overstay my welcome, even between two such lovely ladies. I'll just amble along and see if that nephew of mine is coming. We'll be riding home together."

Varina summoned Edward by one of those slight, almost imperceptible gestures which Maggilee had often tried to imitate, and a few minutes later a boy had brought the colonel's bay horse around to the east front of the house.

Before Maggilee could offer, Varina assumed her imposing height, and took the colonel's readily offered arm.

"I'll wait here and keep an eye out for Ellen," Maggilee said, refusing his other arm. He looked for a minute as if he too would like to wait for Ellen . . . He had always been so fond of the girl, Maggilee wondered for a moment . . . how nice if Ellen could marry such a rich man, old enough so that he wouldn't be looking for a beauty or a woman with great physical attraction . . . She shrugged off her absurd notion. Rowdon Faire must still think of Ellen as the child he had befriended when a lonely girl looked for a father or brother she didn't find at home.

Maggilee watched gloomily as Varina and the colonel

walked together down the porch steps to the semicircular drive around the east front of the house. "A fine business," she thought, "if I'm in such a state I've become jealous of Varina's ancient suitors."

She stood observing them, then saw a horseman coming up the drive on a spotted pony. That would be Jem Faire. An interesting buck, quite unlike the pallid local men. Maggilee roused herself, shook her unruly red hair and smoothed her wrinkling basque. Then, with a swaying walk, she stepped out as Jem Faire leaned down from his spotted pony, offering his hand to Varina. The latter touched it with her fingertips and turned away, wishing the colonel a brusque good night as he mounted his own horse.

Jem Faire appeared unmoved by Varina's rebuff, but Maggilee, always ready to flout her mother-in-law's opinions, moved out across the gravel and standing on tiptoe, offered her own hand. Jem took the small fingers in his. His rough hand was gentle . . . She felt that something about him eluded her. It was an uncommon experience. Had she been a few years younger, she might have made an effort with him. Too bad, because he was a challenge and Maggilee fed on challenge, especially from a virile male.

In a low voice she told him now, "Next time, Jem, you must come visiting with your uncle. We so seldom see you."

His thanks were polite as he rode off with his uncle.

Varina had already gone inside and Maggilee returned to the veranda to wait for Ellen. She stood there several minutes, leaning away from the porch, clutching one of the narrow pillars for support. She wanted to put off going to bed. She stared aimlessly across the south lawn, wondering if it was her imagination, or had she heard masculine laughter somewhere along the woods path?

The path led south toward Gaynor Ferry where Dunmore Creek began its eastward course, meandering through swampy areas and fertile farmland. She studied the woods where the path suddenly burst out of darkness onto the open lawn and for an instant she was sure she made out the silhouettes of two tall men with a female in a striped dress. Ellen, obviously. And Cousin Jonathan? But who was the other man? He must be one of the tenant farmers Jonathan dealt with every day. Strangers were not common here along the Ooscanoto. There had only been one recently—the insolent, good-looking man in the blue uniform. Where was *he* going, and what had become of him . . . ?

"Ellen, honey, are you out there?" she called, suddenly anxious for another human voice. There was no answer except the rustle of birds disturbed in the trees. Her daughter seldom seemed to find the time to talk with her. Probably felt her mother was one of the old generation, like Varina and Colonel Faire. How silly to think of herself as middle-aged, ready for nothing but an old lady's lace cap and a rocking chair!

"I'm *not!* I'm still capable of loving. It isn't ended for me. All it's ever been was work . . . well, there's more, I know there's more . . . I found it once, and lost it . . . I just haven't found it again."

She let go of the pillar and started down across the lawn, toward the Ferry path. The river ran close by now, humming and gurgling near the shore, prowling in among the willows. She felt the grass around her ankles, prickling above her second-best shoes, but there was little joy in the sensation. She had never felt Varina's and

Ellen's passion for the Land. The joy of her hard-driven life had been the drive to success. If she had become a kept woman in New Orleans or an elegant actress in New York City, she would still have had it . . . her strong, motivating urge for success. She glanced over her shoulder at Gaynor House in the starlight. She was proud of it. She'd kept it in Gaynor hands when there was no one to help.

"I may be selfish," she silently admitted, "but by the eternal, there are times when the nice people of the world need a push and a prod from us selfish creatures."

Owning up to the truth about herself didn't help her get to sleep of nights. She'd need a dose of laudanum again. It was a bad habit begun once on a lonely night when she awoke after a particularly vivid dream of her lover's face, so very close to her, and so ineffably dear, she could brush his lips with hers. But although she tried to hold onto the memory, his features kept fading. There were times, sickening, full of self-reproach, when she couldn't even remember the true color of his eyes.

She saw Ellen now, walking toward her through the darkness of the woods, looking for all the world like a tall, slender ghost. She was alone.

Odd. If she had been alone on her walk home, then who the devil was responsible for that clearly masculine laugh Maggilee had heard a few minutes earlier?

* * *

Ellen felt so full of tension and excitement it was hard to calm down and put on the mask of cool indifference that she used toward the world of Tudor County. "Secretive" they were apt to call her, and with some reason. Nevertheless, a glow of warmth lighted her heart toward her mother as she saw Maggilee apparently waiting up for her.

"How nice, Mother, to wait out here for me! Isn't it a lovely evening? It was so cool in the woods."

Maggilee flashed her quick smile. "Cooler than the house, I'll be bound. But then, this is likely our last hot spell. Winter'll be in the air before we know it." She looked over Ellen's shoulder. "I hope Jonathan walked you home. There's cottonmouths around in there, this time of year. But I reckon you know that better than me."

"They don't get on the trail. They stay by the water pretty much."

"Well, somebody should have walked you home. It's only proper."

Ellen noticed that her mother stood on tiptoe to see into the woods, and it came to her with a little twist of disappointment that Maggilee hadn't waited out here to meet her at all . . . she just wanted to see who had walked her daughter home. "Mother, if you're looking to see Cousin Jonathan, he left me at the old poplar and went back. He wanted to get in a little more loading tonight."

Maggilee hesitated. "I—heard someone laugh. It didn't sound like Jonathan."

"No, Mother. It was Nahum. Nahum works for Cousin Jonathan now."

That'll give her something to chew on, Ellen thought.

"Nahum! But it couldn't be. That child?"

"It was Nahum. I'm surprised you're so interested." Ellen looked into her mother's eyes. When Ellen's light blue eyes stared at people the result was sometimes a little chilling.

Maggilee's gaze fell before the challenge. "Well, honey, it doesn't matter. I only wondered . . . What a boring evening it's been. Colonel Faire and your grandmother. Talk-talk-talk. They can't get off the subject of how lovely it all was before the War. The War! I'm tired of hearing about a war that was all over with a quarter of a century ago!"

Ellen saw the tiredness in her mother's face; her mother, who worked so hard and still wasn't happy. Ellen took her arm, remarking, "That's because they're old. You're still young and pretty. You've got so many years ahead that they don't have."

Maggilee clutched her arm like a staff. "Thank you, Ellie. Sometimes I feel so old and dried up and—unwanted—"

Ellen laughed. "You'll never be 'unwanted.' Not you."

It took little to cheer up Maggilee, who, being satisfied that Ellen had eaten supper at the Ferry and needed no motherly attentions, kissed the girl good night and went to her own room upstairs. It was a surprisingly utilitarian bedroom with roughly made furnishings, almost like a frontier cabin. She always claimed she wanted the best furniture to be seen by Richmond bankers when she was borrowing money. "You've got to look like money to get it," she maintained. Even the bed, though large and roomy, was a far cry from the beautiful four-poster with dimity curtains in Grandmother Varina's bedroom.

Edward Hone's niece Ceci, who was working as a housemaid to earn enough money for her own sewing machine, brought up great jugs of water now and poured them into Ellen's old tin hip-bath. Understandably, she wasn't fond of her work. Ceci Hone, born intelligent but not pretty, had the ambition to make something of herself, yet perversely she admired Varina rather than the low-born, ambitious Maggilee. It was Varina, in one of her unexpected charities, who had seen to it that Ceci learned reading and writing. About Ellen, Ceci was indifferent, except when it was a matter which concerned Varina as well.

Ellen scrubbed her body with lukewarm water and jellied soap boiled down from used slivers of the French lilac soap her mother sold in the shop. As the faint, flowery scent rose around the firm flesh of her body, she pictured herself seen like this—quite accidentally—by Captain Bill Sholto. What would he do at the sight of the long, shapely leg she stretched out now in front of her, all dripping with soap suds, the pale flesh gleaming in the lamplight.

A sudden, disquieting thought intruded . . . what, indeed, if Jem Faire saw her naked like this? Those dark eyes burned her flesh, even in fantasy. Embarrassed, she hurriedly drew her leg back as Ceci rustled into the room, which still looked very much as it had looked since Ellen's childhood. The narrow, virginal bed, the dresser with the mirrored shaving stand from a now-forgotten room on top, a rag rug and little armless rocking chair with a plain white muslin seat, and the old clothespress where Ellen had kept cornstalk dolls and paper dolls cut from catalogues along with two wardrobes of her own clothes for winter and summer.

"Mrs. Gaynor wants to see you, Miss Ellen."

To Ceci and most of the household there was only one Mrs. Gaynor. The original. Varina Dunmore Gaynor. Ceci poured a jug of cold water over the girl's shoulders to help shower off the soapsuds, and Ellen gasped at the shock of the water, but rubbed vigorously. With the big, rough-worn towel now modestly draped from her round, pale breasts to her thighs, she groped for her nightgown over the back of the rocking chair. Only after she had slipped on the white cotton gown with its frilled neck did she let go of the towel.

She stepped into her slippers, wondering if Bill Sholto

had noticed tonight that her ankles were slender and her feet shapely. Probably not. He had looked at her a great deal in his rough, flirtatious way. His interested exploration of her as he lifted her over the log bridge on the trail had been daring but casual, too, like an experienced man. But somehow she didn't like him the less for that. She had felt the very pleasant contagion of his warmth, so unlike the wave of emotion she had felt in that encounter with Jem Faire. Surely, this Captain Bill Sholto *was* the man she had waited for all these years . . . and she meant to win him!

As she tied the fringed sash of the cotton robe she wore over her nightgown, she felt a sudden, almost painful happiness sweep over her body. Just having Captain Sholto flirt with her tonight had chased away the old familiar ache of memory, the loss of—what was his name? —oh, yes, Albert Dimster. And even Gavin McCrae. What were they, anyway, but mere paper dolls beside her cavalryman who had, incredibly, ridden into her life on a black stallion?

She'd felt a twinge of fear when she said goodbye to him at the edge of the woods, and he had laughed. A beautiful sound, she told herself. So very masculine, and all the time she could see Maggilee posed prettily on the porch, holding onto one of those silly antebellum pillars. Obviously, Captain Sholto hadn't seen her, because he didn't mention the red-haired beauty. Instead, as he laughed and turned away, he had taken a deep breath of the cool night air, assuring Ellen, "It's not goodbye, Miss Ellen. Not by a long shot."

She hugged her shoulders now while Ceci stared at her, narrow-edged, suspicious of all this excitement in a girl who rarely demonstrated joy or any other strong emotion in front of people.

"Your grandmother will be waiting."

"Yes. Thank you. I'll go see her now."

She went along the hall to the front bedroom, the master bedroom whose windows overlooked both the river and the south lawn. The room was so large part of it had been furnished as a kind of sitting room with a lounge on which Varina reclined, managing always to keep a rigid spine even in the privacy of her bedroom. Her first instruction to her granddaughter after Ellen learned to walk was, "Back straight, child. Back straight. Never slump."

The advice had been useful, though a problem to Ellen, who, like Varina, grew to a height of five foot six inches, several inches taller than the average fashionable female.

"Shoulders straight. Be proud of your height. In heaven's name, don't slump."

Ellen knocked lightly and waited for Varina's low, imperious question: "Yes, yes. Who is it?"

Surely, she knows it's me, Ellen thought, amused at her grandmother's manner of granting an audience. Ellen announced herself, was admitted and crossing the room to Varina's huge, four-poster bed, kissed her grandmother's surprisingly unlined forehead. But as Ellen lowered her gaze to Varina's pale blue eyes and stern, elegant face, she noted that the mouth, which could look haughty or charming when it chose, was thin and pursed with suffering.

"Gran, dear, is it the rheumatism? I'll get a hot brick from the kitchen. Or liniment. Shall I rub your shoulders?"

"Nonsense. Don't fuss so. Do I look like an invalid? Sixty-two isn't the end of the world, you know. It's—well—it's these insufferable pillows. They aren't made the way they used to be. Stupid things!" She threw one of the crochet-edged pillows across the room. The effort must have hurt her but it was clearly worth it.

"Grandmother!" No use in scolding her. Ellen picked up the pillow, brought it back across the wide-planked wood floor, treading carefully on the small throw rugs that had a habit of slipping out from under one's feet. For some strange reason Varina never slipped and fell. Now she patted the bed beside the slender mound that was her body.

"Come and sit down. Don't dawdle. I need my sleep."

Ellen obeyed. "You shouldn't have called me, Gran. You do need your rest." She studied Varina's face. Her recent exertions had definitely given the older woman a malicious pleasure. In spite of the pain she suffered intermittently from her rheumatism, she was never happier than when demonstrating her power over something or someone. In this case, the hapless pillow.

"Where were you tonight? We missed you. *She* said she'd let you run over to that nephew of mine."

"Cousin Jonathan keeps us eating, Gran."

"Now what, pray, has that to do with anything? He can be good-hearted like anyone else. Dreadful mother he had. You never knew Sarah Pluvane. Hopeless. Couldn't make a lady of her if you tried all summer. Never even had much gumption. Died off second year after Jonathan was born. You just couldn't count on her to do anything right."

"Well, Cousin Jonathan has gumption."

Varina studied her long, bony fingers on which the plain gold wedding band and some very large blue veins stood out. Without looking up she asked blandly, "Who's staying with Jonathan?"

Ellen was startled and showed it. "N-nobody . . . Nahum, Biddie's nephew, is learning the business."

"I know Nahum. Gave him his first job. And a good thing he made of it, too, I must say. So don't lie to me."

"I'm not—" She broke off, aware of those shrewd blue eyes on her.

"My dear child, you've nothing to fear from me. So long as you behave yourself and remember who you are."

"How did you know?"

Varina sighed her impatience at such stupidity. "I've eyes, and those windows over there. That little clearing in the woods isn't all that far from our south lawn. I saw you cross it with a man." Before Ellen could speak, she raised her hand. "And don't tell me it was Jonathan."

Ellen took her hand and caressed it absently. She knew Varina was telling the truth, that she would be on her side against Maggilee . . . "He's a western cavalry officer. Used to fight Indians but his regiment was massacred some time ago. Anyway, he was mustered out. He's staying with Cousin Jonathan tonight—"

"Is he attractive?"

"I think so."

"Don't let her meet him." Varina's voice was calm.

"I won't. Oh, believe me, I won't!" There was a silent understanding as to the identity of *her*.

Varina hesitated. It wasn't like her to hesitate about anything she had to say. She glanced around the room and back to Ellen.

"That stupid old he-crow, Dr. Nickels, left me some laudanum last month. Which, I may add, I'd never dream of taking. I'm not one to pamper myself."

Wondering what this was leading to, Ellen refrained from smiling. Except for her rheumatism, Varina Gaynor never hesitated to take the best, whether it was offered to her or not.

"Yes, Gran. What about the laudanum?"

"Nothing. Nothing at all. Except—" With a little smile that troubled Ellen, she ended, "I think *she* stole it. My dear, it's come to this. She is a petty thief. And worse. A weak thief, if she is taking laudanum."

Ellen stood up. "Good night, Grandmother." Whatever her personal grudges against Maggilee, Ellen felt Varina was wrong to gossip about her behind her back. Forgetting her recent resentment against her mother, she kept in mind that Maggilee had, after all, saved them, their home, and maybe their lives.

Ellen was in the doorway when Varina called out, "She owes a great deal of money. Did you know that, my dear? That wretched shop may do a tremendous business—"

"It does."

"But you'll find that the well-to-do customers who patronize shops of that sort are the last to pay their bills."

Ellen automatically reminded herself: *Straighten your back, don't slump, be proud.* Aloud, she said, "Let's hope Mama doesn't lose the shop or you and I will be moving in with Cousin Jonathan again."

"Oh, no, we won't. If the worst comes to the worst, I'll marry that old beau of mine, Colonel Faire. Though I daresay he'd as soon marry you."

Helpless before this absurdity, Ellen closed the door. At her mother's door she stopped. Varina's talk had worried her, after all. She knocked. "Mama? Are you all right?"

A short, breathless wait. Then Maggilee's easy voice, "I'm fine. 'Night, honey."

"Good night, Mama." There . . . nothing was wrong. Ellen went off to bed . . . hoping, expecting to dream of Captain William Sholto.

CHAPTER 6

***

BUT THERE were no dreams about Captain Sholto that night. Ellen awoke to a coolish day with autumn crackling in the air, and remembered some silly snatch of a dream about Maggilee in the arms of Gavin McCrae. Ellen, in her dreams, had insisted on fighting for Gavin, and a ridiculous, childish tussle had followed. What was the sense of it . . . ?

Ellen sat up, leaning on her elbows, thinking crossly, "As if I wanted your old beau who went and married Daisy Wychfield! In fact, if he were here, I'd encourage the two of you. Then maybe Captain Sholto would at least go on appreciating me. If you were married, Mama, he mightn't even want you. Or at least be able to have you."

If . . . Maybe that's what the odd dream meant. But in Ellen's experience most dreams seemed to be based on some minor event of the day, such as Biddie's remarks about Maggilee's flirtation with two bankers from Tidewater Virginia. Anyway, it solved nothing.

She swung out of bed, thought excitedly of her secret man at Gaynor Ferry, and looked through her wardrobe for a more flattering dress than the blue-stripe she had worn the day before. Its shape on her was good, showing off her best attributes, but the diagonal stripe only called attention to her height. Captain Sholto was tall, but still, you never knew . . . he might prefer more "petite" women.

The day promised a pleasant little chill in the air, and though her pink-figured challis might not be warm enough she could always take the lovely cream-white shawl Grandmother Varina had knitted for her. The entire ensemble would be very feminine, and feminity was very much the quality she wanted stressed the next time she saw Bill Sholto. And there would be a next time. There had to be. She didn't think she could bear it if he went away without seeing her again . . .

She had finished dressing, surveyed the results as well as she could in the dresser mirror, which never quite reflected all of her at once, and was worriedly rubbing a piece of red flannel over her lips to heighten their color when Maggilee knocked and walked in, talking as she did so.

"A bright, nippy morning, Ellie. By the way, the bridesmaids will be coming in today to have their patterns and colors chosen. I want you to be sure and—"

Ellen felt her own satisfaction drain out of every pore

as her mother broke off in that startled way and then studied her from head to foot. Trying to hold onto what remained of her self-confidence, Ellen said brightly without turning around,

"Good morning, Mama. You don't think it's too late in the season to wear this?"

"Oh, no!"

But there had been a tiny pause before that quick denial. The old uncertainties, the lack of faith in her own attractions rushed through Ellen's head like the flow of her blood. She took a hard breath and exhaled.

"You may as well tell me. What's wrong?"

"Nothing, honey. Nothing at all." Maggilee hurried across the room. Her fingers smoothed Ellen's sleeves, then her tied-back skirt, and finally removed a thread from Ellen's left shoulder. "You look lovely."

"But . . . ?"

Maggilee's nose wrinkled slightly. She shrugged. "It's nothing to do with you, Ellen. It's that Corrigan girl, Amabel. Her mother met me as I drove past the Corrigan farm last evening. She insisted Amabel has to wear her special shade of pink at the Hunt Ball. I reckon it's pretty near that shade."

Even though her mother's criticism wasn't directed against her looks, it was too late to recover that first pleasure and excitement Ellen had felt when she dressed this morning. She reverted to her characteristic impassive manner.

"Please don't wait for me. I've got to change."

"Ellie, I didn't mean you shouldn't wear it some other time. It's only that Amabel might think you insist on that color for the ball."

Ellen swung around to face her. "Mother, do me a great favor. Don't call me Ellie!"

Maggilee looked at her. "I wish I understood you. All

right. *Ellen*. Let's go down to breakfast. You know how bad-tempered Cookie gets when we're late. But then, we all seem to have gotten up on the wrong side of the bed today. Are you coming, hon—Ellen?"

"I'll be down in ten minutes."

Maggilee hesitated. "Look, I didn't mean you should change. You just come along. You do look—lovely."

By this time Ellen would have gone naked to work before she would wear the pink challis and interfere with her mother's precious business. Somehow, it had all come down to a matter of pride. She knew it was childish, but she couldn't fight it, and all interest in her looks had faded.

Anyway, why would I see Captain Sholto today? she asked her reflection silently. If he goes anywhere, it will be to Tudor Junction, the county seat . . . Who cares what I wear so long as it doesn't interfere with Mama's sales . . . ?

She tore off the pink challis basque, ripping a sleeve seam, and kicked away the skirt before taking out an old gingham now faded to a bilious tan.

Who cares? she asked herself, and getting no satisfactory answer, buttoned herself into the plain, round-skirted, high-necked dress.

Maggilee, drinking cocoa and finishing her buckwheat cakes when Ellen came into the dining room, had forgotten their tiff and waved a fork at her in greeting.

"I know, I'm going to be fat as Mr. Wychfield if I keep on this way, but—cocoa and cream. Cakes and real sugar. Honey, I never get enough of them."

Ellen softened some, remembering how her mother, who always had a sweet tooth, must have suffered from the deprivations of the War and post-war years. Ellen herself could remember the times in her childhood, long after the War, when there was no sugar, no honey, and only the sorghum that could be traded from the neighbors. "Mama, you rush around so much you couldn't possibly gain an ounce and you know it."

Maggilee was pleased. "I do hope that Corrigan woman doesn't come in with Amabel. It's all I can do to handle Irene Wychfield." She flashed her cheerful, gamin grin. "D'you reckon every last one of those girls will want that deep pink shade?"

"Let them." Ellen dismissed the matter with contempt. "If they do, I'll wear the opposite. They pretend to be Bertha-Winn's friends but I hear them snickering behind her back, making their sly remarks about—well, anyway, most of them are so two-faced it makes you sick." She saw that her mother had lost the thread of the conversation and was rubbing her forehead. A sudden worry surfaced. Ellen had meant to ask her mother about the laudanum. It was quite true that anyone could buy it over the counter but it was a very tricky drug and every day people died of overdoses.

"Mama, you've got another of your headaches."

Maggilee's hand jumped away from her forehead as if the flesh had burned her fingers.

"It comes and goes. It's the tension. That damned wedding. If it's a success, the bank will renew. Mr. Wychfield is on the board."

"Mama, you also get these headaches when you take a spoonful of laudanum. I wish you wouldn't."

"Don't nag, Ellie, for God's sake."

The new cook, an elderly black woman with a fine hand at pastries and an uncertain temper, slammed Ellen's plate of buckwheat cakes down and went out, ignoring Ellen's "good morning." She had no particular grudge against Ellen but believed in never wasting words.

Ellen began to eat, watching her mother out of the corner of her eye.

"Now Grandmother is accusing you of stealing her laudanum."

Maggilee exploded. "That old Meddlesome-Betts! Steal her laudanum? I wouldn't take a pleasant smile from Varina! Not that I'm likely to get one."

They both smiled and nothing more was said about the dangerous, sleep-inducing drug. Besides, nagging had never stopped Maggilee, not if she was hell-bent on doing something . . .

* * *

Aside from the silly little ruckus with Ellen, it had started out to be a "lucky day," Maggilee thought. The invigorating fall morning after the Indian-summer heat of the previous day encouraged her on the road into town. Her headache evaporated in the scent of the distant woods and the harvesting.

Maggilee handled the reins of the patient mare as always, having long ago convinced herself that she wanted to save Ellen's hands from calluses. Ellen, embedded in one of her puzzling silences—what *did* the girl think about?—made few objections to Maggilee's erratic handling of the horse and buggy.

Things were less encouraging at the Gaynor Salon. (How she had fought to make people call it "salon" rather than "saloon"!) Mr. Duckworth, down very early from the First Virginia and Dominion Bank of Richmond, was waiting in the shade of his buggy which looked all too prominent on Gaynorville's main street. His horse was tethered to the hitchrail in front of Slagel's Hardware.

"Oh, Lord!" Maggilee muttered. "He must've traveled all night."

Ellen sized up the buggy. "Probably came down yesterday. I know that buggy. It's from Rooke's Livery. That'll be Norfolk. Likely he spent the night there."

"I hope he didn't match notes with Tom Gimmerton of the Norfolk Peninsula Bank." Maggilee leaped down from the buggy before Isaah, the shop's oddboy, could help her out.

Ellen, knowing young Isaah liked to earn his keep, gave him her hand and stepped down, asking her mother quietly, "Is it that bad? You can't pay the installments?"

"Certainly I can. What do you take me for, a bankrupt? It's only that the Wychfield payments won't be in for months, and I have to pay for all materials and labor *now*. I'll take the Peninsula loan and pay off old Duckworth. Then I'll get a new loan from Duckworth and pay off the Norfolk Peninsula. Just a matter of business, honey."

Ellen smiled, though it clearly was too serious to laugh at. "I wish you'd let me do more to help you with the books. I know I could find a passel of mistakes and probably cheating by these wholesalers you do business with."

"Don't you worry about that. Whenever I catch them cheating me I make 'em wish they'd never been born."

Ellen tried once more, knowing she wouldn't get anywhere. "That's just it, Mama. You let that red-headed temper of yours get the best of you, and then you can't do business with them again. You have to point out their mistakes and *very quietly* insist that they make it right on your next purchase."

"Ha! I'm no hypocrite. You get that from your slyboots grandmother."

Ellen threw up her hands and followed Maggilee into the neat, whitewashed building that was GAYNOR'S.

Biddie, already inside ordering around a cleaning

man, grabbed Maggilee's arm as she crossed the heavy Victorian main salon of the shop. "That Richmond man, he's squattin' out yonder like a spider, just readying to snatch up your money."

"He'll get it. Don't you fret about money. I do want him to see the Hunt Ball gowns, though. That'll show him the kind of business we're doing. When are they due?"

Biddie consulted her new lavalier watch, which was a birthday present from her nephew, Nahum.

"I'd say that Mrs. Wychfield might bustle in any minute. For a skinny Yankee with high and mighty ways, that woman bustles and rustles more'n a dozen of you. You need more taffeta in your petticoats, Miss Maggilee. That'll impress 'em bankers."

"You're probably right, Biddie. You usually are. Suppose we get out all the peau de soie, the satin and the silk poplin. And heaps of lace . . . 'Morning, Dora. Are the patt'ns out?"

"All the Butterick ones, Miss Maggilee. And some others. The French ones is hid somewheres."

While Ellen went off with Biddie to get out the yardage, Maggilee considered the pattern problem and suddenly remembered. "I locked them in the sideboard. That Corrigan woman walked away with two of them last month." She gave her ring of keys to modestly curved Dora, on whom she often modeled the outfits she created for the standard-sized Virginia gentlewoman. Then, having finally sent off every employee on some special assignment, Maggilee finished the dusting of the area that could be seen by her customers. All the while she was creating costumes for the ball, considering their figure problems, the elegant setting of Wychfield Hall and, with a glance after her busy daughter, considering Ellen's best points.

Ever the harbinger of evil tidings, Biddie marched by to inform Maggilee with a certain amount of pleasure,

"They're both coming in at the same time. Seems as if they kind of strike a balance somehow."

Before Maggilee could ask who *they* were, Isaah held the front doors open and Mrs. Wychfield came in, chatting animatedly with the banker from Richmond, Mr. Harleigh Duckworth. Maggilee cast a quick, all-encompassing glance around. She couldn't find anything terribly wrong, anything cheap or shoddy that would leap to the eye of the banker. As she had long ago learned, you had to *look* money to borrow money.

Maggilee crossed the wide salon to the entry hall which was likewise shrouded in plush velvet gloom. She took care not to smile at the pairing of stout, fussy Mr. Duckworth with Irene Wychfield. He might almost have fitted under her arm. She was tall, rangy, still spoke with a hard Eastern accent—somewhere around New York, it was said—and corseted in spite of her extremely thin frame until it looked as though she was made in two pieces. Top and bottom. Her smart little feathered hat, the new modified bonnet, sat well back on her high-piled hair and one long pheasant feather slyly tickled Mr. Duckworth's bald pink scalp. All the same, he was enjoying it. Allowing for her lamentable "Northern" birth, the lady wasn't bad-looking.

Maggilee took the gloved hand Irene Wychfield extended. "So obliging of you to come early, dear, knowing how frartically busy we are these days."

Anyone else would have been "Irene" after nineteen years, but the lady was reserved and didn't encourage familiarity. Her husband, Major Ferris Wychfield, scion of an old Maryland family, was serious enough by nature to be called "The Major." They left it to their elder daughter Daisy to win the world of Tudor County with her easy, almost insistent friendliness.

Maggilee hoped that her remarks about the busy

hours ahead for Gaynor's would penetrate the banker's thoughts. She then let him take her hand while she flashed the famous smile, half mature woman, half gamin, which had rarely failed her.

"Dear Mr. Duckworth! And all the way down from Richmond just because we said we'd missed you-all lately." He loved to be teased and as she went on he preened under the picture she drew of him as a gay blade, a connoisseur of beautiful women. "I know what it is. You heard we were having six pretty girls in to choose their ball gowns. Not to mention the gown of our kind friend, Mrs. Wychfield. Of Wychfield Hall, you know."

The little man was torn between admiration for the tall, dark Irene and the small, red-headed Maggilee, who hoped his interest in the fair sex would keep him from being unpleasant about the loan.

Irene Wychfield was polite but had no intention of being part of Maggilee's performance. She proceeded at once across the salon to examine the bolts and rolls of materials lavishly spread across a gateleg table. Dora Johnson's familiar handling gave exactly the right touch of richness and freedom, as though in spite of their cost, Gaynor's could afford to throw them around.

Harleigh Duckworth slipped up close to Maggilee. Her slight size and the innocent flirtatiousness in her heart-shaped face made him feel very protective. "I don't want to alarm you, dear Miss Maggilee, but—" (she took the cue and her vivid blue eyes immediately showed alarm) "—but I'm very much afraid we will have to discuss a certain outstanding business matter—tut-tut, now, you are not to worry." He cleared his throat. "I'm sure the interest might be forthcoming today, and I'm right sure the Richmond Dominion can be persuaded to extend the loan." Maggilee touched his arm and opened her eyes to their widest. She would have forced a tear if she hadn't been so rushed.

"How kind you are! I feel so helpless about such matters. I just have such a time keeping all those figures in my stupid little old head."

"Not stupid at all, my dear. And certainly not old. You could never be old." He gave her hand, which happened to be handy, a comforting pat. "What you need is a male to handle all these problems."

What is he going to do? Surely not propose? She tried to think of some appropriately ladylike way to refuse him. Meanwhile, though the air outside was pleasantly cool, his hand that rested on hers was moist, to say the least.

"I do my best. Really I do," she assured him, limpid-eyed.

"Of course you do, my dear, that is—" he amended so as not to offend—"my dear Miss Maggilee. And for that very reason I think I just might have the way to help you out."

It is coming. My God! He wants to marry me.

Harleigh Duckworth announced triumphantly, "I'm right certain I could find a buyer for this store."

Fury turned her face as red as her hair for an instant. *Might as well sell my own body, my child's body, as sell Gaynor's Salon!*

"Never!" Elizabeth the First, another redhead, might have used that tone to the Spanish Armada.

The banker peered around, then lowered his voice to a discreet murmur, hoping it would be contagious. "Please, my dear Miss Maggilee, no offense meant. Something else can be worked out. Why, just see how much business the store does, and at this hour!"

"The salon."

"Beg pardon? Oh, just so."

By this time she had recovered, and actually managed to squeeze out a tear.

"There, now," he consoled her. "No one's going to take your nice little store—er, salon—away from you. We'll work something out."

She clasped her hands somewhat as he did in church. "How good you are, dear Mr,—I wonder if I may call you Harleigh?"

"By all means. Don't you worry that pretty little head of yours, Miss Maggi. We'll see that the loan is renewed at the interest we charge our preferred customers. You—you, of course, will be able to meet the interest on the past due loan?" he added, a bit anxiously.

"After your generosity, sir? I will if I starve for it."

He accepted this as a joke. "We'll just see that it doesn't come to that. Rest assured."

"You must be our guest at dinner tonight, Harleigh, and we'll do our best to thank you for your kindness. My mother-in-law—she was Varina Dunmore, you know—was saying only yesterday that we hadn't seen you for an age." While he eagerly accepted, Maggilee thought with amusement that Varina had no more notion of Harleigh Duckworth's identity than she would have of a sharecropper on Old South Road beyond the Finch property. However, even Maggilee had to admit that no one played the gracious hostess better than Varina. When Maggilee had to deal with snobs, she always brought them to the house. They were certain to adore Varina Dunmore Gaynor.

The banker had other business in town—who else owes him money, Maggilee wondered. And he left after fulsome thanks for the dinner invitation. Maggilee finally could return to the subject of the Coming-Out Party and the young prospective patrons who fluttered in, giggling, gossiping, delighted at this, the biggest event in their lives since Daisy Wychfield's wedding. Few of them were over five feet, the tallest being five-two and both Irene Wychfield and Maggilee sighed as they saw the taller Ellen.

"Of course Ellen must be there . . . Bertha-Winn insists," Mrs. Wychfield was saying. Then, realizing that this remark had not been put in the happiest way possible, she added, "Not that we would have it any other way. Such a pity she is older than . . . some of the other girls . . . It isn't poor Ellen's fault, of course." Seeing Maggilee stiffen, she hurried on, "And now, let's proceed to business, shall we?"

Maggilee draped the less attractive colors on top, putting the deep pink underneath.

"Mauve for the little Kent girl, I think," Mrs. Wychfield said, pointing to the silk poplin. "A winter ball does require heavier materials. And the deep pink—" She uncovered the bolt, saw the girls all breathless and excited, each hoping to get the bright pink, blue or green. "Amabel Corrigan, I think."

Amabel's blonde curls bobbed with her victory, though she was trying hard to put on a modest air of "Who? Little-old me?" She was happier than chubby, four-foot-eleven Maud Kent, with her dull and uninspiring mauve. All three girls of about Amabel's height received the bouquet of bright colors. Blue, green and deep violet.

To Maggilee's dismay the mustard yellow, which had a depressing gray sheen to it, was left for Ellen, and as Irene Wychfield said to Ellen, who gazed at the material without expression, "Only you can do justice to that shade . . . Indeed, it's almost the shade you have on." Maggilee winced. She more than suspected Ellen hated the drab, faded outfit she was wearing. Maggilee instantly began to plot. Something must happen to this ugly bolt of grayish-yellow silk poplin. It must happen very close to the ball, too close for Irene Wychfield to realize that Ellen would have a much more flattering shade and outshine the pretty "bouquet" of girls. Maggilee determined to find a color suited to Ellen's perfect complexion and her cool blue eyes.

Mrs. Wychfield and the girls bent over the patterns and Maggilee brought her scattered thoughts to bear on the subject at hand.

Isaah had come in and whispered something to Ellen. Seeing a movement at the edge of the chattering group, Maggilee looked up, wondering. There was certainly no reason why Ellen shouldn't receive messages, but the whispering was unusual. Maggilee stepped out of the group and went around to Ellen, whose face was suddenly lighted up. Maggilee was once more surprised at how pretty her daughter could be when she was happy. Almost a beauty, in fact. But what had caused this sudden change?

"Mother, Cousin Jonathan is riding into the county seat. He wants to check a land deed. May I go? I'll work all through Saturday."

Maggilee thought of the endless work, confusion and decisions that lay ahead for the making of party dresses, plus gowns for the chaperones, but Ellen so seldom asked favors it was impossible to refuse her.

"Of course, honey. Have a good time. Maybe I'd better go out and say hello to Jonathan. I haven't seen him for days."

Ellen said quickly, "I'll give him your regards. He's in quite a hurry. Oh—I think the girls want you. That's what you get for being so popular. You 'tend to Gaynor's and I'll 'tend to Jonathan and his friends."

Maggilee, who had kissed her lightly on the cheek, turned back now. "His friends?"

Ellen was already running. "Just a joke, Mother. 'Bye."

Her conduct was certainly mysterious. She hadn't even waited to put on a hat, which was all very unladylike. Maggilee shook her head, laughed, and went back to try and settle a small argument between Irene Wychfield and the girls over which patterns to select. It was chiefly a question of necklines. The girls wanted them low. Mrs. Wychfield wanted them just under the chin.

Meanwhile, Amabel Corrigan had been watching mother and daughter. Sharing Maggilee's curiosity, she looked out through the curtained window of the front door. "Well, I declare! Ellen's gone and got herself a beau."

Maggilee explained, "It's our Cousin Jonathan."

"Not the one I see. He's a soldier." Amabel put on her hat and departed quickly, already thinking that she might go to the county seat herself.

Maggilee thought suddenly of the good-looking cavalryman who had almost run her down the day before. But surely Ellen would have said something at home. What a strange girl she was! So secretive.

. . . I'd better see what the fellow is up to. I wonder if he could be sparking Ellen . . . Maybe he thinks she's rich, what with Gaynor House, the land, the Salon and all . . .

CHAPTER 7

***

ELLEN WAS SO anxious to get away before her mother caught sight of Bill Sholto that she didn't even see Sholto's hand extended to help her as she scrambled up onto the wagon seat. He edged over, putting her in the middle. It was a tight squeeze but neither she nor Sholto made any objection to that. Cousin Jonathan gave her his usual quiet smile and nod but signaled his horse to start so quickly Ellen wondered if he sensed her urgency and was trying to help her. She was glad Bill hadn't worn his blue tunic. The cavalry hat was conspicuous enough when added to the blue of his breeches.

Once they had rattled down the dusty street out of Maggilee's view Ellen didn't care who saw her. Let them talk, she thought. It might do her reputation some good, in a reverse sort of way. She could still hear the voices:

"Dear Ellen never has a breath of scandal about her . . . How lucky you are, Maggilee, that Ellen never took to boys! Such a trial! My husband says the veranda is always full of young men, panting to keep company with my Amabel" Or Maud, or Lavinia, or Persis. Or every other young female in Virginia except Ellen. She shivered.

Bill Sholto looked closely at her. "Cold? I guess we hurried you too much. But I said to Jono here, let's see if the goddess will go along. She can be my witness that the Ferry property is mine."

She flared in defense of her cousin. "Well, it isn't. It never will be. You were just rooked out of your money in a poker game. That's all."

He teased her. "What a vulgar expression on the lips of a goddess! I'm shocked."

Relieved that he hadn't taken her flareup seriously, she responded, "You're about as shocked as an oyster."

He considered this. "You probably know oysters better than I do, but can you really shock an oyster?"

She turned her head to hide her smile but he brought it around again by her chin, nipped between his thumb and forefinger. She thought his grin was devilishly attractive. She wondered—an old habit—if this fellow could be trusted, and impatiently told herself it didn't matter. Whatever he was, she wanted him, even if this was only the second time she had been with him.

Then, briefly, he seemed to spoil it, pointing to the crossroad that went up to Church Street.

"This town surely has some pretty females. Not as pretty as the goddess here, but a whole lot prettier than Deadwood. I almost ran over one yesterday."

Ellen stared at him. Even Jonathan looked in his direction. His easy grin answered them before he explained. "I was going hell-for-leather along that upper street and this buggy pulled out of nowhere. My mount rared up, and his big hooves almost came down on the prettiest little redhead you ever saw. And fighting mad. She didn't like me. Not a little bit!"

Ellen didn't relax until the end of this tale, which was more harrowing to her than he could possibly have guessed. To her relief, Jonathan spoke, obviously trying to get off the subject. Did he always know when the Gaynor women were in trouble? Maggilee once said that he rode to the rescue whenever Varina or Maggilee or Ellen needed him. He said little, but he was there. A strange man. And very, very dear. "Captain," he asked, "you thought over your future plans yet? Just in case you find we-all own the Ferry, after all?"

Ellen raised her head. She felt Bill Sholto's muscular body tighten beside her. He took off his cavalry hat, tousled his hair and said with an exaggerated accent, "Well, now, if you-all own the Ferry, I allow as how I'll just have to tie onto you and share-crop. It's all that's left to me if I want to stay in sight of the goddess here."

"Don't call me 'goddess,'" she said more sharply than she had intended. "Unless you want people to think you're soft in the head."

"I don't think so," Jonathan put in, signaling to the big, powerful old horse by shaking the lines. Ellen was so startled she could only stare at him, but the reaction that surprised and pleased her even more was Bill Sholto's. He did *not* seem surprised at Jonathan's words.

"First time I saw you stalking along in the dust I thought—there goes Ceres, goddess of the harvest. Proud and golden-haired, with eyes like . . ." He tilted her head as if he owned it. "Yep. Like a cool blue lake I once saw up in the High Sierras."

She didn't know for sure who Ceres was but felt flattered all the same, and almost resented Jonathan's conversational leap to the rescue.

"Nothing cold and icy about Ellen. Except maybe when she's mad, and then it's only like frost on a window till the fire takes. Like my Aunt Varina. Ellen's warm and friendly most times."

Ellen blushed, half angry, wondering how Bill Sholto would take this. He felt for her hand and squeezed it, pretending to be afraid of her. Not since Gavin McCrae had any man squeezed her hand, she realized, except a few old male customers buying hats for their wives. Their clumsy, pawing attempts at flirtation made her skin crawl.

"I'd better not stir up all that fury then, had I?" he said, grinning so pleasantly it was impossible not to smile back at him. Encouraged now by his obvious liking for her, she began to make easy small talk, her usual reserve changing to pleasure.

Jonathan said nothing more as they drove on through brown tobacco fields on the east side of the road and dense, deliciously cool-looking woods along the west side. They turned a corner by an old tobacco-drying shed and abruptly saw Ashby, the little county seat of Tudor County. Tree-lined and green, it was almost on the bank of the creek which flowed in an "L" shape from its source on the Ooscanoto near Gaynor Ferry to its outlet northward in the James River.

Ellen couldn't help noticing and rejoicing in the appearance she made before the people she knew in Ashby, in company with a good-looking man who was making such a fuss over her. Imagine! Someone who sees me at my shabby worst and still thinks . . . well, at least *says* he thinks . . . I look like a goddess . . .

Animatedly she proceeded to point out to Bill Sholto various sterling citizens of the county seat, explaining their position in the tight, closed pattern of the little county. All the while she would nod and smile to each person, waving to some, and Bill, in the mock-absurd way she already delighted in, would take his hat off and bow with great solemnity to every man or woman she pointed out.

Jonathan's voice stopped their joking. "I see Rowdon Faire's nephew is in town. Getting supplies, I reckon."

"Probably looking for trouble," Ellen put in.

"I hope they're not making it hard on him."

Ellen apologized to Bill, "We're a bit reserved with strangers."

"Not to my way of thinking," he said.

"Oh, but you're not—"

Jonathan surprised them by his flat comment. "She means you don't have Navajo blood."

Her feathers ruffled, Ellen contradicted her cousin. "I couldn't possibly dislike Navajos. I never knew one before. I dislike Jem Faire only because he is rude and—"

"And minds his own business," Jonathan put in. "I've had him down to the Ferry several times. He's no fool."

Bill Sholto stared frankly at the lean, dark, cleanshaven young man who was heading into the Merchandise Market of Adam Bentincke. After a moment's silence, he said, "Early in the War I was sent off to Arizona Territory. Too young to do much anywhere else. I guess they figured the Apaches deserved me. Anyway, I was a lad, but I learned my way around Indians. Must say I felt a whole lot more in common with them than with the greedy bunch of so-called whites I met out there."

"And yet you killed Indians in the Dakota Territory," Ellen said, and was immediately sorry she had.

Jonathan answered for Sholto. "You do a whole heap of things in a war."

Sholto nodded. "Anyway, you say this fellow's a Navajo?"

"Half." Jonathan's voice was succinct.

Ellen hurried on to explain. "Colonel Faire's sister, Hester, went out there with her brother. Hester and an Indian scout fell in love. They weren't allowed to get married, Colonel Faire says. Anyway, they had a child, Jem. They're both dead now, and the colonel went west years ago and when he came back he had persuaded this Jem Faire to move into his mother's world and work for Fairevale."

Jonathan shrugged. "Jem's more Irish than Navajo. Don't know as that's good or bad." He had pulled up before the two-story brick imitation of an antebellum mansion. He got down at the Court House. "Captain, are you coming in with that deed of yours?"

Ellen was sorry they had reached their destination. It was up to her to keep Bill Sholto interested. She tried to fill her thoughts with all the charm so easily flaunted by the likes of Amabel Corrigan and Persis Warrander, yes, and Maggilee Gaynor . . .

Meanwhile Bill Sholto cooperated with her thoughts as he lifted her down from the wagon and held her there, deliciously teasing her.

"Remember that High Sierra lake I told you about?"

She nodded, watching him, fascinated.

"Well, when I look into those eyes of yours, it's summer on that cool blue lake."

She felt very summery-warm all over. Much, much warmer than she had ever felt with Albert Dimster, or even Gavin McCrae.

* * *

The County Clerk's desk was at the far end of a long, barnlike room used for Judge Warrender's law library, various county meetings, and any purpose which required a gathering of more than six people.

Since Ellen knew Captain Sholto's claim hadn't a leg to stand on, she lingered behind as the two men strolled along to the County Clerk's roll-top desk.

Amabel Corrigan was at the near end of the room teetering in boredom on her little white kid buttoned shoes, while her companion, Jem Faire (of all people) studied a land-rights case in one of Judge Warrender's ponderous volumes.

Seeing Ellen, Amabel sang out, " 'Mornin', honey. You-all got your dress for the Hunt Ball?"

Ellen assured her she had.

"Mine's deep pink, like a peony," Amabel rattled on, her eyes sliding to Jem Faire who had stopped reading when he heard Ellen's voice and turned to look at her with his finger marking his place in the law book. He bowed with studied politeness,

"Good day, Miss Ellen."

Her "Good day, Mister Faire" was equally correct, but she had a feeling he was mocking her—there was obvious amusement in his eyes. And Amabel quickly sensing that she had lost hold of the center of attention, said breathlessly, "Reckon my dress is a mite daring, but Mama's so silly. She just says it's right scandalous. Of course, you know mothers. But I declare, I get the shivers just thinkin' 'bout wearing it."

"Maybe with a shawl over it?" Ellen said.

Amabel was not listening anyway. Her performance had been entirely for Jem's benefit. She tilted her head toward him, her curls almost brushing his chest. "And what fun, I declare! Though I do say so as I shouldn't, I just bet you are the most divine dancer, Jem."

"I never heard my dancing described like that, Miss Amabel," and then, seeing Ellen's tight smile, added, "but we'll find out at the Hunt Ball." Just as Amabel clapped her hands and squealed happily, he looked over her head at Ellen and said, "Won't we?"

She couldn't help feeling pleased at her triumph over the beauteous Amabel. With a turn of her mouth and a little shrug she was about to admit the possibility when her cousin and Bill Sholto came by.

"Would you like a paper to start the fire with?" Bill said, offering her his useless deed to Gaynor Ferry.

"No question," Jonathan rubbed salt in the wound, and started to the door after a nod at Jem and Amabel.

"You're going to have to cheer me up, Miss Ellen. I'm hard-hit." The captain took Ellen's arm.

Unable to resist a glance back at Jem Faire as he left, Ellen saw that he had returned to his law book. It was Amabel who stared.

Walking proudly between her two tall escorts, Ellen felt exhilarated enough to tease Sholto as they came out of the County Court House. "Now what will you do, Captain? Ravage the countryside and scare helpless women and children?"

"No, I'll just be a homeless outcast, starving, like the children of Ishmael."

Ellen turned to Jonathan, hiding her smile. "Do you suppose you could at least give him a piece of cornpone and maybe one little slab of fatback? Just enough for him to keep body and soul together?"

"Well," Jonathan said, "he handles a tiller right well. If he wants to, there's work a-plenty, getting my produce downriver to market. Nahum and I handle the loading at the Ferry and Nahum will oversee some of the planting this winter and spring. So we could use another partner."

"I've got a little money to invest later," Sholto put in cheerfully, "but I'd like to get the hang of it before I lay out ready cash. Even if what you offer does sound like a sea-going deal. Pity I didn't join the Navy. Still and all— is that the river I'm to navigate? Don't look too bad."

Dunmore East Creek ran between tall poplars and crowded willows along the western edge of town. The main street ran on west over a wooden bridge wide enough for a two-horse team and set on banks high enough for barges and small flatboats to pass under, along with their tall bargemen.

"Even a cavalryman could pole his way along that stream," Ellen said.

"Except when it runs lowest, about a month from now," Jonathan reminded her.

"Show me how it's done," Bill challenged her. "Prove I can make it downstream and Cousin Jono's got a new hired hand. Maybe I can get him into a little poker and win the Ferry from him."

"Likely," Jonathan said, "if I was fool enough to let you. I'm stopping off here to pick up the month's supplies. You want to put in your two cents' worth, and I'll get enough to make you a stack of buckwheat cakes and a slab of bacon per day, anyhow."

The captain hadn't been bluffing. He pulled out a twenty-dollar bill from the wallet inside his breeches pocket. Jonathan took it after a curious examination of the bill. The large denomination was not common to a man who dealt in trading commodities rather than money.

"Reckon it's good," he remarked slowly.

Sholto laughed. "Reckon so," he said, and taking Ellen's hand, hurried her across the gravel street to the steep, green-covered walls of the stream ten feet below. "Shall we dive down?"

"What do you take me for? There's a path just behind that split oak tree. It used to be the biggest tree in the County."

"I suppose the Bluecoats did that, too." He sighed.

She refused to rise to the bait. "Lightning split it."

"That's a relief. You had me terrified for a minute. I thought if my checkered past became known, I might be lynched."

"That isn't very funny."

"Sorry. Just a thought."

Going down the little path his foot slipped on the slick grass. He grabbed at Ellen's waist and they slid down together to the edge of the creek, their feet running over smooth stones into the cool water, where they came to a stop and burst into laughter.

"Do you suppose the townfolk will be mortally offended if we take off our shoes and dry our toes?" Bill wanted to know.

Fully aware of his eyes on her, she was caught between a desire to prolong this new intimacy and the fear that he should think her "fast," or common.

Carefully, one foot at a time, she stepped over the pebbles among which the water near the shore still gushed and ran swiftly, until she came to a little area sheltered by willows around a flat rock just big enough for two people. She hadn't come here in years, not since Albert Dimster introduced her to the place and then laughed at her because he had peeled down to his long underdrawers and went swimming while she gaped at him, amazed at this blatant display of his secret parts through the clinging, wet cloth.

Actually there were few mysteries left to a girl who had seen cows drop their calves and mares nurse their foals. The boys of the County swam frequently in the Ooscanoto River and Dunmore Creek stark naked, and Ellen had more than once sneaked glances at them. She had, of course, pretended not to notice Albert Dimster's somewhat mediocre accoutrements, and when he came ashore she had said cooly, "I've got to be going home. Cookie will be mad if I'm late." Somehow the Gaynors always acquired temperamental cooks. Anyway, she should have pretended to be shocked, should have put on a silly display of girlish coyness. She had been too "calm" on the outside.

"What sad thing are you thinking about?" Bill wanted to know. Sitting on the rock he had eased out of one boot but stopped with it in hand and was watching her. The contours of his rough, wind-burned face softened. "Did I touch a nerve? Didn't mean to."

"I wish folks would learn that when I'm resting my face I'm not necessarily sad."

He reached out with his free hand and touched the folds of her skirt. "What ails you, sweetheart?"

He said the endearment so easily it probably meant little to him, she thought, but to her it was like poetry.

She smiled. "Nothing at all," and growing still braver, "I was here with a boy once . . . I just remembered."

"Ah! And he took liberties. You slapped his face . . . Something happened? Something almost happened? Well, then, what did happen that was so sad?"

"The sad thing was—nothing happened."

Dropping the boot, his hand reached out, moved under her skirt hem, and his fingers closed around her ankle. She felt the warmth of his hand through her damp white stocking. It would have been easy enough to shake him off, or stamp away in anger, but she did neither, wanting to savor this delicious, prickling sensation through her body. His other hand began to draw off her shoe.

He caressed her ankle, then the high arch of her foot. "This ought to be done in marble. The curve, the line—you really are quite a goddess, sweetheart."

She tried to keep her balance on one foot but suddenly found herself hopping and had to grab at his shoulders to keep from falling. She lay against him while she caught her breath. He let go of her stockinged foot, kicked her shoe away and stood up, easily raising her to him, against him. He felt almost as hard-muscled as Jem Faire, but his treatment of her was gentle. She was not afraid that he would go too far, nor was she afraid of herself. He teased her as his lips brushed her cheek, the bridge of her nose, and eventually touched her mouth.

"Don't be afraid." He kissed her softly. "You need a little time. Let me teach you." His mouth found her waiting lips again. "I've never taught a goddess before. I'll be very—very careful . . ."

A familiar male voice was calling down to them from the bridge above their heads.

"Quite a beautiful scene."

They broke apart, she feeling guilty as a twelve-year-old.

"What the devil?" Bill muttered, shaken by the abrupt ending of their moment.

Jem Faire was looking down at them from the bridge, his hands tight on the wooden rail, the only sign that he was more than mildly amused at their playful struggle. Ashamed of her own easy part in the embrace, Ellen was aware of how cheap and insincere she must look to the man whose own embrace had once supposedly shocked her.

"What do you mean by spying on us? What business is it of yours, I'd like to know?"

Jem Faire's straight black hair hung as a lank frame for his prominent cheekbones and the full curve of his lips. Someone, probably he himself, had cut his hair across his forehead so unevenly that the black strands made a sharp-angled contrast with the oblique slant of his eyes. His harsh laugh altered the somber planes of his face.

"I'd like to learn just how it's done by dashing Bluecoats these days. Who knows? I might profit by it. Watch her," he called down to Bill Sholto. "She can be violent, I promise you."

He slapped the rail again and moved quickly away, though not nearly as quickly as a furious Ellen could have wished as she felt around for her lost shoe, and reluctantly accepted Bill Sholto's arm as they climbed the river bank.

CHAPTER 8

***

"OH, HELL," Maggi sighed. She had remembered suddenly, after a ghastly day. "I invited that silly old fool Duckworth to dinner." That meant an earlier meal and a big one. Supper might be bad enough. At least the day would be over, and afterward she could go for a walk across the lawn, perhaps along the river path. She could think, and remember other cool, delicious nights on those same paths. Nights when she was not alone. Nights long ago when she would not be alone in the big four-poster bed now appropriated by Varina.

I'm getting old, she thought, and wondered what had brought on that grim reflection. But, of course, it was the memory of the blue uniform she had dreamed about again, thanks to that damned insolent cavalry officer who had almost run her down that other afternoon. Such coincidences still occurred to her once in a while, just when the memory of love and death had blurred for her. Every time a new reminder came to her, she thought: "I'm older than I was when I last dreamed of him. Further and further away from the face I swore I would carry in my memory to my dying day."

She had forced herself to forget the haunting significance of her dreams, but it occurred to her now as she waited for the banker to escort her home in her own horse-and-buggy that she really put aside memories because they reminded her that life was slipping away from her.

Biddie came down from the attic alteration room. "Whyn't you go off home? I'll close up here. You been at it all day. Ain't nobody coming in can't wait till morning. Meaning Miss Ellen, too. Mister Jonathan'll get her safe home to the house."

Maggilee confessed, "I wasn't thinking about Ellen. I know she's safe with Cousin Jonathan. But I've gone and invited that Duckworth man to dinner. I hope Isaah took the news to the house or Cookie will be having a tantrum."

"He went." Biddie did not make a move to leave.

Trouble, Maggilee decided. "It's all right, Biddie. I'll lock up. Good night."

"Sure. 'Night, Miss Maggi." She lowered her voice but managed to keep it quite audible as she retreated, talking to herself.

"Just wonderin'. Miss Ellen might be a little later'n

some folks think. What with good-lookin' gents squeezing her in a real sociable way. 'Night, again."

"Biddie!"

"You said, I could go. I'm going."

"You're not talking about Jonathan, are you?"

Biddie didn't turn back. Her hand was on the doorknob. "Who, me? What d'I know?" She went out the door, put her cane to use, and hobbled rapidly down the street.

Maggilee asked the empty salon, "What the devil is going on under my nose?"

She was still puzzling over Ellen's secrecy when Harleigh Duckworth came up to the door, bowed over her hand, and escorted her to the livery stable. While he took up the reins, explaining the proper handling of a horse and buggy to a woman who had handled one for twenty-five years, Maggilee slipped a tiny satin bag full of coins into his pocket.

"I wouldn't want you to think I'd cheated you, dear Mr.—I mean Harleigh."

It was the interest on her Virginia and Dominion loan. He couldn't possibly know how she hated to give it to him.

"Well, I'll be switched!" His free hand loosened the white shoelace that closed the bag. "And all in gold pieces. Miss Maggi, you are a woman of your word. Your credit's always good at Virginia and Dominion. You can count on that."

Not entirely appreciative, Maggilee wondered if a little less would have made it just as happy. However, it was too late now, so she made the most of her mistake.

"Every last little shin-plaster that I'd collect, I'd say 'This is for Mr. Harleigh Duckworth's bank.' I was right proud of myself. But I'm being immodest. Please pay me no mind."

They had passed the Confederate Cemetery and the banker "cluck-clucked" to hurry the mare, which had a mind of her own.

He still managed to favor Maggilee with his beaming smile. "Never could I do that, ma'm."

She pretended to be confused. "You confuse me, Mr. Harleigh. What do you mean?"

"That never could I pay you no heed."

She gave this effort the bright giggle it deserved and leaned just a bit closer to him, careful to become the entirely proper little lady when he lifted her down on the east front drive of Gaynor House and tried to squeeze her a bit tighter than propriety should allow.

"*Sir* . . ." No need in letting him think he had bought her for one interest payment. But once she was free of his hands she smiled sweetly and motioned to the veranda, where Varina Gaynor waited in stately splendor to greet the guest.

"Varina, honey, aren't we the lucky ones? Here's Mr. Harleigh Duckworth, one of the important gentlemen from that sweet Virginia and Dominion Bank. He's come all the way out here just to have dinner with you."

Varina Gaynor found nothing unusual in this. In fact, it was difficult for her to conceive of guests coming to Gaynor House for any other reason. She didn't move until Harleigh Duckworth reached the veranda. She then obliged him by descending one step and allowing him to take her long, bony hand, once the beauty of three counties but now slightly liver-spotted. She was so used to its gradual change she still saw it as the hand of the Tudor County belle. Oddly enough, so did most of her admirers.

" 'Evening, ma'm. This is indeed an honor." The banker bowed low over her hand, still awed as he raised his head and saw before him the tall, regal figure in a silver-blue bustled gown that was almost the color of her eyes.

"You are welcome to my house, Mr. Duckworth. Do come in and make yourself comfortable. You must be quite blown about in that dreadful old buggy. My daughter-in-law will persist in using the thing. I keep hinting that she should have a new one, but young people are so —what am I saying? And to a young person like yourself, Mr. Duckworth. Come."

It had been several years since Harleigh Duckworth heard himself referred to as a young man.

Maggilee followed them into the house, only once rolling her eyes heavenward . . . *And to think Varina accuses* me *of leading men on* . . . She was also annoyed by the impression Varina gave that the buggy was old because of some miserly quality in Maggilee . . . *When I think of how little ready cash we've got, and how much goes out just to keep this house open!*

Maggilee dressed for dinner in a hurry, afraid of what Varina might say to Duckworth as she entertained him on the river veranda. Last time, Varina had spent an hour giving the Norfolk Peninsula banker and his wife all the reasons why she kept her "little fortune" at home rather than in his bank. It did make things difficult when Maggilee, carefully bonneted and shawled, came to the coastal city asking for a loan.

Maggilee seldom spent much time on her own gowns. People never noticed what she wore. Her personality had always overshadowed her calico and nun's veiling and foulard dresses. It was her proud claim that she hadn't a jealous bone in her body, and she considered that she proved it by spending her business life making other women look their best in Gaynor gowns.

But even her eyes opened wide with several emotions when Ellen came down to join the two women as they escorted Harleigh Duckworth into the elegant old dining room.

Ellen was wearing the blue taffeta dress Maggilee had designed for her last year, with a plaid overskirt pulled back in graceful loops to form what was now being called a "back fullness" where the bustle had swayed in the previous fashion. What a long waist and flat abdomen the girl had! It would serve her well in years to come, Maggilee decided, eying these portions of her daughter's anatomy with envy. The shade had never been Ellen's best. Both she and her mother realized it was a mistake when the dress was being made up. It required a great deal of high color in the face and the throat where the daring square neck revealed considerable white flesh.

But this evening either Ellen had scrubbed her cheeks raw with red flannel or she had borrowed her grandmother's cosmetics. Varina belonged to a generation that boasted of its false coloring on cheeks, lips and even eyes, to the embarrassment of a later and more proper age. . . . There was one other possibility. Ellen's own emotions lighted her cheeks that bright, flattering pink.

Mr. Duckworth could honestly say, as he was seated on Varina's right at the head of the table, "The three Gaynor ladies are certainly the fairest in our glorious State, I do declare."

Her grandmother, too, had noticed the change in Ellen who sat with her mother at the foot of the table. Varina said with a smile directed at Maggilee, "I'm sure we older women are put to shame by this young dazzler. Ellen, you rogue, what have you been up to?"

Ellen's flush only made her more charmingly feminine as she rattled off rather too quickly, "Cousin Jonathan drove me to Ashby—I went down to the creek—I slipped—my shoes and stockings got wet. I know I'm too old for such things but it was fun, and I had such a good time . . ."

After a couple of moments, and seeing Maggilee's puzzled frown, Varina decided to support her granddaughter. "I reckon it didn't give you a lick amiss. You look all the better for it, girl."

Maggilee closed her mouth on whatever she might have said. She was well aware that if this sort of conduct became the subject of gossip, Ellen's reputation would suffer locally. People would begin to say, "What a pity! She takes after the white-trash mother rather than the elegant Gaynors and Dunmores." For herself, Maggilee had long ago ceased to care, but she didn't want her only daughter's life handicapped by such a reputation—

"And how is Jonathan?" she asked, wondering if any of Ashby's sharp-tongued citizens had seen Ellen frolicking in the water with her skirts up around her knees. If Jonathan didn't go with her, had she gone with the mysterious male that Biddie had hinted at?

It didn't seem to matter now. Harleigh Duckworth, at his most gallant, spoke up. "Then we've got the County seat to thank for that mighty pretty complexion, Miss Ellen. I must see if this town of—er—Ashby will have the same effect on my poor, motherless girl. Lina's just at the awkward stage."

Before Maggilee or Varina could respond, Ellen assured him, "I'm sure, Mr. Duckworth, no daughter of yours could be awkward."

As both women stared open-mouthed at the usually silent Ellen, a banker congratulated himself on having achieved the admiration of the three most delightful ladies he had known in years. If only his dead wife could have heard their praise of him, her sharp tongue would have clucked a little less.

I must see what I can do about getting them better terms on Miss Maggilee's loan, he reminded himself.

* * *

Ellen thought the dinner, and the small talk following, would never end. At first it was fun surprising her mother and grandmother by looking her best for a change. In view of the short walk down over the grass to the river that she planned after their guest was gone, it had been pleasurable to see the admiration in Mr. Duckworth's eyes. Surely, if the celebrated banker thought she looked as good as Maggilee and Varina, then Bill Sholto would be pleased, too.

But the longer the dinner lasted, the more she became aware of Maggilee's speculative, puzzled look, as if she knew all the time what Ellen was thinking. Had she discovered that there was another man besides Jonathan who rode to Ashby with her today? For the first time an insidious thought pricked Ellen: if mother takes laudanum tonight she can't possibly follow me out to the lawn.

It was a hateful thought, and she banished it, shocked at the depth of her own wishes. After all, Bill Sholto wasn't the last man on earth. How could she feel so strongly about him when she had only been with him twice. But she did. It would kill her if her mother took him away from her. The important thing was to keep them apart, at least until the captain returned Ellen's feelings in the same degree. Would that be possible . . . ?

It must be. Dear Lord, *please*, it must be!

After dinner, old-fashioned Madeira was served to their guest and to Varina, who never turned down a glass of wine and claimed on the best evidence that no one in Virginia had a better head for it.

Since it was a chilly evening, the women, especially Varina, talked with Mr. Duckworth in the heavily furnished parlor. As usual, they discussed the Good Old Days, and flattered him with the frequent remark, "But I daresay you were too young to remember . . ."

At such moments, the banker, eagerly reminiscing with Varina, found a way to explain his own presence at war-time events: "True. I was a child but I have always had an extraordinary memory."

"He must have been an absolute child prodigy," Maggilee whispered to Ellen, who hid a quick smile behind her knuckles.

But the evening had to end sometime and when full darkness had fallen, Mr. Duckworth, hurriedly stifling a yawn, confessed that he must be on his way back to his friends' home near Norfolk. It would be a long drive and involve crossing the bay on a ferry.

"Edward, our butler, will drive you," Varina announced without consultation with Edward Hone or with Maggilee, who would need the horse and buggy in the morning, thereby compelling Edward to make the long return tonight. Maggilee's mouth twisted in her attempt to hold back a strong protest. Clearly, so far as Varina was concerned, the Emancipation Proclamation had never existed.

To Maggilee's relief and surprise Ellen cut in gently, "But Grandmother, Mr. Duckworth's horse and buggy are at the livery stable in town. You're much too polite, sir, to contradict my grandmother, but we do understand you will want to get your own rig back to Norfolk."

Harleigh Duckworth sighed. "I'm afraid so. If your man will take me to the stable in town, I'll be much obliged."

The Gaynor women sent him on his way happy, and

he stuck his head out around the side of the buggy to get one last glimpse of them as they stood on the step below the east veranda waving to him. But once the buggy was out of range of their hearing, Varina voiced what Maggilee and Ellen thought but hadn't the frankness to admit aloud:

"Thank heaven, he's gone."

Only a little ashamed of themselves, the two younger women laughed and started into the house, one on either side of Varina, whose back had begun to bother her.

Maggilee and Varina never had a word to say to each other when forced to spend any time together, so Maggilee complained of a headache and said she was going to bed. She took one of the kerosene lamps off the drum table in the hall and started up the stairs. On the landing she turned back, leaned over the rail and called to Ellen, "Ellie, honey, you did us proud tonight."

Varina stiffened. "She always *does us proud*—to borrow your vulgar expression. Good night, Maggilee."

Ignoring this, Ellen went to the foot of the stairs and looked up, both touched and pleased. "Thank you, Mama. Have a good sleep."

Maggilee waved and went on around the corner into the hall above.

Ellen felt suddenly guilty after her mother's compliment. Here she was, sneaking out to see her lover—no, the man she loved—and afraid her mother, who had just been so generous, might follow her. She had always been aware of conflicting sentiments where Maggilee was concerned—she was jealous of her mother, afraid of her instinctive power over men, yet she also wanted her mother's good opinion more than she had ever wanted it of any other person, including her grandmother.

Remembering that Varina was still with her in the

parlor, Ellen made a pretense of fanning her face with her hand.

"It seems a little stuffy, doesn't it, Gran?"

"Not to me." The maddening woman eased herself down on the green-knobbed settee and took up her tatting. Her fingers worked the shuttle back and forth, back and forth, in a steady, even motion that always made Ellen nervous to the point of annoyance. Would Varina *never* go up to bed?

Apparently not. Giving up on her, Ellen sauntered out to the river veranda, pursued by Varina's eagle eye and the remark, "Take care you don't catch cold."

"Yes, Gran. My dress is very warm."

"Not in the neck, as I observed at once when you came to dinner."

Ellen paid no attention to that and strolled out across the veranda, down to the grass. There was no moon but the stars made the river waters glitter and sparkle. The thick black border of willows and trees across the river on the Fairevale shore seemed to conceal a certain romance and adventure. But she needn't look on the Fairevale shore. Romance would come to her on the Gaynor side of the river this night.

"Will it ever be quite this beautiful again?" she asked herself, trying to be philosophical, to regard these minutes ahead, her brief secret meeting with Bill Sholto, as a temporary thing, a word, a touch and perhaps a kiss. It just wasn't likely that Bill Sholto loved *her* yet, but if she used her mother's wiles he would learn to . . . Even Maggilee and Mr. Duckworth had remarked on her looks tonight.

She had high hopes.

With her hands crossed, hugging her arms against the chill that crept in off the gently flowing river, Ellen strolled over the lawn and down toward a narrow path near the river's edge. The path was an offshoot of several that emerged from the woods which separated the house from Gaynor Ferry. It was a popular path in summer, used by many of the property owners as well as the workers employed in the scattered plantation houses facing the Ooscanoto.

As she reached the river path she heard the crackle of footsteps on dry autumn leaves and saw a man come out of the woods. Her heart seemed to her to give a definite jump of nervousness. Or maybe it was sheer excitement. Continuing her casual walk, she pretended to believe she was alone. She hoped she looked her best. She had taken a quick glance at her reflection in the glass of the long river-view window as she left the parlor and felt that she had thought of everything. She looked as pretty as it was possible for Ellen Dunmore Gaynor to look. But she worried . . . was there too severe a profile, too cool blue eyes, something in her manner and movement to put him off? That "goddess" business wasn't necessarily flattering. She wanted to look her best as a *woman* for Bill Sholto.

"I'll be all simpering southern belle, like Mama, or like Amabel and Persis Warrender, even if I do think it makes a woman silly, addled, and needlessly inferior. Why must I act like that?"

But she would. Anything was worth it, to have Bill Sholto ache to want her as she wanted him.

Meanwhile the footsteps came nearer. She heard the little crunch of pebbles on the river path, but the bubble and gurgle of the river and the night breeze through the willows smothered the sound and she could still pretend she hadn't heard his approach . . . In a gesture curiously boyish for the experienced Captain Sholto he had slipped up behind her, reached around with his hands over her eyes and whispered in her ear, "Guess who?"

She knew she should play the coy Southern belle, but out of nervousness and still unsure of herself, she blurted out, "Captain!" and swung around in her captor's arms to see the surprised face of Gavin McCraw, pale and aesthetic, his flesh appearing milky in the starlight. Almost exactly as he had looked when he was the great love of her life six years ago, six ages ago. Now, she reminded herself, he was married to Daisy Wychfield, Bertha-Winn's older sister . . . In *those* days he had wanted to marry Maggilee. She wondered if he was happy with the substitute.

"Captain," he repeated in hurt tones. "Ellie, this isn't much of a greeting for an old friend. You've forgotten me. Gavin McCrae? I was visiting at Wychfield Hall back in '82. Fact is, we're visiting there now—er—Daisy and I. For the Hunt Ball."

"Yes. I know." She gave a quick look behind him into the woods, saw no one, and belatedly smiled and assured him, "Congratulations on your own wedding, Gavin. We were all happy for you."

"Were you?" He relaxed a little. She had once considered him "sensitive." Was that only weakness, after all?

With some of Varina's caustic view of the world, she couldn't resist adding, "Yes, indeed. Mother was especially happy. You know how she always liked you young people."

He swallowed. Yes. He remembered. He released Ellen and looked thoroughly lost. "Well—I just thought—I saw you standing out here looking so nice and I just had to say hello . . ."

Warmed by his compliment, and by his helplessness, she saw his hands hanging there in midair where they had dropped away from her eyes. She took his fingers, giving them a brief shake. "Thank you, Gavin. You are awfully kind. I suppose you-all at Wychfield are in a terrible state, what with the excitement of the party plans."

He gave a quick, nervous laugh, shaking her hands as if he didn't want to let go.

"Terrible is right. I had to get away for a little while. Walked a couple of miles along the river bank tonight, wondering about things." He looked up the grassy bank toward Gaynor House. The drapes over Maggilee's window were parted several inches. The lamp was still on.

Ellen guessed he was looking at her mother's room, and wondered what she thought about these sleepless nights, when she didn't take laudanum?

"Mag—I mean your mother—she's doing well?" Gavin got the words out with some embarrassment. So he hadn't forgotten her . . .

"As I said, she's doing very well. With the Salon and all." She hoped his being there wouldn't scare off Captain Sholto. Why didn't Gavin just go *on?* He still had more than a mile to walk if he was returning to Wychfield Hall tonight.

Finally Gavin said, with a sudden, unexpected bitterness, "Yes, I always suspected there wasn't a man in the world could come between her and her shop. Well, I'll say good night." He backed off, studied her up and down. "I must say, Ellie, you never looked better. You're so . . . grown up."

She couldn't help laughing. "Oh, Gavin, I'm six years older."

"But you're really—damn it—excuse me, Ellie, you're—a body'd be right to call you . . . pretty tonight."

Now she laughed again, this time at herself. He was so very much in earnest, and obviously thought he was paying her the finest of compliments. She started to wriggle her hands out of his grasp but her laughter had stimulated something or other in him, and much to her surprise he leaned over their hands and kissed her, almost, though not quite, on the lips. She was oddly pleased, even as she was annoyed and surprised.

But before she could say anything or even draw back from him, she heard other footsteps on the pebbled path and was sure that Captain Bill Sholto had seen her being embraced by Gavin McCrae. Her first reaction was fear that Bill might be turned away by this apparent sign of fickleness. A minute later, with Gavin apologizing stiffly and going on his way, she was delighted to see that, to the contrary, her worth had apparently risen in Bill Sholto's eyes.

He said a pleasant good-evening to Gavin, who nodded as he walked away, leaving the field to the newcomer. Bill immediately kissed her, almost as softly as Gavin had touched her. "This seems to be the greeting down South."

"This isn't *down* South, and that isn't the greeting. He happens to be an old friend."

He sighed. "Ah, that friendly southern hospitality I've heard so much about. Incidentally, this path will have to be paved over if you keep having so many male visitors tonight... Well, dear old Cousin Jono made it quite clear he's expecting me back in half an hour. Hardly time to make mad, passionate love to a lady."

She looked up, her face alive in the starlight. "And had you expected to make mad, passionate love to someone?"

He hesitated. He had moved closer and raised one hand to her face. He surprised her by his seriousness. "No, goddess. You're much too nice a girl."

She snapped angrily, almost tearful, "I'm not a girl. I'm an old maid."

"What? At your age? To me you're just ripe for a

clean young love. Like the bold swain I seem to have scared away." He brought her face close to his . . . if he wasn't going to make love to her, she thought it very cruel of him to tease her. She moistened her lips, wishing she knew what Maggilee would say in a situation like this.

"You—you might as well not waste this silly position we're in," she got out finally. "If we don't kiss, what are we doing here?"

He laughed so loudly she was afraid Maggilee would hear and look out her window. Then he did indeed kiss her, and she poured into her answering kiss all the passion she had hoarded up for him and perhaps for others before him. She did better than accept his arms holding her in an easy embrace. She locked her own arms around his shoulders, pulling his body closer to hers. She knew he wanted her at that moment as she wanted him. She felt no fear at all. Just his easy, almost gentle kiss must mean that he at least cared more for her than those other women he'd known, those Deadwood Calamity-Jane women, the ones who made a livelihood out of sex.

When they separated, finally, she still engrossed in a precious warmth, he managed to say, "You are without doubt the most enchanting goddess in God's entire firmament."

She made a face at the comparison, but as he let her go he added impatiently, "If you were only a little older, if you were just some little—but you're not. When I saw you here in the arms of that—whoever he is—I wanted you more than he did, by a damned sight. But you're going in to bed like the decent young lady you are, and I'm going back to Gaynor Ferry before Jono comes after me with a shotgun. Good night, goddess."

Not that again! She was so frustrated she could only turn around and walk rapidly up the slope of lawn to the house without once looking back.

Passing the open parlor doors on the way to the staircase, she was so deep into her thoughts that she was startled to hear her name called. She looked into the parlor. Her grandmother was still tatting, and hardly looked up long enough to say, "Are we to have a return of that miserable hot weather?"

"What on earth, Gran? . . . Hot weather? . . . But it's quite chilly out . . ."

"Then perhaps you will have the goodness to explain why you are so flushed."

As Ellen stood there wordless, the older woman chuckled dryly. "Never mind. If you had stayed out longer, I'd have had to stop my work and attend to the proprieties. Come and kiss me good night and then go up to those dreams you've got in your eyes."

Ellen ran to her and kissed the cheek her grandmother presented. Varina never kissed anyone. She claimed it was one of the prerogatives of age.

As Ellen left her, Varina asked quietly, "Has Maggilee met him?"

Without turning around, Ellen's back straightened, tension in every line of her body. "No."

"Good girl. Keep it that way."

CHAPTER 9

* * *

MAGGILEE FOUND one consolation in working so hard on the Wychfield Coming-Out Ball. Her usual insomnia was defeated temporarily, giving her a tired-in-every-bone drowsiness that eventually blurred into full sleep. For several days after the renewal of the loan with Harleigh Duckworth's bank, Maggilee was baffled by the changes she saw in her daughter. It seemed hardly possible that the mere presence of the chubby banker could arouse Ellen's latent interest in clothes, coiffures and even some subtle form of cosmetics. It must be

Cousin Jonathan's visitor... Well, she supposed she had better inspect the boy, see if his interest in Ellen was sincere. She hadn't been invited to Gaynor Ferry, and seldom went there of her own accord without being invited, but for her daughter's sake maybe she ought to go, even if Jonathan didn't want her around there. Ellen was twenty, an age when most women would be nursing their second child, but her daughter had always been so shy of men... She'd look the fellow over pretty soon, she promised herself, thus satisfying her burst of maternal concern. If only this damn Wychfield ball were behind her... Well, Jonathan wouldn't let Ellen come to any harm, and Ellen was not the sort to *respond* to any man... Her changed appearance, though, gave Maggilee fresh enthusiasm about Ellen's dress for the Ball. Ellen could easily outshine the other young women in the Coming-Out party if she had the right colors. The style would be no problem. It was one which suited Ellen's tall, slender figure much better than it would suit the pretty, chubby little belles who made up the rest of the party.

"Good. We can begin from there," she told Dora, her assistant, without explaining her prior thoughts. "The style is perfect for Ellen. And the shade must be completely different from what the other girls will wear.

With some alarm, Dora ran her hand over the crumpled yards of dull mustard-colored silk poplin spread out over the table and previously assigned to Ellen's gown.

"Surely not a dark, wintry shade, Miss Maggilee?"

"No. They'll think I've lost my mind. What we've got to do is make all the dresses as planned but say this particular bolt met some horrible fate. Water, I think. If only we had a water pump near this room... Let's pray for rain some time before the party. Less than two weeks now. We'll say a window was left open."

"But by the time we get rain, we mayn't have time to make up Miss Ellen's new dress."

Maggilee grinned. "Oh, yes, we will. We'll make the real dress secretly and then tell Irene Wychfield we worked all night sewing it up. The only question is where I'll find the new bolt of . . . moire, I think. Maybe even silk. I want it the most flattering shade for Ellen. But going to Norfolk or Portsmouth is just too much right now, busy as we are."

"How 'bout the County seat? That worthless man of mine was in Ashby yesterday, drinking up moonshine. But he did say Holderson's Drygoods Emporium was putting up bolts of mighty pretty cloth."

"Holderson's! Old Man Holderson told me only last week that he'd be getting in new goods. Thank you, Dora. I'll drive in to Ashby tomorrow. You and Ellen can take care of Gaynor's, can't you?"

"Don't you worry, ma'm. We'll keep things humming."

"Keep what humming, Mama?" Ellen asked as she came down the attic stairs carrying a red and green plaid taffeta dress whose side seams had been let out again for Mrs. Corrigan.

"Gaynor's, honey. I'm going in to the County seat to get some goods. Lordy, I do hate that long drive." Maggilee fingered the wild plaid in Ellen's arms. "By the way, can you hint—just a mere hint—that this is the last time we can let out the seams in that dress?"

Ellen laughed. "I promise. There's no more material, even if she gains another ten pounds." She turned to hang the heavy gown in the pink fitting booth but stopped as Maggilee muttered to herself, "Maybe I could get Jonathan or Nahum to take me downriver with the cargo, and bring me back by wagon—what's going down today?"

"A passel of watery fruit. Strawberries and some melons and what-not. You'd never be able to do it. It would ruin all your pretty clothes," Ellen said.

"My pretty clothes?" Maggilee gave a careless glance at the three-year-old taupe dress whose bustle had been removed, leaving it with no particular style. Her dress, fitted close around her small waist, almost as an unconscious added feature, called attention to her round, firm breasts and hips.

"I doubt if Jonathan's strawberries would ruin *this* Paris original," she told Ellen lightly and was a little annoyed that her daughter didn't seem to appreciate a joke when she heard one. "However, if the flatboat is crowded, well, never mind."

"Jono's bringing in several crates," Ellen explained.

Maggilee's pale auburn eyebrows went up. "Jono? Where on earth did you get that?"

Ellen picked up the skirt of Mrs. Corrigan's heavy dress and with Biddie began to examine it to see if there was dust anywhere on the plaid taffeta. She spoke casually, but very quickly. Too quickly. Not like Ellen. "Jono? Must have heard Nahum or someone say it. One of the field hands from the old Finch place, I expect. 'Mister Jono.' You know."

It was odd. In fact, Ellen was altogether behaving very oddly. But then Maggilee had never fully understood her daughter. "She's all Gaynor," Maggilee had once complained to Varina with angry disapproval of Ellen's proud, secretive ways.

Varina's smug reply was a slight correction. "All Dunmore-Gaynor. Fortunately."

There seemed no answer to that except to spill out her own red-haired wrath at these constant humiliations, which of course served no purpose except to prove Varina's point about Maggilee's "common behavior." Besides, the old witch was probably right. Ellen had never been anything like Maggilee or her maternal grandparents.

"Ellen, what is all this about Gaynor Ferry?" Maggilee raised her voice, quite unaware that her anger at the oft-played scene with Varina had triggered her sudden cross tone with her daughter. "Nahum has been into town and off to Ashby several times in the last few days. I thought Cousin Jonathan needed his help. Did that drifter who was visiting leave the Ferry?"

"Jonathan does need help. Nahum is helping. That's why he's moving the fruit out before it spoils."

Biddie and Dora exchanged glances. Biddie put in, "Nahum's been made foreman, Miss Maggi. That's keepin' him pretty busy for a lad his age."

"Yes, I know." Maggilee didn't look at the two women. She was looking intently at Ellen. "Is Jonathan alone out at the Ferry?"

Ellen brushed off Mrs. Corrigan's dress before answering coolly, "Certainly not. You heard Biddie tell you Cousin Jonathon made Nahum the foreman."

A heavy heel on the front step, followed by a long pull at the bell-key, broke up this dangerous little exchange.

"Land sakes!" Dora exclaimed, nervously nudging Biddie, "that'll be Miz Corrigan, and this dress wasn't ready a mite too soon."

As quickly as her anger had come, Maggilee was relieved to feel it gone. Thank God for Mrs. Corrigan. She would get to the bottom of the business about Gaynor Ferry right after the business at hand. Meanwhile, as she went to greet the Corrigan woman, she realized the enormous relief felt by all parties in the Salon. Whatever was going on, she seemed the only one left out of it . . . Well, she would change all *that* soon enough . . .

Several hours later she left for the County seat loosely

holding the reins of her mare and enjoying the cloud-swept autumn look of the countryside. She liked creating pictures in clothing and she was mentally discarding various shades of color for Ellen as she rode along.

Several times she passed County people on the road as her mind was busy reliving old days, old thoughts, but Maggilee Gaynor was famous for making up her manners as she chose. When she offended someone by ignoring him (or her), she made up for it at their next meeting by a friendly, almost bewitching enthusiasm. It had always been successful except, of course, with Varina's sort.

Now, as she thought of the joke she would play on the Wychfield Coming-Out party, presenting her daughter as its leading light, Maggilee laughed, a light, merry sound carried on the afternoon breeze, which gusted around her, tearing at her hair, prying her bonnet strings loose. She dropped the reins to grab at her bonnet. The mare, given its head, slowly trotted on around the corner. At the same time the bonnet flew off behind her.

"Pansy! Stop!" she commanded, but the mare, like her mistress, had a mind of her own. "Pansy!"

She knew the mare wouldn't get too far ahead so she jumped down from the buggy and ran back to an abandoned brown tobacco stem which had caught the aging bonnet. She pinned it back on her disheveled hair and started off on the run after the horse and buggy. She was, in fact, in such a hurry that she was more angry than surprised when a male voice called out from the road behind her.

"What the devil are you up to? You want to get yourself killed? You're only scaring that poor beast."

She grabbed at her bonnet, called over her shoulder, "It's my buggy. That damned mare's gone and run off with it."

He laughed, and she stopped, got a good look at the pedestrian. It was, of course, the cavalryman who had almost run her down in Gaynorville.

* * *

For more than a week Captain William Sholto had behaved like an honest yeoman, working hard for incredibly long hours, trying to keep up with the boyish black foreman, Nahum, in culling, packing, loading and then guiding the boats downstream or over the County road by wagon. He wanted to show Jonathan Gaynor he wasn't just hanging about to eat everyone's collards (God, no!) and hog jowls, *or* their catfish. He felt that Jonathan, a peculiar man and very deep, understood his motives. Which was more than Bill Sholto knew precisely about himself.

What was it Jono said last night when Bill returned from those few delightful minutes with the blonde Gaynor girl?

"She's not your sort, you know."

It had sounded like a warning, and his blood was stirred to a certain mean, quarrelsome temper. "How comes it that you know all about my sort, friend?"

Jonathan hadn't answered. He certainly didn't like a quarrel the way Bill Sholto enjoyed it: quick, loud, violent, then over and forgotten. But Bill had been on the warpath. No mistaking the look in those hard gray eyes. Jonathan meant business. He'd shoot a man who brought harm to his lovely young cousin. Bill said so aloud, prodding him, spoiling to ruffle the calm, impassive exterior of this Virginia gentleman.

"I suppose you'd murder me if I took Ellen to bed."

Jonathan looked up from his *History of Crop Failures in the South.* "It's *Miss* Ellen down here—*friend.*"

"Sorry . . . I was only joking." He surprised himself by

explaining. "I used to dream about girls like her, out in the Dakotas. You know. Scrubbed clean and white. Pure. With that long, cornsilk hair . . . You know what I'd like to do?"

Jonathan said nothing. He was waiting. He didn't seem to be breathing. Bill had seen the same waiting look in the eyes of one of Chief Crazy Horse's warriors when they'd met face to face, crawling up opposite slopes of a ridge only one valley away from the Little Big Horn. Bill still carried the scar, so close to his jugular vein he had damn near bled to death before his sergeant managed to drag him back. The Dakota warrior was less lucky. He took Bill's bullet in the mouth.

"Jono, what I'd like to do is unfasten Ellen's—Miss Ellen's—hair and just run my hands through it, like it would clean off the past. That's all I meant."

Jonathan said a curious thing. "You can't clean off the blood of the past. Shakespeare had it right."

"Who's talking about blood and killing? I'm talking about marriage."

Jonathan stared. He wasn't any more surprised than Bill Sholto, who heard his own words with astonishment.

"You know, I haven't talked about marriage since I was eighteen and asked the madam of a bawdy house to do me the honor." His face lightened at a memory.

Jonathan smiled, asked, "What did she say?"

"Molly-O? Dear Molly O'Devlin! Prettiest thing west of Wichita. She just laughed. Offered me a discount any time I wanted it. She was a great girl, was Molly-O. Common as pig tracks but let me tell you, she was dead straight. Any one of us would've given her our name, a ring, the whole business, just to make sure she belonged to us alone."

"Did she marry a general?"

"No." The brightness in his face faded. "She died in a cholera epidemic. Caught it nursing the boys."

"Don't sound much like Cousin Ellen to me. Not that she isn't a good nurse when a body's taken bad."

Bill rumpled his hair, thinking this over. "No, Ellen is a dream. Untouchable, you might say. Some goddess you just never quite own." He saw Jonathan raise his head and added quickly, "My, now, you're a touchy man. I didn't mean *own*. I meant—understand. Yea. Understand. It's one of her attractions." He kicked the log fire into flame with his boot-heel. "But she's part of why I came east."

"Don't tell me Dabney Bavier sold you on the Gaynor women, too."

"Hell, no. But I did come for a wife. And a place with roots. You see, I may not be good enough for Ellen in your eyes, but in a lot of ways she fills the bill for me. And don't get on your high horse if I tell you she's ripe for loving, too . . . All right, all right! I better say good night. I'm bedding down on the porch. It's too damned touchy in this house."

By the time Bill Sholto took a few hours off to do some of Jonathan's shopping in the County seat, he and Jonathan were friends again. He didn't at all resent Jonathan's prickly attitude about his young second cousin. Matter of fact, Sholto admired it, and he assured himself that whatever intentions he had toward Ellen were as honorable as Jonathan could have wished. But all the same, one of his reasons for the long walk to Ashby was the hope that somewhere along the way, either on the road or in Gaynorville, he might meet Ellen Gaynor, purely by "accident."

And now, having failed to meet a soul he knew in Gaynorville, he saw on the road to Ashby that gorgeous little redhead who reminded him faintly, but endearingly, of Molly O'Devlin, favorite of the Seventh Cavalry. Sure enough. The redhead's temper and language were just as peppery as Molly's, once she saw who he was, but unlike Molly she tried to cover up both.

She called, "Good God—I mean—good heavens, is there no escaping you?"

The air was bright and lively. He felt its vigor. Here was a girl to quarrel with, to squeeze and tease and watch that red-haired temper explode. He told her, "This time you can't blame me, Red. I'm on foot, after all."

"Well, you startled me. Pansy is racing off right out from under me." She really was a glorious creature, her exciting little body all tense, her breasts barely encompassed by that wide neckline and the way she pivoted with a graceful hip motion as she waved a fist at him and held her bonnet on the back of her head with the other hand.

"Get along. Go about your business."

"Now, now . . . Why are all redheads so touchy? I'll get your precious horse and buggy if you give me a smile." If she had been a lady, someone like Ellen Gaynor, she would refuse his advances cooly, but he made a bet with himself that this successor to Molly O'Devlin had never learned ladylike hypocrisy. Sure enough, she smiled. It was a wicked smile, as if he were the butt of her secret amusement . . . She wasn't a girl. Maybe older than she looked. Well, all the better. He wasn't in the mood to court two inexperienced girls at the same time. It had been bad enough keeping himself in check with Ellen when her response clearly told him that she was so ripe, but had to be gentled first.

The redhead was now saying, "Well, you might as well help me, at that. You've probably scared my poor mare into the next county."

She was a minx and he liked her for it. With one arm he pulled her along and started after the horse and buggy. Running beside him she displayed neat ankles. Her body pressed back against him. When he reached his arm around under her breasts, pretending to hurry her, he felt her heart beating. Good. The contact had excited her, too.

The brim of her tipsy bonnet brushed against his nose. He sneezed and with his nose edged the hat away. His chin touched the crown of her head with its fine red hair, now tousled by the wind.

"You really are a little thing, aren't you?"

"Big enough to handle you, if it comes to that."

He laughed. His lips grazed her ear and he could tell by the feel of her body that her desires easily matched his own. He said into her ear, "Do you know, you smile like a smug little puss just before she scratches? Not that I mind. I like a good tussle."

For some reason he had said the wrong thing. She shivered against his arm, and not from pleasure. Damn! Just when they were getting along so well.

"Sweetheart, don't tell me I've offended you."

"What made you say that?"

"Say what?" She had caught him by surprise. "That you're as unpredictable as a cat?"

"It's not that. It's just that I've heard it before. It seemed odd to hear you say it the same way."

"I reckon I should have said 'kitten.' "

"Don't be silly. I'm much too old to be kittenish. Oh, there's Pansy."

Who the hell was Pansy? He had thought they were all set, at least with a promise for the very near future. She certainly had an enticing body, and a tantalizing way about her . . .

A farm wagon full of country folk passed, returning from Ashby. Bill looked around. Maggilee laughed and drew him behind a tree. "Don't let them see. Those are the Putneys. Tenant farmers from down-country. Pansy is my mare."

He didn't want to let her out of his arms. He hesitated, but she wriggled away from him.

Nearby, nibbling at a stream of oats from some farmer's broken sack, was Pansy, that damned mare, still pulling the buggy. As the redhead started after him Sholto called out, "Tell me at least who you are, Red. You owe me that."

"Just think of me as Red," she called back, and having found Pansy's reins she looked around, asking in her most charming manner, "And who's my rescuer? Are you staying with any of the folks down-country?"

"Don't worry, Red. You and I are going to know each other a damn sight better. But if you have your mystery, I'm entitled to mine."

She shrugged and turned away cooly. Any man worth his salt, she thought, would have gotten in beside her and ridden into town with her.

He considered whether she expected him to ride into town with her, then decided to surprise her, leave her with her damn beloved Pansy. He could find out more about her later. She seemed disappointed, and he hoped she was. She deserved it, working him up into a state and then leaving him like a teasing bitch.

He raised two fingers to his hat in salute, and walked behind her right into town.

CHAPTER 10

***

*T*WO NIGHTS before Bertha-Winn Wychfield's Coming-Out Ball, several of the young ladies gathered in the large front parlor of Wychfield Hall for a festive evening of gossip, fuss over Bertha-Winn, and some last-minute practice in the dances of the evening. The girls had been escorted from the poplar drive to the splendid three-story Georgian brick hall by their male relatives, who then retired to Major Wychfield's study. Their mothers joined the other ladies who arrived from Fairevale and Ironwood plantations across the Ooscanoto

Bridge, or from Gaynor House and the County seat at Ashby.

Ellen was surprised when Varina agreed with Maggilee that the two younger Gaynor women must arrive by carriage, with Edward driving. Varina complained, "That wretched horse and buggy! But we can't let the Faires and those Cavanaughs of Ironwood give themselves airs. Newcomers, every one of them. The Faires barely arrived here just before the Revolution. By that time a Dunmore had already been governor of Virginia, when it was a Crown Colony."

"Unfortunately, that particular Dunmore was thrown out," Maggilee couldn't resist muttering.

Ellen heard and tried not to smile, but Varina countered quickly, "He left of his own volition, thank you. *He* wouldn't play the traitor to his kind. At all events, Ellen," she added, picking up her tatting, "your Gaynor grandfather saw Ironwood built, and that was a century and a half after the Gaynors had settled here. So don't you let them put on airs with you."

Ellen had heard it all before, but she said, "They never do, Gran. They're all friends of mine." She thought it over and amended, "Friendly neighbors, I'd say."

Maggilee reminded her, "You'd have more friends, honey, if you unbent a little. You're always so . . . standoffish."

Ellen thought wryly: much you know about it, Mother. Much you ever knew about me! But then—do I really know you?

She felt a little sad at the realization, and had to be snapped out of her mood by the jubilant Maggilee as she climbed into the buggy and they trotted off toward Wychfield Hall.

"Honey, you're going to be a triumph. You do love the new dress, don't you?"

"It's wonderful, Mother. Though I'm having a little trouble with my conscience, carrying this stupid mustard dress, pretending I'm to wear it."

"My Lord, Ellie! Do you really want to look like a dowdy old maid? Because that's how you look in this impossible dress."

"Maybe I *am* a dowdy old maid," Ellen told her. "And there's so much conniving in this change of dresses. I mean—if you pretend the mustard colored one got wet, why didn't the others? And how could a complicated dress be whipped up overnight?"

Maggilee slapped her hand in a friendly way. "Leave that to me. Dora and Biddie and I presumably slaved away all day and all night over your dress after the rain ruined this mustard one . . . Smells like rain, don't you think?" (Wishful thinking, Ellen decided, but joined her mother in the hope.) "Anyway, honey, the whole County will say we are noble creatures to get you ready in time."

Ellen looked down at her hands, examined them carefully. "It just seems so sneaking. So dishonest." She knew her mother was disappointed and said quickly, "But I'm awfully grateful. This mustard dress takes all the color out of my hair and makes my skin look positively blue."

"That's the girl. You'll be a real advertisement for the Salon when they all realize what can be done, especially after seeing you in this thing." She pointed to the heavy package across Ellen's lap. "The new French silk is a wonderful shade for you. You looked downright impressive when we fitted you this morning."

Ellen had a sudden impulse to lean over and kiss her mother's flushed cheek, but this sort of spontaneous behavior was discouraged long ago by her teacher and preceptor, Varina. Nor had Maggilee ever been demonstrative with her daughter as a child. So Ellen merely smiled her gratitude and sat very straight, hoping she would do justice to all her mother's hard work. They rode up to Wychfield Hall just as the new moon was obscured behind a wind-driven mound of clouds, and Ellen wondered with amusement and some awe if her mother was going to produce the first rain of the season by sheer concentration.

Major Ferris Wychfield, a serious man who loved best to argue politics with his cronies when safely away from the women, stood at the portico to greet the two Gaynor women. His wife embraced them both in a civil if unenthusiastic way.

"My dears, how good to see you! I might almost say, Maggilee, without you and your shop, there could not be a Wychfield Hunt Ball."

Maggilee, almost without thinking, replied: "Irene, darling, if it weren't for that good-lookin' husband of yours, we'd never have come."

While the two women went inside together, Major Wychfield bowed over Ellen's hand with old-fashioned pre-war gallantry and told her she was indeed welcome in his house. He had been heard to say that Ellen Dunmore Gaynor was "the only sensible, serious-minded young woman in the County," a compliment Ellen was forced to live with. He escorted her in through the spacious central hall, where her coat was taken by what seemed to be a dozen invisible hands, while Daisy Wychfield McCrae and her husband Gavin greeted her.

Daisy was a likeable chatterbox. She now elbowed her husband so hard he winced. "I just set myself out to capture this handsome creature, and by the Lord, I did!

We're related by marriage, but tut to that, I say! You-all can't blame me, can you? Poor Gavin! I'm making him blush, but it's true and I'll not deny it. Now, the next thing is to find someone for you, Ellen. Nice and handsome and very, very tall."

Ellen couldn't help remembering how Gavin McCrae had kissed her in a kind of panic less than two weeks ago. She wondered if he would spend his life always wanting the women he didn't have. She was almost ready to think "poor Daisy," but it occurred to her that Daisy wouldn't comprehend the pity. If anything happened to her marriage, she would find happiness some other way. Daisy took hold of life.

Ellen returned Daisy's quick hug. "Thank you, Daisy, but I'm an incurable old maid, I suspect."

All the same, Ellen knew a secret satisfaction. There was an attractive man at Gaynor Ferry who acted as if he wanted her. She needn't be an old maid. But even if she became one, she was fairly sure one Captain Bill Sholto felt about her *almost* the way she felt about him. At least he showed every sign of it. Since meeting him, she couldn't understand what she had ever seen in that hang-dog intellectual Gavin McCrae.

Daisy was chattering away as they went to join the girls upstairs, and Ellen said abruptly, "Daisy, you're an old married lady now, but you've had dozens of beaus—"

"Oh, honey, not dozens. But several interesting ones, I confess."

"Suppose one of them was very . . ."

"Physical?"

"No. Of course not . . ." And she had a quick, unwanted memory of Jem Faire and that near-violent encounter. "Not at all. Very romantic, I was going to say."

Daisy gave her a side glance. "Not physical?"

"A gentleman!"

Daisy giggled. "I'd figure he was pleasuring himself with someone else."

Ellen considered. Even now, this very moment, she *felt* the memory of Bill's strong arms and his kisses. She could appreciate the smooth, soft, gentle way he want about it, but she of course knew there must be more. She thought of his lips touching other parts of her body. His caressing hands had known just how to hold her . . . but he hadn't tried to go further. She assumed she would have fought him off as she'd fought off Jem Faire, but all the same, she wondered that he hadn't tried. Was she really so prim and proper? And had he gotten his real satisfaction from some woman in the tenant farms beyond Gaynor Ferry, the way the likes of Jem Faire must carry on?

"Even if a man did that—you know—with somebody else, it wouldn't be love," Ellen said finally.

"Lordy, no. Lust, the Bible calls it. Thanks be that Gavin isn't lustful. He's such a good boy. Behaves beautifully." She didn't look as though she was all that thankful, however.

Ellen looked back down the great double staircase, wondering as she often did why she admired the graceful white staircase at Gaynor House so much more. Even aside from a lifetime's affection and childhood memories of the smaller, more perfectly arranged house in which she was born, there was something so grand about Wychfield that she could never feel at home in most of its long, high-ceilinged rooms . . . Fairevale, across the Ooscanoto, was in some ways even worse. The biggest place in two counties. But at least it had the personality of Colonel Faire to make it warm and inviting to the visitor. In her childhood Ellen had loved Fairevale, as a haven largely, because of the genial, garrulous Irishman who was master.

Daisy's curiosity had been aroused by Ellen's unusual question and she broke in: "You aren't going to leave the subject like that, Ellie, you tease! What is this about lust?"

Ellen shrugged. "A book I was reading."

"You and your books. You are getting as bad as your Cousin Jonathan. Ellie, honey, you won't find your lustful gentleman in some silly old book. If I told you the wiles I used to snare my sweet Gavin at White Sulphur Springs —well, they're not for a maiden's ears. Here we are. I declare, we're crowded. All that impossible 'back drapery' takes up every inch of room."

"But it will be a lovely ball!"

The dancing-master, a tiny, ancient Frenchman, Monsieur Bonet, was pirouetting about the Wychfield ballroom, demonstrating dips and turns of the waltz to several young ladies who were dancing in pairs. There were shrieks of merriment and much stumbling over skirts, with squeals of pain when they trod on each other's toes. Worst of all was Bertha-Winn, looking wilted, overtrimmed, hot and sweating. She left a disgruntled partner, Amabel Corrigan, and confided to Ellen, "Thanks be, you-all came. I'm so scared."

"But Daisy says your escort will be Mister Carroll. You aren't scared of him?" It was an open secret that Bertha was exceedingly fond of a young distant cousin, Wilbur Carroll.

"I'm scared of falling all over myself. But how could I be afraid of my dear Wilbur? I know everybody thinks he's funny. He's not romantic the way they are in plays. But I like him just the way he is. He's not pretty, Lord knows, but he makes me feel comfortable . . . even beautiful."

For an instant her ungainly body stood straight and

full of grace. Her complexion, which looked muddy against the oyster-white of her dimity gown, became warm with a flattering blush. Ellen was impressed by these true and perhaps deepest effects of love. She wondered if her own looks would improve so dramatically when—and if—she might marry the man who was quickly becoming the center of her world. She touched Bertha's cheek lightly with one finger. She seldom allowed herself to demonstrate emotions, but she felt an old tenderness toward this homely, endearing girl who, though younger than Ellen, had been her friend from childhood.

"I reckon that's what love is all about, dear."

Bertha studied her solemnly. "Ellie, you are so smart."

Ellen laughed at that. "I'm probably more stupid about love and its ways than any woman in this room. And all the girls except Daisy are younger than I am."

"You're smarter. I don't care what you say." Bertha-Winn leaned forward and touched Ellen's cheek with her own. "I love Daisy," she whispered in Ellen's ear, "but sometimes I feel closer to you. We understand each other."

"Yes, I think we do, Bertha. You must have a happy life, you and Mister Carroll. I think Daisy will, too."

Bertha said carelessly, "Of course she will. If she doesn't, she'll pound life into any shape she wants. In a way, I envy her."

This can't be all there is to love, Ellen insisted, but silently. She still dreamed of a great love, and its fulfillment . . . and I will know it with Bill Sholto, she vowed to herself. *I will.*

The older women marshaled the girls into some kind of order. To the tune of a Strauss waltz played on the Wychfield pianoforte by Miss Eliza Faire, Colonel Faire's spinster daughter in her funereal black, the girls divided into pairs again, dipped and swayed and even marched to the Lancers step, looking awkward without male counterparts.

Ellen, her mind on other things, moved easily and mechanically through the intricate dance.

"That will do, young ladies," Irene Wychfield called from the wide, fan-shaped foot of the staircase. "Pick up the beat now. Miss Eliza, the music, if you please."

It was not until more than an hour later that the feminine rehearsal ended and everyone gathered to view Bertha-Winn's recently received eighteenth-birthday presents in the long, many-windowed music room, between Daisy's unused harp and an ancient harpsichord on which Bertha-Winn had practiced many a lesson to no avail.

Suddenly a sharp voice, too sharp in the circumstances, interrupted this warm scene. Miss Eliza Faire, looking a little like a crow, suggested, "Bertha, bring the ladies some of the refreshments." She nodded to Maggilee, said, " 'Evening, Ellen," and went back to assist in supervising the girls.

As a child Ellen had been befriended very early by both Miss Eliza and her father, but it was obvious to everyone there had been no love lost between Eliza Faire and Maggilee Gaynor. It annoyed Ellen tonight to see this dislike so nakedly displayed and she murmured to her mother, "Miss Eliza seems to have left her manners upstairs."

But Maggilee only winked. "We couldn't both marry your father, and Eliza saw him first. I was the Beausnatcher." She laughed at her own joke.

"So she's gone into eternal mourning ever since. Did you ever see her in anything but rusty black? Surely Father wasn't the last man on earch, or even in Tudor County."

They laughed together and went over to the sideboard for a cup of punch. There was a pleasant feeling of companionship between them. Only minutes later, it was broken by Maggilee.

"Honey, I think we should be getting home. I've got to get to town extra early tomorrow."

Surprised, Ellen offered, "I'll go with you. I don't mind. The earlier the better. We can get more done."

But Maggilee refused, almost brusquely. "No, no. You take your time. I have a few last-minute touches I want to make to that special ball gown of yours. I can work better alone. But thanks anyway, honey."

After another protest, Ellen gave up.

Maggilee remarked in passing, "By the way, God's in his heaven . . . it started to sprinkle about ten minutes ago. It'll rain tonight. Not much. But enough." She winked at Ellen, who laughed at her prophecy, while those nearby were impressed by this apparent close relationship between mother and daughter.

* * *

Maggilee walked briskly over the harvested and rumpled autumn fields behind the old Ashby Road. She hoped to arrive by way of a certain grove of trees between the East Dunmore Creek and the Confederate Cemetery just a few minutes before the Bluecoat cavalryman passed through the same grove.

Three days ago she had left Ellen at home fitting Varina in her new gray silk for the Ball, and had taken the buggy alone to Ashby for a much-needed bolt of fabric. Outside the cemetery she met the man in the cavalry hat. He had walked into town from the direction of the Finch properties beyond Gaynor Creek and jokingly flirted with her for half an hour. It had been a great boost to her spirits. For some reason he called her "Molly-O" while she, equal to the occasion, kept the secret of her real identity.

Aware that the sight of them together would give the town gossips something to chew on, Maggilee had deftly moved into the fenced off graveyard where—between flattering propositions from the captain—she pointed out the various noble dead. When there seemed no way they could prolong this tour of the cemetery, Sholto had said boldly, "When will I see you again, Red? I'll be by here tomorrow."

"I won't," she said tartly.

"You can't stay hidden forever. Sooner or later you'll be passing by. Before you do, I'll catch you in that little clutch of trees over there."

"Likely!" She turned quickly from him and the edge of her mantle caught on a button of his homespun jacket, tearing the button off. As he and Maggilee stooped to pick up both button and mantle, their contrived closeness brought his mouth to hers. Her warm, moist lips with their sensuous curve had been his first goal and he made the most of his opportunity. She returned his long, hard kiss with a passionate hint of her arousal. They stared at each other. He grinned.

"I knew it, sweetheart. I've been looking for you ever since—" He broke off. "Well—somebody I knew long ago. Dead now, bless her. But I've found you, Molly-O. And you're not going to get away again."

"I'm getting away now, Mister Captain." She gave him a knowing smile and, with a sway of her skirts, walked out of the cemetery, swinging the gate closed hard behind her. The gate latch caught and she was gone before he could follow.

The next five days were an agony for her. She could think of nothing but the hard strength of his arms and the warmth of his kiss. Finally she abandoned her earlier one-week resolve. That she'd see him again, she had no doubt, but best to wait. She had known several other physical attractions since the real love of her life, but this was the first time she had felt again the overall attraction as strong as she'd once, and only once, known. The excitement of the rehearsal had made up her mind. She'd go to his clutch of trees tomorrow morning.

Maggilee left the buggy now and took the steps over a stile, through another field, and crossed the creek bridge. Beyond the creek, lined by dogwood and half-hidden violets, was a clumb of curiously intermingled trees: dogwood, willows, poplars and oaks, while the undergrowth, damp from the previous night's light rain, felt like a mossy green carpet under her feet. In an unusual concession to fashion—and appearance—she wore neat kid pumps that revealed her ankles.

She chided herself: Why should he be here at this hour? He probably spent his nights making love to some black or white wench from the Finch tenantry. It didn't seem likely that even the most love-besotted suitor would be up and walking this early in the morning.

The day began to warm, and wisps of steam rose from the dewy underbrush. Maggilee had already made her way beyond the willows, and begun to step carefully to keep from slipping on the still-soggy leaves, when she suddenly walked into the captain. He must have been watching her cross the bridge. He was here. He had let her come to him, actually to his arms. He reached for her now, confident of her. His breath in her ear made her shiver as he drew her close to him.

"You're late, Red. Are you going to keep me wet and gloomy for another whole, wretched day?"

He was certainly sure of himself, but she didn't mind that. She raised her head and forced an impudent, challenging look. Not enough to put him off but enough so that he'd never feel he'd bought her cheaply.

She asked, "Is it the Yankee or the Western part of you that makes you so crude?"

He laughed, warning her, "Don't look at me like that, you red-haired bitch, or I'll take you right here and now in the wet grass."

It was *good* to be alive again. Maggilee's heart raced, stimulated by his manner, his talk, his closeness. She was glad to feel against her body the proof that she had stirred him to the same hungry feeling.

"There must be dry grass somewhere."

Her words were whorish, her smile sweet and teasing. The combination he found irresistible. Both arms were around her waist, with her face close to his, her warm breasts pressed against his body. He lifted her now, like a tawny little cat, unsure whether she would bite, scratch or purr. But when she insisted, "Set me down! I didn't say—you wouldn't dare . . . you don't even know who I am," . . . it was too late.

She'd been careful not to let her protests discourage him. She weighed very little and was easy enough to lift over underbrush through a narrow space between poplars and willow rushes leading to a broken-down log house whose roof was gone and whose single room had a dirt floor.

Long ago, before the War, one of the Gaynors had experimented with drying tobacco here. It hadn't worked and, for a brief time after the War, runaway ex-slaves up from the Carolinas had lived here. Now it was so sheltered and overgrown even children had stopped playing inside its inadequate three walls. Bill Sholto must have picked it out long before meeting her this morning. Was he *that* sure of her . . . ?

She was surprised, and a little touched, to find he had spread a heavy winter poncho on the dirt floor. He knelt with her now on the rough cloth. She murmured simply, "You are a practical man. I like that."

Afterward, they would both marvel at how few preliminaries there were between them. They knew what they wanted, what they needed. They were neither virginal, nor hypocrites, and there were no reproaches on either side.

Maggilee welcomed him as he came down upon her, drawing him to her with her arms and legs locked around his body, her own body ready. She wore two petticoats under her dress, and when his hands moved softly but firmly over the warm flesh beneath her skirts, she moaned in the satisfaction of an old hunger. She hadn't expected him to be so gentle, and when he entered her waiting body, the release of their growing passion was almost simultaneous.

"Sweet, adorable Molly-O, we were made for each other," he whispered.

So he thought of her as some young sweetheart of his youth . . . well, she didn't mind. She pictured herself as that early love taken into maturity by this passionate man. She liked the portrait of Maggilee Favrol Gaynor as a pure and inexperienced girl that he'd seduced long ago. She wouldn't spoil the moment by asking him to tell her about the virgins he'd had . . . that would come later, but she grew more and more interested in the idea that she had become, for him, the embodiment of that lost, innocent girl he had once known.

And meanwhile, there was this marvelous release of long pent-up tension in such a simple act as making love to the right man . . . Dear little Molly-O, she thought . . . I wonder what you were like. Well, I shall take your place . . .

CHAPTER 11

***

MAGGILEE HURRIED lightly up the servants' stairs of Wychfield Hall closely followed by Dora, who carried a long box. Maggilee's hair had escaped from its old-fashioned knitted snood and was beaten by the misty wind into a mass of auburn curls. It made her heart-shaped face look as young as any of the debutantes present for Bertha-Winn's Coming-Out Ball, but the similarity ended there. Her poplin dress was old, worn, and more suited to a poor-white than to the widow of a Virginia plantation owner.

Irene Wychfield gave her a brief up-and-down survey, compressed her lips, and then, carried away by the excitement of the occasion, bustled around, gathering up the giggling, nervous bevy of girls.

"I see your mother has finally arrived, Ellen. Now, young ladies, we must leave our Ellen to dress. And the sooner the better. I reckon we might just form our line for the Receiving. To be all ready . . . Maggilee, my dear, you *will* hurry?"

Sweeping her dust ruffle up over one arm, Daisy followed her stepmother into the adjoining bedroom, calling over her shoulder, "Ellie, honey, just *dress* . . . nobody's going to care how you look . . ."

To Maggilee's great satisfaction, that set Ellen's back up. Before the door closed on the girls, Ellen said, very much Varina Gaynor's granddaughter, "Mama, do hurry . . . *they are going to care very much how I look, I guarantee you . . .*"

Out came the yards of moire, taffeta and fine lace, in a shade deeper than blue ice, bearing no resemblance to the popular pastels worn by the other bridesmaids. It was a color, or lack of color, that suggested a regal, almost forbidding, elegance. But Maggilee's eye for the most flattering colors hadn't failed her. By the time the gown had been eased on over Ellen's petticoats and the pad which provided the silhouette of a bustle without including this gradually outmoded style, even Ellen could see how the curious shade perfectly matched her eyes and seemed to give them new depth.

"Miss Ellie!" Dora breathed, getting her first look at the overall vision of Ellen in the new gown. "Your complexion! I never saw the like. Pure china."

Maggilee agreed. "Porcelain. Look at yourself, Ellie, honey. Ever see the like? Not even Varina ever looked like that."

Ellen stared, seeing the tall young woman in the pier-glass, hardly recognizing her. The gown followed the long, slender lines of her torso. Below her hips the material flowed out behind her in a smooth, fan-shaped train, untrammeled by ruffles or bows, but gently rustling as she moved. The bodice was close-fitting, high-necked at the back with a square-cut décolletage in front. The pale flesh of her throat was covered by lace so nearly matching her own complexion it appeared that her throat and upper bosom were bare. The tight sleeves were three-quarter length, finished with lace frills that flattered her long, thin fingers. Maggilee drew out a few fine-spun strands of Ellen's high coiffure, softening this frame of her face.

Ellen caught her breath. "You don't think it's a bit daring?"

Dora said emphatically, "Law, no, Miss Ellie. Elegant. Like Miss Varina, 'n kinda bold."

Bold, thought Ellen, straightening her shoulders . . . That's the difference between Gran and me . . . she can afford to be bold . . .

"She'll do. My girl will do," Maggilee agreed. "She'll show them, for both of us."

Ellen stepped out behind the shifting, shuffling procession of girls. The rustle of her skirts and small train called their attention to her. One by one, they looked around. It required all her will-power to prevent her shoulders from sagging to conceal her height, and to prevent her hands from lingering over the lace insert covering her throat and bosom.

They were shocked. That much was certain. Amabel and Maud and Mrs. Wychfield clearly didn't like what they saw. It obviously upset all their pre-set images of plain Ellen Gaynor.

Irene Wychfield's eyes had opened a little wider as she considered the ugly duckling-into-swan transformation, but except for two little lines carved at either side of her mouth, she gave no other hint of disapproval. She waved Ellen to her place beyond the Wychfield girls.

The lilt of a waltz met the arriving guests moving past the Wychfields and the girls, along the hall to the ballroom. Every girl, inspired by the music, the grand occasion and her own special gown, felt as if she were curtsying to the new President, Grover Cleveland, himself.

Dozens of faces stared at them. Ellen saw her Grandmother Varina standing between Judge Warrender and Colonel Faire, never looking more imperious or lovely. She wore only the Dunmore pearls in her pierced ears and a tiny gold comb—once outlined in similarly matched pearls—in her simply coiffed white hair. Varina had never explained the missing pearls, but Ellen grew up believing she had sold them one by one to keep Gaynor land intact. Her gown's gray-blue shade enhanced all her most admired qualities.

She was apparently the first to see Ellen with Amabel and Persis Warrender. Ellen, watching her, saw her eyes glow with innate pride.

"She *is* proud of me," Ellen told herself and tried not to think of the trick played on the party. Everyone adores Varina, but that isn't what I want. Admiration is so cold. I want love, the way Mama knew it . . . She blotted that out hastily. No, I want the kind of love Captain Sholto can give me, not Mama's flirtations.

Keeping her head up, her shoulders straight, she opened up her silk and ivory fan with relief. It wasn't until she had fanned herself vigorously and moved to the far edge of the receiving group that she allowed her eyes to wander.

Daisy's vibrant personality overcame the slight awkwardness of her stance in too tight a skirt. As for Bertha-

Winn, she might be perspiring and uncomfortable in her gown but her face radiated love and hope when the chubby, beaming Wilbur Carroll passed along the receiving line.

Ellen's glance flickered over the guests. Varina's eyes had wandered as well. She was studying the new drapes at the long river windows. Cheap quality—Ellen could almost read her thoughts—but of course Gaynor House has a better view. And then, this house is new, scarcely more than fifty years. No tradition . . .

How nice to be so sure of yourself, Ellen thought, but couldn't like her grandmother the less for that . . . queens and empresses were allowed.

Late in the proceedings, Ellen saw Maggilee upstairs, standing with Dora Johnson and the Wychfield servants, all of them leaning over the heavily carved upstairs bannisters to watch the festivities. Maggilee didn't look unhappy or isolated. Like Varina, Maggilee looked proud, and perhaps with better reason. She was seeing all her own creative talent come to blossom in the group below the stairs. Ellen smiled up at her mother, indicating with an expressive eyebrow that Maggilee should join the guests, but Maggilee was determined to let Ellen shine tonight, and pretended not to notice Ellen's signal.

The line of arriving guests thinned out, groups mingled, the hired orchestra of five took over from Miss Eliza, and Ellen found herself the center of her own little coterie. After a moment's self-consciousness, which caused her to react cooly, she responded to the genuine interest of Colonel Faire, banker Harleigh Duckworth, even Major Ferris Wychfield. The latter went directly from kissing Bertha and Daisy to kissing Ellen. He didn't even spoil his gallant salute with his comment: "Good to see you looking so elegant. Positively regal, m'dear. A fine, sensible female." *Sensible* . . . she could have done without *that* . . .

Close behind him came Colonel Faire. His face was ruddy, partly due to his pride in her and perhaps a little more to the whiskey he and other war veterans had put away beforehand in Major Wychfield's study. He grabbed Ellen's shoulders, gave her a bourbon-flavored kiss, which she returned affectionately. She sometimes thought he cared more for her than any member of her own family did. Before letting her go, he tickled her ear with his whisper. "My nephew's here." (She tried to look around him but he blocked her view.) "I think he'd like to partner you in the Grand March."

"Did he tell you to ask me?"

"You know Jem. Never asks favors. But he's sure as hell—pardon—sure as fate looking at you. Not that I blame him."

He moved on to bow gallantly, if a trifle unsteadily, over dark Persis Warrender's hand, as the girl curtsied. Ellen now had a clear view across the long ballroom.

Sure enough, there he was against the far wall, the tall, trim young man with a scowl, looking like a black and white monolith thanks to his formal suit and the white shirt with its brightness immaculate against his bronze skin. He wore one glove and beat the other impatiently across his bare palm. Around Ellen the girls were buzzing about him. Although he was presentable down to the last detail, with his blue-black hair just in place, Ellen suspected he was excruciatingly bored.

She heard Amabel's well-remembered giggle as the girl announced in a sibilant whisper: "He's sure to stop for me. You mustn't let it go further, but he's very taken with me. Of course, he doesn't like to show it. He's painfully shy."

About as shy as a snorting black stallion, Ellen thought. Most of the younger men against the far wall were also gossiping among themselves, selecting their partners for the Grand March around the ballroom, to be led by Bertha-Winn and Wilbur Carroll, followed by Daisy and Gavin McCrae and then the other girls with their chosen partners. It was clear that none of the girls expected Ellen to provide competition. They were already dividing the eligible males among themselves.

To bolster her fading confidence Ellen had a devilish notion. Why not show up those girls who were so sure of their own attractions? She fixed her attention on Jem Faire across the hall and mentally willed him to look at her. He turned his head, finally, and his bored, almost sullen gaze caught Ellen in the most dazzling smile of which she was capable. It was a clear enough invitation but he frowned, probably wondering whom the smile was meant for. He raised his eyebrows. She nodded, still smiling. He made his decision somewhat deliberately, then strolled across the floor.

Ellen held her breath. She would never get over the shame of it if he turned her down in front of all these people.

Both the Wychfield girls and Persis Warrender had already been claimed, and the chaperones, led by Irene Wychfield, were herding them into line. Amabel Corrigan began to shuffle her dancing slippers nervously as Jem Faire approached. He wasn't looking at the girls. He seemed deeply interested in the glove he eased on over his fingers.

Suddenly, he was standing before Ellen, and she thought how good it was to look upward into a dancing partner's eyes instead of levelly, or worse, downward.

Amabel and Maud Kent were stricken to silence even though they were the object of attention from two nervous, sweating young men.

"Was that an invitation to me?" Jem asked her bluntly.

Ellen kept the smile fixed on her face. "Really . . . I do think, sir, that you presume—"

Taking her hand, he pulled her away from the others. "Next thing I know, you'll be fluttering your lashes and rapping my knuckles with a fan."

She gritted her teeth. Mortified to think she might have exaggerated her flirtatious manner, she wouldn't dream of letting him know he had hurt her. "I give you full permission to retreat right now," she said, "though I must say you'll be the first coward in the Faire family."

He laughed at that and she permitted herself to be led into the line of march.

The Grand March served to show off the young ladies' gowns, the nervousness of their partners, and prospective matches for the chaperones to gossip about. Ellen, who thought it all a pretty silly business, couldn't think of a single thing to say to Jem. Probably nothing would interest him, she decided, and she didn't dare to practice any flirtatious tricks as she would have done, say, with Captain Sholto—*Bill* Sholto, sophisticated, worldly . . .

On the other hand, it was hard to find fault with Jem Faire's public manner, in spite of what he had said to her privately, and she didn't miss the way Amabel Corrigan and several other girls almost unscrewed their necks trying to observe her with Jem.

The first man who asked her to dance, however, was Jem's uncle, Colonel Faire. Fortunately, the Lancers could be danced in his present condition. He need not even step on her toes, though he admitted during a few seconds into the dance that he felt a trifle dizzy.

"Do better after a wee dram of fresh air," he told her at the end of the dance.

She promised to save a dance when he recovered in the fresh air, but reminded himthat the night threatened rain.

"All the better," he mumbled, then smiled ingratiatingly. "Thin out the whiskey I've nipped."

She laughed and when he had taken her to the old-fashioned settle beside Varina, she watched his stiff-legged progress out toward the front doors.

Someone, probably Daisy, had persuaded the orchestra to play a peculiar, lively dance that some of the more knowledgeable ladies informed Varina was "The Apache Stomp."

"Land-alive!" Mrs. Corrigan breathed heavily. "It must surely be a shock to a lady of your refinement, Miss Varina."

But Varina refused to be patronized. "Not at all, madam. In my youth, when some of this country was very young, the frontier folk danced jigs and went to routs that made this affair look very tame by comparison. *In my day,* our liveliest pastime was shocking our elders."

Ellen laughed and kissed her cheek, whispering, "Bravo, Gran."

Ellen danced the waltz with Judge Warrender, a stately white-haired and -bearded old gentleman with no light conversation, either.

"I certainly can't practice a light manner with him," she thought, and managed to reply soberly when he devoted the dance to a discussion of a land dispute with the Cavanaughs of Ironwood House in the next county. But Ellen was soon relieved that the conversation required no sparkle on her part. She became too busy watching the other waltzers, especially raven-haired Persis Warrender being whirled around and around in the arms of dark, exciting—admit it—Jem Faire.

As the couples passed in the dance, Ellen came face to face again with Jem. She hadn't time to do more than smile before the judge determinedly guided her away. She was rewarded for her good humor at the end of the dance by seeing Jim Faire usher his partner to Judge Warrender and casually glance at Ellen a yard or so away. Once again he raised his eyebrows. Ellen shrugged. He looked as if he might take this for a refusal, but the music of a bright, toe-tapping reel started up, and he offered her his arm.

It was a reel Ellen had danced as a child and one she loved. In surprisingly little time her usual inhibitions were all but gone. Jem, she saw, was affected by the music, the air of festivity, and perhaps his partner . . . His arm went around her lithe waist, hard and secure. She had forgotten what his laughter could do in provocative contrast to his somber good looks. The caller's voice halted for an unexpected throat-clearing. Everyone laughed at the caller except Ellen, who found herself close enough to touch Jem's mouth.

I won't think of that, she promised herself, but suspected from the amused look in Jem's eyes that he too was thinking of it. Her tongue flicked quickly over her lips, giving her away, and she was relieved when the caller's voice went on.

"No slaps tonight?" Jem asked as the dance ended.

"No kisses. No slaps." But she felt warm and not quite in control of herself.

Fortunately, her grandmother kept her from going any further along that dangerous line. "My girl, there's a friend waiting at the door to escort you home. I'd like to have a word with you about that."

Jem had Ellen's arm in his and looked now beyond the ballroom at the hall and the east front door . . . where Captain Sholto lounged against the newel post in his blue uniform that made several ladies shy away from him in distaste. No one was making him feel at home and yet he had been kind enough to come into a den of enemies just on her account . . . She freed her arm from Jem's in order to wave to Bill, and he returned her hail with his cavalry hat in hand.

"Why, Gran," she said, "I'd no idea you'd even met the captain." She remembered her dance partner then and started to make her excuses, but he had beaten her to it. With assistance from Varina's cool air, Jem inclined his head slightly to Ellen, thanked her in what she considered his "arrogant voice" and went off to that silly, yellow-haired Amabel Corrigan and her clan.

If Ellen hadn't known herself so well she might almost have thought she was jealous of his attentions to Amabel. Actually, she explained to herself, she was only sorry that he had such poor taste. Then she turned to matters of more immediate concern.

"Gran, where did you meet Captain Sholto, for heaven's sake?"

The merest shadow of a smile appeared on Varina's face. "He asked for me. I knew at once he was your secret gallant. I warned him that your mother and I, with Colonel Faire and his daughter, will be returning to Gaynor House in a few minutes for a midnight stirrup cup. At that time I'd like you to be present, my girl. So you had better be on your way now." She paused just long enough to place extra emphasis on the next innocuous words. "Maggilee was in here half an hour ago . . . She may be back . . . I believe her headache is getting better . . ."

Ellen recognized the warning to go off with Captain Sholto before her mother saw him. She glanced up the staircase.

"Go on, child, don't keep this young man waiting," Varina advised firmly. She lowered her naturally deep-pitched voice to a murmur. "He has over six thousand dollars he's earned or won—heaven knows how. And he intends to invest it in land hereabouts."

Ellen was startled. "Gran, you wouldn't sell part of the Gaynor land!"

"Who talks of selling? There's more than one way to skin a cat. Or persuade a headstrong young man to make a good investment."

It sounded odd to hear a forty-year-old man called "young," but Ellen was so relieved at what seemed to be Varina's blessing on the relationship that she didn't go further and question her motives. She hugged the older woman, promised to go straight home, and went off to join Captain Sholto.

He tipped his hat gallantly and said to her behind its shelter, "What a woman you've become! Where has this glorious creature been hiding all this time?"

She winced at the reference to her usual plain appearance but he teased her, "Let's get out before I have to fight off every red-blooded male here."

"There's only one with *real* red blood." She laughed. "And I'm not sure he wants to steal me from anybody. He'd apparently rather steal Amabel Corrigan."

"What? Well, I'm mighty pleased to hear it. He's welcome to those corkscrew curls." He didn't wait but hurried her out to the drive.

A few minutes later Ellen found herself beside the

captain driving out between the Wychfield wrought-iron gates on their way to Gaynor House. In spite of the faint mist, somewhere to the south the moon was trying to make its presence dimly felt.

Bill Sholto had borrowed Cousin Jonathan's horse and buggy for the occasion. Having looked Ellen over until she was worried that something had gone wrong with her Cinderella finery, he said, "I like your grandmother."

Surprised, she smiled. "I'm glad. So do I. Very few do, though. They admire her, and respect and—heaven knows—they fear her. But *like?*"

"She is very good-natured."

Increasingly astonished, she stared at him. "How did you happen to meet her?"

He grinned. "They weren't going to let me in. Not invited, you see. And they weren't exactly overjoyed at my uniform."

"Neither is grandmother. I'm amazed she even spoke to you. Sometimes she acts as if the War ended yesterday."

"Well, she did back off at first. But I said I'd come to collect you after the ceremony, and for some reason she told the Wychfield butler I was a guest of the Gaynors. I thought she was your mother, at first. You do favor her."

Ellen nodded. "I'm always being told that. Did she say anything about mother?"

"Just that she was busy upstairs and wouldn't be able to meet me." He added abruptly, "You don't want her to meet me, do you, Ellen?"

Flustered at his nearness to the truth, she asked, "Why shouldn't she?"

"Be honest, honey. An aristocratic lady of the Old South, widowed by us Bluebellies . . . you know."

She was so relieved she laughed. "It's nothing like

that. Not in the least." He didn't seem to be hurt by his suspicions.

"Anyway, your grandmother was a deal politer than I expected. Kept telling me how pretty you were, and how sweet. Not that I needed telling."

She reddened, hoping Varina hadn't overdone it. She said, honestly, "Mother is prettier, and she can be nicer, than either grandmother *or* me."

His eyebrow went up. "Not by what your grandmother said. She said the old—I mean your mother—hated soldiers, blue uniforms, and I'd better keep out of her sight. Tell you the truth, I don't much want to meet her. I've never known any Grand Dames. Except you." Before she could deny this, he surprised her with a total non-sequitur: "Why doesn't Jono attend any of the County affairs?"

She was relieved, though it was hardly a subject that interested her . . . Besides, she was long accustomed to Jonathan's hermit life.

"Reckon he just doesn't like swarms of people around him."

"Maybe. But he's been a mighty good host to me. Good boss as well, for the time being."

She didn't like the sound of that "time being." Was he already thinking about leaving? If only she had the talent, the clever ability of her mother to hold a man . . . Did women ever hold a man by the reserve she'd used for so long to camouflage the turmoil she felt inside? Perhaps all these years her training had been a mistake. She must demonstrate her own true feelings to receive his love. How else would he know that there was genuine emotion beneath her too-calm surface?

She smiled at him, not casually, and moved a bit closer to his warm, hard body. He studied her face. She thought his rather cynical look softened. It didn't matter. She was sure she loved everything that was part of him, the cynicism as well as the bruised good looks.

"Sweetheart . . ." he began.

She raised her eyelids slowly. "How lovely that sounds—" and then, to her own disgust, habit spoiled her effort and she laughed, "as if you'd had a heap of practice."

He winced. "If you were anyone else—like a certain Molly-O that I—that I knew once, I'd say practice makes perfect."

"Well?"

His free arm pulled her against him. Nervous now that she seemed to have aroused him, she wanted to draw away but managed to force down the inhibitions of a lifetime. The buggy bounced along. How unromantic, she thought, acutely aware of the rattling and swaying of the buggy as Bill Sholto kissed her. But under the impetus of her heady success at Wychfield Hall, she seized on that gentle, proper kiss to give out all her own pent-up feelings. She had learned about violence and passion from another man . . . Jem Faire, in spite of his violence, taught her there was more to her own kiss than a mere outpouring of playful flirtation. All she knew was that her mouth responded to Sholto's gentle caress with an abandoned, uninhibited kiss, fighting his own careful restraint, forcing his lips and his body to betray the passion he probably saved for his "Molly-O" women. Whoever they were . . .

She wanted this love-making to blot out all the sensations she had begun to learn from a less gallant, less gentle man. She also wanted Bill Sholto to forget forever the cheap and trashy mistresses that must fill his past. "Molly-O" indeed!

Feeling the sharp draw on its reins, the horse slowed to an amble. Bill Sholto had responded as Ellen hoped, but now she grew frightened. He was going further than she intended . . . or thought she intended . . . but all of her craved him as he looped the reins, secured them, and reached under her cloak, over her silk-covered hips and commenced to unbutton the long basque bodice that covered her. How practiced he was . . . not like fumbling Gavin McCrae or that light of her fourteen-year-old life, Albert Dimster.

Though Sholto was neither violent nor brutal, she began to panic, began to push him away with her elbows, whispering, "Not here, not like this, later . . ."

But he was no longer playing a game, a flirtation. He'd had enough of protecting her against herself . . . He had been aroused and meant to be satisfied.

"Sweetheart . . ." He whispered into her ear as his hands moved under her camisole to her warm but now reluctant flesh. Her thoughts were in a turmoil, confused by her desire that he *never* take his hands off her body . . . She wanted these exquisite moments to last forever. She had made him forget his Molly-O . . . perhaps too well . . .

His mouth and hands had roused her to a pitch that matched his own. She gasped, felt herself drawn closer to his body, her hands crushed hotly against his thighs. She no longer held back—

And then they both heard hoofbeats along the road behind them, two horsemen riding home from the ball while their ladies followed more sedately in carriages.

"Damn!" Bill let her go.

Feeling dizzy, she pulled her cloak over the unbuttoned bodice of her gown, doing nothing about her corset and camisole and lace-trimmed underthings in disarray beneath. She had almost been seduced, and she had *liked* it. Her own reaction shocked, but all rather pleased her. She felt that she could hardly wait until that act of love was completed . . .

Sholto did something with the reins, managing to tear the leather, and then signaled to the oncoming horsemen, who had obviously seen the stopped buggy and would suspect the worst. While Ellen, looking flushed and her hair disheveled, listened with what she hoped was a bored, faintly annoyed expression, Bill explained that the line had frayed and could they give him a little help. Before either Mr. Corrigan or Dr. Nickels could do more than rein up their own mounts, Bill got the leather tied, apologized, and sent them on their way. Cousin Jonathan's good-natured old horse then calmly ambled along in their wake.

"You did all that business, breaking the line and all, to protect my reputation. . . ."

He shrugged, then grinned at her. "Thought I'd see how it felt, just for a change. Protecting a lady's honor, I mean."

With a directness that startled herself, Ellen said, "I love you. And please don't laugh. I *do* love *you.*"

He covered her twisting, nervous fingers with one calloused hand. "I love you too, my sweetheart. And I won't laugh. Matter of fact, I think I'd sooner bawl."

"What?"

He did not look at her but kept his eyes on the Gaynor turnoff in the road ahead.

"Because you're kind of special . . . I swear I never knew a woman like you. Knew her well, I mean. And yet, it's no use . . . there'll be others. You came to me, sweetheart, about twenty years too late . . ."

Daring everything, feeling desperate, she slipped her

hand out from under his, touched his thigh and rested her hand on his leg. "I tell you, I am like all the others. I want you to love me"—and in case there was any possibility he didn't understand—"make love to me, I mean . . ."

He looked down at her hand. After a brief silence, during which she felt the ripple of muscle as he moved his leg, he cleared his throat and said uneasily, "Sweetheart . . . I've got a pretty little wench on the string right now, going to meet her later tonight, in fact . . . we're two of a kind . . . You, darlin', need somebody special. I've done things—lived in ways you'd never imagine. I've killed my share. Hostiles, mostly, but once"—he cleared his throat—"well, we found out later that half the dead were squaws, even some little—"

"Don't!"

"Sure. Just want you to see it's all wrong. You and me." But he stared at her finally and in spite of all his arguments, she knew he wanted her. After he had made love to her, she was certain he would marry her. He was that sort. Decent, never mind what he said. They *belonged* together. She knew it. She would make him forget that field girl . . . or *whoever* his precious "Molly-O" might be . . .

CHAPTER 12

***

VARINA DUNMORE GAYNOR picked up her tatting shuttles and eyed Harleigh Duckworth as Marie Antoinette might study Georges-Jacques Danton. She ignored any good qualities he possessed, concentrating on the matters which concerned her.

"Do sit down, Mr.—er—yes. Duckworth, of course. Of the Baltimore Duckworths, I believe." He corrected her. She agreed, "Richmond Duckworths . . . yes, of course . . ." This, along with his bow as he raised her hand to his lips, brought a slight note of approval to her voice as she said, "Do sit down, my daughter-in-law and the Faires will be down shortly. They are primping upstairs. Then we may all enjoy a little warmth."

Mr. Duckworth began to beam.

Missing nothing, she added, "A tea tray will warm us nicely." The beam faded. Varina began to examine the row of pink lace in her lap.

The banker murmured with a nervous display of enthusiasm, "Lovely work, ma'm. May I ask, what is it to be?"

She held it up. "The oldest Corrigan girl is in the family way. With such people it is a way of life."

He smiled tentatively, not sure whether she had intended the pun. She looked over her spectacles at him and he quickly rearranged his face. After an awkward few minutes of silence, Varina asked in her imperious fashion, "Would you mind ringing that little bell on the sideboard? My granddaughter should be arriving home."

Duly summoned, Edward Hone arrived at the same time that Maggilee and her guests came down the stairs from the bedrooms. Before Varina could speak, Hone said to her, "Miss Ellen has just gone up to her room."

"She is late.

"Yes, ma'm." Hone seemed to take quiet pride in forestalling her criticism. "There was a slight accident. A broken rein, I believe Miss Ellen said."

Maggilee, who had been discussing repairs to the passementerie in Miss Eliza Faire's black-taffeta dress, turned to ask casually, "Who brought her home, one of the town boys?"

"I believe not. It was Mister Jonathan's buggy."

"But Cousin Jonathan wasn't there."

"So Miss Ellen says."

The Faires were moving into the elegant parlor to join Varina and Duckworth. Maggilee let them go. She glanced up the stairs.

"Ellen is there now. She didn't stop in to see us."

"She went up the back steps, Miss Maggilee. She seemed—agitated."

"Over a buggy ride? Edward, what *has* she been doing?"

Maggilee saw that she and the butler were alone. She knew he was the only member of the household who looked to her as its mistress. She was the only person who called him "Edward," and not, coldly and indifferently, "Hone." They both felt themselves outsiders in this relic of the Old South.

Edward considered her before answering. "I never saw the . . . gentleman before. The soldier, I should say. In the cavalry."

Maggilee took hold of the newel post. Her voice sounded much too light to her own ears.

"Really? A cavalryman? Wonders never cease. Edward, is the tea tray ready?"

She felt sick to her stomach . . . My God! He's after *Ellen* . . .

Edward said, "All ready. Ceci is bringing it in. Will you pour, Miss Maggilee?"

He had to repeat his question before she heard him. "No . . . yes . . . that is, I've something else to do tonight . . . or, I had." His calm, correct face asked her no questions, yet she had a strong compulsion to explain—at least as much as she could. "I was going out. I mean, back to the shop. You see, I lost so much time at the ball tonight . . ."

" 'Fraid I didn't quite take your meaning, Miss Maggilee. Are you pouring? The tea, I mean." The whiskey decanter was close to his hand but he pretended to ignore it.

"Reckon I'll have to." She gave him a saucy grin that made her pert face look all of sixteen. "I do hate teas." She added in a whisper, "And dull old officers reliving the War."

His eyes told her he understood perfectly, though his expression scarcely changed. He signaled to his daughter Ceci, who sailed past him and Maggilee, headed for Varina. The latter was now surrounded by her admirers, including Miss Eliza Faire and her father the colonel, but she took time to whisper an order in Ceci's ear. The girl hesitated, then nodded and left the room, avoiding Maggilee.

Varina cut across the small talk to demand of her daughter-in-law, "Where is Ellen? These County boys know better than to dawdle with my grandchild."

Maggilee saw the quick interest of the Faires and Harleigh Duckworth and tried to contain her indignation at this hint of her own guilt.

"Ellen is twenty. I think she may be trusted to behave properly, like any other well-brought-up female." Before Varina could reply, Maggilee ended, "Ellen's escort had difficulties with a broken rein, but she's here now. She will be down in a minute. Shall we all have a drop of the Gaynor bourbon to warm us for our little journeys?"

Harleigh Duckworth and Colonel Faire leaped at this suggestion with enthusiasm just as Ellen came in.

She had arranged her ball gown but her cheeks were still flushed and her eyes full of sparkle. Maggilee eyed her carefully. Yes . . . it was infatuation with some man, all right. Maggilee knew the symptoms too well . . . But Bill Sholto? Had the man deliberately set out to seduce a respectable and decent young virgin, her own daughter . . .

The hurt was surprisingly deep. Maggilee took a full swallow of whiskey, asking herself to face whether her concern for her daughter was greater than her own jealousy. She was still facing it when she raised her glass to her lips again and saw over the rim of the glass the thoughtful, very thoughtful, stare of her mother-in-law. Did Varina suspect . . . ? Her gaze seemed to grind its way into Maggilee's soul.

Varina offered Ellen a cup and saucer which she accepted, and Maggilee noted that for some reason the older woman seemed especially satisfied with her granddaughter. Secrets there? Or just their usual close understanding?

Ellen and Eliza Faire chattered on amiably. They had always gotten along very well. Perhaps Eliza saw something of the dead Beauford Gaynor in Ellen, though what those qualities might be escaped Maggilee. Her husband had been sleek, insincere, a fickle charmer. Ellen was his opposite in every way. Or at least had been, until a few minutes ago . . . *Was* it Bill Sholto who had produced the spark and excitement, the womanly, knowing appeal in Ellen tonight? . . . Meanwhile, Eliza and the gentlemen were outdoing each other to praise Ellen's appearance now and at the ball.

"So like your dear papa," Eliza Faire murmured. "That same fine look when you descended the stairs with dear Beauford's grace . . . I remember at *my* coming-out . . . He had been turning pages for me on the pianoforte in the upstairs music room. We walked down the stairs together. I'll never forget . . ."

"None of us will, my child," Varina agreed, adding what Maggilee knew was a calculated stab at her. "We all thought that night you and Beauford would—well, it was not to be." Her sigh was studied.

Still basking in the glow of her own much more recent memories, Ellen paid no attention to this usual sniping. But not her mother . . .

You bitch! Maggilee thought . . . Varina . . . you vicious old *cat* . . . Maggilee had also been debating whether actually to meet Bill Sholto as they had planned—and give him a piece of her red-headed temper, or just ignore their rendezvous. Stimulated by the whiskey and the not so veiled insults passed, she got up. "You must excuse me. I have things to do at the Salon. Some orders that must be ready for delivery to Portsmouth and Norfolk tomorrow."

Though Eliza Faire was shocked at this sudden departure, Harleigh Duckworth speedily bounced up. "Do let me escort you, Miss Maggilee. It's too late for a lady like you to be out alone."

. . . And wouldn't that be jolly, if he saw Bill Sholto! It would be all over Tidewater Virginia in no time. "No, no, my dear friend. I couldn't deprive our guests of your good company. I'll hurry, perhaps I may return for a late supper. I'm sure we'll all be famished."

Then she had Ellen to contend with. The girl insisted, "After all you did for me today, Mama, with that lovely dress, the least I can do is help you tonight."

Even when Varina cut in sharply, "Don't be rude, child, we have our guests," Ellen persisted, and Maggilee had to tell her firmly that she preferred to work alone, that she had some creative thoughts that required peace and quiet.

Just as Colonel Faire and Harleigh Duckworth started with her to the horse and cart on the gravel drive, Miss Eliza and Varina exchanged looks that plainly showed their agreement on her bad manners. Maggilee laughed. She felt reckless. An impending quarrel often made her feel reckless, especially when nourished by a stiff glass of spirits.

"Take care, Miss Maggilee," Edward Hone said in his quiet way as he gave her Pansy's reins.

With the battle light in her eyes, Maggilee thanked him, wanting to say, You might warn Bill Sholto. He's the one in trouble! But she merely waved to him and then to Pansy and set off.

The mist had passed over. Weak, watery moonlight softened the shadow. Much like last night. Her body and Bill's together in the tack room just off the hay, feed, and grain store. Warmly fitting, as if Bill were the incarnation of that other love, long ago. Outside, she remembered now, there had been intermittent rain. Then the even splash-splash of water drops off the roof into the rain barrel below the window.

Maggilee called to the guiltless animal, "Get *on*, Pansy!"

She moistened her lips, felt the pressure of Bill Sholto's mouth upon hers. Hard and thoughtless. All emotion. No consideration. That was all right. She had thought only of the pleasure he gave her. She stiffened. A pleasure he practiced on alternate nights with her daughter?

"No, by God, no!" Not her innocent Ellen . . .

An innocent of twenty?

"What was I doing at twenty? I had been widowed for almost four years. I had a daughter to support, and my precious mother-in-law. That blackmailer . . ."

She heard herself laugh, a harsh sound in the autumn night. Her thoughts came sharp on each other. And wasn't I a blackmailer too? We are well matched, Varina and I. Chained together for life . . .

She shuddered, telling herself she deserved a little

happiness. The shop was a success but only the work mattered to her. She had no real interest in the results, at least for herself. Changing styles were only important as they brought her the idea of success. The ball tonight had been a good advertisement for her shop, but above all, what a delightful revenge it was against those planter families who had never accepted her since her marriage to Beau Gaynor! Today their simpering little girls were completely eclipsed by the elegant beauty of Maggilee Favrol's daughter.

She saw that she had reached the graveyard fence. Gamble's Hay, Feed and Grain Store was off to her left, the unused tack room deserted except for the gas street-globe on the corner, whose flickering glow had been enough for Captain Bill Sholto and his easy redhead, "Molly-O"... She had felt more excited than at any time since the black day in '65 when the world had exploded for her...

She got out of the cart now, unharnessed and rubbed down Pansy, who began to munch on a heaped pan of oats. "Well, my pretty, shall I send him on his way with a flea in his ear? Shall I lay him cold with old Adam Gamble's musket? The pin's broken but the barrel ought to crack his thick skull... Oh, I'm a fool, Pansy. Face it ... I *want* him." Pansy's large right eye regarded her warily, and Maggilee felt in duty bound to defend herself ... "After all ... Ellen has her whole life before her. Besides, she's a cool, careful girl. She doesn't need this the way I do."

Pansy nudged her arm out of the way ... Maggilee's hand had gotten between Pansy and her little meal. Maggilee laughed and slapped her smooth flank. "All right, girl. No sympathy from you, I can see that."

She turned, started up the open, creaking stairs to the

long, unused tack room. Only a moment after she sensed someone behind her, she felt herself lifted off her feet by two calloused hands closed tightly under her still young, admirably rounded breasts. She called out, partly in surprise, partly because it was expected of her. Pansy's head moved, but only with casual interest . . . She had heard such scenes before.

"You damned Bluebelly . . ." She tried to think of the vilest words she had heard in her girlhood during the War, but it was all so long ago. And besides, since '65 she had never thought of men in blue uniform as the Enemy.

"Damn you! . . ." getting down to personalities. "Let me go. I know exactly what you've been up to . . ."

His rough chin rubbed against the softness of her cheek. "All right, Red. Now just what've I done?"

He had the nerve to ask. Chasing after her daughter, a decent young lady . . . and betraying her in the bargain.

"Done? You've been doing your best to seduce a respectable girl—"

He kicked her in the seat—not too hard—and lifted her into his arms in spite of her shriek of outrage. He laughed, his mouth close to her ear, as she struggled like a bug on its back.

"A little late for you to be calling yourself respectable, Molly-O. But you can call yourself a girl forever, for all of me."

The trouble was that in more than twenty years she hadn't known such pleasure as she felt now in his arms. Her struggle only added to it . . . It became easy to forget her daughter Ellen, except as a rival . . .

Finally she cried out indignantly, "You did! You drove Ellen—Ellen Gaynor—home from the Wychfields."

"So I did. A fine, lovely young lady. And I've no doubt you've done a little driving home with your own local swains. You couldn't be this good in bed without a bit of practice, my Molly-O."

"And don't call me Molly-O."

"What else, sweetheart? You're so damned secret. Young Nahum told me there's a pretty redhead down by the river. Came over from Charlotte County. Mighty hospitable. I said I knew her. I do, don't I?"

... If I tell him the truth, will all this end?, she asked herself, suddenly terrified ... Will he feel I'm too old? A grown daughter ... will he resent the truth? He *might* even prefer the daughter to the mother ...

She couldn't bear it.

Sulkily, as if forced to the truth, she murmured, "Charlotte County was so tiresome. No future there ..." Not quite a spoken lie. She had never visited Charlotte County. But he could accept the implication. He did, and was amused. He wanted her to be the trashy redhead from one of the river houses. It suited her, and him ... How long she could keep up the charade she didn't know, but if she felt in the future as she felt this minute, she would never want to let him go.

He dropped her onto the pile of worn, patched summer overalls and shirts, plus feed bags and canvas scraps. He'd thrown down the curious, picturesque serape collected in his western travels, and its roughness against her flesh acted to further excite her. She held out her arms to him.

He dropped down on her, knowing from previous experience that she was more quickly aroused by his weight and strength. In practiced haste she opened her basque bodice.

"Thank God for you, Molly, sweetheart. There's no holding back with you. No company manners and acting the gent. I'm not cut out to hold back."

Knowing he must be thinking of Ellen, who certainly wasn't his type, she took his head between her hands and guided his face, his rough mouth to the warm hollow between her still shapely breasts. Only her large, highly colored nipples were those of an experienced woman, and especially enticing to him.

All the built-up and unsatisfied desires aroused by his struggle with Ellen could now be poured out to the mutual satisfaction of himself and his "Molly-O."

. . . You're right, sweetheart, he thought, as his lips brushed the sweet warmth of one breast . . . I've known all along that Ellen Gaynor wasn't for the likes of me. Maybe I just never got Molly-O out of my blood . . .

But was this redhead only his dream of the vanished Molly-O? Or was she a real love, special for and of herself . . . ?

He heard her gasp, but doubted he had hurt her as his finger coaxed her aroused breasts. "Now, sweetheart, you never complained before."

"That—the door—" she whispered, struggling to break his hold.

Understanding finally, he looked around. A young black woman, neatly dressed in a dark, hooded coat, stood in the doorway, her mouth open, her knuckles pressed against her teeth to keep silence. Then she turned abruptly and clattered down the stairs.

"Who is it?" Sholto demanded. "Are you married? Was she spying on us for your husband or—"

"Oh, God! God!" she muttered, scrambling to her feet, fastening her bodice, ignoring her disheveled hair and skirt. He persisted in his question and she snapped impatiently, "No, I'm *not* married, but that's Ceci Hone. She hates me. She's loyal to—to my worst enemy."

It had been a rough night for Bill Sholto. First, there

was cool, aristocratic Ellen Gaynor who had turned out a dazzling tease. He should have known better than to let himself be aroused to such a state with her. But to have the thing happen a second time in one night, with his fiery little redhead, of all people, it was too damn much. He felt strongly inclined to knock her down and complete what he had started. But he could laugh at himself, and did, with an irrepressible chuckle that infuriated the redhead. She slapped him hard across the cheek. What a wallop! And when that didn't stop him, she pushed out the door and went after the vanished Ceci Hone.

Maggilee's fury only masked her deep anxiety. Ceci had probably been put up to this by Varina. What would Varina make of it? The worst, obviously. More blackmail.

CHAPTER 13

***

SHAKEN BY the sensations of her moments with Sholto, Ellen could never recall the details of the hours that followed, during which she substituted for her mother and even her grandmother as a gracious hostess. She made conversation with Colonel Faire, her hand in his red, weathered palm as he assured her she was "a darlin' young colleen. You pleasure the eyes. Put me in mind of those glorious days before the War. Never saw you looking better, m'dear. A true belle of our beloved Old Dominion."

Ellen overlooked his pompous tinge. He was a good man. He had been her father's commander late in the War. She couldn't forget how often she had made the long walk along the river bank past Wychfield to the big bridge, crossed the Ooscanoto and been received with stocky, florid Colonel Faire's usual good nature. The stories he told her of neck-and-nook daring in the War had seemed a trifle absurd to her practical mind, but even then she appreciated his kindness in not saying, "Run along home, child. Don't annoy your elders," as too many others did . . .

Miss Eliza squeezed Ellen's arms now as they stood on the east porch waiting for their buggy. "Dear Ellen, how splendid you looked tonight! And how you brought back the memory of your gallant father!"

"Thank you." She was uncomfortable over excessive praise of her father. She knew quite well that he had betrayed his young wife, betrayed Ellen herself, before he died. She loved him dutifully and sometimes with a sort of pity, but she never made Eliza Faire's mistake of setting Beauford Gaynor on a pedestal.

Miss Eliza patted her hand. "Once again you show you are the true mistress of Gaynor House. After Miss Varina, of course."

"As you say. After my grandmother. And Mama," she said stiffly.

"I understand. The whole County knows you are a good and loyal daughter, my dear."

Annoyed, Ellen turned away from her to wish the banker Harleigh Duckworth good night. He seemed upset and she had an unpleasant feeling that Maggilee's abrupt departure had cost her an extension on the bank loan. She tried to think of some way to soothe him. Her mother certainly couldn't afford to antagonize a banker.

"My mother will be so sorry, Mr. Duckworth! She told me how much she looked forward to her little—chats with you."

His small eyes seemed to brighten. "Did she now? But of course we may have many another—chat."

"Indeed, sir." She smiled teasingly. "One splendid dividend, as you might say, about her loans from your bank is that she and all of us are privileged to visit with Virginia's foremost banker."

He tried hard to appear modest. "Well, now, I wouldn't go so far as to say the—foremost."

"But I would, sir. A girl may always quote her mama."

He went off a happy banker.

Ellen returned to the big, elegant parlor in time to see Varina making her way up the stairs to her master bedchamber. She waited for Ellen, who ran lightly up the stairs, kissing the cheek Varina presented.

"Gran, what a night! You were splendid. No back trouble? No neuralgia?"

"Certainly not with guests present."

"Sleep well, Gran."

Varina turned, looked down the stairs. Her grim face broke into a faint smile. "After I hear from Ceci Hone. Send her to me when she returns, no matter what time it is." She went on to her room, supporting her right arm with her left. She might be in pain but she seemed so pleased with herself Ellen felt sympathy was unnecessary and even unwelcome. But she did wonder what errand Ceci Hone was to have carried out for Varina.

After the excitements of the day and evening, Ellen should have been ready for bed when she went upstairs but she was far too charged up to sleep now. She spent a few minutes fingering the stiff, gorgeous surface of her ball dress, holding it up in front of the glass, smoothing its folds against and around her slender, supple body.

Surely, what she saw in that reflection was more attractive than her mother was . . . *I can really get up courage and introduce Captain Sholto to Mama if I look like this*... Her conscience hurt a little with the reminder that Maggilee was responsible for her transformation, but Maggilee could win anyone. Bill Sholto was the only man who belonged to Ellen. She had discovered him. Her mother, thank God, didn't even know him.

"I'd best wait a little longer. Until the captain has gotten over his ridiculous notion that he and I somehow aren't equals..." Maddening! Of course they were equals! She slapped the mirrored reflection. *Purity. Much good that had done her!* Then, smiling wryly at her stinging palm, she reasoned, *it isn't as if his past were here. It's back in Deadwood. Or wherever he fought those Indians.*

She wondered if he might, just possibly, be outside on the grounds, walking near where she had met him the other night when it had looked for a minute or two as if he might overcome such resistence as she saw fit to put up, and take her there on the grass. Hanging up the lovely blue dress, she went to the window and looked out across the lawn to the trees on the south and the river to the west. Wasn't that a shadow out there, feebly cast by the misty moon?

She decided not to go out. Another time, when she was more—when she looked better, in one of her best gowns—when she could give herself without doubt.

What a coward I am! No time like the present. She reached for the first coat she could find, a black wool Directoire redingote two years old with a torn lining. It had always made her look mature for her years but in this instance it might be all for the best. At least Captain

Sholto couldn't accuse her of being too young for him. Varina had liked the coat and seemed flattered when numerous townspeople mentioned how much the black redingote pointed up the resemblance between herself and her granddaughter.

Ellen rushed out of her room and down the stairs, still fighting to get her arm into the right hole in the silk lining. By the time she reached the grass she couldn't see any sign of Captain Sholto. The night was wet and chilly, though the mist had moved on. Maybe he hadn't been here at all. She stopped, listened, and heard voices below the east porch, low at first, what appeared to be a challenge—that was the male voice, followed by high-pitched indignation. The woman was Ceci Hone. The man was her father, Edward Hone. Ellen moved silently across the grass and under the south end of the porch.

Ceci was saying, "Pa, Miss Varina *sent* me to follow Miss Maggilee . . . I only did my job. I saw her and a—"

"I don't want to hear what you saw, Ceci. Go on up to your room. I want to talk to you."

"I got to see Miss Varina."

"You'll see nobody. Mind that!"

Ceci shrugged her way past her father, giving him a sulky look before disappearing.

Ellen came around up the step of the porch. "Mr. Hone, can we stop this sort of gossip now? Before it goes any further?"

"I hope so. I think so, Miss Ellen. She has always obeyed me." He moistened his lips, then confessed, "But a parent never can be sure, not these days. My girl was brought up to her duties by Miss Varina and naturally feels a certain loyalty to her." He studied Ellen while she wondered what he was thinking. He seemed satisfied that he could trust her and went on, "I won't let her hurt Miss Maggilee. I give you my word. I'll call my own an out-and-out liar if I have to."

"Thank you. I don't know what this so-called scandal is . . . and I don't want to know. I hope we can all forget this thing ever happened."

"Nobody's going to bring shame to Miss Maggilee. Least of all any kin of mine. Good night, Miss Ellen."

She had to be content with that, but for an hour or two she lay in bed wondering in what "scandal" her mother had been caught. Very likely Maggilee had met Harleigh Duckworth, and continued her flirtation with an eye to the next business loan.

She finally got to sleep, only to be awakened by Varina stamping on the floor with whatever weapon happened to be closest to hand. Ellen sighed, and got up.

By the time she reached Varina's room the older woman looked as composed as ever, having apparently arranged her hair and wrapper before arousing anyone. Ellen, on the contrary, was disheveled, in her nightgown, and barefooted.

She sighed when she saw her grandmother sitting there on her chaise longue looking pink-cheeked, her eyes almost snapping . . . with anger, or anticipation?

So it was all true. Varina *was* back of Ceci's spying. "She came in some minutes ago, about the time I went to sleep," Ellen told her.

Varina ignored this hint. "And why didn't she come to see me at once?"

"She had an errand for you?"

"I said she did. Now, don't lie to me. What has happened?"

Hoping she would be able to settle this without a quarrel, Ellen said, "Maybe she had no message, after all.

Do you really think I would lie to you, Gran?"

"Most likely. I reckon I'd lie to you if it served my purpose."

Ellen didn't doubt it. She yawned elaborately and dug her cold, bare feet into the thick carpet. "I'll go back to sleep now, if you don't need me."

"I didn't need you in the first place. I told you that. I need Ceci Hone."

Since she was still asking about the maid, Ellen could be relieved on one score. Edward Hone had kept his daughter from betraying whatever secret she knew about Maggilee. "Ceci has gone to bed. And if you aren't suffering any pain, Gran, I think you should do the same."

Varina snapped, "I'm always in pain. But I surely don't intend to parade it for my enemies to gloat over."

Ellen smiled and kissed her faintly sweating forehead. The older woman pretended to turn away, ignoring this demonstration of sentiment. The faint sweat, however, told Ellen that Varina probably did suffer, even while she stubbornly discouraged all sympathy.

"You don't have any enemies, Gran. Why . . . you've outlived them all."

Varina chuckled. "By the eternal, that's true enough!" She waved her granddaughter away and then, suddenly, her play-acting attitude was banished as she said, with all her old, keen attention, "That's your mother. I know her step. Send her in—no! Don't. I must think."

Ellen left her, realizing that whatever scheme she was planning needed ammunition which Ceci Hone had failed to provide. Meanwhile, Maggilee looked as if she had been running as she reached the top of the stairs and stopped short at the sight of Ellen in nightgown and bare feet.

"What's happened? Has Varina had an attack?"

She was certainly unnerved. Short of breath and wide-eyed, she puzzled Ellen, who was used to seeing her independent mother very much her own mistress, afraid of nothing. But even before Maggilee asked, "Has Ceci Hone come in?" Ellen realized the truth. Her mother knew she had been spied on. To relieve her of that worry, Ellen said quietly, "Ceci's father talked to her. She had some gossip she wanted to spread around but he sent her to bed."

Maggilee clutched at her breast . . . How very unlike her to display such fluttery feminine behavior. Ellen started forward anxiously.

"Mama! Are you all right?"

"Yes, yes. Just ran up—stairs. Then Ceci didn't—"

"Mama, do stop worrying. Gran likes gossip but there'll be none tonight. Hone won't let his daughter spread her little lies."

Maggilee was still breathing hard but she seemed to be at least somewhat reassured. She touched Ellen's hand lightly. "Thanks, Ellie. Thanks be!" and she went into her room. At once she stuck her head out. " 'Night, honey." She did not wait for Ellen's good-night kiss, and Ellen thought as she went back to her room that it seemed pretty sure that Ceci Hone's "scandalous gossip" was based on truth . . . Except what kind of scandal could Maggilee be involved in at the shop? It must be that lovesick Harleigh Duckworth. No wonder he had been in a hurry to get back to town.

Ellen found it surprisingly easy to sleep that night. The triumph of the evening and the long hours of standing and dancing had completely tired her. The tension of finding herself at her best in that special gown had also been wearing. Afterward came the tempestuous minutes in Captain Sholto's arms, and at the end of the evening the anxiety about a new bitterness between her mother and grandmother. Well, she was too tired to lie awake worrying . . .

* * *

For days and unbelievable weeks afterward, Ellen discovered her appearance at the Wychfield Hunt Ball had suddenly made her popular with the males of the County. She found herself receiving compliments not only from men like Rowdon Faire and Major Wychfield, but an assortment of attractive male visitors, along with Daisy and Gavin McCrae, the latter looking a little like a whipped dog in Daisy's charge. Daisy must be a strenuous wife. True . . . no word came from Jem Faire, but she hadn't really expected any. She had obviously offended him when she went off with Captain Sholto. Or maybe she had just bored him by what he must think of as her "flirtatious antics." Each Sunday that fall at Gaynorville's Community Christian Church she was the center of a flattering little group, predominantly male, and she made it a point to wear her best church clothes, remembering Sholto's reference to her plainness.

One Sunday in late October Cousin Jonathan and Captain Sholto arrived just before the first hymn; the neatly groomed cavalryman flashed a big, sassy grin at Ellen as he entered. Ellen was feeling confident enough to think about presenting Sholto to her mother and whispered to Varina, "I want Mama to meet the captain. Where's she gone?"

"Stopped off at her beloved shop when the Corrigan brothers were talking to you." Over her shoulder Varina too had seen Sholto and bowed her head in a regal acknowledgement of their tenuous acquaintance. To Ellen she remarked, "Your mother has better things to attend than church, I dare say. Either she or Edward Hone sent his Ceci up to Richmond for some bugle beads, of all things. She's always keeping that girl from me. Indeed, I *still* have not received any answer to a small errand I sent her on some weeks ago."

"Why should she do that, do you suppose?"

Varina looked at her sharply. "You might ask your mother. And I suggest you also ask her to meet your captain. Soon."

"I will. Today." She felt sneakily relieved that Maggilee had come to church in her usual faded green mantle with a small, out-of-date bonnet perched on her red curls. Maybe, Ellen thought, just maybe he will see the change that other people have found in me since last month. In the last three weeks she had seen much less of Sholto and he was careful never to overstep the boundaries of a proper, even staid, courtship. Their meetings had been accidental and entirely too civil to suit Ellen.

It was also a little unsettling to look out the church's south window and see Maggilee talking to Jem Faire with such animation. He was another man who almost deliberately avoided her now. He and Maggilee were laughing. Jem stood with his back to Ellen, and she could not help but notice his easy, almost feline grace. He has no rear, Ellen thought, as her eyes slid down the broad white triangle of his back to the slim, flat hips. His whole body spoke of strength in repose. After a few minutes he asked a question. She pointed to the red-brick Community Church, said something and he glanced that way. But he didn't start to the church. He went off toward Gamble's Hay, Grain and Feed Store.

Ellen looked around at Captain Sholto and Jonathan in the back of the church. I've got to introduce the captain to Mama, she reminded herself, and then, by way of encouragement to herself . . . I'm different now. He'll not even notice her . . . I hope.

All the same, when the service ended Ellen was unnerved by her grandmother's determined sweep toward Bill and Jonathan. She permitted her nephew, Jonathan to kiss her cheek and then, as Ellen was wishing the matter could be postponed, Varina turned graciously to the captain.

"Well, sir, here you and my nephew are business associates and never once invited to Gaynor House. You-all must come to dinner this very evening."

In a cowardly spirit Ellen suggested, "Gran, maybe this is too soon. Maybe Cousin Jonathan—"

Jonathan was looking at the two women in a puzzled way. He felt the undercurrents but obviously couldn't comprehend why a Yankee soldier should be welcome in Varina Dunmore Gaynor's house. Varina was, after all, still an unreconstructed Rebel. Jonathan himself never came to Gaynor House, for quite different reasons, as his aunt knew very well, but he gave his usual answer. "Reckon I'll have to take the will for the deed, Aunt. I can't be away from the Ferry twice in one day. I've my stock to feed, and the rest."

But Captain Sholto, putting on his best Sunday manners, took Varina's hand, made a gallant pretense of kissing it and assured her, "I'd be right proud, ma'm, if you'll have me."

He then took Ellen's hand, looking directly into her eyes. She was aware of a difference. He wasn't clowning now, and she couldn't mistake the message there. He did care for her. How much he cared must depend on how she persuaded him that she was not a porcelain goddess but an adult woman. His unexpectedly serious eyes seemed to ask that question. She tried to give him her promise without words.

Varina let her own attention wander to the street, where Maggilee and Jem Faire had been standing earlier. Then she gave Captain Sholto her regal smile.

"Do come to dinner, Captain." And to Ellen she added easily "We'll just keep this a little secret and surprise your mother. You know how she likes company. Captain, I'm sure you will be pleased to meet Ellen's mother. You mustn't be frightened of her... At all events, we shall try to make dinner interesting for you."

CHAPTER 14

* * *

THE CAPTAIN left town in an excellent humor. He couldn't have mistaken the receptiveness in Ellen Gaynor's delicious eyes. Was it possible that the likes of Bill Sholto might actually end his days as the husband of such a lovely, gentle young female, one who would preside over Sunday socials with the neighbors, *and* offer a good bed-partner when he came home after a long day's work riding the estate as owner and overseer . . . ?

Whose estate?

Well, he had to admit that his bride would furnish the estate. But to judge by the way the Gaynor acres had been let go, they badly needed a strong hand and, by God, he had some cash he'd gladly spend to bring life back to the fallow land. Without seeming to, he studied his companion, Jonathan, who now walked beside him over the Gaynor trail to the Ferry. Old Jono had done wonders with the vegetables and the fruits he cultivated on much smaller acreage than the big Gaynor spread, and in spite of Jonathan's taciturnity he clearly could teach a man about making a success of the land . . . As the two of them made their way through the underbrush, trying to preserve the stiff Sunday look of breeches, uniform jacket, and Jono's ten-year-old coat, Bill asked abruptly, "You mind my going to Gaynor House for dinner?"

Jonathan barely grunted.

It was like digging through cement. Bill tried again. "I mean, seeing as you don't seem to spend much time there yourself. Don't you like the old lady?"

Bill felt Jonathan's tension, though he said calmly, "I'm not a visiting man."

The sudden tension intrigued Sholto. It was all part of the mystery that surrounded him. Bill felt his way through the conversational swamp. "I take it Miss Ellen's mother is a rare tartar. The family's tried their level best to keep me away from her."

"You been asking around about the Gaynor ladies?"

"Lord, no. What d'you take me for?" He grinned, trying to make his good humor contagious. "But I notice Miss Varina just as much as called her an old battle-ax. Think she's dangerous?"

For the first time there was a slight break, a shadow of amusement in Jonathan's grim countenance. "Depends."

"On what, for God's sake?"

"On what you call dangerous."

Bill was getting nowhere. He began to feel some uneasiness. He wanted to look well in the eyes of Ellen's mother, but he also had his own pride. Still, if he failed to win over Ellen's mother as he had obviously won the stately Varina, he would have to rely on the easy conquests like "Molly-O" for the rest of his life. He had seen many an ex-soldier on the frontier wind up as a squawman or the kept stud for some fading madam.

It would be a hardship to give up his special new redhead, his second "Molly-O," but he believed that with a little patience and a great deal of affection he could teach Ellen Gaynor all the redhead's spontaneous feeling. The tall, lovely blonde was already smouldering; some manly attention would create a fire that warmed as it burned.

Was it possible to love two such different women at the same time? Not only was it possible, but he had succeeded at this very minute.

"Ever been in love?" he asked Jonathan as they came in sight of the Ferry house.

Jonathan gave him a hard look—no friendship in that look.

"You given much thought to moving on?"

Bill Sholto wet his lips, took and breath and came back, "Sorry, Jono. I should've made myself clear. I was thinking about me. Not you. I just mean—I reckon I'm in love and I sort of wanted to find out how it feels." That brought nothing, so he ended lamely, "Feels fine, I think, though kind of confusing."

To his surprise Jonathan Gaynor gave a quick bark of laughter. "You're too old for sulphur and molasses, so you're likely in love."

Relieved at his host's change of mood, Bill agreed. "Anyway, now all I've got to do is win over her battle-ax of a mother."

* * *

"Ah, if it isn't m'darlin' colleen!" Rowdon Faire called out across the street in the stentorian tones he might have used on the battlefield.

Varina, sedately arranged in the Gaynor buggy, winced and nudged Ellen. "I daresay he means you, child. He does have a vulgar streak."

Amused, Ellen waved to the colonel, whose curly snow-white hair was blowing around his sturdy face.

"No, no," he insisted. "Come on up in the wagon and let Jem and me take you home to Fairevale for lunch. Eliza's got a sick headache. You'll cheer her up. Jem's fetching along some grain at Gamble's but he'll be by in two shakes."

Ellen hesitated. There would always be pleasant memories associated with visits to Fairevale across the Ooscanoto from Wychfield and Gaynor House. But though Miss Eliza, in her severe way, welcomed her and even seemed to like her, there was now the problem of Jem Faire. She couldn't understand why she should want Jem Faire's good opinion, but the feeling persisted . . .

"Go along," Varina encouraged. "The colonel is fond of you and you may as well have a little practice in a ladylike flirtation. You will need all your wiles for your guest this evening.

Ellen shivered but kissed her grandmother's cheek and hurriedly climbed down from the buggy with the help of young Nahum.

"You sure lookin' mighty pert, Miss Ellen," the thirteen-year-old assured her. "Colonel there, he's got his eye on you."

Much good that would do! With a slight sense of her own ingratitude Ellen reflected that it was no special credit to look good in the eyes of "Rowdy" Faire. She could never remember a time when the good-natured Irishman hadn't been her defender, protector, and pretended admirer. The trouble was, she had become used to his gallantry. In many ways he applied the same garrulous charm to Varina and Maggilee. How could a girl give any weight to his praise?

Nevertheless, it was hard not to like a man who so obviously sought out her company, and before the entire town. She thought she just *might* practice a little flirting with him, in preparation for the nerve-wracking ordeal tonight when she introduced Bill Sholto to the exciting Maggilee Gaynor for the first time.

The colonel got down, boosted Ellen up into the wagon and crowded in beside her. It was going to be a very tight fit when his nephew arrived, but though Rowdon Faire enjoyed close proximity to a pretty young woman, he was so busy waving, bellowing and calling out to various county neighbors as they came out of church that he didn't annoy Ellen by any sly tricks with his hands or his hips as they sat there together. "Vulgar" he might be in some ways, but to Ellen he was simply a rough gentleman.

In between shouted greetings to Major and Mrs. Wychfield and jokes about "old married folk" to Daisy and Gavin McCrae, he gave Ellen's knee a smart slap, remarking, "Honey, you Gaynor women are a sight easier on the eyes than that Wychfield clan. The older you get the better you-all seem to weather."

Amused at this peculiar but well-meant compliment, Ellen laughed. She felt so free and easy with her old friend that she could, she decided, easily afford to practice her wiles on him . . . "We Gaynor women always look our best in the eyes of our favorite gentlemen."

He gave her gloved hand a quick little slap. "Now, don't you tease an old rooster, honey," and then deafened her as he bellowed an answer to one of Irene Wychfield's questions: "Oh, she'll be right sassy and chipper in a while. These headaches take my poor Eliza now and again. Always was a sickly one. Not like the rest of us Faires. Took after her maw." This didn't quite penetrate, what with the noise of other departing vehicles and the stir-up of dust; so he repeated while Ellen cringed, "I said—*took after her sainted maw!*"

He settled back beside Ellen. "I'd give a plenty if my poor Eliza was more like you, Ellie. And don't you blush now. You know right well you're the prettiest little thing in Tudor County."

No one but Rowdon Faire called her either "little" or "pretty." Although he was scarcely an inch taller than she was, he had always gone out of his way to regard as as a "dainty little piece." In his presence she could almost imagine she was the beautiful Maggilee . . .

"Coming from the finest gentleman in Tudor County, that's a compliment indeed," she assured him, and meant it. She had looked around earnestly, couldn't see any sign of Jonathan and Captain Sholto, and begun to count the blessings of a gallant fellow like Rowdon Faire.

He laughed, called her "a flattering little minx" and made her the threat or promise he had made ever since she was five: "When you're a grownup lady, miss, I'll be bound if I don't marry you."

They smiled together at the old, worn joke, and then he shifted around, begged her pardon but pointed out, "There he comes now, my nephew."

Jem Faire had come down from Gamble's Hay, Grain

and Feed Store, and as he stepped out of Church Alley Ellen busied herself arranging her hair, so she could watch him between her fingers. Though it was the Sabbath, he wore buckskin trousers, a homespun shirt, and flat moccasins. The moccasins were the only sartorial sign of his father's people. Nonetheless, he would never be mistaken for a Caucasian or a mulatto. There was a rough, exotic look about his coppery complexion, as well as the structure of his face.

"Someone really should cut his hair evenly across his forehead," Ellen thought, and to her horror realized she had murmured it aloud.

But the colonel wasn't upset. "His mother was like that," he explained. "Everybody loved her out in the Territory. Went her own way, though. When she fell in love with Natani there wasn't anybody would marry them. They just had their own service, Injun-style. Anyway, she wore her hair like Jem's—what you ladies call a fringe across her forehead—but every bit as crooked. He's a good boy, though. Loyal. Like a son to me."

The "boy" was in the mid-twenties, Ellen guessed, and began to wonder how such a dark, mercurial-tempered fellow could get himself so well liked by both the colonel and the girls in the County. Not that he wasn't attractive enough, heaven knew . . .

He moved through the milling churchgoers, hailing the Corrigan family and then the Warrenders. He caught the attention of at least a dozen people who stared after him with silent curiosity. For one thing, he was carrying a load of grain over his shoulder, and on a Sunday!

But Ellen wished she could carry herself with his easy, unconscious grace. It was impressive in a land where he was at times alien to both the black and white populations.

For his uncle's sake as well as her own conscience,

Ellen determined to try harder to win his friendship, not that he seemed to have forgotten his stolid interest in her.

She greeted him brightly. "A lovely morning, Mister Faire."

Her voice caught him as he shoved the grain sack back into the wagon. He stopped for a second before getting up beside her. For a minute he looked surprised at her enthusiasm, gave her a sardonic grin. "Lovelier all the time, wouldn't you say?" He took up the reins.

He hadn't inherited his uncle's garrulous Irish disposition but Ellen was satisfied that at least he might be getting over his grudge against her. Colonel Faire rambled on, telling a much embroidered tale of his dealings with a carpetbagging lawyer representing the Freedman's Bureau back in '65. Some people found his repetitive tales boring, but to Ellen they evoked dreams of romantic struggle against the mysterious, faceless enemy. Mysterious and faceless because other Northerners Ellen had met seemed quite normal . . . perhaps lacking in a certain intuitive charm she found in her relatives and friends, but still nothing like the ogres of Reconstruction days.

He broke off only to say several times, "All this chitchat's given me a devil of a thirst—begging your pardon, Miss Ellie."

She was intensely aware of Jem Faire's interest in her. Or was it curiosity? Did he think she would be bored or make fun of Rowdon Faire? To show him how wrong he was, she became especially attentive to the older man, looking closely at him as he acted out his story. She laughed gaily, enjoying not only an unusual awareness of her own popularity but also a genuine pleasure because the colonel seemed so happy. His lively blue eyes snapped. His tousled hair and natural animation made him look ten years younger.

"Well, he high-tailed it off the Fairevale land, and never stopped his running till he reached Washington, I'll be bound."

She could see it all vividly, and the colonel, much inspired, continued in that strain. The more he talked, acting out both grand triumphs and ludicrous defeats, the more she laughed. Much of her tension over the coming night seemed to fade away. In spite of the fact that her good relations with the colonel didn't seem to please his nephew as much as she'd supposed they would, she greatly enjoyed the ride. The rain-washed countryside sparkled in the late October sunlight and made a background she would remember a long, long time.

There was only one small difficulty and it didn't come from Jem Faire. On the contrary, during the moments when the Irishman stopped to complain about his thirst and she had time to look around, she noticed that Jem was gazing at her as if to memorize her face. He *seemed* to be a bit jealous, with a darkening scowl when she hung on his uncle's every word. It might be, of course, that he resented playing second fiddle to someone not of Faire blood. Whatever his interest in Ellen, it excited her and she began to see where her grandmother had been quite right about her lunch with the Faires. She would certainly have practice before facing her major challenge . . . keeping Captain Bill Sholto from falling hopelessly in love with her captivating mother the minute he met her.

The colonel broke off in the middle of yet another story in which he was the butt of the joke . . . "There'll be that spalpeen Corrigan, footing it into his barn. He promised me a jug of something to warm the innards on a wet day. Well, now, here's m' little lady present, so I'll be asking your pardon while I have Jem just fetch in some good mountain whiskey."

Rowdy Faire's thirst was no surprise, but he seldom drank heavily in the presence of the Gaynor women. Ellen felt faintly uneasy, especially when his perspiring hand clasped hold of hers, then touched her fingers in his teasing way. "You see, Jem, m'boy, my friend Ellen isn't one of those Carrie Nation battle-axes. She accepts a man for what he is. Off with you, boy. Let's sample that whiskey."

For just a moment Jem caught Ellen's eye, and she remembered how much he disliked his uncle's well-known dependence on whiskey, and the argument with her that had led to their kiss that afternoon in late summer. She wondered if he remembered it too.

Jem pulled up now before the gates of the Corrigan place. There was no yawning, bored gatekeeper to let in the wagon as there might have been in the old days. The land had once been Gaynor property, part of the great Gaynor Plantation, but the Yankee Corrigans had made a success of their parcel and no one questioned their profits these days, though the actual ownership of the land was as muddy as the waters of the Ooscanoto River.

Jem leaped down and started along the short dirt road to the Corrigan house veranda, where Ellen could see Amabel Corrigan flirting with one of the young tenants of the Finch properties. Jem hailed her and asked a question. She tossed her curls as she indicated where he might find her father down at the barn, but Ellen, watching curiously, noted that the girl had stopped teasing her young man long enough to follow Jem's figure as he strode through muddy runnels to the barn.

The colonel became more and more impatient, swerving around, shading his eyes and squinting into the sunlight after his nephew. Suddenly he patted Ellen's shoulder, muttered, "Just be a minute, don't you fret now." Without another word he climbed down and started off, his shortish legs marching along in a near jog trot. He turned off and headed for the barn after saluting Amabel and her admirer, who were suddenly joined by her mother, too late to receive the greeting of Fairevale's master.

With a sinking feeling Ellen saw Jem and Mr. Corrigan come out of the barn with Rowdon Faire between them. In spite of all her experience with the colonel, she suddenly remembered tales of his excesses when he'd had too much to drink. Now he was pulling and hauling at the burlap-covered jug in Jem's hands.

Mr. Corrigan, a quiet-spoken, hard-working farmer who actually had been born on the Old Sod, tried to reason with him. By the time they all reached the wagon, Jem had apparently decided further struggle was either undignified or pointless. When he saw that Ellen was witness to his uncle's foolery, he surrendered the jug and Rowdy Faire hugged it to his chest.

He could hardly be drunk yet, but they had no sooner said good day to Mr. Corrigan and started up again when Ellen saw how much freer his tone, his voice and gestures had become. For a while she was afraid the heavy jug would fall over into her lap, but the colonel retained a tight hold on it with both arms. Still, in Rowdy Faire she always made allowances. It brought back memories of days when she had sat on the long front steps of the Fairevale veranda while he drank his juleps and entertained her with his marvelous tales of derring-do. She could forgive almost anything from the man who had been the *best* of fathers to her . . .

They reached the Ooscanoto Bridge without further

problems, and as they pulled up before the pillared and porticoed riverfront facade of Fairevale they saw Miss Eliza on the veranda accompanied by old Taffy, the spaniel, who greeted them with a feeble wave of her tail. Miss Eliza's thin black-taffeta-clad figure looked like a frieze of perpetual mourning as she pressed a hand-sewn bag of hot sand to her forehead to relieve the headache from which she was obviously suffering. But she waved to Ellen with her other hand.

"I see Pa persuaded you, Ellen. Did he use all those gallant manners he gets up when he wants to?"

Ellen laughed warmly. "He didn't have to use them all. You Faires set a mighty good table. Miss Eliza, I hope you're feeling better."

Jem swung off the wagon on the opposite side and held his arms up. As he lifted Ellen down, taking his time about it, he murmured, "No thank-you kiss?"

Relieved that he at least held no grudge, she promised lightly, "And no slap."

"I wonder if it would be worth trying it." He laughed at her pretense of indignation, added, "Probably not," and let her go.

She smiled to show that she assumed he was joking before she went to meet Miss Eliza. They embraced sincerely. Neither had had a very happy childhood and neither had been a belle during her young womanhood. And although Eliza's open dislike of Maggilee made Ellen uncomfortable, they did share one unacknowledged secret —they both blamed Maggilee for the loss of the men they had loved.

Eliza waved Jem on with the horses, the wagon and grain sack, but it was unnecessary . . . he'd already started to drive away. Her treatment of him, though, surprised Ellen. Surely, the colonel's two nearest and dearest ought to get along better than this.

Meanwhile Colonel Faire had taken another long swig from the whiskey jug, then tucked it under his arm with some difficulty and strolled into the long, dark parlor overlooking the river, "escorting" a young woman on each side, until he stumbled over the loose rug between the entrance hall and the parlor.

"Reckon Pa needs a little food," Eliza suggested as she knelt to straighten the bright-colored rug with its curious designs, which looked like black-lightning strokes on a cheerful fire-red background. She guessed it was an Indian design, before Miss Eliza confirmed the fact that the rug was a gift given by Jem Faire to his mother's family.

"Rather barbaric, it seems to me," Eliza remarked, squeezing the hot-sand bag against her reddened forehead with angry force, "but Pa insists on keeping it in plain sight."

Ellen didn't like to contradict the highly sensitive older woman, who was famous for her easily hurt feelings, but she also couldn't resist her enthusiasm for the Navajo work. "But it's beautiful! And so different from our usual Virginia carpets. And it brightens the hall so."

Two magnolia trees, very old, thick and spider-infested, cut off the light from the long parlor, but Eliza shrugged off Ellen's view of things with, "Too much brightness brings on my headaches. I'd as soon have a softer light."

"Well, all the same, I envy you. It's so beautiful," Ellen said as she stopped to straighten the fringe of the rug where the colonel had scruffed it up, her fingers caressing the stiff, rich threads.

She was startled when a shadow crossed the rug and she looked up to see Jem Faire standing beside her. He had returned from the outbuildings, and though his tight-fleshed features showed little, she thought he was touched by her obvious admiration for his gift to his uncle.

"I never saw anything like it," she said.

"I have another. It's blue," he said casually. And as if there were some mysterious connection in his mind, he added, "It's your color."

She didn't know if he was hinting that he might give the rug to her, a gift she could never repay, but his compliment was a more immediate gift. He seemed to be studying her intently.

Miss Eliza called abruptly then, "You, Jem! Will you get Pa to the table? We're lunching in the dining room."

"Damn that woman! She's everywhere," he muttered. He didn't look around but put his hands on Ellen's shoulders. "Ellen, can't we just—"

Miss Eliza demanded, "Jem! Are you coming?"

Ellen wasn't sure what was in his mind. "Yes?"

He looked as if he might go on, then, hearing Miss Eliza's heavy step, dismissed whatever it was. "Never mind, later," and he left her.

Regretting the interruption, Ellen followed Miss Eliza into the dining room. "I'm told in town that Jem has made practically all the Fairevale fields pay. Even Major Wychfield says he wishes he had a nephew of Jem's ability."

Eliza sniffed. "Well, I'm sure I do the best I can. But what with these headaches—and the trash help you hire nowadays—I often wish Pa would marry again, take a little of the load off my shoulders."

Jem was crossing the hall toward the colonel's library, but then hesitated. Ellen glanced quickly in his direction. His fingers closed into his palm. He didn't like Eliza's suggestion. That was clear.

It wasn't Ellen's concern, but she wondered what would happen in this strangely antagonistic household if

Colonel Faire *did* marry again. It seemed to her that it would be like setting a match to gunpowder.

On the other hand, in spite of the whiskey jug, when the family finally sat down to Sunday lunch, Rowdy Faire was reasonably sober and his own friendly, talkative self. Jem sat opposite Ellen, with Miss Eliza as hostess at the foot of the table. The dining room, on the west front of Fairevale, had six long windows with direct afternoon light. Beyond the drive was a border of red roses, then grass, and beyond that a splendid stand of virgin timber, which the colonel pointed out proudly.

"Thought a while ago I'd start cutting down the woods there but Jem talked me out of it. Said they were the future."

Miss Eliza put in sourly, "And we had to take the field profits to pay the taxes."

"Well, Miss Ellie," the colonel boomed, "how do *you* feel about it?"

Both Miss Eliza and Jem looked at her, Eliza clearly expecting her support. Ellen, sensibly, wanted to be noncommittal, but it was difficult . . . she had too many memories connected with the Fairevale woods. "I'm sure it's worth a great deal of money. Only—you see—I keep remembering picnics in those woods when I was a child. I'd hate to see it all cut down."

Jem's look of approval was immediate, but Miss Eliza snapped her napkin out of its ring with a gesture like the wringing of a chicken neck.

"Not that it's any concern of mine," Ellen added hurriedly.

"Oh, I'd not be going so far as to say that," the colonel said. "If my friend Ellie would just say yes, she'd be running the household. And the estate. How many's the times I've asked you to marry your old friend, eh, Ellie?"

Ellen laughed, treating his proposal as a joke, her usual fashion, but at least she couldn't be mistaken this time. Miss Eliza flashed a triumphant look at Jem Faire, whose bronze jaw tightened noticeably.

Actually, Ellen thought, it was a rather pointless discussion ... She wanted to blurt out the truth, that tonight she hoped to persuade quite a different man she was worthy of his proposal. Today's visit to the Faires had given her more confidence in herself. She could hardly wait for the evening. And Captain Bill Sholto.

CHAPTER 15

***

WITH HER mind put at least temporarily at rest by Ceci Hone's trip to Richmond, Maggilee worked on her accounts at the shop that Sunday morning. She repeatedly told herself there was nothing to worry about. Ellen would never believe Ceci, even if Varina backed her nasty tale. Ellen was a loyal daughter. She had never made trouble for Maggilee like the sassy, obnixious Corrigan girls and some of the others. Even if Ellen had flirted with Bill Sholto—and Maggilee couldn't imagine her cool and distant Ellen actually *flirting* with anyone—no, Ellen

couldn't have been serious about the raw cavalryman
. . . And as for Bill himself, Maggilee knew something
about men. He couldn't have loved anyone but his
Molly-O.

"And now *I* am his Molly-O."

But every few minutes she took time to look out the
side window upstairs until she saw her cousin Jonathan
and Bill Sholto walking along Beauford Street toward the
Gaynor Ferry trail. So Bill hadn't stayed to exert that
damnable charm on Ellen. Poor Ellen might have been
impressionable, but she was all wrong, so very wrong, for
a man like Bill . . . She deserved someone better—anyone
better . . .

There was Ellen now with Varina in the street below.
Colonel Faire had called to her. He had always been devoted to her. Ellen's future would be secured, it occurred
to her, if only she could become mistress of Fairevale. A
pity she wasn't wise enough to recognize the jolly colonel's good qualities . . . She's not like me, Maggilee told
herself. She just doesn't have the . . . taste for the vulgar
struggles of life . . .

Jem Faire would understand, she thought. There was
hot blood in the young halfbreed. He must be all of
twenty-five now. Wouldn't *he* be a marvelous lover!
For someone else, of course. For Maggilee it was Bill
Sholto . . .

She pulled the window closed now and started down
the stairs, and was within four steps of the salon floor
when the stuffy air became alive with a humming sound.
Confused and dizzy, she realized the humming was inside
her own head, a sign of faintness, and she fumbled for the
bannister, holding on tightly until the giddiness passed.

After a few minutes she was able to remind herself,
"You're getting on, Maggi. All this running up and down

the stairs as if you were Ellie's age . . ." She never slept too well at night. The laudanum doses would have to be increased. That was it. But she hadn't fainted, or even been dizzy for years . . . a disturbing symptom, a warning . . .

A little while later, having given up the attempt to concentrate on the passementerie trimming for Eliza Faire's new black go-to-church moire suit, she started to walk home through the fields. She felt much better now. The dizziness that had almost turned her stomach was relieved by the brisk, clear air. All the same, she would be glad to get home, shut herself into her own room and, to borrow one of Varina's habits, simply lie down and recoup her customary energies. With nothing planned for dinner or supper she might actually sleep for a little while. But how much easier to sleep in the arms of . . .

In one bright gleam of sunlight she seemed to see an unforgotten face, and her thoughts ran back to that other time, which had been all too painfully short. No difficulty sleeping then, in his arms. And now she might return to those nights, with Bill Sholto. She hugged the idea to herself, and reminded herself that before this could happen it was necessary to be quite certain that poor young Ellen didn't become seriously involved with him. It would be a little sacrifice for Ellen. Ellen was young; she had never looked better than she looked after the Wychfield ball, and she certainly provoked interest among the eligible males of the county.

More than usually tired after her walk from town to Gaynor House, Maggilee almost fell into the arms of Edward Hone, who helped her upstairs to her room. He assured her earnestly, "Ceci has never disobeyed me, Miss Maggilee. She knows better than to go about peddling gossip."

"She is also very devoted to Miss Varina," Maggilee reminded him. She was so bone-weary after climbing the stairs she didn't even feel like discussing the matter, but the truth had to be faced. "She's sure to be back in a day or two."

"Maybe Miss Varina won't believe her,"

Maggilee looked at him. His own gaze lowered. They both knew the answer to that. Maggilee said, "The main person is Ellen. I don't want her troubled by all this talk. It would hurt her."

"Miss Varina said young Miss was invited to Fairevale after church. The colonel and Miss Eliza are very fond of her."

Relieved to hear that, Maggilee went into her room, partly closed the curtains, and to her own surprise rested through most of the afternoon. There was a nagging pain in the small of her back, but she almost banished it by concentrating on plans for her next encounter with Bill Sholto. The affair, of course, held an added spice because he didn't know who she was, treated her like that lost love of his, Molly-O. But when he knew her age, that she was the widow of a Confederate hero and had a daughter as old as twenty, she might inevitably prove less irresistible to him. She prayed that this revelation would be put off for as long as possible.

She sat up, tried to see her reflection across the room in the small walnut shaving mirror on top of the Queen Anne dressing table that Varina had spurned as an imitation. She couldn't see her face at this distance and in this half-light, and got up warily to discover if she looked as bad as she felt.

There was a knock on her door. Varina looked in, dressed as usual in the height of the fashion she had chosen for herself some ten years ago. Also, as usual, she was apparently trying to annoy Maggilee by a reminder to dress for dinner.

"You aren't going to wear *that* old gown for dinner, I trust."

Challenged, Maggilee reacted as she always did, raising her chin, saying, "Certainly. Why not? I'm fully clothed. What else is necessary?"

The annoying thing was that she could have sworn Varina had seemed content as she went on to her own room. Not that it mattered. Maggilee knew she looked her worst, both in face and dress, but one hardly had to dress in Sunday best to please one's daughter and mother-in-law.

Varina's visit had brought on a new surge of aches and even nausea. Maggilee could no longer put it off. She got a teaspoon and bottle from the back of her dresser drawer, measured laudanum drops, took one more for good measure, and swallowed the spoonful.

* * *

Still in the glow of her expectations, Ellen sorted through her wardrobe for the prettiest, or more important, the most flattering dress she owned. She knew she had looked well enough to the male eyes at Fairevale, attracting not only the admiration of the colonel but even the surly Jem Faire. And on her way home in the colonel's buggy she had been stopped by Gavin McCrae. Out for a Sunday stroll, he said. But he had certainly appeared to be lingering about the Wychfield end of the high Ooscanoto Bridge, and when the Fairevale buggy rattled over the wooden planks of the bridge she could have sworn he expected it. Politeness demanded that she ask him if he wanted a ride to the Wychfield carriage drive half a mile away.

"You did that with alacrity," Ellen teased him as he leaped into the buggy beside her.

"With what?"

She laughed. "Nothing. I've read it in so many novels I just wanted to hear how it sounds."

He smiled obediently, but soon brought the conversation close to the forbidden. "It sounds mighty fine when you say it, Ell—Miss Ellen."

She tried to ignore the tension and depth in his voice. "Well, on such a gorgeous day, everything sounds fine."

"You always were modest."

Beginning to be annoyed, she asked casually, "How is Daisy?"

"Same as always. You know Daisy. She's down among the tenants, telling 'em all how to do things her way. Not that she isn't right, mostly." He coughed to change the subject. "By the way, looks like I'll be practicing law here."

"Here?" The news surprised her. She certainly didn't care for him . . . That emotion had been banished some time ago, and replaced shortly after her meeting with Bill Sholto. But Gavin McCrae's sober, intelligent face with its wisp of mustache outlining an over-sensitive mouth reminded her of the pain she had endured, and perhaps for the same reason.

"Not in Gaynorville. Over in Ashby. It happened all of a sudden. After Bertha-Winn's wedding I just got to thinking—but what's important is that I was always happy here when visiting in Tudor County, and what with Daisy being so fond of her family, it seemed logical. So I talked it over with the major and it's just about settled. What do you think, Ellen?"

"Wonderful, Gavin. Here's the turnoff to Wychfield House."

He didn't want to leave. He tried to keep the conversation going by begging more of her opinion of his move. There was very little she could say except to congratulate him again. He stared at her while she waited for him to get down. "You've grown up. You're even prettier than—Miss Maggilee."

It had taken a long time to hear it. He now meant nothing to her personally, but the *favorable* comparison with her mother, on top of her most pleasant time at Fairevale, was enough to give her confidence for the tense meeting ahead. She owed Gavin McCrae something for that, and as he finally got down to trudge up the road toward the big Wychfield Planation house, she gave him her warmest smile. "I wish you great success, Gavin, you and Daisy. Whenever we have legal problems, I guarantee we'll take them all to you. That's a promise." She held out her hand. He took it, managed a half-articulate thank-you, and went on his way, followed by her sympathetic gaze.

Late that afternoon, when she was considering all her dresses for this most important dinner, she still was full of the warm knowledge of her popularity with so many men today. It seemed to be a sign, pointing to success with Bill Sholto. How careful he'd been the evening he took her home from the ball! She knew he must have had many women, prostitutes and women of all kinds out west, but she had felt his desire for *her*, and he had been gentle. Careful. Surely, this indicated a more serious feeling toward her . . . True, she had made advances to him that astonished herself. Result? He not only responded to her advances but very nearly made love to her then and there. Yes . . . he loved her, she wasn't imagining it . . .

She finally chose a square-necked evening dress of black lace over rose pink, with a back detail of pink moire.

She had never liked it. It seemed much too... noticeable, not very ladylike, with its clashing colors and low neckline. But this was a time when she needed to call on every resource, every advantage. If only she had some jewelry, she thought, as she entered the river parlor.

Varina, enthroned in her green-knobbed chair, suddenly sat up straight. Evidently her back troubled her because she had been hunched forward over her tatting, a pose that would have looked like discouragement in anyone else, but at the sight of her granddaughter, pain was forgotten. "You surprise me. I don't think I've seen that gown before."

Ellen tried not to let herself become embarrassed. She shrugged off the fact that the dress was a year old and never worn until this evening.

"I had it made up in Ashby for the Corrigan wedding but I lost my courage. I didn't want to hurt Mama's feelings... I wore my brown foulard instead."

Varina's heavy eyelids lowered, narrowing her gaze. Ellen had the brief sensation of being inspected by a serpent's head but managed to keep her poise and at least a pretense of confidence.

"Very good. It ought to serve tonight to make any male forget"—she broke off at Ellen's quick movement—"forget his previous loves," she finished firmly. "Now, we'll not call your mother until our guest arrives. We don't want to disturb her. She undoubtedly needs her rest. She missed church today so she certainly must have been working hard." She made it sound as though "working hard" were the sinful result of having missed church.

It seemed terribly underhanded, and Ellen's conscience told her that her mother should be warned and have time to dress, to arrange her lovely red hair and maybe put rice powder on her nose. On the other hand, she recalled too often in the past when Maggilee appeared in all her radiance contrasting with her daughter's quieter looks, and the consequences . . . Just once, Ellen decided, she would borrow without restraint Varina's devious mind.

No matter how confident Ellen felt, though, her pulses jumped noticeably.

"Watch yourself, child. You are only greeting an admirer, not a future husband."

Ellen almost opened her mouth to correct this misconception but decided not to. Let events speak for themselves. She sat cooly erect as possible while Edward Hone came in to announce without fanfare, "Miss Varina, your guest, Captain William Sholto, has arrived." He addressed the older woman but with a side glance at Ellen. As Varina nodded, gathering herself together to present a picture of regal condescension, the butler asked Ellen pointedly, "Shall I tell Miss Maggilee there is to be a dinner guest?"

Before Ellen could speak, Varina cut in. "No. Send Bethulia to me. I'll have her give my daughter-in-law any help she needs."

"Yes, ma'm." But he gave Ellen another look before leaving.

Ellen got up. "Gran, we can't do this. We must tell her."

Bethulia, a stout, pretty woman Maggilee's age, came in just ahead of Bill Sholto, who entered at the far end of the parlor in his cleaned and brushed uniform, his worn but newly polished boots. If she was his goddess, he was her god—no question.

He walked the length of the room while Bethulia leaned over Varina's chair, receiving her instructions:

"Remember, simply the word that dinner will be served immediately."

"Gran!" Ellen warned Varina aloud, though her mind was fixed on Sholto's grand appearance as he grinned at her before turning to Varina.

"Very well," Varina added to Bethulia, "simply say that Miss Varina has invited an old church friend to dinner. That should take care of the matter." But she needn't have been concerned over her granddaughter's conscience. The arrival of Bill Sholto had put everything else out of Ellen's mind. She watched him bow to Varina, take up the old woman's hand with a gallant air and earn from her a rare and grudging smile.

"I must say, you Federals have learned manners since my day."

"I assure you, ma'm, this is your day." He turned finally to Ellen, took her hand, held it in his. He started to say something, broke off and finally said without any of the professional gallantry he had used toward Varina, "You surely are a sight to behold . . . You're so—damned —lovely—" He worried over Varina's reaction behind him and apologized, but Varina benignly ignored his language and Ellen was far too delighted to object. She'd seen him play the gallant flirt before, but he was certainly sincere now. She couldn't be wrong about that or about his intentions. He was both careful and tender with her; yet even as he answered Varina's questions about "all those wild places west of the Alleghenies," Ellen caught him studying her in a puzzled sort of way, as if he perhaps didn't understand his own feelings.

She decided that this was because he had never loved anyone so deeply before. I'm different. I'm not like his other women. No wonder he's puzzled . . .

Bethulia stuck her head in. "Miss Maggilee says she's

coming. She's feeling a mite poorly but she's coming anyway."

Ellen put in quickly, "Then perhaps she shouldn't come down. What's happened?" She explained to Bill Sholto, "Mother sleeps badly and then she works too hard. I'll go and—"

Maggilee walked into the parlor, looking as if she'd just crawled out of bed with all her clothes on.

"Mama," Ellen said with real concern, "are you all right?"

Sholto's back was to Maggilee now, but as Ellen got up to go to her, he winked at her, whispered, "The lady just wants to avoid me. That's it, isn't it?" Then he turned slowly, curious to see Ellen's gorgon of a mother but obviously wanting to appear calm about it.

At the far end of the room Maggilee said, her fury barely under control, "You *might* have told me you had company."

In spite of all Varina's preparations, Ellen was shocked by her mother's behavior. Maggilee's disheveled, uncombed hair clearly told Ellen that she had come out of her room without even a glance at herself in the mirror. She was wearing the faded green poplin dress she had worn all day. It was now wrinkled, with a stained bosom and uneven hem. If Ellen hadn't known better she might have suspected her mother was drunk. Maggilee blinked as if she found it difficult to make out the group in dinner clothes at the far end of the room. In a flat, almost dead voice, she asked, "What are *you* doing here?"

Ellen explained hurriedly, "He's Gran's guest, Mama. He's been helping Cousin Jonathan. Captain William Sholto, my mother, Miss Maggilee—"

Captain Sholto stared dumbfounded at the woman who was Ellen Gaynor's mother. "Holy Christ!" he muttered, nearly blurting it out. He seemed in a state of shock.

Ellen pushed by him toward her mother, but Maggilee stopped her with a tired gesture. "Couldn't sleep . . . might've overdone . . . medicine . . ." Then, on a sudden bright note, if pitifully artificial, "But I'm starving. A good meal. That will wake me up fine . . . Please take me in to dinner, Captain Sholto."

She held out her hand, which shook badly. He hesitated and glanced at Ellen as he reached for Maggilee's hand, which she abruptly snatched back. Her voice was hollow as she turned her hand over, examining it. "Looks drunk, doesn't it? It's not, you know. Just a little . . ."

Varina, who had been studying the upholstery knobs on her chair with concentrated interest, looked up now to say, in her "sensible" voice, "I suggest we go in to dinner. Cookie is an artist of temperament, as we-all know."

Maggilee moved toward Bill Sholto with a shaky smile, stepped on the hem of her skirt, and promptly fell against Ellen and Bill. They caught her between them. Over her tousled head Bill asked Ellen, "Is she all right, do you think? Shouldn't she be lying down?" There was something Ellen couldn't quite fathom at first in his face and manner. He seemed furious. His sunburned skin was redder than usual. Either he felt a trick had been played on him by Varina and Ellen, implying her mother was a fierce gorgon, or, more likely, he felt an ordinary man's upset at the sight of a woman who appeared drunk.

While Ellen and Bill walked Maggilee through the various rooms of the ground floor, Ellen could hardly wait to get the captain alone and explain that she hadn't meant to mislead him about her mother. It must be clear already that Maggilee didn't dislike him, but her condition was so somnolent it was necessary for them to shake her lightly and raise their voices to get her attention. Bill avoided speaking to Maggilee, so Ellen was forced to keep up an inane monologue, as though she and her mother were both showing their guest over the house.

But each time he allowed himself to look at Maggilee, he seemed to show greater annoyance... Finally Ellen had to remind him with some sharpness, "You needn't disapprove, Capt'n Sholto. It's never happened before. She accidentally took a dram too much laudanum. It can happen to anyone—"

"Not to me. I saw my old man—the fellow who took me in as a boy—die of it. He'd had too much rum. And then this damned stuff to cure his head. It's more dangerous than gunpowder."

"That's all very well, but you don't know my mother. She's very highly strung and volatile—"

"I don't doubt."

"Please don't be flippant about it," she said edgily. "You're acting very peculiar tonight. You don't really know Mama well enough to pass judgment—"

"I know her well enough... her sort... I knew one like her a long time ago, only the one I knew was an honest woman. Your mother—" He broke off at her frozen expression. "I'm sorry, don't listen to me. It's just that I don't like drugs."

She had to let it go at that. Well, she had, she thought, considered everything about their meeting except this— that Bill Sholto should actively dislike her mother. It was absolutely the last thing she might ever have guessed...

When they finally decided it was safe to sit down to dinner, Varina's disdain became more vocal as she was seated at the elegant oval gate-leg table. Like most of the Dunmore-Gaynor furnishings it was smaller than the great formal tables of neighboring estate homes, and oddly suited to the lifestyle of the Gaynor women. Ellen and Sholto tried to settle Maggilee comfortably in her chair, and by now she seemed to be improving. At least, she was becoming cross.

"*Don't* fuss over me, please. I'm perfectly fine. All I need is a little food." She looked from Ellen to Bill Sholto, closed her eyes a second and then said gaily, "A glass of Grandfather Gaynor's French brandy should do it."

"Heigh-o," Varina murmured, apparently to herself. "That would be a splendid way to start dinner, I must say."

"We'll all have some when dinner is over, Mama," Ellen promised her, hoping she would forget about it.

They were all somewhat relieved after the first course—a delicate oyster chowder—was finished and the table was then heaped with ham, chicken, candied sweet potatoes and creamed corn cut off the cob. There was so much passing back and forth of platters, so much praise heaped on each dish, that it almost seemed they were involved in a conspiracy against silence.

Although the cross-currents were very strong, everyone insisted there had never been a finer meal, and when the fresh-churned strawberry ice cream was finished, Ellen began to hope things would continue to go better. For one thing, Maggilee seemed herself again. Varina questioned the captain about his experiences with "those wild aborigines in the Dakotas. We have one in our midst, perhaps you've heard about Colonel Faire's overseer?"

"Not an aborigine, Gran! For heaven's sake, Jem Faire is as civilized and educated as we are."

" 'Fraid that puts him one above me," the captain said. "I never had much of any book-schooling. I guess that's why I appreciate your granddaughter so much, among other things. It isn't often you meet an educated young woman who's beautiful and a lady besides."

Varina began to wonder if things weren't going even better than she had hoped. She rose to the occasion with what, to Ellen, was an out-and-out lie. "You'll find agreement on that, sir. When I think of the young gentlemen of Tudor County who have come to me asking if they might pay court to her! Yes, it will be only the best for Ellen."

"Grandmother!"

Maggilee took a quick sip of water, said abruptly, "Excuse me. I'm still not well, I'm afraid . . . the—the medication—" She got up, knocking over the tall Hepplewhite chair, and went out of the room. Ellen started after her.

Varina said, "Let her go. She needs to be alone. She will be a right as a trivet in the morning."

By this time Ellen had reached the hall door and Maggilee was climbing the stairs on Bethulia's strong arm. She looked down now at Ellen, shook her head.

"Go back to your company. I'll be fine . . ."

"Didn't you like him, Mama?"

Maggilee smiled tiredly. "A roving eye if ever I saw one. But pay me no mind. I haven't been very smart about men in my life . . ."

Back in the dining room, Ellen found that the captain had taken Varina's arm and was escorting her to her favorite chair in the river parlor. The old-fashioned oil lamps were flickering across the river. Fairevale, like Gaynor House, had not yet been connected up for gas lighting. The colonel and Varina shared a common dislike for the smell and danger of gas, and held to the soft lights of candelabra and oil lamps. Hone came in now and drew the portieres.

"If you don't mind, Miss Varina," Bill Sholto was saying, "I've got something to say to you about Ellen—Miss Ellen."

Ellen stopped, breathless, in the doorway.

"I want her for my wife. And I'd make her a good husband . . . I know, I know, I've had a rough life, but I'm done with those other things—the running, the fighting, the rest of it. I think she needs me, and I *know* I need a loving, gentle girl like Ellen—"

"Bill!" Ellen called out, trying to forestall some crushing dismissal by her grandmother. "Ask me. Gran has nothing to say about it."

He began to laugh, and held out his arms to her, still laughing.

"Loving—gentle—and no fancy games," he said, and held her in a tight embrace. She returned his tender kiss with a force that seemed to Varina the height of bad manners, to say the least. Her little scheme against Maggilee was going altogether too well.

Pounding her fist on the chair arm and trying to get up unaided, she said, "Ellen, you are behaving like your —like some trollop—stop this at once."

Ellen was only dimly aware of her voice, like a firefly's light in summer.

CHAPTER 16

***

"PLAYING WITH me, she was!" Bill Sholto shouted while Jonathan, busy dumping pipe-dottle into the fireplace, seemed not to be listening.

"Playing her little games. The fancy lady from the great house wants a little roll in the mud with a poor bastard she thinks isn't good enough to tell the truth to."

"You're talking about my Cousin Maggilee, I reckon."

"Who else would I mean? Not her daughter. Now that one's a real lady. Jono, Ellen's everything any man could want. You should've seen her standing up to old Miss Varina. I was so proud I like to have crushed the life out of her, in plain joy of her, you understand."

Jonathan merely examined his pipe before sucking on it. "What did Aunt Varina do?"

"Oh, she's not a bad old girl. A good deal like Ellen in some ways. You can get around her, but you never forget she's a lady. And I've got over seven thousand—no, sixty-three hundred—saved up that I'd like to put into renewing all that fallow Gaynor land. Won it fair and square across the poker table, plus a bit of faro here and there."

"Yes, that ought to do it with Aunt Varina. And don't think I'm not grateful for the seven hundred you've put into this place. Repairing the barge, for one thing."

"It's little payment for what you've taught me about making money off the land."

Jonathan didn't deny it, but his mind was clearly on another matter. "What happened to Cousin Maggilee?"

Bill reverted to his original grievance. In fact, it seemed to occupy him even more than his possible marriage to Ellen. "She made a damn fool of me. Made me think she was an honest piece. Never once hinted she was a lady with a fancy name and all. And tottered in tonight not even troubling to fix up. No doubt didn't think me worth it. Looked real awful. You can't imagine, Jono. For a minute there I was worried for her, but then it come to me how she tricked me. You just can't imagine how she looked . . ."

"Yes . . . I can."

"When I think of how I was crazy about that woman, like a flame burning inside you, she was."

"But you didn't think of marrying her."

Old Jono seemed to be misunderstanding. "Look, you

don't marry women like her. You marry for a family, and a future. Women like Maggilee Gaynor don't have children, or don't care about them if they do—"

"Seems to me Ellen has turned out pretty well."

"Sure and certain. But the old lady raised her. It shows in her breeding, her—"

Jonathan looked steadily at him. "You talk about marriage. Ever think about love in that marriage? Like should marry like, as they say. What do you and Ellen have in common? Will you ever wish you'd married a woman who burned, as you say, like a flame inside you?"

"Don't you worry about that. Miss Ellen and I—you know—we'll be just fine. I'm going to forget all about Molly-O, I mean, Miss Maggilee. Ellen's the helpmate I need . . ."

Jonathan got up, trying to hold down his anger. "I'm off to bed." He stopped in the doorway. "You'd best give more thought to what you really want. And which woman will be hurt most. I tell you, if it wasn't for that seven hundred I owe you, and those wild-west tales of yours that I don't put stock in for a minute, you'd be out on your backside. Still," he added almost to himself and without any sign of humor, "the Gaynor women always did have a taste for gewgaws."

* * *

Bill Sholto continued to have dreams about gorgeous redheads, which was odd, seeing that he went to such great effort to avoid meeting one. He had numerous good excuses for not showing himself at Gaynor House when Maggilee might be there, including the fact that Jonathan was busy getting all his produce cleared out at the onset of the winter season.

There was one difficulty, though. He wanted to get better acquainted with Ellen and, almost as importantly,

Miss Varina. He was still a little in awe of both of them. Old Jono was right about one thing. He had felt a good deal more at home with Maggilee, damn her, but he hated a lying woman, a woman who made love in a meadow with the first stranger who came along and then made him ache for her afterward.

Stopping off at Gamble's to pick up some winter feed for Jono's livestock, the captain found himself a focus of interest among the customers and hangers-on. He ordered a little feed for the peanut-eating pigs across the creek who had run out of leavings, then some hay for the milk cow Jonathan treated as one of the family, and grain to fatten the countless ducks and chickens who had the run of Gaynor Ferry.

Most of the men in Gamble's Hay, Grain and Feed Store were watching a checker game between Colonel Rowdon Faire and "Stonewall" Gamble, owner of the store. Sholto glanced at the stairs to the loft above, remembering the last time he and Maggie had made love there.

"Who's winning?"

Gamble, a long, lean, mournful-looking man, said without looking up, "Got him cornered, I'd say."

The colonel, who was drinking something steamy out of a pewter mug, remarked sociably, "Mighty good stock you carry, Stonewall. Makes it a pleasure to lose to you, so it does." He looked over the mug at the newcomer. The others had accepted the cavalryman as Jonathan Gaynor's friend, a good fellow who paid his bills or Jonathan's, drank a drop when the ladies weren't by, and according to the young black overseer, Nahum, carried his weight in the work of the Ferry.

"So, my lad, it's a suitor you are. I hear you're thinking to walk out with Miss Ellen Gaynor." The colonel took another swig of something that smelled like old-fashioned hot buttered rum. He set it down on a milking stool and carefully swiped his mouth dry with the back of his hand. Sholto had heard about Rowdon Faire's long interest in Ellen Gaynor, and considered the older man's behavior mostly paternal.

Apparently, from the colonel's next remark, he hadn't lost that warm regard for her. "All I'll say, Captain, is that Miss Ellie is a prize worth winning, and the finest young female in the County. Ask my nephew. Sure, now, you've cut him out."

The nephew, a slim, hard-looking young man with curious green eyes and a red-gold complexion, had come in silently with a saddle slung over one shoulder. Sholto studied him with some interest. The halfbreed obviously didn't like him, gave him a sardonic, narrow-eyed survey as hard as his own, but asked his uncle in a surprisingly pleasant voice, "You ready, sir?"

The colonel sighed. "No way out of it. Cornered me, he did."

"Maybe the colonel's the reason we lost the War," one of the idlers put in, and Rowdon Faire joined in the general laughter.

"I lost a few skirmishes, won a few. But I lost the last, reckon that's all that counts. Jem, this is Captain Sholto. He's working up at Gaynor Ferry."

"We've met," the nephew said. Sholto, who had previously only seen Jem Faire at a distance, wondered if the fellow had been watching him, and why.

"He's paying court to Ellie Gaynor," his uncle added.

This time there was no mistaking the dislike in Jem Faire's eyes . . . The damned fellow *is* jealous, Sholto realized . . .

"I've got the buckboard outside," Jem said abruptly.

"Sure, sure." The colonel got up a little heavily. His nephew put a hand under his arm, steadied him. Rowdon was far from drunk but a deep mug of liquor did affect him a trifle, even on these cold, frosty days. He stopped, politely offering his hand to Sholto. "Good to know a soldier, even in blue, sir. You'll be doing me honor, so you will, if you come by Fairevale now and then for a bit of a drink and some good talk about the old campaigns."

Sholto agreed with pleasure and then watched Jem Faire pilot his uncle outside.

"Injuns always make me jumpy," Stonewall Gamble admitted when the two were gone. "Ain't that I don't trust that fellow. He's real good with Rowdon. It's just that he's so danged quiet. You think you're alone. You look around, and there he is. Like the Sioux took Custer."

Another of his cronies suggested, "Ought to make him wear them pinching boots you're so quick to sell us, Stonewall. You can hear them a mile away."

They all laughed, as Bill Sholto stood at the edge of the circle.

"Sure thought Miss Ellen would end up an old maid. Seemed like the type. Not my sort. Too cold by half, and never one for funnin'. Now Miss Maggilee, there's a whole other thing."

With a look at Sholto, Stonewall said firmly, "Here, you take the black. I'll take red this time."

Which effectively stopped talk about the Gaynor women.

With his vivid and unwelcome reminder of Ellen's mother, Captain Sholto waved to his friends among Gamble's cronies and went out to Jonathan Gaynor's wagon, loaded the first of several bags into the back of the wagon and moved slowly behind the Fairevale buckboard, where an aged spaniel bitch raised her head wearily and gave him a half-hearted bark of warning.

He went back into the store to get the other two sacks, passing Colonel Faire and his nephew going out. Jem's words to his uncle made it even more clear that he was jealous of Ellen and any man.

"You were talking with that bunch about the Gaynor women again," he was saying. "You want them gabbing about *her?*"

The colonel considered this before punching his nephew's shoulder lightly. "Jemmy, boy, if only Ellie had taken to you! Looks like I'll have to marry her to keep her in the family, and stop all that gabbing."

Jem laughed harshly. "No reason why she should like me. She finds me a savage. You secure there, Taffy?" he asked the old spaniel, who licked the back of his neck in reply.

They drove off, unaware that Sholto was watching the tail of the buckboard as it rattled into Church Street, and as he watched was thinking some mixed thoughts . . . Angry as he was at Maggilee, he also felt a certain resentment over their cold talk about her, not taking into account at all that she supported her daughter and mother-in-law with her shop earnings, and that even if she was a woman who— Hell, I've got no call thinking about her . . .

To get her out of his mind he walked over to Gaynor House after delivering Jonathan's supplies, where he was careful to check with the reserved and not too receptive butler Edward Hone to find out whether Maggilee had come home yet.

Hone certainly disapproved of him.

"Miss Ellen just arrived from the salon. She's upstairs dressing for dinner, I believe. Miss Varina is in the river parlor."

"Thanks. I just wanted a word with Miss Varina. If you'll see that Miss Ellen knows I'm here in a few minutes."

"Certainly, sir."

He sounded ice-tipped. The butler left him to find his own way to the parlor, into which he walked unannounced, in time to note that Ceci Hone, the butler's daughter, was leaning over Miss Varina's chair in earnest *sotto voce* discussion with the old lady.

Distinctly uneasy at the sight of the girl who had spied on him and Maggilee, Sholto cleared his throat and stopped. The black woman started at the sound, glanced nervously over her shoulder. Miss Varina appeared angry as she took note of him. Obviously she must have heard the worst from Ceci Hone.

She said roughly, "Well, well, come in. Don't just stand there. You are not as ornamental as you imagine."

He crossed the room, bowed over her hand, tried a whimsical smile that had no effect at all on that glacial face. "Must I guess, ma'am, what your maid was telling you?" and hurried on before she could answer . . . "She's told you I tumbled your daughter-in-law in the hay, so to speak. Down in Gamble's loft."

The old lady blinked, in at least a hint of admiration at the frankness of his remark. "You're an honest sort of scoundrel, I'll say that for you, and I suppose it was all her doing. Enticed you—"

"No, ma'am. I reckon you'd say it was even. I hadn't had a woman in some weeks—excuse the frankness—and there she was. I'd no notion she had anything to do with the Gaynors."

Miss Varina watched him like a cat at a mousehole. "I can't say I blame you for that, she's *not* a Gaynor. Except by the stupidity of my son."

"As I said, ma'm, it was my fault. Not the lady's."

"Lady, hah! You are gallant about it, though. A quality we used to rate rather more highly than they do these days. Come here."

He stood close beside her.

"What precisely are your feelings for my granddaughter?"

"I always thought a girl like her was beyond me. I still think she is, but I want her anyway. I think she needs a man. I think you do, too—"

"What!"

"You need a man to get the Gaynor lands operating at a profit, to see that the tenant farmers make the land pay. Jono's done well with his property—"

"So you'd marry my granddaughter to get at her property."

"No, ma'm. I'm going to ante up over six thousand dollars to start things. It's not much, but it's a start to get the land going. And Ellen *is* the Gaynor land. She's lovely, and lonely, and she needs attention. She should be put up there as belle of the county, where she belongs. She deserves better than she's had. And so does the Gaynor land."

She studied him. "I wouldn't be surprised but what you're right. You expressed it crudely, but straightforwardly. We *could* use your money, God knows. And Ellen does need attention—she *and* the land." She offered one hand to him, and he felt the sharp end of the tatting shuttle in her palm. Surprised, he let it fall through his fingers. He started to pick it up. "Never mind," she snapped. "We have a bargain, you and I. You will marry Ellen, make her happy, and restore the properties. If you can make Gaynor pay, we no longer need depend upon the charity of that . . . woman . . ."

They'd shaken hands but he pulled away at her last word and she reminded him, "You surely don't expect to keep her under the same roof with yourself and your wife . . ."

She had barely finished when they heard Ellen speaking to the butler in the hall, and Miss Varina motioned silence to Sholto, who understood that there was to be no "crude" or "straightforward" talk with Ellen.

He went to Ellen, took her hands and kissed her forehead, and led her over to her grandmother. He had to hurry. Maggilee would be getting home from her shop any time now and he was not anxious to meet her at this moment in particular.

"Sweetheart," he said to Ellen, "Miss Varina gave us her blessing."

Ellen was looking her best, her tall, slender figure surprisingly provocative in a bright spring-yellow dress that swayed as she moved. She hurried to Sholto and almost at the same time was warmly encircled in his arms. "I knew it. Darling, I knew she would . . . Dear Gran, please be happy for us."

Varina raised both arthritic hands, but there was no mistaking her affection for Ellen, who whispered as she touched Varina's cheek with her own, "I'm so happy! Thank you so much . . ."

Sholto felt her warm, relaxed body close against him, and had curiously ambivalent feelings. He wanted to protect this lovely creature who had just made herself part of him before a witness as stern as her grandmother, but at the same time he was—face it—a little unnerved at the idea of being Ellen's and Varina's savior forever . . . He was accustomed to women who pursued what they wanted, women who were no better, maybe even worse, than he was. He was uncomfortable with such superior females, wondering in a daze what he was doing here among these strange, thin-blooded aristocrats, even with such as Ellen Gaynor as the prize. He loved her, looked up to her, but diffident respect, even awe, were new and difficult emotions for Bill Sholto.

"You will stay to supper with us, won't you?" Ellen asked, and, sensing his hesitation, reminded him with a slight hint of reproach, "It will be the first time since— since we found out we were in love."

"Not the first time, sweetheart. That was when I tried to steal old Jono's house and lands. I loved you from the evening I first saw you." Without intending to, he caught Miss Varina's too clear blue eyes. Cynicism was in them, yet she smiled in her tight fashion.

Ellen adored every word of it, and with her arm around Sholto she fairly glowed, no longer the porcelain goddess.

"Well," Varina said, "we can't keep the captain from his work . . . No doubt Jonathan needs him . . . And we won't be having supper alone, child. Your mother should be here at any time." Her pale eyebrows raised and Bill Sholto was sure they were a signal to him. She shared his concern that he shouldn't come under Maggilee's spell again . . .

"No, sweetheart. I really do have to get back to the Ferry. So I'll be on my way now."

Ellen no longer urged him, word of her mother's impending arrival making her share the concern of the other two. She certainly didn't need Maggilee's charms working at this crucial moment. They kissed, Bill almost hesitant, as if afraid he would crush her, and Ellen passionately, as if pressing the memory of her slim arms and her body onto him during all the hours they would be apart.

They said good night again on the river veranda. The

gold of Fairevale oil lamps across the Ooscanoto gleamed on the water. Sholto wondered if the colonel and his Navajo nephew were over there watching the lights of Gaynor House and envying Bill Sholto for his conquest of the supposedly unapproachable Ellen. They kissed again, but now Bill let the invitation of Ellen's lips and the knowledge that Varina couldn't see them turn the kiss into a long embrace.

When he left her he cut across the grass, inhaling the brisk winter air. He was trying in his mind to separate the forest odors—the maples, scrub pine and catalpas, the reeds and dogwood along the riverbank, and the dying grass. He had almost reached the woods when, looking to the east and the field path from town, he caught sight of the silhouette of a small figure in a dark mantle and hood. He had seen Maggilee wear them during wet weather. He of course knew who it was and for one feckless moment thought of disappearing into the woods . . . anything to avoid meeting her face to face, all his anger melting under the memory of the wild sweetness of her touch, her soft, deliciously molded body.

She was limping. He changed his course quickly and started toward her. She saw him before she reached the eastern edge of the driveway and he thought she was going to turn and run. Like him, she braved it out and stood in the shadow of a leggy boxwood hedge.

"Good evening, Captain." She greeted him as primly as her daughter might once have done. Her face looked pale and taut as he stood in front of her, barring her way. Her ankle must be giving her pain, and in spite of himself he felt that pain with her.

"You shouldn't be walking on a bad ankle. It might be broken."

He wasn't sure there was amusement in her laugh. "You needn't worry, I mend easy. I only twisted it. Stepped in a rabbit hole. I thought I knew this path. *Don't let me keep you.*" She put her small hands on his forearms as if her slight weight would move him away.

He felt the heat of her touch through his coat and tunic to his bare flesh. It triggered a craving for her that was frightening, he couldn't afford it . . . God, not now . . .

"I'll get you to the door," he said abruptly. "You can walk in, no one will know. And don't argue."

"I'm not arguing."

He picked her up, enjoying the delicate weight of her in his arms, wondering how someone so light could create this overwhelming desire in him . . . It was impossible to take her to the house as he had promised. Without thinking, he had swung her around in the opposite direction, toward the fields, fallow now in winter and still damp with the recent rains. She had lied to him, true. Made a fool of him, no question. And still, hating his own body's betrayal, he *wanted* her, must have her . . . Reason had nothing to do with it.

She startled him then by the hard edge in her voice. "Don't think you'll use me and then marry my girl, *Captain* . . . You made your choice. I'll give you nothing."

But, damn it, if she didn't want him, why did she look at him like this, her enchanting mouth moist and ready, her eyes large and mockingly innocent. She was *still*, damn her, the lovely, earthy female who had given herself to him with a freedom that might have put to shame even that long-ago Molly-O in the Dakotas. It wasn't a question of betraying Ellen . . . He loved and respected Ellen, he *wanted* Maggilee the way a drunkard craved his bottle . . . Only once more, he reasoned with himself. Then, never again. His marriage to a fine, decent girl like Ellen would cure him of this sort of craving. He told himself what he wanted to hear.

"You want me, just the way I want you," he said tersely. "At least let's not lie to ourselves."

"No."

"The last time . . . Who are we hurting? No one will know—"

"I will."

"You weren't so fancy before . . ." He swung her over the plant debris left by one of the local peanut farmers who had experimented with this patch of ground. "There's that old slave cabin around here some place. I've always thought of it as ours—"

"We're through, damn you . . ." But the timbre of her voice told him something else.

That she really cared for him, after all? He couldn't be sure, but he knew now with an awful certainty that he could never forget her. Could he ever stop wanting her?

She had begun to struggle in his arms. The moonlight suddenly gleamed on her face and he saw etched by it the features that had so attracted him . . . But there was suffering, too, pallor and dark smudges under those seductive eyes. The effect was poignantly moving. His grip lost its cruel force as he stepped back with her into the shadow. There was a tenderness in his touch now. He whispered softly, "Darlin', I didn't mean to—"

"Put me down, please. It's too late . . . it was too late when you let my daughter believe you were in love with her."

"But that's different and you know it."

It was an effort for her to say it calmly, but she managed, "Please, Bill. Just say good-bye."

She raised her head. The long red wisps of hair brushed his mouth. His tongue touched the hair and then entered her parted, waiting lips. A pleasure to be enjoyed for the last time.

CHAPTER 17

***

"GRAN, YOU know what I'd really like to do? Shout the news from the very peak of the roof." Ellen swung around, hugged Varina, who made a weak attempt to shrug her off.

"Now, now, all this emotion over a simple engagement. It's been going on for quite a few years."

"But me! He'd rather have me than—oh, hundreds of pretty girls he's seen in his life." Guiltily, Ellen went on. "He hardly paid any attention to Mama at that Sunday dinner. It wasn't fair of us not to tell her a good-looking male was coming. No wonder she took that laudanum. Working such long hours at the shop and leaving so early in the morning. And servants gone—I saw Ceci Hone in the hall. Why on earth did she have to be sent to Richmond? Why not someone at the shop?"

Varina smoothed the tight lace choker which gave her something of that upright look. "I've no doubt your mother had reason. Or maybe it was that butler."

"But why, Gran?"

"Well," Varina said, "she's back now and their purpose failed if they wanted to keep her away from me."

"Keep Ceci Hone away from you? But why, Gran?"

"Never mind. I was just going on . . . You know me . . ."

It wasn't like Varina to be uneasy, unsure, Ellen thought, and then dismissed it . . . She was too happy to linger over any unpleasant or worrisome notion.

"I wish Mama would get home. Maybe I should go out and see if she's in sight. It's so dark. And it looks like frost before morning. I'll take her winter coat."

But Varina was irritable as always whenever Maggilee's habits inconvenienced the household. "She certainly knows the weather as well as we do. If she insists on spending all these hours at her beloved shop, we can at least go on about our lives. I suggest we have supper. I want my tea. Hot, if you please."

Ellen went to see if Cookie was ready, and in the hall she heard Ceci calling quietly to her from the head of the stairs, and then saying, "There's people out there, miss, come and see."

Ellen started to call Edward Hone but Ceci motioned frantically "No, ma'm . . . It's easier to see from your window."

Ellen went up the stairs. It did occur to her that Ceci

wanted to avoid her father, who might come out into the lower hall at any minute, but she was curious enough to follow the girl's directions. It was odd too that Ceci hadn't confided in Varina, to whom she was devoted.

"Yes, Ceci, what is it?" Ellen asked at the top of the stairs, but Ceci was already leading the way to Ellen's room. With her hand on the polished brass doorknob she asked, "May I, miss?"

"You've gone this far, you may as well go further." Even to her own ears she sounded exactly like her grandmother.

Ceci opened the door, and her neat brown traveling dress swept past Ellen's furnishings until she reached the window. The portieres had already been opened a few inches, probably by Ceci on her previous visit to the room. Ellen started to touch the lace curtain as well, but Ceci's voice stopped her.

"Don't let them—see you."

Ellen was annoyed by the girl's conspiratorial manner but instinct made her go along. She motioned Ceci to turn down the oil lamp beside her bed. She studied the lawn. Nothing. The woods at the south end of the open space were silent and dark. Nobody could see anything there. A regiment could hide within the heavily timbered area between Gaynor House and Gaynor Ferry. But to the east, beyond the driveway, she made out a figure as it moved from the foliage toward the drive. A clumsy form? No, a big powerful man carrying someone small in his arms. Maybe a child. He set her down. A woman.

For a couple of minutes the two were visible in the faint lamplight from the east front of Gaynor House. They melted together. Again they were one bulky shadow.

Ellen's fingers caught in the lace of the curtain. She tore her fingers away impatiently.

"See 'em?" the girl prompted her. "Prowlers, you think?"

Two tenants from one of the farms along the east border of the Gaynor fields, Ellen told herself.

The woman, of course, was wearing Maggilee's mantle and cowl. Lots of women had them. The man was wearing a uniform of some kind.

They separated. For an instant his blue jacket was visible in the lamplight pouring out from the ground floor of Gaynor House.

"Why, miss, you've gone and torn the curtain," Ceci said, but there seemed no mistaking her satisfaction.

Downstairs the front door opened and closed. Maggilee and Ceci's father were exchanging a few words about the prospects for snow. In another room Cookie was arranging a few hot dishes for supper and in still another Varina waited impatiently for that supper call.

All normal. All . . . except Ellen's life. She told herself that her mother's outrageous beauty had caught Sholto unawares. She'd used her all *too* familiar charms. Sholto had kissed her . . . he was human. But they had gone their separate ways. No looking back. It was a casual thing, what else could it be . . . ?

Ceci was staring at her. "There don't seem to be prowlers about, after all," Ellen said. "You *might* watch that imagination of yours, you've almost made me late for supper."

"Yes, ma'm," but she didn't look very sorry. She knew her father had always favored Maggilee, and so anything that tended to reflect on Maggilee tended to please her.

Ellen passed her, without any outward sign of her profound upset. She went down to the dining room, meeting her mother in the lower hall, her mother who was limping but managed an impish grin all the same.

" 'Evening, honey. Turned my ankle. I know I'm late. Tell Cookie I'll be down in a minute."

Ellen seized on this new possibility like a reprieve. Captain Sholto had seen her mother limping and had gone to help her. *Nothing* more natural.

Maggilee brushed her daughter's cheek with a kiss. Ellen asked if she could help to wrap the swollen ankle.

"No, thanks, you go along and make my peace with the dragon. I'll be at the table in no time . . . Are you catching cold? Your voice sounds hoarse."

"Does it?"

But Maggilee was already on the way to her room with her mind on other matters. She held tight to the banister, moving with some difficulty, as if her ankle troubled her, though she had refused help.

Ellen went in to supper.

It was a silent meal, enlivened only by Varina's apparently artless prattle. Unhappily for the other two women at the table, much of her talk was in praise of Captain Sholto and the assets he would bring to the family.

"You've done very well, Ellen, I must say. His antecedants are nothing to boast about . . . the less said of that the better . . ." Waving a half-eaten biscuit, she brushed aside the prejudices of a lifetime and then carefully rubbed her buttery fingers on a napkin. Then, after calling for spoon bread and the jam put up from Jonathan's recent crop, Varina announced, "An early wedding, I think. We will certainly need his—shall we call it a dowry? —in time to put down new crops. What do you say to sometime after the holidays? Around the second week in January. Does everyone agree?"

"Unfortunately, I have to be in New York over Christmas," Maggilee said.

Ellen set her teacup down. Sharply. "Why? You

never go up north this early in the season."

"Yes. And you remember those second-rate bolts they sent down. Claimed I'd been too late. The new weaves, those soft silks and crepes... that popular zephyr cloth. I couldn't order any for spring. All gone, they said. This time I mean to get there first."

While Ellen digested this, wondering because it was so unusual, Varina was relieved, and made her feelings evident.

"It hardly seems fair for poor Ellen to put off her wedding because you must go off to New York. And in view of the need to get the crops in as early as possible, the wedding can hardly be postponed beyond the new year. What does the bride-to-be say?"

"The sooner the better, although it will shock everyone in the County," Ellen said. She was drinking the last of her tea, now cold and bitter, but she didn't notice. Without seeming to, she studied her mother over the rim of her cup. "What do you think, Mama? Is it too short a time? Will they gossip about me?"

Maggilee shrugged. "Ellie, they'll gossip whenever the wedding will be, but it will be all right. They are fond of you." She had eaten hardly anything and was playing with bits of bread, shifting them around on the tablecloth.

In spite of animated talk about the wedding, the supper had been a nightmare to both daughter and mother. The latter excused herself, claiming her ankle ached, and she went up to her room, asking that a hot footbath be brought to her. Ellen watched Maggilee... watched her closely until she was out of sight. An *incredible* thought had begun to eat at her. Incredible? No. Unacceptable...

"Thank heaven she's gone," Varina remarked. "Come and read to me, child."

But Ellen had already gone after Bethulia, who was carrying the deep basin of steaming water up to Maggilee. "Never mind. I'll take it."

She found her mother as she expected to find her, lying on her bed, staring at the ceiling. Her hands were spread over her abdomen, as if to warm her cold, shivering body. The lamp had been turned down and the room was deep in shadow, her white hands and face glowing palely in the dim light.

Ellen set the basin on the old gaming table which had been banished from the "company" rooms.

"Do you have a stomach ache, Mama?"

Maggilee's hands moved quickly to the cool bed coverlet. She tried to sit up but fell back and waved impatiently. "No. It's nothing. I ate too much of Biddie's preserved melon rind this afternoon. I knew I should have taken it home but—*why* are you looking at me like that, Ellie?"

Ellen took a step, stood with her knees against the bed to give her strength. Standing there, looking down at Maggilee in the light and shadow of the oil lamp, she couldn't know how terrifying her stony face and tall, slender form looked.

"Mama, are you pregnant?"

Silence. Ellen told herself that innocence would have brought a shocked and indignant denial. Very slowly, her mother turned her head on the pillow, looked up at her. "Ellie . . . it wasn't his fault."

Ellen stared at those great eyes and wanted to burst into tears. Woman to woman, mother to daughter, Maggilee Gaynor was asking for pity and understanding of her daughter. This woman who had gotten every man she glanced at . . . and now she asked forgiveness. Ellen wanted to forgive her, wanted to . . . but the strong inheritance of the Dunmores and the Gaynors demanded payment of some kind . . . *I will not make it so easy for her* . . .

"I'm *sure* it wasn't his fault."

"Ellie, honey, listen to me," her mother began, sitting up and trying to take her hand, which she avoided and stepped back, hoping for a return of her own strength of will, remembering what had been done to her, and to the unborn child that should have been hers.

With glacial calm she asked, "Why were you going to New York? To get rid of it?"

Maggilee winced, closed her eyes and sank back. She looked suddenly haggard, old. "What else is there? He is promised to you. He will honor his promise."

The last knife thrust: *He will marry you because he must honor his promise.*

"You're a *liar* . . ." It had the crack of a whip and Maggilee cringed away from her, as though instinctively protecting her baby. The gesture infuriated Ellen, demonstrating as it did a weapon she would be powerless to fight against.

And then it occurred to her, a private revenge . . . of course, Sholto *had* to marry Maggilee. Nothing else was possible, thanks to what probably had been Maggilee's intention all along. But what if Bill Sholto was forced into "honorable" marriage while he was known to be still in love with Ellen? Sooner or later her mother would know, know that she had lost for winning.

Ellen felt in better control of herself. She'd been a fool to betray her deepest feelings in front of her rival. And she had always known Maggilee *was* her rival . . . "I'll send for Captain Sholto," she said quietly, with a strong hint of Varina's steel underneath. She noted with some satisfaction the fear in her mother's eyes.

"Don't, Ellie. Please. Leave things as they were."

"Are you afraid? Maggilee Gaynor, desired by every man in Tudor County? By Albert Dimster and Gavin McCrae and God knows how many others—"

Maggilee raised herself up on her elbows, staring at her. The first genuine puzzlement in her eyes now gradually changed to understanding . . . "So that's why you hang on to him so . . . Because of *those* children, silly schoolboys, the sort to flirt with and laugh at—"

"To you, not to me . . ."

"Oh, Ellie, please don't get even with me by trying to take away from me the only man I could love, the way I once—" She sighed and collapsed back against the pillow. "Go ahead. Send for him. Talk to him. Don't tell him about me. I never intended him to know—"

"Why? Wasn't that how you got my father, by getting pregnant and telling him about an unwanted child?"

Maggilee's voice was an exhausted whisper. "Oh, my God . . . oh, *God* . . ." It sounded like a cry for help.

In the silence that followed she seemed to recover. Her voice held a new firmness. "You'll find, Ellie, it's me he wants, even without knowing about the child. He's marrying you because you have one thing I never had. And it's not the property. I am Beau Gaynor's widow. Gaynor House is mine before it comes to you. No, it's quite a different thing he admires in you."

Ellen allowed herself to hope. Dry-lipped, and trying not to show her eagerness, she asked, "And what is that?"

"*You* were born a lady. Proper, inaccessible, like Varina. He's marrying a woman like *Varina Dunmore Gaynor*, but he will *never* get over his need for me—"

Ellen turned away, unable to listen to it. But she had to hear the denial from Bill. At once. She couldn't wait. If she had time to think about it, she might come actually to believe what her mother was saying . . . She left the room, feeling an awful emptiness. In those last few minutes she had lost her mother—whatever the outcome with Bill Sholto, the cruelty of Maggilee's words—and her own —could never be forgotten . . . She left her mother's room and began to run.

She was still running, breathless and icy cold, when she found herself at the foot of the narrow servants' stairs. An old storm cape belonging to Bethulia was hanging on a hook by the open pantry door. She couldn't wait here until Bill arrived. She had to get out of this house—the house she was born in had become a symbol of pain, and loss. Her first sense of a building hatred was directed against this house . . .

She started walking along the river path toward Gaynor Ferry, tucking her hands inside the cape and wrapping it close around her. She welcomed the prickle of the ice-tipped air; perhaps it could somehow numb her consuming pain. But her thoughts kept dwelling on the awful picture of Maggilee and Bill Sholto, their bodies rolling and twisting only minutes after he had *so* gallantly turned aside her own diffident advances, talking about how *pure* she was and how much he wanted her . . .

Well, was Maggilee right after all?

What had it been like in the last two months? Did they lie in some secret place making love while they laughed at ignorant Ellen, the spinster, the "Miss Eliza of Gaynor House," the woman no man could possibly desire?

But why had Bill bothered to fondle and kiss her if he had no serious interest in her? Maggilee was wrong, too sure of her own attractions and too desperate to have a father for her bastard child.

Across the Ooscanoto River the bulk of Fairevale loomed as a haven, its lights haphazardly shining on the water from wherever someone had left an oil lamp untended. But within that rambling house were people who cared a little for her, with no ulterior motive. Maybe she should run off to Fairevale before facing down Captain Sholto.

But it had to be done. She swung around, disoriented, one foot slipping into a reed-choked pool of runoff from the river. She dragged her foot out of the water. Her high-buttoned shoe had protected it, though her stocking felt damp. She went on, scarcely noticing.

She missed the spot where the path turned away from the river and across the woods to Dunmore Creek and the Ferry. Backtracking, she found the path and went on, more carefully now, no longer running. She had begun to be afraid, not of the old dripping locust trees and spongy undergrowth, or even the darkness, but of Bill's real feelings. Maggilee had shaken her confidence, made her once more doubt, as she had all her life, her own adequacy as a woman . . .

From the north side the old Gaynor Ferry house looked dark. The shutters were closed. Not a ray of light escaped and she felt sick at having to wait still longer for Bill Sholto to reassure her. But when she made her way around to the combination porch and wharf extending out into Dunmore Creek's rushing waters, she saw the rays of firelight through the uncovered porch window. She stepped up onto the porch, causing a flurry of wings and raucous honking from her cousin's geese.

She raised her hand to knock, wondering for the first time what Jonathan's attitude would be. He had always been her friend and partisan, but though he seldom mentioned Maggilee she had heard rumors that as a boy he adored his Cousin Beau's red-haired young wife.

Before she could knock the door latch was raised and

the silhouette of Bill Sholto appeared in the frame of the door. He was bare-chested, dressed in his cavalry breeches. She moved back quickly. He squinted into the darkness.

"Is that you, Jono? Who's here?"

He reached out, saw her face, and called to the gander, "Quiet, Pompey! Stop that squawking." Then, as he pulled Ellen into the warmth before the fireplace, "Good lord, sweetheart. You must be frozen."

She made much of his concern as a good sign, and of his gentleness in holding her icy hands enclosed by his own. "What is it, Ellen?" And louder, "Are they all right at the house?"

"Where's Cousin Jonathan?"

"Over at the Finches. One of his cows got into their river pasture. Sweetheart, what is it?"

She was weighing every word, every gesture he made, as a plus or minus . . . and it seemed to her sensitive ears that his anxiety about "they" at the house was greater than the concern he had greeted her with.

She looked straight at him. "Bill, do you love me?"

"Of course I do! Haven't I told you so? Who could help it, sweetheart?" His expression lightened. "I know what it is. My lovely girl just wants to be told . . ." He drew her to him with that gentleness she had always supposed was a sign of his deeper love. But this time in his arms she did not thaw. She remembered the many times her Cousin Jonathan had held her, consoled her in her troubles. Even Colonel Faire had held her like this as a child when she fell and hurt herself. She left herself in his embrace, her face against his muscled chest. He kissed the crown of her head, then asked again with something that sounded like real urgency, "Ellen, sweetheart . . . you haven't told me—are they all right at home . . . ?"

Her answer was her own urgent question. "Captain, why do you want to marry me? Honestly."

"Because I never thought I'd be lucky enough to win a goddess, a lovely, golden goddess—"

She shivered, and mistaking her reaction, he tried to warm her by holding her close. "If you married me," she said, "and we had children, would you mind very much?"

"Mind! Sweetheart, I came east to plant roots, to find you, to marry you and start a family."

"Soon?"

"The sooner the better."

"... Would you also marry my mother?" She waited. The heavy beat of her heart was stifling.

His grip tightened around her shoulders and he looked down at her. "You saw us tonight."

"Yes. Are you going to tell me you don't love her?" She decided he must be asking himself whether truth or a lie would serve him best.

He let her go, except for her hands. It was colder outside his embrace. He shook his head. "Ellen, a man has several needs . . . When I met Maggilee, I need—needed her, but in a different way—"

"You needed an experienced *woman* . . . say it . . ."

He didn't deny it. He looked at the deep-glowing heart of the fire. The color of Maggilee's hair, Ellen thought, and wondered if the thought had occurred to him too.

"Why didn't you ask her to marry you?"

He laughed shortly. "Can you really see Maggilee as a loving wife and mother?"

And Ellen recalled her mother's quick, instinctive gesture, during their argument, about the child she was carrying . . .

Ellen freed her hands. "You're in love with Mother.

You never did love me in the same way, you can't—"

"I do love you, Ellen . . . I'm more fond of you than of any woman I've ever known . . ."

He made a move toward her, but she stepped back. She looked taller now, with her head up, her gaze level. She really would rather have died than let him know what she felt. The awful confirmation of what her mother had said. She moved to the door.

"Ellen, wait, you've got to understand about Maggilee. It wasn't something we planned . . . We didn't know how it would be with us . . ."

"You wanted a family. Well, Captain, my mother is now in a condition to give you a family. And an estate, as well. Incidentally, this is one child she seems inclined to love. Good night, Captain."

Her last glance told her the news had stunned him. And delighted him too. She couldn't mistake that. He went for the door but she slammed it in his face and stepped out into the dark shelter of the woods.

For a few moments tears blinded her, then she heard him call her name . . . Knowing he always took the river path to Gaynor House, she wandered out on the town road and kept walking, mechanically. The night wind beat across her face, dried the tears. But not the ones inside.

CHAPTER 18
***

SOMEONE WAS trying the doorknob. Either Ceci or Bethulia. Maggilee forced her way back from a laudanum-induced sleep and fumbled for the big turnip watch that had belonged to Major Clinton Dalkett long ago. It lay on the table beside her bed lamp as always.

Was it only an hour since Ellen had stormed out? It seemed like years. Maggilee mumbled, "Go away, Ceci. Don't bother me until morning."

When the doorknob rattled again she got off the bed with an effort and wove her way across the room. She had difficulty squeezing her fingers around the doorknob and then found it pushed open against her. Confused by what appeared to be the door's own free will, she stared at it and then, in a blur, saw Bill Sholto step inside looking wet and cold. He'd pulled on a shirt over the breeches but hadn't put on a coat.

Breathing heavily he closed and leaned against the door, not taking his eyes off her.

"Is it true?"

She tried to avoid his eyes by folding her arms over her breast and looking as outraged as she could in the circumstances. She was recalling him that Sunday afternoon when he saw her in her laudanum daze.

"Get out of here! Do you want *everyone* in this house to know my daughter's fiancé is my lover . . . ? My God, haven't you done enough . . . ?"

He ignored her tirade. *"Please*, tell me the truth. The child . . ."

He reached out, touched her hair, which had tumbled around her face, and before she could move caught a handful of it and held her there motionless.

"Don't come to me with your questions. Go to my daughter. *She's* the one who's going to be your wife."

"I've already seen Ellen." Then, firmly but with great care, his hand wound in her hair, and he brought her close to him. His other hand raised her chin. "Your daughter is a fine young lady. She'll make a good wife for a better man than I am. Sweetheart, you want that baby as much as I do. And don't bother to deny it."

The idea that he had come back to her only for that reason made her angrier than ever. "She was a fool to tell you. And she hates me now. She would never forgive me if you and I do this thing to her."

"If you and I gave that child of ours a name and a

decent background? ... Maggilee, you don't know the first thing about that daughter of yours. I honestly believe she came to break off her engagement to me, to give us her blessing."

"Her blessing? Bill, are you crazy? Varina's granddaughter give us her blessing when we've broken her heart and betrayed her?"

"Yes, sweetheart. I mean just that. She wasn't heartbroken. She was very calm about the whole thing." He raised her hair, kissed the warm, soft flesh of her neck, and she felt the familiar rush of desire. She fought it, closing her eyes, trying not to let it work.

"That can't be true. You weren't here in this room. She accused me of the most dreadful things. She hates me."

He smiled at her. "Sweetheart, that's the wonder of it. She had time to think things over while she walked down to the Ferry. She practically ordered me to marry you." Maggilee raised her head to speak but he stopped any protests with a kiss.

When they parted he tapped her nose with his forefinger. "And no more of that stuff for your nerves ... We want our daughter born a healthy, gloriously beautiful young lady. *Like her mother.*"

"Or our son?" she answered, astonished at herself for beginning to believe that any of this was possible.

"Or both. Look at me. William Sholto, family man. No burials alone in the goddamn Dakota hills for me. I'm going to be a family man, believe that, my red-headed sweetheart."

In the strong comfort of his arms she now felt anything was possible. She looked around the room where, just minutes before she'd been wondering when she could possibly go to New York to end the life of this man's child.

Even laudanum hadn't blurred that horror. But now she was free of it . . . She broke away from him.

"I have a present for you."

He watched, marveling at his own luck in finding this woman who could give love so joyously, give him a family, the home and roots he had come east to find. She reached far back in a drawer of the high chiffonier and brought him a flat, tight-necked bottle of liquid. She held it in her hands as if to warm it, and offered it to him.

"Bill, I saw your face the other Sunday when I thought you knew I'd taken laudanum. I want this to be my first gift to my husband. Along with my promise. No more, as you say, of that stuff. I don't need to blot out old memories any more."

He didn't understand, but supposed she must be referring to her worries over the child. He reached for the bottle, then hesitated.

"Put it back where you found it, sweetheart. Let it stay there the rest of our lives. I promise you, you'll never want it again."

* * *

Ellen had lost her way. It was ridiculous. As a child she ran through these woods day or night. There wasn't a tree or a shrub she didn't recognize. But tonight she had stumbled along in a kind of madness, pushing her way between rushes and willows, wading across pebbles through inches of overflow from the river channel. She must have crossed the Ooscanoto on the footbridge half a mile below the Ferry House. She was on Fairevale land.

There was a pain in her chest. Too much wild, aimless running. She slowed to a stumbling walk and came to a halt against a spreading oak tree, its branches now stark against the foggy sky.

Her head ached unbearably. She refused to believe it

was from unshed tears. She would not cry. No man was worth it. But Maggilee . . . my own mother. She'd done it deliberately, just the way she took away Albert Dimster and Gavin McCrae . . .

The fog curled around her, soft and restful. Confusing. Her knees gave way and she sank down on the cushion of soggy oak leaves, trying to get her wits together, think how to gather strength for the endless walk back across the river to the familiar comfort of her dark bedroom . . .

She must have briefly lost consciousness. She was roused by the bright rays of a lantern somewhere nearby. The rays kept appearing and disappearing as if the lantern was being swung in someone's hand.

She tried to speak, cleared her throat and called out for help.

Long, milky gleams of lantern-light cut through the fog and she tried to get to her knees. Behind the blinding light she made out a tall figure in a bright fringed serape such as she had seen thrown over chairs at Fairevale. She heard Jem Faire's sharp intake of breath at the sight of her.

He leaned over her. "Are you hurt? Just tell me—yes or no."

"No . . . tired . . . so tired."

He set the lantern on the ground and, reaching under her body, lifted her into his arms, took up the lantern in his left hand and started off.

"I'm all right," she said, gathering her thoughts into some kind of order.

"Be quiet," he told her, and held her in a near-suffocating embrace.

Her relief at being cared for turned to a nearly hysterical need to be set free. She squirmed in his arms. "Put me down, damn you . . . I can walk . . ."

He paid no attention. His stride was long and easy, and time blurred for her. Later she would remember the rough texture of his serape and the strong beat of his heart.

There was a confusion of voices and lights, Miss Eliza's shrill scream, and Colonel Faire wanting to know if she had fainted, and shouting for whiskey "to restore the poor little mite."

By the time Jem had set her in his uncle's big leather armchair in the south parlor and was chafing her hands, Ellen had recovered most of her equilibrium.

"I'm really all right. I only walked too far, and got lost."

"Eliza," Colonel Faire bellowed, "where's that whiskey?"

Which upset Jem. He looked around. "Uncle, she will choke. For God's sake, she's in shock, she needs quiet."

Ellen roused herself. "I'm not, I just found—I decided not to get married. That's all. I'll take the whiskey."

She saw the two men look at each other.

"There's my girl, she's right as rain." The colonel was delighted by what seemed to be her abrupt recovery and promptly held a cut-glass goblet to her lips. She clutched his wrist, literally holding on for dear life. The whiskey was strong, but it heated her. Between sips she asked Jem, "How did you find me?"

"I was burying old Taffy. She died today."

Taffy, the ancient spaniel, had supervised the Fairevale land for almost eighteen years. Ellen tried to express her sympathy but Jem didn't want to discuss it. He changed the subject abruptly. "Hadn't I better take Ellen —Miss Ellen—upstairs to rest?"

The whiskey had given Ellen courage. "Thank you,

all of you dear friends. But I've got to go home sometime. I want to get it over. Could someone take me tonight?"

"My poor child," Miss Eliza told her, having gained an inkling of the real story. "You shouldn't have to live there with that woman . . . I knew she was responsible for . . . well, for whatever happened . . ."

Ellen couldn't bear the idea that Jem might find she'd been jilted. She wasn't sure why, but of all people, he must not know the humiliating truth. Nothing to do but deny it . . . "She had nothing to do with it. I just decided I didn't want to marry the captain. Is that so strange . . . ?"

"Of course not, my dear." The colonel took hold of her cold hands. "You won't marry *anybody* but your old friend Rowdy Faire," he told her with a straight face, "and that captain can just take himself back to where he came from—Jem, where are you going?"

"I'll get the buggy and take her home."

Ellen panicked. She didn't want to be alone with Jem. He would be sure to remind her that she had been a fool over Captain Sholto, that she'd been betrayed by her grand cavalier, that he was not so bad, after all . . . it just might be . . . but right now she was in no mood for *any* man pressing himself on her . . . Her pain and loss were double . . . She despised Bill Sholto for his weakness, but for her mother's treachery . . . She took Colonel Faire's hand. "You take me home, please."

It would be more *comfortable* with Rowdon Faire. No painful involvements with him. No physical attraction to cut her more deeply . . . only a safe, fatherly warmth and concern . . . safe . . .

"She needs a decent woman's care," Miss Eliza put in with sudden decision. "We'll both go with her, Father. You and I. Jem won't be needed."

Ellen avoided Jem's eyes, but she knew he had been

hurt. His mouth looked grim as he shrugged. "Suit yourself," and went out to get the horse and buggy harnessed.

Ellen called after him. "I do thank you, Jem." He didn't seem to hear her.

Miss Eliza took her upstairs to wash her face, lent her some lavender cologne, and as Ellen combed and put up her hair, said frankly, "I may as well tell you, Papa and I never thought that Bluecoat would be faithful. Of course," she confided, "I suspect Papa was jealous."

Ellen, startled, stopped pinning up wisps of hair. "The colonel thinks of me as a daughter."

Miss Eliza ventured a bleak little smile, a rarity on her flinty features. "*I'm* his daughter. It's not the same, I assure you. Besides, I don't want him marrying one of those County beauties who'd like to get her hands on his money and Fairevale. Amabel Corrigan was over at Fairevale yesterday making eyes at him. I was never so disgusted. I thought right there and then that if a friend of mine, a decent, sensible woman like you, were there instead—well, imagine that trashy Corrigan family running Fairevale . . . Are you ready, dear?"

Ellen wasn't ready, but the return to Gaynor House had to be gotten over. The women went down the stairs together. By the time Jem pulled up the horse and buggy before the east portico of Fairevale, he looked as if he'd been chiseled from stone. Ellen was sorry but in no mood to give him a chance to say, "I told you so."

As she rode off with the colonel and his daughter, Rowdon Faire turned to Ellen and took her hand. "You've finally seen through that fellow, I expect."

"I expect."

"You mustn't mind. Some day you'll be glad. Wait and see."

Wait and see. It wasn't the happiest reminder. She

didn't want to wait that long for the pain to ease. Ellen released herself gently, touching his face with her hand. "Thank you. You've always been my friend—you and Miss Eliza," she added with a glance at the woman in black. "And you will tell Jem that I appreciate all he did for me—"

"Of course, my dear." And under the eyes of Miss Eliza, who sat watching them, he kissed Ellen's hand.

Miss Eliza smiled.

After that, they drove most of the way in companionable silence. Ellen's emotions were in such a state she welcomed this peace and thought how easy it would be to spend her life like this, loved and cared for by a man as kind and loving as Rowdon Faire . . .

They let her off at the Gaynor House east veranda, where Varina Gaynor stood in white-lipped silence, wrapped in an old cashmere shawl. She asked the Faires to come in and have a hot toddy before their return home, but they declined and Ellen and Varina were grateful for their thoughtfulness.

Expecting the worst, Ellen started to explain but had barely stammered out the first words when the old lady recovered herself and said briskly, "You're freezing cold. Come along with me."

For once Varina made no impatient move to shrug off Ellen's arm when it went around her waist in gratitude for the old lady's understanding, and once they were in Ellen's room, she explained in tight, clipped words, "He told me, that precious Bluebelly. At least, he had more decency than she did. You understand, of course. They must marry. The Gaynor name is not going to be shamed by that woman—"

Ellen said tiredly, "I understand, Gran . . . don't worry. I'll be fine . . . I feel much better now . . ."

"Excellent." Varina paused. "Rowdon Faire is very fond of you. Not quite a Dunmore, but a man of integrity. You could do worse, you know—"

"Please. I'd rather not talk about it. I think I'll go to bed . . ."

Varina clapped her on the back. "That's my girl. Mind you, no sorrowing over that worthless pair. Better things are in store for you."

The old lady kissed her cheek and went out, firmly closing the door behind her.

Alone, finally, Ellen went to the window, pressed her forehead against the cold glass and looked out over the foggy grounds, wondering if this was how it felt to be dead.

Out on the drive the Faires were riding away. Ellen watched them go and automatically waved as the colonel stuck his head out of the buggy and looked up at her window.

The colonel . . . She closed her eyes but couldn't banish the thought.

PART TWO

CHAPTER

1
***

ROWDON FAIRE'S Christmas-night marriage proposal to Ellen Gaynor provided endless jokes for him, even before the wedding, and though the females of Tudor County grew heartily sick of them, the males guffawed every time he re-enacted them.

"Took me up on one joke too many, so she did," he would confess. "And me never guessing all the while that I'd sold my freedom down the Ooscanoto." He would wait for laughs and jeers, then add warmly, "but I'd do it all over again, so I would. Should have done it years ago, but who would have thought she'd have me."

The entire county, regarding itself as arbiter of their destinies, was also stirred by Ellen's announcement that she did not wish to be married from Gaynor House. Varina frostily reminded her that all important Gaynor or Dunmore weddings since the turn of the nineteenth century had been held at the house.

But it was at Gaynor House that Ellen had learned the truth about her mother's condition. It was not the setting she wanted to begin her own marriage. Even though Maggilee and Bill Sholto had tactfully absented themselves two days after their engagement, going to Portsmouth to marry and on to New York for a business-honeymoon, Ellen couldn't bear to spend any more time in Gaynor House than absolutely necessary, until she could go, feeling warm and loved, as the wife of Rowdon Faire.

Miss Eliza suggested Gaynorville's Methodist Episcopal Church, where both families had been christened. It seemed the logical wedding choice.

Since it was impossible to exclude Varina Gaynor from these wedding plans, Ellen found, at least outwardly, that her relationship with her grandmother was unchanged. Privately, however, she made it a practice to choose Miss Eliza for her confidante and companion during the weeks of preparation before the wedding. It was a foregone conclusion that Miss Eliza must be her maid of honor. It remained only to convince the spinster that her habitual rusty black would be impossible. Miss Eliza herself was so excited over the discussion of Ellen's wedding among the ladies of the neighborhood that Varina remarked, on a slightly sour note:

"One would think you were the bride, my dear Eliza. I do believe you care more about these details than my granddaughter does."

Eliza blushed without embarrassment, while Varina went on, "My granddaughter is, I grant you, a lucky girl, and Rowdon only confirms my high opinion of him by demonstrating such good taste in his choice of a wife."

Everyone hastened to agree, then returned to the wedding plans . . .

. . . How carefully no one mentions Mama and Bill, Ellen thought as she listened to Varina, Eliza and Irene Wychfield politely disagree about details which normally should have been exclusively the province of Ellen's mother. Ellen herself wouldn't admit it to a soul, and hardly even to herself, but there were times when she wondered what on earth all these women were doing here, discussing her marriage to one man while her heart and—face it—her dreams were still painfully full of another . . . At this very minute that other man was probably walking about New York City arm in arm with her mother, and tonight, and all the nights during the last two months, they had slept in each other's arms. God, how she hated him . . . Yes . . . nice, calm, cool Ellen could have such a shocking emotion . . . emotion*s* . . . love, and hate . . .

She became aware that the voices had stopped. The women were all looking at her. Eliza repeated her remark, punctuating it with a little laugh to soften the accusation, "My dear, I hope you aren't overdoing all these tiresome preparations. For a minute there you looked quite—" She didn't speak the appropriate word, but Varina cut in with . . . "Quite savage, I would say." With a wave of her tatting shuttle which made her wince at the rheumatic twinge, she added, "But that's all over. I must say I am rather taken with your wedding dress. I had hoped you would wear mine but I daresay hoops and crinolines would look a trifle odd in this modern age."

"And having a Baltimore modiste make it for you,"

Eliza agreed. "So much nicer than some local seamstress like . . . well, so much nicer, I always say."

Varina put in . . . "Now, wouldn't it be a scandal to delight the gossips if Ellen had asked *that* woman to make her gown . . ."

No one needed to ask who *"that woman"* might be. Ellen was annoyed by her grandmother's deliberately provocative words, but Eliza's face flamed with anger.

"That would be the last straw! I personally do not ever intend to acknowledge *that* woman, if I must publicly cut her on the street."

Nothing new about that, Ellen thought . . . You always have cut her since she married Beauford Gaynor . . . Why two women should be enemies over my father is more than I know. Didn't he betray both of them for some female up in northern Virginia? At least, with Bill Sholto it was only two women at a time, not three! She had to smile in spite of herself . . . And at the same time wondered, as she had a hundred times before, whether Bill Sholto perhaps did think of her once in a while . . . whether, damn him, he ever regretted the choice Maggilee had forced on him.

Outspoken Daisy Wychfield McCrae had come in on this public discussion of Ellen's private affairs and blurted out now, "It's a shame about you, Miss Varina. After all these years, too."

Everyone glanced nervously at Varina, who looked a little upset herself. With a huff she inquired, "May I ask why I should be pitied?"

"Well, because"—Daisy looked around, belatedly realized that she had blundered—"because Captain and Mrs. Sholto will be living at Gaynor House, of course. I only wondered where Miss Varina will be living."

"And what makes you think I will move out of my

own house to oblige that woman merely because her husband intends to spend a few thousand on the land? I did not find it necessary to move out when that woman married my son. I played in this house in my childhood. I came here as a bride when I was fifteen. I'll leave it in my coffin."

Ellen remembered what Maggilee had said, that as widow of Gaynor House's last male owner, Maggilee was its owner now until her own death. This reasoning had probably never occurred to Varina.

Everyone assured Varina that Daisy hadn't even hinted at her departure from Gaynor House, it was all a misunderstanding. But Varina had already gathered up her basket and limped out of the sewing room, trailing behind her a ribbon of white tatting that would eventually decorate Ellen's bridal petticoat.

Ellen watched the older woman until she was out of sight. Somehow there was something a bit pitiful about all that tatting for what was supposed to be the happiest day of a girl's life. She wondered how Varina really felt about the rapid change in bridegrooms. She had seemed delighted when Ellen gave her the news, but ever since she had taken to watching Ellen at odd moments . . . Ellen suspected she wanted to offer sympathy about Bill Sholto but didn't know how. How like Grandmother! She could handle everything except a show of kindness and sympathy.

"Ellen," Daisy interrupted her thoughts, "aren't you simply ecstatic, marrying the richest man on the Ooscanoto?"

Ellen was well aware that she would be hearing this frequently until she proved herself as Rowdon Faire's loyal and loving wife.

"I'm ecstatic because he's always been my dear

friend and now he'll be my husband. Not many wives can say that."

"Surely not me," Daisy agreed in what Ellen suspected was a true reflection of her relationship with Gavin McCrae. "I never know what my Gavin is thinking from one day to the next. By the way, Ellie, that indiscreet husband of mine wanted me to find out from you how Miss Maggilee is enjoying her honeymoon."

Eliza gasped. "Really, Daisy! I think you've said quite enough."

Daisy quickly went over and hugged Ellen. "You know I want you to be happy, honey. You always were older than your years . . . The colonel will be *perfect* for you, you mustn't mind what I say—"

"I never do," Ellen told her sweetly, returning her embrace.

Not one to take offense Daisy laughed heartily and, leaning nearer, whispered, "In a month you'll never know that wretched captain existed. Maggilee will whittle him down to a poor stick of a man," and, swinging her full plaid-covered hips, Daisy went on her way, leaving behind the customary turmoil in Ellen's heart as she displayed bits and pieces of the bridal outfits.

Miss Eliza chattered on, apportioning the slight changes of style, white flowers and coiffures to the bridesmaids according to heights and weights. Ellen watched idly, finding herself relieved that at least she had not ended like Miss Eliza . . . she had found another man, and need not ever be referred to as "poor Miss Ellen."

. . . If only she could have slept in Bill Sholto's arms just once, known the joy that her treacherous body cried out for. She even thought of Jem Faire, the promise of his kiss . . .

Stop it . . . I don't dare to think of that, not with Jem

in the same house. I must be very, very careful never to encourage him.

Or myself.

* * *

Opinions differed as to whether it was bad luck for both bride and bridegroom to be present at church rehearsal, but because everyone loved the colonel, they deferred to his wishes when he complained that he had seen little enough of his lovely bride during the two months of preparations and was not going to be dislodged from the church that rainy February night.

The rehearsal went with surprising ease. To Ellen it seemed mechanical, but Bertha-Winn Carroll, newly returned from her honeymoon, dropped in as an interested witness and assured Ellen, "You're lucky. Remember the nightmare of my rehearsal? Nothing went right. But . . . oh, Ellie . . . if you can only be as happy as my Wilbur and me, that's all I ask . . ."

Ellen had been touched by the colonel's good-natured complaint about not seeing her, and agreed as usual that he should have things his way. Driven by her own strong feelings of both gratitude and guilt, she tried to respond to him as generously as possible, in every way that made him happy . . . including the bed they would share. She might spend the rest of her life trying to make him content, she thought, and still do no more than repay him for his lifetime of kindness to her. He had capped all his previous goodness by asking her to marry him at exactly the time when she desperately needed to fill the aching emptiness in her. He had asked no questions. He knew her circumstances, yet he offered himself, his whole life. From all she knew of his trusting, open nature, it would never even occur to him that a wife thirty-five years younger might betray him.

Well, I *won't* disappoint you, dear Rowdon, she vowed to herself the night of the last wedding rehearsal. She was moving in a lockstep down the aisle of the darkened church toward the altar where the Reverend Archibald Sheering waited for her, his long, lean face looking even longer than usual under the new gas lights. But not even the gaslights could make Wilbur Carroll's cherubic face look sinister. The colonel had agreed to let Bertha-Winn's new bridegroom stand in his place for tonight . . . since Jem Faire had flatly refused to do so.

According to Miss Eliza, it was all the colonel could do to get his nephew to act as his best man, a concession Jem had made only on condition he need not rehearse for it.

Glancing at her husband-to-be, Ellen saw many features about Rowdon that she somehow had never noticed before. There was a genuine nobility in his easy assurance, a most uncommon goodness in his nature, and strength of character in just about everything he did.

Reaching the dark, cold wood floor below the altar, Ellen smiled up at the colonel, who was nervously rocking back and forth on his heels. Ellen suspected he would have liked a good stiff drink of bourbon. He responded to her smile with one of his big, jaunty grins, his heavy-jowled, ruddy face looking positively handsome to her at that minute.

Afterward the colonel and certain cronies from the War, the Occupation and Reconstruction years, were going off to celebrate his "last night of freedom." Jem, who seldom drank, had declined the gathering and agreed to take Ellen and Miss Eliza home to Gaynor House where they would both be spending the night.

Outside the red brick church Ellen put her arms

around the colonel and kissed him on the lips. He was always a little hesitant when he embraced her, and she thought it likely that despite his continually expressed love for her, down deep he still thought of Ellen Dunmore Gaynor as the lonely little girl who came to him for comfort and friendship. It was a suspicion that made her even more tender, more anxious to show him he needn't ever be afraid of loving her.

"Dearest, good night," she told him, then teased, "don't have such a good time you forget to wake up tomorrow."

He held her slender form, promising, "There'll be that you may count on, sweetheart."

In spite of herself, she winced at the endearment. It carried with it too many memories of Bill Sholto . . .

"Did I hurt you, Ellie? There, you run along with my other girl. Both of you, be good now."

They gave their promise and went off to Gamble's Hay, Grain and Feed Store, where Jem waited with the Fairevale buggy. The light of the lamps in Gamble's office window gave Jem a tense look that made Ellen uneasy. She was sure he misunderstood her reasons for marrying his uncle.

"So you're going to marry a rich father, not a husband," he'd said.

She didn't argue with that but she resented the fortune-hunting barb, and she and Jem had barely spoken ever since.

Miss Eliza seemed pleased at the failure of Jem and Ellen to get along—her attitude reminded Ellen of Maggilee's claim when Jem first came to Fairevale . . . "Ellie, I tell you that ridiculous old maid is in love with her wild young cousin . . ." And ever since Eliza's brief attempt at charming him had failed, her frustration seemed to have turned into a virulent dislike . . .

She was saying to him now, "I don't know why we have to come back here to this awful place, with men spitting everywhere. You *could* have come around in front of the church—"

Ellen hurriedly stopped this tirade. "I think we owe Jem our thanks. He might have gone off with the bachelor party."

Jem looked at her, startling her with what seemed to be genuine concern in his eyes and voice.

"Never mind that. Why don't you both come along to Fairevale tonight? I could get you two there in no time. You'd be with the rest of us"—he hesitated—"I mean, with the colonel tonight."

While Eliza complained that it made no difference that she could see, Ellen felt that his suggestion was at least well meant. The question was—why did he want her and Eliza to avoid Gaynor House? Did he know something they didn't know? . . . "Has anything happened? Is my grandmother ill?"

"Do let's go," Miss Eliza insisted. "I'm freezing and it's starting to rain again."

Jem studied Ellen, apparently decided not to pursue his objections and waved the women to the buggy. Eliza placed herself in his way so he was forced to help her up first, putting her in the middle between himself and Ellen. As Ellen felt herself boosted up in his strong arms, she mentioned Gaynor House again.

"Is there some reason why we shouldn't go home?"

But he simply wasn't talking now. He shrugged, left her, and went around to take the reins.

When they reached Gaynor House it looked white and silent, very much as it always did when the household was asleep. Ellen politely thanked Jem, he received her thanks with the same rather formal politeness and drove on toward Fairevale across the Ooscanoto Bridge.

Trying to puzzle him out, Ellen watched him until he was gone from her sight . . . and was interrupted by, "Do come inside, dear, out of this rain." Eliza was calling to her as Edward Hone hurried to the veranda, said something to Miss Eliza, who gasped and ran outside after Ellen.

"Stop him!"

"What? You mean Jem?"

"We can't stay here. Your butler says not to."

"But of course we can. All my underwear and stockings and even my shoes for the wedding are here. Anyway, it's too late now." Ellen put her arm around Eliza and propelled her stiff, resisting form back into the house.

Before Edward Hone could reach Ellen, Varina had come out into the hall in her nightgown and a ragged purple mantle. Her hair, as always during the night, was in two neat white braids down her back. But unlike her normal, collected self, she was so furious she could barely speak.

"My child—both of you—you mustn't come any further."

Terrified, Eliza said, "Don't spare us, tell us the truth. That wretched butler said we should go on to Fairevale . . . It's yellow fever, isn't it? I know there was an outbreak in New Orleans only last year—"

Which seemed to restore some of Varina's chill self-control. "Good heavens, Eliza! Don't be so nonsensical. It's nothing like that." Then, seeing Ellen's own growing panic, she added, "That woman has come back. To get some things for the night, she says. But i know her. Come to steal the glory from your wedding."

Ellen dropped down on the hard ladder-back chair in the hall. The blood seemed to have drained from her. "I don't believe it. Even she couldn't be that cruel."

"Oh, but she *could.*" Eliza's voice was venomous. "And she will. She knows they'll all be looking at her tomorrow instead of you, it was the same in the old days when we went to church . . . deliberately arriving during first prayers so everyone would look at her, always some excuse about business at the shop but they never looked at anyone else after she got there . . ."

Nothing did Varina so much good as needing to cope with weakness in others. "Do hush, Eliza," she said impatiently. "You babble as if you were deprived of your senses."

Eliza subsided.

By this time Ellen had pulled herself together. "I'll go and have a few words with her."

"I tried," Varina said, "but, as you might imagine, she ignored me."

"Is he here?"

"He wouldn't dare. He brought her and he's coming for her later tonight. They intend to sleep at the old Winchester Coffee House in Gaynorville tonight."

With a calm she was far from feeling Ellen reminded her, "She won't bite, you know."

"No. She will cry."

While Eliza lamented, in lower key, the return of "that evil woman," Ellen went upstairs to face Maggilee, to test her own well-concealed, at least up to this moment, weakness . . .

Maggilee had a very small, helter-skelter pile of night clothes on the bed, including a long-sleeved but diaphanous nightgown of flesh-colored crepe de chine that somehow made Ellen's honeymoon gowns look maidenly.

More important than this little pile was the contents of her travel cases, which she was busy hanging in the wardrobe. Evidently she was moving back into Gaynor House after the wedding. At the warning creak of the door, Maggilee turned around. To Ellen she had never looked more beautiful. Her condition might not be apparent, thanks to the low, pointed basque of her two-piece corded green silk walking dress, but either pregnancy or a happy new married life gave her face a near-translucent pink glow.

Ellen thought: I might have been that happy.

She stood in the doorway, heard her mother call out with all her old charm, "Ellie, honey, please forgive me for not telling you we were on our way, but when we heard you were to be married in church we couldn't resist coming back to see your happiness." She hurried on, getting no response from her daughter, "It's no surprise to me, really. Rowdon has been in love with you for ages."

Ellen closed the door. She didn't want those eager listeners on the floor below to hear this. It was nearly inconceivable that her own mother could be so insensitive . . . Not only did she come home flaunting as a prize the man she knew her daughter loved, but she implied that like a disappointed child Ellen had easily transferred her love to a more expensive toy. And just as Miss Eliza predicted, Maggilee would walk into the church in all her New York finery to eclipse now as a bride the daughter she had eclipsed throughout her life.

"Are you planning to stay here afterward?" Ellen asked, avoiding mention of tomorrow's wedding.

Her mother seemed defiant, which was not a characteristic quality. "Long ago your grandmother and I made a pact, which I've never dishonored. She may regard Gaynor House as hers until she dies. But it was left to Beau as the male of the family, by her husband's will."

"I know all that."

"When Beau died it became mine. I paid the taxes on it. And I paid the price in many other ways, as all of us after the War when we were no longer Virginia Commonwealth but a federal district. Now Bill wants to invest in the land, make it pay again." She became anxious, aware of Ellen's paleness, her expression freezing into icy rage. "It's only natural . . ."

All of it might be expected . . . Bill Sholto had wanted Gaynor House, he'd married to get it . . . I've got to remember that, Ellen told herself . . . whenever I'm jealous of her I must consider that if I had been the legal owner I would have been in his bed tonight. God *knows* how far the gallant captain would have gone . . . if Varina had still owned Gaynor House he might have offered for her!

Which struck her so funny she burst out laughing, which shocked Maggilee more than a slap.

"Ellie, please don't."

How she hated that damned nickname . . . she'd told her mother a thousand times . . .

"Don't worry, Maggi—" Her mother started at this disrespectful use of her first name. Ellen looked at her . . . "It was just something funny I remembered about your husband. Oh, don't worry, you'll no doubt be able to handle it . . ."

That certainly disturbed her . . . good. Give her something to think about when she came sweeping into the church in her glorious new wardrobe tomorrow to steal the show. Ellen turned to leave but couldn't resist asking one question. Worse, she couldn't freeze the emotion out of her voice.

"Do you intend to be at the church tomorrow?"

"Well, honey, you *are* my daughter. I'd never forgive

myself if I didn't come . . . It's why we hurried home as soon as we heard. We thought . . . since you're marrying Rowdon . . . well . . . that you'd feel less bitter toward us. We do want to be friends with you. Honey, can't we go and see you on the happiest day of your life? And you will be happy. You'll see. He's such a good man . . ."

And Ellen thought, "a good man" . . . but you weren't so interested in marrying a good man, were you, Maggilee? You were interested in bedding with a young, virile man . . . Well, Maggilee, I'm your daughter. In some ways, like it or not, we're not so different in our wants . . .

"Then you are coming?" she said aloud.

"Unless you forbid us. Ellie, we do want to be there and wish you well. Perhaps it will bring us together again, like in the old days . . ."

We were never together . . . didn't you know that?

"Who has a better right?" Ellen found herself laughing again, afraid she'd be unable to stop, hating this sign of hysteria. She just managed to burst out, "Why, honey, if it weren't for you I wouldn't even be marrying Rowdon Faire, so isn't it perfectly *ridiculous* to keep you away? Of *course* I want you there . . ."

Her voice trailed her as she quickly turned away and went down the stairs to face Varina and Miss Eliza . . .

CHAPTER 2

***

MAGGILEE SAT up in bed and stared at her husband, who was actually primping—no other word for it—before the half-unsilvered mirror in the small room of the Winchester Coffee House. He smoothed his hair again and then his mustache, both sides. He raised his chin—never his strongest point—and got a good luck at his jaw, which he tightened dramatically.

"Handsomest man south of Baltimore," Maggilee teased him.

"And who'd you see in New York or Washington that

you thought was prettier, you red-haired little—" He threw a discarded string tie at her, which she deftly caught and drew under her bare bosom, raising her small, round breasts that shone so white in the rainy morning light.

"My dog collar, O Mighty Master! You see how well trained I am?"

It took three strides for him to reach the bed. He tucked his fingers into the string tie. He pulled it to him against her own fingers, which were locked into the string at both sides of her breasts, swelling them until the areoles stood out against the tempting fullness. He was smiling, but his smile was not so pleasant.

"Your master? Maggie, how many others did you try this trick with? How many others took what you offered? Knew you'd sleep with the next man you fancied?"

She twisted her body but that only hurt her. The game grew uncomfortable. She fumbled with his fingers, but he drew her to him as he knelt on the lumpy bed with its ancient goose-feather mattress, and caressed the bare breasts.

"Don't play with me, sweetheart. I'm not like the others. I don't care a damn about your past—"

"Don't you?" Her face was close to his, her tongue moving over her lips.

He kissed her, pressing hard, taking the soft mouth she offered him . . . "No . . . I don't care, no more than you do about my past," and then, grinning, he got up from one knee and brushed himself off. "Better get dressed, mother-of-the-bride. It's almost noon."

"Never *mind* . . . What did you mean about your past?" She raised the wide neck of her gown, covering her breasts and at the same time remembering her daughter's infuriating taunt. Was it possible her reserved, proper Ellen actually had carried on an affair with him at the same time he was begetting himself an heir with her . . . ?

He twisted her nose between his fingers. "Never you mind, sweetheart. It's you I married, and it's you I love. So stop your chatter."

She wanted to press it, but was experienced enough to know it was pointless. For now, anyway . . . After all, she had to get ready for a wedding.

By the time she was washed and dressed, she saw Bill looking out the window at the muddy road below.

"Too bad it has to be raining," he said, more or less to himself.

Maggilee went quickly to the window, running her fingers along his coat sleeve and inside, to linger on his wrist. She felt uneasy, unsure of herself . . . of him? . . . ever since she discovered her pregnancy.

His detached comment hardly helped. "Quite a bit of traffic going into Gaynorville, I suppose for Ellen's wedding."

She moved his arm and stuck her head under it to look out the window. "I hope she's happy," she said, almost to herself. "My God, I truly do . . ."

He looked at her. "I thought you said she always cared so much for the fellow."

Maggilee shrugged. "I certainly believed so. After all, it took only a month for her to accept him. And here they are, a mere two months later, all set to marry. Still, respectable young women take a good deal longer to make such decisions—"

"You didn't."

"Ah, but who says I'm respectable?"

He found her mouth and kissed her again, and she held tight to him, shutting out her fears. For the moment.

"Anyway," Bill reopened the subject while Maggilee was dressing, "if she still resented us, I doubt she'd have invited us to the wedding." His hands were moving slowly over her warm shoulders.

Maggilee wished Ellen *had* invited them. She had not forbidden them, but that was not the same thing. And certainly she had aroused her anger again by her talk about owning Gaynor House. The subject need never have come up at all. After all, Ellen would be living across the river as the grand lady of Fairevale . . .

"You aren't going to wear that, are you?" Bill said. Maggilee was getting into a dark foulard dress she had owned for the past five years. It had one important asset . . . the folds across the upper half of the skirt concealed her condition, although she carried this child as she had carried Ellen, with very little sign of its presence. It didn't matter too much, in any case; she had already been "cut" by several women yesterday evening in Gaynorville. Only Jem Faire, whom she met at Gamble's, had been his usual pleasant self . . . She wondered what he thought about his uncle's belated second marriage. She had always suspected Jem of an interest in Ellen, odd as it might seem. The cool, aloof Ellen didn't appear to be the sort of woman who would appeal to a young man with what she suspected were strong passions just beneath that stoic surface. She was seldom mistaken about the existence of such male passions.

"Don't you have anything more natty you can wear?" Bill was saying. "I'd like to see you looking more like—"

"Molly-O?"

"Matter of fact, sweetheart, Molly-O was always very well dressed, although you—"

"I'm sure she was," Maggilee cut in.

He took hold of her shoulders, kissing her. "Look

here, beauty, there's no one to beat you . . . It's just that I don't want that gaggle of old hens turning up their noses at my wife, thinking I can't support her." He went over to the window again and Maggilee felt a stab of fear. Was he possibly thinking that a fine church wedding alongside a tall, elegant—and *young*—bride might have been his if he hadn't been forced to marry a thirty-eight-year-old mother and mother-to-be instead?

Whatever his thoughts she was relieved to hear that he'd discovered a friend on the old highway below the window.

"Now, that's what I call handsome . . . Jono's come to escort us to the church. Those old biddies will have to accept us with him along."

Maggilee ran to the window to see Jonathan stalk across the muddy street in his best fifteen-year-old frock-coat and ancient stove-pipe hat, his austere face bearing an even more than usual resemblance to Abe Lincoln *and* President Davis of the Confederacy.

"Dear Jonathan," Maggilee said quietly. "He always seems to be there when I need him most."

Bill looked at her curiously. "You often have such crises that require him?"

"Not since"—she caught herself—"not for a long time . . ." The thought of Cousin Jonathan took her back momentarily to the old and terrible days, his memory of which she was sure was one of the reasons that had driven Jonathan to his hermit life. In spite of their devotion to each other, they both wanted, needed, to banish the memory that seemingly locked them together.

Bill went out in the dingy hall to meet Jonathan, and when the two men came in Maggilee was relieved to see that their friendship appeared unchanged. Jonathan kissed his cousin on the cheek, scarcely responding to her own impetuous embrace. His lips were dry and rough. He looked her over.

"Do I look happy?" she challenged him with a sparkle in her wide eyes.

"I reckon. Thing is, does Ellen look happy?"

They were both startled at his frankness, and Maggilee was hardly pleased by Bill's, "Well, is she? What do you think? The fellow's a decent sort, they say, but damn it, he's old enough to be her father—"

"Grandfather." Jonathan took off his hat, rubbed the rain spots with his sleeve and said mildly, his eyes on the hat, "I suspect she's had enough of these young bucks. Not too steady, they do say. You all set to go?"

Maggilee nodded, anxious to end this, and went to get the old brown mantle and bonnet she used in bad weather.

"I really had every intention of getting to the church early," she told Jonathan.

"Glad of that. She goes down the aisle on my arm. You sitting up front with the bride's family?"

Maggilee forced a smile. "No, I'll spare Ellen that. Can't you just see me sitting beside Varina? She'd stab me with a hatpin or one of her icicle looks. No. In the back of the church. Or in the balcony with the blacks. Dear old Biddie will welcome me anyway. She and Florine and their family will be there."

Jonathan gave her dress an approving remark. "You had the good sense not to deck out in your frills and feathers. That'll be appreciated."

And for the first time Bill understood some of the reasons for the rather drab outfit. He took her hand, whispered, "I'm sorry, sweetheart. I didn't understand."

And again she forced a smile.

* * *

"I never knew the church to be so cold," Ellen complained. For what seemed hours she had been forced to stand completely still in her petticoat in the middle of the Reverend Sheering's study while the tiny modiste from Baltimore, Madame Vandeleur, crawled around the floor on her knees, adjusting the hem. All Ellen could see of the woman was a head of suspiciously black hair, but when she looked around at the other advisors, each offering a different opinion as to the proper length, she wished devoutly that she had never heard of a wedding proposal. As the minutes ticked off on the minister's old grandfather clock, she had an impulse to run and hide . . . from all the fuss? Well, yes . . . but also perhaps from herself, and her unease at what she was about to do . . .

Varina, whose rheumatism gave her considerable pain, sat in the minister's stiff desk chair watching the proceedings. Her discomfort did not prevent her from looking resplendant in silver-gray silk. "The girl is shivering. Haven't any of you the sense to put something around her shoulders?"

Miss Eliza, Mrs. Wychfield, Daisy and Bertha-Winn rushed about searching for something besides the pool of white bridal veil or the satin gown and its heavy, six-foot train beaded with seed pearls which lay spread over three of the chairs customarily used in the Sunday School.

. . . I wish I were sitting quietly over at Gaynor Ferry, with nobody but Cousin Jonathan, Ellen thought . . . feeling panicky . . . I wish I were *any*where else . . .

"Finis!" Madame announced in her birdlike squawk, and stood up. "Now the gown itself."

Bertha-Winn immediately dropped her end of the train and the bottom of the gown and was ordered off with barely suppressed anger by her mother. Then Mrs. Wychfield, with the help of Daisy and Eliza, carefully got Ellen into the gown. The style had been taken from medieval drawings. Its high waistline, long, flowing skirt and tight, wrist-length undersleeves with wide, turned-back oversleeves, again trimmed with seed-pearls, had been chosen to flatter Ellen's best features.

Dora Johnson, who had worked on its final touches between hours in Gaynor's Salon, confided to Varina, "I never did see such a sight, ma'm. No. Not even Miss Maggilee when she married Mr. Beau—"

"I should say not. You're quite right."

"Looks like a queen in one of them history books, so she does."

The others were too busy for compliments as they arranged Ellen's shining blonde hair in its high-piled new coiffeur, then settled the medieval headdress on top of it like a small cornucopia from which the veil descended, to flow out behind her over the long train. Ellen was afraid to breathe, but Irene Wychfield assured her, "It's fastened solidly. You may move your head as you choose."

The modiste suggested that mademoiselle keep the headdress on while the other young ladies made their own small final adjustments . . . "It will help give mademoiselle that so necessary confidence."

She was right. Especially about mademoiselle's need . . . The other bridesmaids came in, were fitted, combed, brushed and decked with flower holders full of tiny hothouse lilies of the valley to match the narrow wreaths crowning their hair.

By this time the procession was made up of four bridesmaids, then Miss Eliza in gold peau de soie, her *first* non-mourning dress in twenty-five years. "I do this only for my beloved Beau's daughter," she confided to Varina, who dismissed her "sacrilege" with the brusque assurance, "I've no doubt he understands."

As a new matron, Daisy was not included in the procession of Ellen's four bridesmaids. Three of these were daughters of Tudor County households, who found her boring and spinsterish before they were invited to take part in her marriage ceremony. The fourth bridesmaid was Bertha-Winn. But, having seen the elaborate preparations for her wedding, thanks to the expense borne by Colonel Faire (so gossip said), the girls now found the future chatelaine of Fairevale well worth cultivating.

With everything ready, the bride indeed looking like a princess in a medieval tapestry, her flustered maid of honor, the four bridesmaids in yellow watered silk, Varina went out into the vestry with the Wychfields and the modiste. Leaning heavily on the arm of her nephew Jonathan, Varina was escorted to her seat in the front pew nearest the altar. Then Jonathan went back down the nave of the crowded church, glanced only briefly at the red-haired woman and her handsome husband sitting three quarters of the way back, and went to the minister's study.

Miss Eliza declared, "Oh, dear, I do wish I were out there playing the processional, I'd feel much more at home," as in the distance Ellen heard the first unnerving notes of the Wedding March and Jonathan opened the door. The four bridesmaids, stifling nervous giggles, passed him on their way to the nave of the church. Miss Eliza looked back in panic. "Ellen, I'm so scared."

"You look splendid," Ellen assured her truthfully as Eliza passed her, her nervous walk transformed to a dignified lock-step. This slow pace revealed Miss Eliza as no one had seen her since her girlhood, her gray hair a softened coronet for her usually tired features, her sagging, middle-aged body now straight and firm in the full-skirted silk gown with a graceful frill at the wrists and high neck.

Jonathan stuck out his sharp elbow. "Ellen, you ready?"

Inside her head: "What are you doing here? What happened to your dreams... Run away before it's too late..." She asked aloud, "Are *they* here?"

"Sitting near the back. On the bride's side."

"How appropriate... and do we have a good turnout?"

"Place is full. Not a pew with a vacant space."

She raised her head. "Well, this deserves a good audience."

He started out the door with her but couldn't help saying, "You don't much sound yourself. Are you well?"

"Perfectly." She shook his arm impatiently. "Come, Cousin, you're out of step." They had moved forward to enter the aisle with the altar at its far end when she whispered, "Nudge me as we pass them."

Seeing the looks on the faces turning to stare at her as she entered the aisle, she felt nearly drunk with a delicious pleasure altogether rare for her... all that admiration... It would doubtless never happen again. She allowed herself to smile as a murmur swept through the crowded church, audible even above the thump of the church organ... "Beautiful... Is it really Ellen...?"

The hennin with its streaming veil no longer weighed down her head. The train slithered along of its own will. She had never felt more secure, more self-confident, and she owed it all to Colonel Faire, to his generosity, his desire for her...

"Well, I shall at least try to make it up to you, dear friend," she promised him silently, and looked straight ahead to see the stocky figure of the bridegroom standing there at one side of the altar in his formal black. His face was beaming but his hands worked nervously at his sides. Bless him! He was afraid, too. She had never felt so warmly toward him. She smiled again, a lovely brightening of the austere picture she presented in her medieval gown and headdress. She even forgot to give Sholto that triumphant, dazzling look she had mentally rehearsed all night. At this moment, neither he nor her mother mattered. Only Rowdon Faire did. He had, after all, made this moment possible.

As she and Jonathan followed Miss Eliza and the procession to the altar she noticed Jem Faire for the first time. He wore a tight black jacket such as the Spanish and Mexicans wore. It also fitted him very well, showing off his lean, hard figure. No weakness about it. His clean-shaven face with its strong profile seemed far more manly, somehow, than the weak-chinned men of the congregation, most of whom covered up with mustaches or beards. How proud the colonel must be of this nephew he had unofficially adopted. Ellen noticed the quick glance Miss Eliza gave him as she approached the altar and turn away with the four bridesmaids.

Now Ellen stood beside Rowdon Faire. She forgot Jem's dark good looks, forgot Bill Sholto, even forgot her mother. The colonel looked at her eyes with an uneasy excitement beyond the familiar, warm affection. Halfway through the responses his voice built to its usual confident bellow, and she pressed close to him, raising her own voice, almost defiantly, to answer, "I do."

Jem Faire passed over the ring, a plain gold circlet quite unlike her engagement ring. For the ceremony she wore the enormous single diamond on her right hand. She would have preferred any one of a thousand simpler rings but she hadn't been consulted. With the best intentions in the world the colonel had chosen to surprise her with this opulent symbol.

The colonel's hand shook while he pressed the gold circlet on her finger and he began to sweat as he failed to get it beyond her knuckle. Beside him, so unobtrusively no one but the Reverend Sheering and Ellen knew it, it was his best man who finally eased the ring over her knuckles. She didn't look down, kept her gaze tightly focused on the colonel.

The slight pause appeared to be natural. When the minister pronounced them man and wife the bridegroom moved his unsteady hands to raise Ellen's veil.

She laughed softly. "The veil is in the back." She took his hands between hers. Over their hands, each pair borrowing warmth from the other, they kissed. A full, exuberant kiss. They turned together, hand-in-hand, to the laughter, chatter, and congratulations from the bridal party. Ellen was vaguely aware of several embraces, of Varina with tears in her eyes—Varina actually crying!—and of Major Wychfield, Jonathan (a quick and reserved kiss), Harleigh Duckworth the banker, and then Bill Sholto.

He looked big, almost hulking, with that brazen admiration she remembered so painfully. Marriage and prospective fatherhood seemed to agree with him.

"Just wanted to wish you well, Mrs. Faire," he said, and would have kissed her cheek except she took a quick step backward, suddenly unwilling to risk contact with him.

As if he understood, Rowdon told Jem Faire, "Your turn, boy. This is the last time I'll be giving away a chance to kiss my darling wife."

The best man swung her around out of Sholto's reach, her skirt and train tangling themselves about her feet. In her confusion she saw only the narrow dark eyes with their bright, intense circle of light, and then Jem's mouth was full on hers. She had known he would be hard, not soft, and before he released her into the bridegroom's arms, it had become a sensuous experience that upset her more than she'd thought possible . . . bringing back memories, even fantasies, that she'd fought so hard against, reminding her again of needs she had denied herself but that would not be denied.

Laughter around her. Everyone pressing knowing advice on the bridegroom, who had the last laugh when Ellen said, "Can we go now, dearest?"

"Ellie, dear, any little thing your heart desires." With his arm around her the colonel kicked aside her train and cleared a path down the aisle through a swarm of well-wishers which did not include Jem Faire. She didn't see him again as she swept the train over her free hand and with a dazzling smile fixed on her face walked with her new husband toward the open church doors.

There Maggilee stood, alone. Her bonnet had fallen back onto her neck, held by its frayed ribbons. The rainy afternoon light filtered through her red hair. She held out her hand diffidently.

"Hello, honey." When Ellen said nothing, she went on, "I never saw anyone so beautiful as you were today. I know you'll be happy. And you, Colonel. You are a lucky man."

Uneasy, the colonel took Maggilee's hand, thanking her with a gruff attempt to hide his own tangle of feelings. His action had given Ellen time to recover from that first near-disastrous weakness on seeing her mother alone, looking small, with no defenses . . . For a moment there she'd wanted to put her arms around Maggilee, lend her strength, show the love she herself had so long been starved for . . . "Mama, it's good to—"

Interrupted by Bill Sholto, who'd elbowed his way to stand beside Maggilee.

"May I join my wife in wishing you a happy future? As happy as our own."

Ellen's back stiffened. The bright, fixed smile returned to her drawn features.

"Thank you. So thoughtful. And thank you, Maggilee. It was nice that you could come . . . Darling, shall we go? Heavens, we'll never be on our way at this rate."

And they ran down the three church steps, followed by the shouts of their well-wishers.

CHAPTER 3

***

MAGGILEE WAS pushed aside by the crowd rushing to watch the bridal couple ride away. A man stepped on her foot and when she cried out, he turned to apologize. It was Jem Faire. Maggilee waved away his apology.

"Of course. What a crowd! Your uncle is certainly popular."

"And your daughter." His voice was pleasant, but she sensed that he was deliberately reminding her. It didn't matter.

"You're quite right." She turned her sweet smile on him, all innocence. "It was a beautiful ceremony. I know they will be happy."

"Do you?"

"Yes. Really. You may find it difficult to believe but in a way they've always loved each other. They're well suited."

She felt suddenly very tired. She knew her color was bad. She had scarcely recognized her face in the glass window of the church as she passed on the outer aisle. Apparently, Jem thought so too as he said quietly, "I hope you are right," and then, "Are you well, Miss Maggilee?"

"Mrs. Sholto," Bill corrected him, arriving suddenly on the scene and taking Maggilee's arm.

Jem's glance at her husband was full of a contempt he didn't bother to hide. "Sorry. Mrs. Sholto." He nodded. "Good afternoon."

Young Persis Warrender, a little brunette with a seductively innocent face Maggilee had never trusted, came rushing along with a dark mantle covering most of her bridesmaid's gown and stopped Jem. "Dear, *dear* Jem, will you-all be a sweet angel and ride me home? Papa said he had business in town and I'm such a little silly, I told him I'd get home safe and sound without him, but I forgot about this awful dress, so many yards of satin," which she displayed to him by swinging around.

"Come along," Jem agreed cheerfully and took her arm. "What's so awful about your dress? You look very pretty in it."

"Oh, Jem, really?"

They went out onto the muddy street, where it was necessary for Jem to pick her up and carry her to the Fairevale buggy.

"My Lord!" Maggilee sighed. "I do believe he actually likes that little fool."

Sholto looked after them. "Pretty, though. Except for the black hair, she kind of puts me in mind of how you must have looked when you were young."

An unfortunate, if doubtless accidental choice of words at the moment, but Maggilee felt the sting in them.

"What did young Faire want?" Bill was asking her.

Maggilee's voice sounded lifeless, flat to her own ears. "He doesn't seem to think Ellen and the colonel will be happy—"

"And you . . . ?"

She didn't answer as they started out of the church and she clung to him like, she thought, a loyal squaw, and remembered her daughter's proud stance, the gracious way she accepted the arm of her . . . mature husband.

Strange, Maggilee thought. Ellen, her plain daughter, might well be the stronger of the two. Ellen might break, but she would never bend as she had done. Pride. That's what the Dunmores and the Gaynors had. Much good it might do them!

* * *

After a brief honeymoon in White Sulphur Springs Colonel and Mrs. Faire took the steam cars to Kentucky for a four-month stay, as was customary in the marriage of such socially prominent names. It was the proud colonel's notion to show off his young, aristocratic bride among various relatives who had moved out to Kentucky and done well in the tobacco trade after the war-time devastation of Virginia.

They were in a Pullman compartment with the rural beauty of the Virginia countryside rushing by. Woods and rivers, stark and cold against the late afternoon sky, were separated by over-cultivated fields now lying fallow.

The South needs fresh blood, Ellen thought, and wondered if she and her husband might ever have children. Bill Sholto's child would bring fresh blood to Virginia. She had thought a lot about having Bill Sholto's children when she thought, dreamed of marrying him . . .

The colonel was working on the interminable buttons sewn down the back of her gown. As the Pullman car swayed around curves, rattling and lurching over the rainy tracks, the colonel's hands fumbled, dropped from her satin-clad body with a button torn off in his hand.

"Christ-damn!"

Ellen laughed. This sounded more like the raucous, drinking colonel she had known all her life. Nervous as she was over the consummation of this odd marriage, she thought they might both behave with less inhibition if he felt free to sip his usual Kentucky bourbon. She took the button out of his sweating palm and, still amused—her laughter just a trifle forced this time—she said, "Darling, you need a sip of something. You go get the porter and we'll both take a sip. Drink to all the years ahead."

Standing there in his black suit that was old-fashioned and too tight through the shoulders, he immediately relaxed at her suggestion. In fact his face bloomed.

"Just a nip to—to get us going?"

"You do have a glass every night at your bedside, don't you? Well, tonight we'll both drink. From the same glass."

"Sweetheart, I'll tell you the truth . . . you're the best wife a man ever had." He opened his arms and she went into them, her dress off one shoulder but not quite unbuttoned yet as far as the hips. He held her to him until she said jokingly, "Colonel, that was a bear hug."

"Sorry, honey, don't know my own strength. Now, I'll

just get out that good Kentucky corn—"

"What? You villain! You had it all the time."

He winked, snapped open his heavy leather valise and felt for one of the bottles wrapped in his nightshirt. He glanced in Ellen's direction but she pretended not to see the nightshirt and went on carefully unbuttoning and slipping off her gown until it lay in a pile of folds around her feet.

The colonel found a silver cup, poured two fingers of bourbon into it, considered his bride's lovely bare shoulders, and poured back half of it. He cleared his throat, held out the cup to Ellen.

"A wee dram, as old Angus Huddleston says."

Well, if he felt more sure of himself with a drink, maybe it would work for her. "Here's to Angus Huddleston," she called more loudly than she'd intended, and sipped the whiskey, then whispered, "and here's to my dear friend, my husband." She sipped from the cup again. The stuff burned, which was all to the good. She needed something to warm her spirits.

Much cheered by his wife's comradely acceptance of the whiskey, the colonel took long swallows from the bottle itself, one to the old Scot and the other to "the prettiest bride that ever was seen, barring none, sweetheart."

The word "sweetheart" still brought back hurting memories, which, of course, the colonel could not possibly know. She took a sip again.

He took another swig at the bottle before she set the small cup down and came to him, falling into his arms as she swayed with the lurch of the train. He still had the bottle but when she regained her equilibrium she corked it and set it back in the valise.

She began to ease his coat off. Befuddled by the train's movements, the whiskey, his own secret fears about making love to this maiden he'd for so long thought of as a daughter, he hesitated, then let her remove his coat and the stiff collar that gave him a double chin. By the time she started to unbutton his vest, the scent of her perfume, the closeness of her half-clad body and her light-fingered touch had done their work.

He backed away. "No, now, this'll be my job. You just stand there and keep looking like you do now. Fact is, you look good enough to eat, so you do, but turn away . . . so I can get m'self ready . . ."

She flushed, and was aware of a pleasant, tingling glow through her body. She told herself she would learn to desire his love as much as she might a younger man's . . . and in spite of herself felt for a moment as she had when Jem Faire kissed her with that hard force at the altar . . .

The Pullman berth was not yet made up for the night, but she tried to feel a sense of anticipation. She expected him to emerge naked. Instead, he now stood there in the nightshirt that disguised his strong, bullish trunk and accentuated his short legs. She did her best to present exactly the picture that would best arouse his self-confidence. She looked pink, fragile and a bit scared. Damned desirable. There was nothing avuncular or fatherly about the feelings she aroused in him now. He started toward her. She instinctively backed against the Pullman couch, lost her balance and fell over onto the narrow couch, where he pinned her down with her arms over her head and one of his knees across her ankles. He raised her body, pushed a pillow under her hips and before her muscles could stiffen with tension he had entered her, forcing himself, and forcing her, to receive him without preliminaries. She struggled, but it was only a reflex action

. . . She saw from his sweating features and abrupt withdrawal that he blamed himself. He freed her and stroked her hands over and over.

"Honey, I'm sorry. I'm so sorry. Forgive me."

She forced a smile. "Don't be silly. It will be better"—she corrected herself—"easier next time."

"Next time. Oh, sweetheart, I'm sure the luckiest man in the world."

She drew his head down to her breast, caressed his rumpled white hair. "You deserve to be happy, Rowdon. And I solemnly promise to try to make sure that you are . . ."

Over his bowed head she saw a long strip of birch, black oak and pine woods, and then the distant horizon. Somewhere on that western horizon was a jagged blue opening in the gray sky.

She hoped it might be an omen of something better than what she had just endured.

CHAPTER 4

***

*E*VERY MORNING, rain or shine, and occasionally snow, Bill Sholto rode the acres he had come to think of as the property of his prospective child. Boy or girl, the young Sholto would one day inherit the Gaynor estate and he meant to have it a paying proposition by the time his child was old enough to appreciate the value of this material inheritance. Everything else could fade, be lost, give back nothing in return, as he had found. But if you gave just a little to the ground, in his case money and care, it could give back life.

Old Jono proved that, and following his example, Bill had begun the same thing. Employing a poor white and an itinerant black field worker to plow, fertilize and rotate crops, the dormant Gaynor fields were beginning to waken with new life.

Growing things began to fascinate Sholto. He thought of tobacco and peanuts, both successful in this area, even rice in the low wetlands, and vegetables and fruits, of course. There were fertilizers that could help the long-starved fields.

Through less than four months of work and the investment of his savings, Sholto had proved it. Most important, the tenant farmers would have to produce results— either money, which they had owed the Gaynor women for years, or a raise in the yield of their crops, a share of which they likewise owed but seldom paid to the original land-owner, the Gaynor Estate. He would have to go to court to get some of that bottomland back from the Corrigans, but he was used to fights.

"My daughter or son is going to inherit everything they're entitled to . . . They're *not* going to grow up with a mother gone, working day and night in that blasted shop." . . . The thought of Maggilee working incessantly all those years to support Varina and Ellen strengthened the feeling he'd acquired during his frontier years, when and where females were scarce and prized accordingly . . .

Now, on a soft, flower-scented May day he rode his stallion Oglala down across the Corrigan land, which bordered the north-south fork of Dunmore Creek, and speculated that the Corrigans had cheated the Gaynor women out of at least several thousand dollars during the last few years. Some of their lands were purchased dirt-cheap at the time they arrived in 1866 as carpetbaggers from the

North. But at least a third of the now-cultivated bottomland still belonged to the Gaynors, and was "rented" so long ago with a continuous report of "no profits" that the lie came to be accepted as fact by the Gaynors. Probably because none of the women knew enough about such matters to question them.

With a building sense of satisfaction at his own acumen Bill rode on into town past the Confederate Cemetery, left Oglala in the care of Gamble's best horseboy, and crossed through Church Street to the back of Maggilee's Salon.

She met him on the run. Her condition was now apparent in spite of the full front folds of her dress. The youthful curve of her cheeks had gone and her flesh looked blue-white and a bit puffy. But as usual she was so busy she couldn't spare the time to do more than greet him with a kiss, and the breathless excuse, "Dreadful hurry, darlin'. Two old biddies down from Richmond. Really! Recommended by Harleigh Duckworth, of course. He wants his loan paid off and he seems to be furnishing customers to pay it. Got to rush!"

"Yes, but sweetheart, that's what I want to talk about with—" She was already off into the dressing room, leaving him talking to himself. A common enough practice these days. Old Biddie came hobbling by to look him over with her steel spectacles pushed far down her nose.

"Oh, it's you. Reckoned as how it might be a customer. She's sure doin' right well if they'd only pay what they owe."

Sholto laughed, mostly at himself. "I'd see more of her if I was a customer. Biddie, isn't there anything we can do to keep her off her feet? It's dangerous for her, with the baby due in a few weeks."

Biddie shook her head, cautioning him, "None of

that, Mister Bill. It's not due for two months and more. It's just accidentally going to be beforehand. You take my meanin'?"

"I take it, Biddie. I just forgot for a minute."

"Well, don't forget. It's Miss Maggilee's good name that's being saved. So keep the thought right handy. The baby's due in July. Late July. It just so happens, what with one thing and another, it'll be arriving a mite early. By two months. My Florine's boy, Nahum, is over to Gamble's getting supplies for Mr. Jonathan. If you see him you tell him to be a good boy."

Young Nahum, competent, self-sufficient and rapidly becoming Jonathan's heir to Gaynor Ferry, had loaded grain on a wagon and was getting ready to leave when Bill arrived. The lean young black man looked older than his years. Not surprisingly. He had supported his mother and sisters for three years and was barely fifteen now. He and Jonathan suited each other well. When Bill had been staying at the Ferry it was Bill who did all the talking. Jonathan seemed genuinely interested in his wild-west tales but it was obvious to Sholto that Jonathan and Nahum could share the same house in companionship without ever having a word to say to each other. Nahum went out with the daughter of black parents working the Finch properties, but otherwise was nearly as solitary as Jonathan.

As Nahum passed the checker players, with a nod for Sholto, Bill asked the question that was frequently on his mind: "How are the newlyweds? Has Jono heard from them this month?"

Nahum didn't stop but tossed the answer behind him. "Miss Eliza says they've been havin' one good time. Miss Ellen's been the belle of Kentucky, so they say." And just as he was leaving, Nahum added, "Mr. Jono is going over to Gaynor House tonight to see the—the daguerreotype picture the colonel sent Miss Varina. Real fancy. Of the colonel and Miss Ellen in all their fine feathers."

"Well, I'll be damned," Gamble announced. "First time old Jono's gone to Gaynor House in I don't know how many years. He does care for his family, and no mistake."

Bill had his mind on more important things than Jonathan's peculiarities. Someone must have delivered the picture while Bill was out riding the Gaynor acres. He very much wanted to see it . . . He would never be sorry he had married Maggilee . . . the pleasure of her fascinating body, her endless erotic ways, his child-to-be, his very own daughter, or son, who would bear his name . . . But there was no getting around it. When he had pictured himself married and settled down beside a lovely Southern girl who would be the First Lady of the County, it had been a girl like Ellen he'd thought of . . .

"Reckon I'll have to beat you another time," he promised Gamble. "Got to be on my way or Miss Varina will skin me alive. She's a stickler for the exact dinner hour."

The ride home was not all pleasant even though the fields were gorgeously colored with wildflowers spread over the meadows and the first plantings in full flush. But his pleasure at the sight was somewhat dimmed by the reflection that he still hadn't made clear to Maggilee she was going to have to give up that damned dress shop.

As he reached the Gaynor carriage road, he saw Jonathan walking ahead of him and was about to speed up Oglala when the actions of the walking man interested him. Jonathan's stride slowed to a saunter as he came in sight of the whitewashed bricks of Gaynor House. He stopped, stared up at the house and then went around to the east front, formal entrance, although the river door was much closer. Curious.

Bill dismounted, led Oglala to his stall, where dinner and a good rubdown waited for him. The stallion was old now and probably not up to anything like an actual campaign, but Bill's dreams also included having Oglala live long enough to seat Shelley Sholto. Male or female, either way, Maggilee had agreed that the child was going to be called Shelley after the trapper who had raised Bill. And Shelley was going to love Oglala as much as Bill did.

With Oglala seen to, Bill quietly entered the east front of the house. He had no compunctions about eavesdropping to find out if possible why Jonathan never visited Gaynor House.

Jonathan went immediately to the river parlor, where he waited alone for a few minutes.

In the reception hall Bill started nervously as Edward Hone tapped his shoulder. In his low voice he explained like a fellow conspirator, "He's waiting to talk with Miss Varina. She's been told of his arrival."

"Hone, tell me . . ." Bill moved into the still deserted dining room where the table had been laid with the Wedgwood china and Waterford crystal. The pieces didn't match, but the setting bespoke a lifestyle new to Bill Sholto.

The Gaynor women always lived high, even when they had nothing, Bill thought, before getting down to more important matters. "Hone, isn't it true that Old Jono —I mean Jonathan Gaynor—doesn't visit here very often?"

"True, sir." You could never tell what Hone was thinking. He was devoted to Maggilee, Bill knew, but whether he liked or even hated Bill himself was impossible to say. "I myself haven't seen him here since Miss Maggilee—I mean, Mrs. Sholto—was stricken with influenza back in '82. Miss Ellen went to fetch him. He came and spelled Miss Ellen, sitting at Miss Maggilee's bedside until she was on the mend."

"Why do you think he's here tonight?"

"It's about Miss Ellen. Mrs. Faire, that is. He wants . . . to be certain she's happy . . . he thinks maybe Miss Varina persuaded Miss Ellen to marry the colonel—"

"How do you know?"

Hone shrugged. "Talk gets around here."

And they blame me, Bill told himself . . . If Bill Sholto hadn't come here they'd still be going along the way they were before . . . and they'd rather have it that way . . . God! Am I responsible for Ellen's marrying that senile old goat? He'd fought against the idea, accepting Maggilee's constant reminder that Ellen and the colonel had always been devoted to each other, with the marriage a natural result. But the more time that passed the more he disliked this Rowdon Faire . . .

After he heard Varina come down the stairs and enter the river parlor he went back into the hall and unashamedly listened in on the conversation between the old lady and her nephew. There was clearly not much love lost between them.

"So you've seen fit to distinguish this house with your presence at last, Nephew."

"Not by my wish, Aunt Varina."

"Well, well, don't just stand there. You always were a gawky sight, to be sure, and age hasn't improved you. Sit down and tell me what you're here for."

"They told me you-all heard from Ellen."

"True. Ring for tea. Or coffee, if you choose."

"Neither. Is she happy?"

"Of course she is happy. She married the finest man in the Virginia Commonwealth. She will return to Fairevale, a place worthy of the Dunmores and the Gaynors. What more can she ask?"

Jonathan's abrupt answer was, "May I see the picture they sent?"

"Certainly. It is here in my sewing box. I do wish you would sit down. You look like a ridgepole standing there. Will the evidence of your eyes satisfy you? Here."

Finally self-conscious about his eavesdropping, Bill looked away, but he could still hear Varina, who talked on as Jonathan examined the stiff daguerreotype.

"My boy, why not let bygones be bygones? You have my permission to visit Gaynor House any time you like. After all, you are a Gaynor on your father's side. Besides, they are on their way home. It says so in his letter."

Jonathan ignored this. "They look happy enough. Him, anyway. Good night, ma'm."

Before Bill could enter the room he heard Edward Hone at the front door exchanging courtesies with Maggilee, who had just arrived. She sounded exhausted, as well she might. Bill took a few rapid steps, took her in his arms.

"Come on, sweetheart. What you need is a hot brandy. Hone, could you see to it?"

The butler might be Maggilee's friend but Bill felt that loyalty didn't extend to Maggilee's husband in spite of all his efforts. Bill didn't like to feel that anyone disliked him, he was never satisfied until he had won over everyone. In spite of the breakup of his engagement to Ellen, he knew Varina still had a sneaking liking for him . . . They got along very well in the household, with Bill acting as buffer between the two women, but neither Hone nor that Navajo nephew of the colonel's had any use for him, even though he was always careful to be friendly with Hone, at least.

Varina heard their voices and called to them.

"Is that you, Maggilee? William? Your Cousin Jonathan is here. Actually entered the house, can you imagine? Come and encourage him to stay for dinner."

To Bill's surprise Maggilee broke away from him and, tired as she was, ran into the river parlor, Bill following. She was wearing her old brown mantle, which hid her figure, but he knew from the look on her face and her color that her pregnancy was not an easy one. It was hard to think of her as thirty-eight. In many ways she seemed younger and more impulsive than her daughter, but running like this was hardly something to be encouraged during a pregnancy . . .

"Dear Jonathan! This is the most wonderful thing that could hap—"

But Jonathan's tall, reedy figure was already passing her in the archway, waving to her only, and then was gone out the front door.

Certainly an odd fellow, Bill thought, but he had his hands full with Maggilee, who had unaccountably burst into tears.

Varina got up while Bill was comforting Maggilee. "Forevermore! *What* is the matter with her?"

Still caressing his wife's back while he held her in his arms, Bill answered her sharply, "It's her condition, why shouldn't she cry if she has a mind to?"

Varina unexpectedly smiled. "Well said, my boy. Maggilee, you should know better than to expect anything but incivility from that reprobate nephew of mine."

Maggilee wiped her eyes anew and insisted, "Cousin Jonathan has a right to feel any way he wants. But why did he come here at all, after so many years?"

"To see the picture the colonel sent me of him and his bride. I'm afraid he hasn't much interest in you and me these days. He did nothing but ask about Ellen. Not that I blame him. She's done very well for herself," Varina added. "Now, would you mind dressing for supper? It seems to be too late for dinner."

Bill led Maggilee out of the parlor and up to their room, keeping her sheltered within his arm all the while. But Maggilee clearly had her mind on some painful memory, and he began to lose patience when she took so long washing and changing.

"All this tiredness of yours could be avoided, sweetheart," he said, opening the subject he'd been rehearsing all day and for several weeks previous . . . "You've got the baby to think of, you know . . ."

Maggilee was busy getting into one of the few dressy outfits she could still wear and was having trouble with the skirt. "Avoided? I wish I knew how. This is one of the Salon's busiest seasons—"

"They're all busy seasons," he reminded her, watching her dress and still fascinated by the physical charm she held for him, a fascination that was then complicated by thoughts of the other men she'd made love to . . . His annoyance at the thought was directed on a far more mundane matter . . . "All this running around, these long work hours, they're likely to lose us the child. Have you ever thought of that?"

She swung around on him. "Is that *all* you care about? The child? What about my feelings, the things I need, my work, my own place, the money you could have lent me for my shop instead of fixing up those damned pastures—"

"Your so-called shop has got you into this fix about money."

"What do you mean—fix?"

He tried again. "You started the shop to make money

and save the Gaynor land and Gaynor House, didn't you?"

It was true. She didn't bother to deny it . . . He wanted to ease up, worried at how ill she looked, but if he could persuade her to give up the Salon, it might be worth the risk . . . it could change and give her a whole new life . . . "All right, then, sweetheart, just stop and think. You know right well you can't take care of a baby and still work these late hours at the shop."

She seemed rigid with anger. "My shop, as you call it, kept us from starving, Bill Sholto."

"True. I'd be the last to deny it. But now, in a few months the land will be paying up. We needn't depend on the shop. We'll have crops. Even the tobacco is coming on, if we can keep the damn worms off it."

She shuddered. "Worms! I'm making money out of beauty, lovely materials, careful workmanship. And you talk about worms."

"All right, I'm sorry, but I can get an offer for the shop and you're not going to be able to attend to business while you're nursing the baby. So please, darling, let me sell it to Handsel's Emporium in Norfolk for whatever you can get—"

She stared at him as though he'd tried to murder her. She was shaking. "Sell Gaynor's? I'd as soon sell my child. Gaynor's *is* my child. It saved us all in times you Yankees can't even imagine—"

"My God, am I still one of the enemy? Is that all it's meant to you, what we have?"

"Don't be silly," she said, abruptly subsiding. "Do help me. If I have to fumble with these damn shoe buttons any more I'll be sick to my stomach."

He took her small foot on his knee, buttoned the dainty white shoe and set to work on the other foot while he felt his way verbally in what appeared to be quicksand.

"I do have an offer. Major Wychfield says the Norfolk offer is a real one. They'll take Gaynor's off your hands, pay off your debts, both loans, and still give you a handsome profit. Then you can devote your full time to the baby. Think about that . . ."

She tried to pull her foot away but he held onto her ankle, looking up at her. She was dangerously upset, and red as fire. "If you *dare* do anything while I'm laid up with the baby I'll sell off the land. I am the owner, you know. Think about that!"

He soothed her hastily. "We'll see, sweetheart. Ready now?"

They went down to dinner in silence. Fortunately, Varina had the box containing a letter and the daguerreotype, which they all pounced on as a safe subject.

"She looks well, wouldn't you say?" Varina asked them, playing down her own enthusiasm. Bill marveled at how well Varina had adapted to living with Maggilee and himself, as if she had favored the match all along. Still, he couldn't help feeling that Varina was just biding her time before working out some sort of subtle revenge. He did admire her, but damned if she didn't frighten him.

Maggilee studied the dark picture. "Ellen certainly looks rich . . . Aren't those the sapphires Rowdon's first wife used to wear?"

"Yes. The colonel told me before the wedding that he intended to divide Mrs. Faire's jewelry between Eliza and Ellen. Of course, Eliza never wears anything but onyx and mourning beads. Ellen seems to have done very well for herself."

Bill put in, "Then why isn't she looking happier?"

"She's smiling," Maggilee said.

"Not with her eyes."

Varina was impatient. "And so would your smile be

forced if you had to wait while those ridiculous photographers fussed with their machines. I never saw an expression that didn't look forced."

Bill badly wanted to know what the letter said but didn't like to call attention to his interest in it. Contrary to his hopes, Maggilee didn't bring up the matter, so he asked as casually as possible, "Does the colonel tell you when they're coming home?"

"Any day, or so it says. The note is short. Rowdon never was a lettered man. One would think Ellen might have written to me."

Maggilee and Bill avoided each other's eyes. Bill read the scrawling, childlike hand aloud:

Dear Madam,
All good things must end and we began the journey back by steam car from Cincinnati yesterday. We have great plans to refurbish Fairevale, make it more cheerful and livable, including ideas from daughter Eliza and nephew Jem, of course. I am the luckiest man in the world, as this daguerreotype shows. My Ellen is an angel.

Obediently yours,
Rowdon Faire

"Hmph," Varina put in, "we Dunmores are noted for many things, but angelic behavior is not one of them."

Maggilee didn't appear to be listening, busy as she was with her own thoughts. Finally she said, "Just think! With the kind of money Rowdon has, all of the notes on the Salon could be paid off at the same time."

Bill studied his plate of ham, chicken and sweet potatoes, trying not to reveal that he knew this was a dig at him. She was still bitter because he hadn't sunk his six thousand dollars in her precious store. He wanted to point out how much free time she would have without the shop, its financial worries . . . all the time in the world to be with her baby—well, didn't every woman want that? But he said nothing, only reached for her hand under the table and squeezed it affectionately, hoping there would be a few weeks more to wait for the baby. She certainly looked too frail to bear it now.

Four hours later, as if a perverse fate had read his mind, her labor pains began, and he was much too anxious about her life and that of their unborn child to remember what they had quarreled about.

CHAPTER

5

***

ALL THE way across the country both Ellen and the colonel had been looking forward to their arrival at home, Ellen because she hated living in other people's houses, and the colonel because he pictured his gracious young wife as the hostess for all the gregarious days and evenings he enjoyed so much.

Ellen still received no physical satisfaction in their lovemaking. Even after four months her husband's precipitous lovemaking gave her little or no time for her own gratification, but since she was very fond of him, she told

herself that this was a small enough sacrifice . . . When
they reached "home" things would be different . . .

They arrived at Fairevale on a hazy warm day at the
end of May to find the fields ripening under the supervision of Jem, and the meadows still with sweet-smelling
grass and a few remaining wildflowers. They had come
down from Washington past Chesapeake Bay, around Old
Point Comfort on a steamer and been met by Jem with a
very pretty girl whose long, glossy black hair lashed
around her laughing face. For some reason this sight of
Persis Warrender so cozily ensconced with Jem gave
Ellen a start. It might have been Persis' arch, proprietary
air, or the way Jem's arm went around the girl's waist and
squeezed her briefly before Persis excused herself to
them all and threw herself into the arms of her father, the
judge, who was also a passenger on the steamer . . .

Jem welcomed his uncle and new "aunt" with what
Ellen regarded as exaggerated respect. She was sure he
was making fun of her . . . taunting her . . . There was a
distinct amusement in his eyes and his voice as he helped
her into a new surrey with elaborate care, as though she
were an invalid. She thanked him with equally excessive
politeness. She knew she must be on her best behavior.
She was very much aware that the whispered talk had
even reached Kentucky—when a woman of twenty marries a man of sixty, it must be for his money and estate
. . . There was no outward way she could prove them
wrong . . . He showered her with jewels and clothes, and
the more she tried to show her gratitude, the more apt he
was to give her presents.

She was curious to know how Maggilee and Sholto
were getting along . . . She only knew from Miss Eliza's
long, gossipy letters that they'd quarreled several times
over his wanting her to sell the Gaynor Salon. She wants
it all, Ellen decided . . .

"Likely-looking filly, that Warrender girl," the colonel remarked, giving Ellen a breath-catching nudge and a wink. "Kind of taken a fancy to her, have you, boy?"

"Matter of fact," Jem said, "I owe it all to you."

Ellen wondered what "all" he referred to but didn't like to go into it.

The colonel, however, demanded, with full good humor, "How'll that be? Explain yourself."

"I met Persy at your wedding. A charmer."

And well she knows it, Ellen thought, but had the sense to agree. "Persis was always the prettiest girl in the County."

"Rather like your mother, I always thought," the colonel put in.

Ellen sat listening to this, aware that Jem had looked at her curiously. Was there a *little* warmth in that glance? Sympathy? He said nothing.

At Fairevale the colonel got out, feeling the effects of several "farewell bourbons" with friends on the steamer, and announced that he must carry his bride over the threshold. Both Miss Eliza, waiting on the portico, and Ellen herself objected but finally his daughter confided in low tones, "You may as well let him. Papa can be stubborn as a mule."

So the puffing bridegroom swung Ellen out of the surrey and through the river portico. The first thing that caught Ellen's eye was the beautiful white building across the river, much smaller and infinitely more graceful than Fairevale. Was Bill Sholto there at this minute, with Maggilee? No. Maggilee preferred her shop. How were they really getting on? Shouldn't the child be born soon? If it was my child, she thought, I'd give up all the shops in the world for his child . . .

Recalled to duty, she kissed her husband, made a fuss over his gallantry, and was rewarded by his obvious pleasure in her attentions. Jem watched the three on the portico until Miss Eliza stared at him. He turned away then.

Eliza confided to Ellen, "How lucky you didn't arrive two days ago! That Sholto came riding over here to find out if you'd returned."

Too aware of a quickened heartbeat, Ellen said, "Really? Now why would he want to know that?"

"It was about your—about that woman."

"What about her?" Probably, she thought, Maggilee had dispatched him to try to patch things up . . . Typical . . . Once she'd gotten her way, she always wanted everyone to be friends, never could see why others held grudges longer than she did . . . Rowdon was speaking, "Coming in, honey? Eliza? Come on and see what we brought you."

But the women ignored him. Miss Eliza said, "He came to bring you to your mother. It seems they thought she might die. She didn't, however. The—ah—birth was successful."

"Birth!" The colonel burst out. "Ellie-honey, you've got a brother. Or a sister. Well, tell us, Eliza. Boy or girl?"

"How is she now?" Ellen asked, feeling her mouth go dry. "She isn't—"

Eliza said, "A girl. Seven-months, they claim. Very likely, I'm sure."

"How is she? My mother."

Miss Eliza's smile was tight. "Doing well, naturally. During the birth, I hear, she lost considerable blood, then rallied. The servants tell me that she is weak but definitely on the way to recovery."

"Good lord! Look, honey, we'd best pay Gaynor House a visit. Just you wait till we get all this junk put away and we'll pay a nice neighborly call on the Gaynor ladies." The colonel was entering the big, gloomy house with his valet, Joseph, a wizened man in his late seventies who as a slave had accompanied the young Captain "Rowdy" Faire to war in '61 and, as a free man, brought him home safely in '65.

"Thank you. I'd like us to go together." Ellen couldn't explain even to herself why she was so anxious to see her, but she was both anxious and afraid to see Sholto alone.

"We'll go this afternoon. Wait. How about bringing a little something as a gift for the baby? Do we have anything suitable, Eliza?"

Flustered, and resentful, Eliza looked to Ellen. "There's nothing suitable. What do you think, dear?"

"The christening would be time enough for that, but if you would like to go over and wish them well with us, they might appreciate that."

"Personally, I will wait until the christening. But if you do go, Ellen, would you please notice the relationship between Sholto and that woman? See if the gossip isn't right. According to Miss Varina they constantly quarrel."

"But only about the shop."

"Well, quarreling is quarreling."

Ellen tried to ignore the malicious hope behind the words but was aware that she too was curious to see what had become of the love that had been so powerful it had changed four lives. She said to her husband now, "Darling, you're always popular at Gaynor House. You know how my grandmother enjoys your company." This was unfortunate, suggesting a similarity in ages. She pushed on, "They'll love seeing you. And imagine the baby . . . actually, my own sister."

The colonel squeezed her to him with one arm. "And think of this, the baby's going to be *my* sister too, by marriage."

Rowdon was still laughing at the thought when they

entered his bedroom. He proudly called her attention to the dark and enormous Jacobean bed. The room was hung with draperies that shut out all light.

"In this very bed we'll raise the future Faires, won't we, Ellie-honey?"

She managed to respond, ran a finger over his cheek and lips, knowing that every night that passed made it less likely he would ever sire another child. "We will, darling."

He kissed her finger, noisily.

Within an hour, various suitcases, boxes, valises and a big trunk with a hump top had been unpacked, and the colonel and Mrs. Faire departed for Gaynor House.

Eliza whispered to Ellen as they left: "Do notice their situation, how they are getting on."

Ellen nodded. Really, Eliza could be tiresome. She and the colonel arrived at Gaynor House late in the afternoon. The dainty house seemed crowded with visitors, plus Dr. Nickels and Bethulia, who had acted as midwife.

Ellen had prepared herself for the first meeting with Bill Sholto, so she was more in command than he was when the Faires were ushered into the river parlor by Edward Hone. The butler looked anxious, and his face reminded Ellen of his loyalty to Maggilee.

"How is my mother?" Ellen asked at once.

"Better, ma'm. It was a close thing yesterday. She had a relapse."

"And the baby?" the colonel asked hopefully. Negative talk always bothered him.

"Doing excellently, sir. A fine, healthy girl."

"In spite of the early arrival?" the colonel asked in all innocence.

"Luckily, the child appears to be quite perfect."

Thank God for the baby's health, Ellen thought, grateful too that her mother was recovering. Nevertheless, it was strange how *lucky* Maggilee seemed to be. All things went well with her. Ellen was certain by this time that it was all but impossible for the colonel to give her a child. His performance in bed, thanks in part to the whiskey he consumed, hardly was promising. Recently she'd been trying to cut down his drinking, but so far with little luck. It was a habit too old for him to break, and her concern over it was the only thing about her that annoyed him . . .

The female Corrigans, along with Mrs. Wychfield and Daisy, were waiting in the river parlor to see the Sholto baby, and Ellen could imagine the gossip that must have gone on just before she and her husband came in. All the female heads swiveled around to greet the new arrivals, but she hadn't missed the picture of them seconds before as they exchanged whispers.

There were greetings all around, fresh congratulations for the newlyweds, and Irene Wychfield assured Ellen, "They do say the child is perfectly formed . . . in spite of its early arrival. Very unusual, but Maggilee always was in a hurry about things. I understand Captain Sholto is quite the proud father."

Amabel snickered behind her hand but caught a look from Ellen and subsided.

The colonel was oblivious to all these not-so-subtle cross-currents. He rubbed his hands together, said he couldn't wait to see the "little tyke" and that if there was one thing he was good at it was swinging children up over his head. The ladies all found this highly amusing and Ellen reminded him with gentle humor, "Not until she's just a little older, darling."

Daisy said loudly, "I never saw you looking better,

Ellen. Anybody can see marriage agrees with you. Wherever did you get that elegant dress?"

Ellen took the colonel's arm. "It's all thanks to my husband."

She looked up, saw that Bill had come into the room and both seen and heard her possessive little byplay with her husband. He looked pale. Feeling herself blush, she recovered to say brightly, "We came to congratulate you, Captain."

She hated the thought but he had never looked more . . . alive to her.

"Thank you. You are—you-all are very kind." After his first jealous reaction (didn't he know she would bring her husband?) he was all smiles and polite good humor like a proper new father.

"I'm sorry we seem to have lost our hostess, but I hope Ceci and Hone have brought you coffee and sherry. Miss Varina is lying down this afternoon. She had very little rest yesterday, what with presiding over the food and drink for the doctor and our midwife, Bethulia, and all the well-wishers. I'm afraid her temper won't improve until she's had her nap."

He looked at Ellen as he said, "Dr. Nickels says you may see little Shelley Ann for a minute or two. One at a time."

They all assumed Ellen would be the first to go with Sholto. She said, "Thank you," stopped to kiss her husband on the cheek, said, "Wait here, sweetheart," and went after Bill. On the stairs he said in a tense, low voice, "You're pretty obvious, aren't you?"

She knew at once what he meant, and was pleased. "What on earth do you mean?"

"I know you married him out of—of—"

"Despair?" she asked in an irritatingly light way.

"Spite. But when I see you actually fondling that gross old devil—"

Her head snapped up, her eyes flashed. "That's enough. One more word about my husband and I'll go out of here and never come back. I'll leave you to explain to your *wife.*"

He quickly said he was sorry, reached for her hand. She evaded him. He made no further effort to win her over but couldn't keep his eyes off her and just before they entered Maggilee's room, told her, "You really look marvelous, Ellen."

"Thank my *husband*," she said.

He nodded and opened the door.

Maggilee was sitting up in bed. Someone had brushed her hair, which spread out over the pillow around her like a fox's brush. Dora Johnson was beside the bed, stolid but busily taking notes on a pad of rough paper. Others were in the room, Dr. Nickels in a corner leaning over the long basket which had been the cradle of Gaynor babies for a hundred years, and Bethulia tickling the baby and looking radiant. Obviously, Bethulia had adopted the new baby as her own.

Ellen was torn. Whenever she looked at the lovely pink-and-white beauty of her mother she remembered the deep anguish of her own suffering when Maggilee admitted her pregnancy. Not only was the child Bill Sholto's daughter, which meant it might have been her own daughter, but it was actually her little sister, almost surely the only one she would ever have. She smiled cooly at her mother. "Hello, Maggilee. They say you are doing well. Now then, where is that remarkable baby I've been hearing so much about?"

Maggilee sank back against the pillows, while Ellen followed the proud father to Bethulia's charge. He had reason for pride. Ellen had seen numerous babies in the tight-knit County, but there was no doubt Shelley Ann Sholto, as her father called her, was the prettiest newborn baby she had ever seen. Still a bit red, the child also had feathery auburn locks and a face featuring beautifully moulded high cheekbones and eyes that looked more hazel than the usual baby-blue.

"Did you ever see such a beauty?" Sholto demanded, lifting the baby out of the straw cradle in a very practical way. "Pretty as her mother, I swear."

Ellen glanced at Maggilee, who had tensed up to watch Ellen and Sholto together as they huddled over her baby. Maggilee laughed at the implied compliment and, returning to business, went on dictating.

"Now, Dora, I want a thorough report on how far they've gotten with Mrs. Warrender's summer wardrobe for Sulphur Springs. And that little Maud Kent's Coming-Out dress. That should be ready by the end of the week."

Ellen saw that this swift return to business bothered Sholto. His hands tightened their grip on the pink blankets wrapped around Shelley Ann.

When Dr. Nickels left the room to give instructions about Maggilee's dinner, Bill began to talk hurriedly, trying to block out his wife's businesslike voice, and Ellen found her sympathy going out to him in spite of herself.

"Ever see such long legs on a baby this small? She'll be a tall one," he was saying. Suddenly she became aware that he'd taken one of his hands from the baby and had covered Ellen's hand with it. Starting to pull her hand away, the sharp setting of her engagement ring scraped across his palm. "Oh, I'm sorry," she said, not wanting him to think she had tried some deliberate, petty revenge.

He smiled. "It's nothing." Looking into her eyes, he sucked the cut flesh until he saw what had scarred him, and the smile faded. Unaccountably, she felt ashamed of the ring and turned the stone inside. "It—I didn't choose it..." Not that it mattered. She knew he must be thinking that the expensive ring, along with her blue moire suit and other signs of wealth, showed very clearly why she had married Rowdon Faire. The irony was that she had no particular interest in elegant clothes or oversized rings, or the other accoutrements of rich wives. What Rowdon really contributed were two qualities she rated high—devotion and compassion, neither of which she'd enjoyed much during her life.

"Better than I could have done for you," he whispered.

She stared at him, hoping to put him in his place. Apparently he chose to ignore his own role in what she had done.

She was relieved when Dr. Nickels returned with the colonel, who rubbed his hands and proudly proclaimed, "She won't be the first baby girl I've held in these arms. There was my Eliza. And then my dear Ellen. I'm an old hand at it, as you western lads would say."

Sholto gave him a very forced smile, and the colonel strode across to the bed, bending over to kiss Maggilee on the forehead.

"I've the right, you know, Miss Maggie. You are my mother-in-law, after all."

Maggilee burst into her deep, contagious laugh. "Thank you, son-in-law. Now go and see your little sister-in-law. But don't scare her with that great Irish face of yours."

Colonel Faire tiptoed absurdly across the room to make a fuss over Shelley Ann. As always with children, he was a great success. The infant waved her feet and hands at the same time and the colonel exclaimed, "You-all see that? She knows me. See there. She took my finger. You've got quite a grip there, little girl."

Ellen watched her husband, grateful for his presence which, she told herself, helped to make her overlook the proud father.

"Darling," she said, the endearment making Bill raise his head quickly, "I hate to think about it, but hadn't we better be on our way? We've just gotten back, you know," she told the others, "and there's always so much to do the first night after a long trip."

"Yes, yes, honey. One more smile from Miss Shelley Ann. Took my finger again, she did. That's the girl."

Ellen touched the baby's pudgy, active little hand. The child clutched her finger. Ellen felt a rush of affection toward her enchanting little sister, felt she could have stayed all day with the baby . . . if only the child's father hadn't been there . . .

The colonel said, "You're a lucky man, Captain."

Sholto seemed touched. "Thanks. I think so. Glad you came by. Both of you. It was neighborly. I suppose we'll have to have those harpies up here now."

The colonel and his wife wished everyone well and left Maggilee's room, with Ellen looking back to get one last glimpse of Shelley Ann. Maggilee stopped dictating long enough to call, "Ellie? You will come back and tell me about your trip? And where you got that dress? What were they wearing in Cincinnati, Ellie? . . . Ellie?"

"Your mother is calling you, honey," the colonel told her in the hall.

"Yes. I know. It's business. We can talk business some other time."

"As you say. Want to get home with your old Rowdy, do you?"

She hugged him just as Varina came out of her room.

"Very pretty, I must say. One would think you were newlyweds."

Ellen turned and hurried to her, and that controlled lady actually went so far as to hold out her arms, her thin, fragile flesh enfolding her granddaughter. Finally Varina waved to the colonel. "Take her off. I can see you've done more for her than I ever could. You are happy, then?"

"Of course," Ellen said.

The colonel kissed Varina's forehead. "Never more so. She's my angel."

"Very likely," the old lady returned, and watched as they went down the stairs and out to their buggy.

Ellen was thoughtful as they rode away, and the colonel, smarter than most gave him credit for, read her thoughts. "Wish little Shelley Ann was ours, don't you, sweetheart?"

"She might as well be. I doubt if Maggilee knows she exists."

The colonel looked at her curiously, but not without understanding and real tenderness.

CHAPTER 6

***

ON THE night of Shelley Ann's fourth monthly birthday, Maggilee hurried home through the tall, yellowing grass on the western edge of the Corrigan fields. The low sun reminded her of the lateness of the hour and she began to run. Shelley Ann was such an unusual child Maggilee half-believed the claims made by both Bill and Varina that Shelley not only recognized everyone she met but could even count the fourth month of her life on her toes.

Maggilee's thoughts were chaotic. "And here I am—

hours late, damn it! I should have left that tiresome Kent woman to Dora Johnson. What was there in it for me? The money will be the same, payments endlessly delayed as they all are. Why must I run everything myself?

Minutes later in the silent evening she heard the sway of drying summer grass as someone passed through nearby.

"Who is it?" she called uneasily, though she had made this trip hundreds of times in the dark and seldom if ever met a stranger. With relief she saw Jem step into the path.

"Sorry. Did I startle you?"

"No. I'm grateful. I was afraid for a minute it might be one of the Corrigan boys. After they've had a few drinks at that tavern on the James River road they sometimes go on the warpath." Realizing this was something less than the most diplomatic thing to say to him, she slapped her hand over her mouth. "Good heavens! I didn't mean that the way it sounded."

He laughed. "No offense. The Corrigans can be rough but they mean well. They're soon over it and then the apologies flow free as the whiskey." Although he'd been headed toward town, he now walked along with Maggilee. She wondered. It was uncommon for them to spend time together. They were friends but he had never flirted with her the way most of Tudor County's males did at one time or another. Lately, there was gossip that he might be paying court to Judge Warrender's daughter, Persis.

"I hope I'm not taking you from business in town, Jem. Though I must say I appreciate your company."

"No. I intended to meet you. I thought we'd walk to Fairevale together."

"How good of you, Jem! Just when I was feeling a little depressed. I'm late for my baby's party . . . yes, every month we have a party for Shelly Ann. It's my husband's idea," and she added hastily, "not that I'm against it. I think it's lovely, but I can't help feeling the baby is in danger of being hopelessly spoiled. Day after day, everyone who sees her—I don't know . . ." And to herself, I failed with Ellen for different reasons . . .

"How is the child?"

"Marvelous. Though when I come home at night I'm hardly allowed to play with her. I'm kept from my own child by her—what would you call them? Her guardian angels? Her wardens?"

He pushed aside the wild honeysuckle bushes that laced themselves across her path and said flatly, "I thought mothers had to stay home to feed babies."

She shook her head. "I never was able to feed Ellen either. No milk. Bethulia's niece, also a new mother, obliged with Shelley . . ." And again to herself, Is that why I lost Ellen so early?, and knew in her heart it wasn't.

"My uncle's—that is, Mrs. Faire—seems very fond of her baby sister . . . She seems to be there more often than at Fairevale."

Maggilee smiled. So that was it. Jem might have a heritage of stolid Indian blood in his veins, but to Maggilee he was a man barely able to disguise his feelings for her daughter. Jem did not like Ellen seeing overly much of Bill Sholto. Was it jealousy?

"Remarkable how a small baby can prove such an attraction to a newly married young woman," she said innocently.

"Very true." Jem had the wit to blush, his bronze, well-chiseled face deepening. "Here's Fairevale, we'll join them all in the big attraction."

* * *

The colonel was saying, "Look at that, will you? Shelley Ann won't let go of my wife's finger. You've mighty good instincts, little lady . . . Ellie, she's sure all-fired fond of you."

"Thank you, dear," Ellen murmured, brushing his cheek with a light kiss.

He turned to Bill Sholto. "Now, Captain, what were you saying about your war with the Corrigan family?"

"Not a war, sir, it's just that they've had the use of Gaynor land for twenty years. I'm going to court to collect. Either the land or what they owe."

"I don't know, Captain, it's not quite our way of dealing with neighbors."

"Still," put in Judge Warrender, standing close to Miss Eliza, who didn't seem to notice how close, "it is a legal matter. The captain has a point."

Persis Warrender stood at the long river windows tapping her fingernails against the glass, looking north toward the Ooscanoto Bridge. Ellen was certain she hoped to catch a glimpse of Jem, who'd gone off, heaven knew where, at the time Sholto and Bethulia arrived with Shelley Ann. He certainly had no use for Bill Sholto, who remarked on it to Ellen when they were alone in the pantry a few moments later. The colonel had asked his wife to "be the darlin' girl and fill up that whiskey decanter, I don't like Jem to come back and find it empty, you know his funny ideas," and had then explained to Judge Warrender, a man of similar drinking habits, that "that nephew of mine, if he wasn't my own sister's son, I'd think he was spawned by Carrie Nation!"

The judge, who seldom showed the amount of liquor he consumed except for an increase in his gravity and the stateliness of his walk, replied stiffly, "Well, sir, it is a sad day when young men can dictate the habits of their betters—" Interrupted by Shelley Ann's beginning to cry.

"Ellie-honey—" The colonel raised his voice. "Hurry back. Your baby sister's crying for you."

In the pantry Ellen found the whiskey jug, and with Sholto's help poured the contents into the elegant Waterford decanter.

"That *nephew*"—Sholto always placed emphasis on the relationship—"he's not too fond of me, went off the minute we arrived."

"Maybe he's smarter than some others of us."

"Watch it, my lady," he said, trying to put an arm around her, which she angrily avoided, "or someone might get the notion you weren't too fond of a member of your own family—"

"Don't call yourself 'family'—oh yes, I suppose in a way you are—my stepfather, I believe . . ." Which, she was pleased to see, at least put him off sufficiently to cut short one of his snide insinuations about her romantic—or lack of it—life with her husband. In fact, he was so angry he stalked back into the parlor, leaving her to carry the decanter.

She came into the parlor herself just as Persis Warrender stopped tapping her fingernails on the windowpane and exclaimed, "Here he comes now."

"Who? More guests?" Ellen asked innocently, ignoring the quick glance Sholto gave her. She set the decanter down on the sideboard the full length of the room away from her husband, and was crossing to join the group around Shelley Ann in her basket when Persis added . . . wailed, was more like it . . . "Oh, no! He's brought someone with him . . ." "Someone" clearly being a female.

The judge chided her gently, "And why not, my dear? Young Faire isn't your property yet."

Ellen heard that "yet" and wondered if there was an understanding between them. Not, of course, that it mattered to her . . . It seemed obvious Jem would marry eventually . . . except silly Persis? He might as well choose that addle-pated Amabel Corrigan and be done with it—

"It's Maggilee!" Persis broke out.

Her father's warning recalled her to some manners, and she murmured in Sholto's direction, "I'm sorry," adding under her breath to Miss Eliza, "but she *is* old enough to be his mother . . ."

Not that that would matter to Maggilee, Ellen thought . . .

Maggilee was already in the parlor, greeting Judge Warrender, Rowdon and, of course, her devoted husband, Captain Sholto, as she made her way to Shelley Ann in her basket, holding tight to the wide opal bracelet on Ellen's wrist. Ellen took her hand away as her mother approached the basket. She watched the animated group, marveling at the way her mother, in last year's dolman jacket and the nun's-cloth dress she wore in her shop, could stir up males more than a younger woman in the brightest Paris fashions of 1886 . . .

She watched Jem come into the room shortly after, walk past the cluster around Maggilee and seemingly head for her, when Persis floated across the carpet in her gauze-and-silk dinner dress, and after the briefest of glances in her direction his dark eyes shifted to take in Persis. She linked his arm. He rested his hand on it, dark against her fair skin, and she began to whisper in his ear. He nodded and whispered something back, which put her into an absolute paroxysm of giggles.

Miss Eliza remarked quietly to Ellen, "It really is quite something to see how he manages to put himself forward with a nice, decent little girl like Persis."

"It looks as though Persis is the one who's putting herself forward," Ellen answered, and was immediately sorry to be so revealing.

Meanwhile Maggilee was saying to her admirers, "No, no, we really must go. I know how Shelley loves being with you, Colonel, but she needs her sleep. It's far too late for her to be up." She reached in to pick up the baby, but Shelley, who had been soothed to sleep by the brief absence of faces and attention, burst into wails as soon as her mother picked her up. Maggilee did her best, bounced and swayed the child, while everyone offered conflicting advice, and Sholto reluctantly announced, "My wife is right, I'm afraid, it's really my fault. It's much too late for her. We must be going."

Ellen sent the colonel's valet Joseph to interrupt Bethulia's talk with Ma'm Doe, the ancient Fairevale housekeeper, and the judge asked Sholto if he had "room for my girl and me, sir? We walked over here before dark but I fear it's a little late to be making our way back at this hour."

"Nothing easier," Sholto agreed quickly, with a nod to Persis, who found herself mentally looking from the handsome captain to Jem, and deciding, "But I thought— didn't you ask to take me home, Jem?"

Surprising Ellen and the colonel, Jem, in effect, came to Persis' rescue, said she was right, and, to Sholto, "Never mind, Miss Persis and I are walking." The judge wasn't too happy at this, apparently worried that she might get serious over Jem and hoping for a more suitable husband for his pretty, only daughter, but he gave in to her looks and cajolings after Jem promised to have her home within half an hour.

* * *

Out on the portico Ellen and the colonel stood in the warm summer night. The colonel, with a good deal aboard, had a little trouble getting the words out.

"S'nice night, sweetheart. The . . . there's smell of flowers in the air. You no'ce?"

"I notice. But it's my cologne."

She knew he was trying to be sweet and gentle, but she also knew what to expect tonight . . . He'd fall on her, fumbling, failing, and then he would be sick, and after that, as always, would come the task of cleaning up, because she couldn't bear that the servants should know. That would be the night's end, and that was part-payment for her decision made in the bitterest hours of her still young life . . . It *was* her own fault, she couldn't blame Rowdon no matter how desperate she felt . . . She'd been so sure when they came to Fairevale after the honeymoon trip that she would have no time to think of the what-might-have-beens . . . of lying in Bill Sholto's arms, or what might have happened a year ago if she hadn't been so *shocked* at what Jem's single kiss could do to her . . .

She had spent the past four months of her marriage refurbishing Fairevale, making some of the rooms cheerful, carefully having Miss Eliza's magnolias pruned so gradually the spinster wouldn't notice, but enough to bring light into the long parlor, organizing better meals, hiring servants for better pay and more efficient work . . . all things she had learned from her Grandmother Varina. She had supposed if she worked hard enough in the daytime she would be too tired to do more than fall asleep after Rowdon had done so.

No one had told her—or she had denied to herself—that these things wouldn't satisfy her other hunger . . . No one but Jem had intimated how strong that hunger might be . . .

. . . Maybe, just maybe, tonight will be different, she told herself without conviction, and took her husband's hand. He clasped his fingers over hers, assuring her that he was very much his own man. Maybe his conversation was a bit thick, but he had walked out on the portico without stumbling. He stood straight. He had behaved beautifully after five hours of drinking. And besides, she did love him in so many ways . . .

Lights moved through various rooms at Gaynor House across the river. Grandmother is off to bed, she thought with sudden affection for the days of her girlhood and her dreams that still made everything possible . . .

"Shall we go in now?" she ventured as the colonel seemed hypnotized by the beauty of the night.

He inhaled deeply, his fingers fumbling over hers. "Beautiful night. Yes, sweetheart, let's go."

Movement, however, brought on the inevitable. He lurched heavily against her as they walked into the house, and his valet Joseph was there to take his other arm. The colonel then became stubborn. "I'm—have wee dram 'fore bed. Always do, don't I, Jo—Joseph?"

Joseph and Ellen glanced at each other. Before she could catch herself she said sharply, "You've had enough!"

Which only put the colonel's back up. "Sw—sweetheart—don't s-start—nagging wife . . ." His greater strength easily forced the decanter out of Joseph's hand.

Realizing her mistake in tactics, Ellen backtracked with, "Darling, for my sake—"

"Your s-sake, sweetheart—why I'm—one night- . . . cap."

"No, darling, you'll be too sleepy." She hated saying this in front of Joseph. Her consolation was that she had few marriage-bed secrets from him. He knew the colonel's condition from years of putting him to bed.

The colonel waved his decanter. "One. Promise. You g-go on."

Short of wrestling him for the decanter, there was nothing else to do. She was nervous, on edge, trying to preserve somewhere within her consciousness the memory of what she'd felt at Bill's touch earlier in the evening. She very much wanted to scream. At her husband? Or most of all, herself? She said to Joseph, "Don't wait up. You go along to bed, and thank you."

He hesitated, thanked her and after removing Judge Warrender's empty glass and straightening chairs, he left the room. Ellen watched her husband a few minutes longer, but he'd settled into his big leather chair and waved her away. The first fresh swallow of whiskey seemed, strangely, to act as a momentary sobering agent.

"Go along to bed, Ellie!" His tone was unmistakable —the Colonel in the Peninsula Campaign. "I don't like you staring at me. Put me in mind of Miss Varina."

No point in staying. She went quickly up to the huge bedroom, which seemed dank even on a late summer's night, and tried to blot out all the evening's memories by concentrating on the needs in this room. The huge, dark bed with its heavy posts, the furniture all Jacobean and ancient enough to be valuable, even the heavy brown drapes were "necessary," according to Miss Eliza. "Heirlooms from Mama, you know, my dear."

Ellen killed time for a few minutes, not wanting to get undressed until she knew whether she would have to contend with an inert body or a drunken, over-active man in bed. She got undressed at last. He might be asleep in his comfortable chair downstairs. If so, she would leave him there. She washed and then dismissed Verna, the upstairs maid, who had brought up the hot water. Fairevale hadn't yet piped water to its upper floors, another project she had in mind. She got into one of her silk and lace honeymoon nightgowns, took down her hair and began to brush it.

The house seemed unusually still. She could hear each brushstroke as it snapped along its course to the ends of her hair. Corn silk, someone had called it. She examined a strand. Much good that did her. She was absently studying her reflection, wondering if she really did look like her forbidding grandmother, when she heard a noisy thump as if something heavy had dropped.

She knew. Dropping the brush, she rushed out to the dark-paneled Jacobean staircase and, as she'd feared, saw the colonel sprawled halfway up the stairs, his arms flailing the air, his feet some steps below trying to propel him upward. In her relief that he seemed to be unhurt she got down on her knees, examining him. "Really, you are worse than a child! Are you hurt anywhere?"

"I tripped."

"I know, dear. Just put your arm around my shoulder, and for heaven's sake, open your eyes!"

"I'm sleepy."

"Well, you're not going to sleep on the staircase. Now, do try and give me some help."

She was still kneeling above him, bending over to stop his arms from flailing about, when the front door opened beyond the foot of the stairs.

Jem Faire came in.

Ellen saw him stare up at her for a brief moment without uttering a sound. Not surprising when Ellen looked down at the low neckline of her nightgown and the full view of her breasts as she bent over Rowdon. She straightened up quickly, flushed with embarrassment. And an overwhelming urge she tried not to admit to herself.

CHAPTER
7
***

JEM MOVED quickly. "Don't worry. I'll take care of him." He came up the long flight of stairs, several at a time.

Knowing how he felt about her and her supposed reasons for marrying his uncle, she said hurriedly, "He just stumbled. I don't think he's hurt."

"Never mind. Leave him to me." Jem sounded curt.

Feeling increasingly obliged to apologize for him, she began again, "He just had a little more whiskey, and when he started to climb the stairs—"

"He's drunk. Say so."

"No. You don't understand. He—I heard him when he—"

With a calm that puzzled her until she realized it was an old story to him, he waved her away. "He never hurts himself. Don't worry. Go and get something on. It's chilly outside."

Suddenly furious, she stood up, not giving a damn that the silk and lace panels of her gown revealed very clearly the rest of her body. "I've been helping my husband for nearly five months."

Jem had raised the colonel to a standing position with surprising ease, and he was now tugging in a stupefied way around Jem's neck.

"Up you go," Jem said, very much like Ellen in the voice of a stern but kindly parent. "Aren't you gone yet?" he asked Ellen as an aside. He was certainly going out of his way to be rude to her.

She went up the stairs ahead of them and turned down the sheets and blankets on Rowdon's side of the bed.

Jem had his uncle's full weight on his shoulders and stopped in the doorway. "I'd better take him to one of the spare rooms."

"No. Bring him here. I've seen him like this before."

He didn't argue but half-supported, half-dragged the colonel to the bed, where his heavy body bounced as it fell onto the mattress. Instinctively, he raised his legs, shoes and all, onto the clean spread. Jem took one leg, Ellen took the other, and they began unbuttoning his shoes. Jem said suddenly, "I sometimes figure it's the only real fault he's got."

"I know that."

"It's not as if he rampaged around town, or got involved with other women. Or gambled, or beat his wife."

She smiled. "I do realize all that, you know. And I really could have handled him, even if you hadn't come."

This time he looked at her with the colonel's shoe in his hand. "Has it been bad?"

"No." Pride goeth . . .

He began to undress the colonel and she said, "I'll do that."

He waved her away. "Will you, for God's sake, do one thing for me? Get something on."

She reached for an old linen wrapper hanging in the wardrobe. It was still in her hands when she heard Jem's sudden, angry, "God, I knew it!" He ordered her over his shoulder, "Ellen, get out of here."

"Don't be silly!" She heard all too familiar sounds coming from the colonel, threw on her wrapper, grabbed a towel and forced it into Jem's hand. "Use that," she said, "and I'll get the basin."

"Want—fight, boy?" the colonel said as Jem washed him.

Jem rolled his eyes heavenward, and Ellen couldn't help smiling.

She went downstairs to wash the chamber pot. The night was so still she could hear the creak and crack of old timbers. She finished her work, stood there leaning on the kitchen pump, with the faint, cool breeze from the open pantry window cooling her body, ruffling her gown and linen wrapper. Briefly, she felt relief. She would like to have been chilled to the bone, then the rest might go away, the pleasure she'd known a few minutes ago in the close presence of Jem . . . and the intense unease at her own weakness.

Now that she was married to his uncle she simply could never let Jem know . . . She put out her wrists, one at a time, and ran water on them from the pump. Feeling the gush of cold spring water she was relieved to find herself calming down. She splashed cold water on her face, made no effort to wipe it away. A reminder.

She took the clean chamber pot up the stairs and met Jem at the top, as if he had been waiting for her.

"You had better sleep in a spare room tonight," he told her, standing in her way.

"Is he all right?"

"Asleep now. He'll be fine tomorrow."

She was only one step below him and he undid her calm by observing, with unexpected humor, "Your face is wet." His forefinger grazed the soft flesh under her eye. She wanted to avoid him, avoid his touch, step backward. Instead, she stood there below him, biting her lip, her eyes betraying something of her feelings.

"I'm glad," she managed finally.

"About what?"

"You said—I thought you said he was all right."

He nodded, let her pass him and looked around after her. He appeared to be making some judgment about her. She put the chamber pot away in the commode. He had been right. She couldn't sleep here. The colonel was snoring loudly as he always did when he lay on his back after drinking. There was nothing to be done about that. He would feel terrible when he woke up. Not until coffee, ham, eggs, corncakes and grits were laid in front of him would he feel like living again.

She went along the upstairs hall behind Jem to the next room. Miss Eliza's large room was at the opposite end of the hall. Jem had a small room downstairs that had originally belonged to Hester Faire, his mother. A girl of independent ideas, she hadn't wanted to be where her parents or brother could watch her every minute, and it was whispered that more than once she'd been seen returning late at night through the ground-floor window after meeting some local on the extensive Fairevale grounds.

"Will this do?" Jem asked, carrying a double-globed lamp into the spare room next to the master bedroom.

"Very nicely. Thank you."

He set the lamp on the mahogany night stand beside the modern four-poster bed, which looked a good deal more comfortable and less imposing than the master bed in Rowdon's room. Fortunately Ellen had kept all the bedrooms dusted and cleaned. Almost every weekend there were guests who filled the house, to the gregarious colonel's pleasure. Still, it was not pleasant to find herself in a strange bedroom and expected to sleep calmly through the night after all that had happened.

She didn't want to get into bed until Jem was gone. She said a reserved "good night" and turned her back, hoping he would take the hint. She heard the door close with a thud, like a hard kick. Was he angry with her, or with his uncle? Or both . . .

She took a step toward the bed, removing the wrapper as she did so. She gathered the linen robe with its blue ribbon and lace trim and started to throw it onto the foot of the bed. A dark hand took the wrapper out of her fingers, dropped it onto the carpet as the palm of Jem's other hand closed over her mouth, stifling her scream of surprise.

He must be crazy, she thought, to try such a thing in his uncle's house, a house full of witnesses. As she struggled, astonished by this animal behavior in a man who *might* have taken her with gentleness, she kicked at him but her bare feet could do little damage when one of his powerful legs got between hers, and her feet struck out harmlessly against nothing, like a cat lifted in midair, its paws dangling.

She tried to bite his hand, tasted only the salty sweat of his curved palm. His face was close above hers, his long blue-black hair hanging forward, lank and straight. In the oblique slant of his green eyes she recognized the same glitter of purpose and desire she had seen that other time. He meant to have her, no doubt, but in his own way. She tried to shake her head, his hand clamped tighter over her mouth. Scrambling and fighting like her drunken husband half an hour ago, she was thrown on the bed. Before she could do more than twist her body away to avoid him, his smothered hers, pinning her to the embroidered bedspread. It was hardly as she had pictured it an hour ago when she saw him flirting with Persis Warrender. For an instant his hand left her mouth, which felt paralyzed. She whispered, "Not this way, not—"

His mouth pressed down hard on hers. She began to respond to what seized her body in spite of all her efforts. It was as if his kiss, brutal as it was, impregnated her with his own angry passion.

Heavier with guilt than with the weight of his body, she made a final attempt to struggle before he raised her hips and roughly entered her. Their joining made her cry out, but his hand, more gentle now, passed across her mouth and she was lost in their mutual fulfillment.

Jem's hands moved over her now, his lips caressing her thighs, only the top of his head visible to her eyes. She stroked the straight, coarse hair and then, together, she and Jem reached a climax, the first of her life. And she knew, she understood, finally, far more about her mother's behavior than ever before in her life.

He drew away from her. The joy ended with her first sight of his eyes. He was still angry with her. He hadn't made love to her. He had raped her. She tried to rise but he held her shoulders pinned to the bed while he told her in that hard, low-pitched voice, "Why do you think I stayed here?" He shook her.

She tried to move her bruised lips, but couldn't speak.

"You think I wanted to nurse this lush country that wasn't my own? I've burned to know you like this since I first came. I was a damn fool. I actually wanted to marry you then. But you wanted to be a great lady—"

She didn't recognize her own bitter laugh. "I wanted some peace, an escape."

"You'll get it," he promised her with a quiet fury. "You've escaped from that Bluebelly and that milksop Gavin McCrae. I see the way they look at you. Just remember. You belong to me. Forget your pretty little soldier-boy, because I'm the one you're going to remember."

She raised herself, hugging her bare shoulders against the shivering that had seized her. "If you want me to scream—it's a little late, but I can bring down the house. And our lives with it."

He touched her lips with one warning forefinger. "You won't, though. I'll give you that. You know what you want . . . You like to be Mrs. Rowdon Faire."

She dragged herself out of bed, clutched at the wrapper and put it on with shaking hands. Vaguely, she was aware of the honeymoon nightgown, torn and disheveled on the carpet where Jem had thrown it. He was at the door now. With a swiftness that even surprised Jem, she put her hand out in front of him, stopping him. "I made a vow to my husband. As long as I wear his ring—"

"My ring," he reminded her. "I put it on your finger. You made that vow to me." He opened the door.

She slapped at the door hard, noisily. "Stay away from

me, Jem. I owe him more than I can ever repay. So stay *away.*"

His smile frightened her. He lowered his head to kiss her. She pushed past him. The door opened at the far end of the hall and Miss Eliza stuck her head out. Her graying hair was neatly confined in two braids.

"Is something wrong? I heard so much noise." She stared suspiciously at Jem, who looked very much as he always did, though his color was even deeper.

Ellen said quickly, "It's Rowdon. We just got him to bed and I've no place to sleep. May I share your bed?" She didn't glance at Jem but hurried to join Miss Eliza, who pulled her inside and bolted the door with an ominous snap. She stared at Ellen. "That dreadful man. He tried to make love to you, didn't he?"

"No . . . I was wearing nothing but this wrapper when Rowdon became ill, then Jem saw me trying to wash the basin and offered to help. After Rowdon fell asleep, I suppose Jem thought I was immodestly dressed—"

"Horrible man, I wouldn't put anything beyond him. I've always been very careful to be fully dressed around him. My dear, you're all flushed. Come to bed. You may have that side. I'll take this. And don't cry over a small matter like his looking at you. He can't hurt you, you know. Papa would never permit it."

CHAPTER 8

***

BILL SHOLTO patted old Oglala's flank, promised to be back soon, and went into Judge Warrender's small one-story frame office next to the Tudor County Courthouse. The white-haired old gentleman looked more formidable than ever, studying some kind of legal-appearing letter through his spectacles. His daughter Persis made things a bit difficult, running her finger over the back of his neck and demanding, "Do be serious, Daddy. When did Jem say he'd be here? Now stop that reading and 'tend to business."

"Daughter, he's going to expect this agreement to be signed, but I can't oblige if you keep pestering."

Sholto took it all in. Persis, with her kittenish ways, reminded him a lot of how Maggilee must have looked and acted in her younger days—not that there was anything very wrong about Maggilee at her present age . . . when she chose to be charming, and didn't insist on that damned job being so important.

"Good morning, Miss Warrender. Judge."

Persis gave him her hand with its soft mitt leaving her fingers free. She was a real little teaser, he thought. She tried too hard. But at least she wasn't as obvious as the Corrigan girl. Mowbrey, the tenant farmer who worked the Gaynor east pastures for Bill, had told him Amabel Corrigan and one of the boys from Ironwood in the next county were doing a lot of heavy sparking along Dunmore East Creek. He surmised the girl was going to have to be married off pretty fast or wreck all her ambitious mother's plans.

But Bill reminded himself he wasn't at war with the Corrigan females. Only the three males. And his war had nothing whatever to do with the pert daughter of Judge Warrender. Bill let go of her hand with an elaborate show of reluctance, which she clearly enjoyed.

"My, my, Miss Persis, you do defy the laws of nature."

"How? Me?"

"You get prettier every day."

She beamed and he turned to her father.

"Sir, may I count on your help to protect my bottomlands on East Dunmore Creek?"

The judge took off his spectacles, rubbed the lenses on his handkerchief. "The Corrigan properties you're referring to, naturally."

"Excuse me, sir. The Gaynor properties."

"Quite so, yes, most difficult."

Bill's veneer of courtly charm wore thin. He had to remind himself that he wasn't dealing with corrupt Indian agents or warring Indians. Arrogance or strength were not weapons he could use with Judge Warrender and these polite Virginians. "But, sir, the County records clearly show that all the land along the west bank of the creek was originally deeded to the first Jonathan Gaynor. There can't be any legal doubt, surely."

The Judge replaced his spectacles with a deliberation that warned Bill not to lose his temper. "Legally, young man, you are in the right. But we don't deal here with mere cold legality. The Corrigans have done splendidly with their fields—"

"Our fields."

"Indeed," the judge said, adding, "that is the precise problem we are faced with. The Corrigans have certain rights awarded to them by the Federal government at the end of the War." Sholto opened his mouth, but the judge raised one hand and silenced him. "Not precisely the bottomlands you are contesting. Very true. But if you were to win back those bottomlands, you would cut apart the Corrigan north and south fields. You are farmer enough to know what that means. The water rights, the creeks and brooks, even the planting, the fertilizing of the fields . . . If you were to take over these disputed bottomlands—"

"If? But I intend to do so, sir. I thought everyone understood. Especially those carpetbaggers who came down on the tails of the Freedman's Bureau."

"Sir! Are you implying that I would side with carpetbagging riffraff from a Yankee Freedman's Bureau? *I* am not the man in this room wearing the uniform of the Union Army."

My God, Bill thought . . . if we get the Civil War mixed into this, he'll never settle the business.

"Now, Daddy," Persis put in, "the captain doesn't mean you're a damn Yankee."

"Persis, attend to your language."

Which gave Bill the chance to retrench. "I see we both have the same idea about those days when the state was under martial law, sir. But I did want to be certain that the validity of the Gaynor claim was recognized under the law. That's about all, Judge."

Only partially mollified, Judge Warrender made his displeasure with Sholto clear by being more affable than usual to Jem, who walked in just then, much to Persis' pleasure.

"Jem, you're dreadfully late," she reminded him with a pout.

He didn't make out Sholto at first in the dim, dusty recesses behind the judge's rolltop desk and made his explanation to both the Warrenders. "Sorry. I had a little business with the Corrigans. They have some land trouble, and they're talking violence. They won't listen to legal remedies. But that's your department, sir, not mine. All I could do was advise them to do what I'm doing."

"Ah, yes. Very wise." The judge looked up under his bushy white eyebrows at Sholto. "Mister Faire has purchased the acreage between the Ironwood and Fairevale lines. A very civilized method, if I may say so."

Bill stepped out of the shadows and said evenly, "I've no use for Corrigan money, sir. After all, they made it off Gaynor land. It would be a little like being paid with my own money. I'm afraid that makes me uncivilized, by Mister Faire's definition."

"By mine, sir. By mine!" the judge cut in.

Persis laughed uneasily and clutched Jem's arm.

The judge again filled the awkward moment. "Will that be all, Captain?"

"As long as I'm assured of the Gaynor rights. I'm putting in my tenants to work tomorrow. Good day, Miss Warrender." And threw in, "From the talk around the County I wonder if congratulations will soon be in order." He made it doubly clear what he meant by glancing from Jem to Persis.

"Thanks, Captain," Jem said. "The deal was worked out by the judge. Fairevale made the offer and Ironwood accepted. That was what you meant, wasn't it?"

Sholto knew when to back off. He grinned, nodded, and left the judge's office.

He was already in the saddle when Jem came out and said, "I'll ride with you to Gaynor House. My uncle and his wife stopped off there on the way home from White Sulphur Springs."

Strange. Bill was fully aware that Jem, to put it mildly, disliked him, and he had a pretty good idea why.

Persis interrupted his thoughts as she came running out after Jem, asking him to stoop over while she confided a message to him. "You're very brave, Jem. Daddy says, 'Thank you.'"

Jem's first reaction was annoyance, but unexpectedly he smiled at the girl and then rode off.

. . . Now, why the devil should he break his neck to ride with me? Bill asked himself again, and why should the Warrenders thank him?

Bill galloped to join up, wondering if Jem wanted to give him some message. If it hadn't been for the Warrender girl's gushing thanks, he might have suspected the halfbreed wanted to bushwhack him somewhere along the way. Wouldn't be the first time . . . It was a little like riding under flag of truce with old Crazy Horse himself . . .

To make conversation and with no immediate ulterior motive, Bill remarked, "So your family is back. To tell you the truth, my wife was surprised that they left so soon after our visit to Fairevale. The very next morning, Miss Eliza says Maggilee thought it was funny they never mentioned it to any of us that night."

"It seems to have been a sudden idea."

"Of the colonel's? Or—"

"I wouldn't know."

Sholto said, "I can see why. That big, old house. And poor Ellen surrounded by ancient reminders of the former Mrs. Faire." He caught himself, added, "Present company excepted, of course. Must've been lonely this last month, just you and Miss Eliza."

"They had to come back sometime. I knew they couldn't stay away forever." Jem said this with a smile that Bill didn't at all like. He wondered how often Ellen did find herself alone with her "nephew." He decided he'd better get Maggilee to warn her. Ellen would hardly know how to handle a man like Jem Faire, and her husband, God knew, was not much help.

"You've never had any trouble with the Corrigans before, have you, Captain?"

"You're riding shotgun for me against the Corrigans?"

Jem gave him a look fully returning Sholto's dislike. "The Corrigans happen to be friends of mine. I don't want to see them hanged for putting a bluebelly out of his misery."

"I see. All you natives stick together."

Jem caught the dig, ignored it.

Instinctively, the two made a race of their ride and

by the time they reached Gaynorville Oglala was winded. Jem on his neat, spotted pony was the winner, but to Bill's surprise Jem reined in too when they started west on the side road toward the old plantation houses along the Ooscanoto.

"He's a good animal," Jem remarked of the old black stallion. "Break him yourself?"

"Took him from a dead Sioux. Had him since he was little more than a colt."

The exchange had, unintentionally on either's part, given them a slight bond, and Sholto found the riding actually companionable . . . In other circumstances, in fact, he might even have welcomed such a man by his side in a skirmish. But shortly afterward they came to the bridge over the waters of East Creek, now running lower as autumn approached, and on the west bank were the Corrigan fields. Sholto looked out under the brim of his cavalry hat but saw no one around the Corrigan house beyond the big white gate. Smoke came from the chimneys at the rear. The women were probably supervising preparation of three o'clock dinner.

Jem, bareheaded, merely watched the road. He seemed uninterested in his surroundings but Sholto had seen men like him before and knew that hardly a blade of grass in those fields would move unnoticed by him. It put Bill on his guard, too. He could almost imagine he was back in the Black Hills, moving over sacred Sioux ground . . .

And what if this halfbreed *was* actually leading him into a trap? He was surely capable of it . . .

As if to try Sholto's nerves, Jem raised his hand suddenly, called, "Finding any game, Timby?"

Out in the field, rangy Timby Corrigan unfolded himself out of the high grass. He was armed with an old shotgun that he waved casually at Jem. "Nothing but rabbits. It's stew tonight. Want to set down along of us?"

Jem laughed and called, "Not tonight. Make it wild turkey and I'll pull up a chair. Rest of the family crawling around with you out there?"

"Nope." Timby still avoided looking at Sholto. "Pa and Sean, they're out huntin' skunks."

"Must be something better to do with their day."

This time Timby Corrigan made it a point to glance at Sholto. "Just funnin', Jem. Just funnin'."

But as Sholto and Jem rode on, Sholto couldn't help wondering if he would have been able to ride along now, unhurt, if it hadn't been for Jem's presence. It wasn't a good thought. The last man in the world he wanted to be beholden to was this damned halfbreed ladykiller.

* * *

Maggilee threw the ledger down on the little kidney-shaped desk. Dora Johnson sat opposite the desk rubbing her fingers together nervously. Even Nahum was uneasy. He was a literate young man, thanks to Jonathan's books and his own deep interest in history. Perhaps he was remembering the ancient custom of killing the man who brought bad news. Only Jonathan Gaynor seemed unmoved, calm despite this being his first visit to the distinctly feminine world of the Gaynor Salon.

"Jonathan, are you going to stand up all day?" Maggilee asked finally, after looking from face to face trying to find a victim. "I'm just as anxious to get away as you are. My daughter and her husband are waiting for me at home, and my husband and Shelley Ann will be expecting me."

Jonathan recrossed his arms. "I came along because I figured you might not believe Nahum alone."

Maggilee threw up her hands. "Why not? If Norfolk

bankers do their talking near the kitchen door of the Winchester Coffee House, why shouldn't Nahum—or the whole world—hear them, if it comes to that?"

Dora said the obvious: "If only you knew who was back of it, Miss Maggilee."

Maggilee shrugged. "Even if I knew, I couldn't stop them from buying up my loans. I've always managed—"

"Sweet-talking them," Biddie put in from the doorway. She leaned on her gnarled stick and reminded them all, "Takes money to buy up loans, seems to me. You know anybody with fresh shin-plasters? If you do, and you've made an enemy, that's your man."

"There's not a soul I know who's come into money recently," Maggilee said. "We're not in the best fix in this state and the only way a body makes money these days is if they inherit or marry it." She felt rather than saw the quick exchange of looks between Biddie and Dora Johnson and suddenly, with a stab of pain, realized what they suspected. "Look, Nahum, tell me exactly what you told Mister Jonathan."

Nahum got a nod from Jonathan and cleared his throat.

"I didn't think too much on it right away, Miss Maggi. Was just when Mister Jono said go see you that I figured it might be something you-all never heard about."

"You were in the kitchen at the Coffee House."

"Yes'm. Waiting for Nellie-Jo that works there. Her family's sharecropping on Finch land. And this Mr. Gimmerton of Norfolk, he come to the table and Nellie-Jo waited on him and a fat, pink-face gentleman from Richmond. He's a banker too."

"Harleigh Duckworth," Maggilee muttered, and reached for her ledger again.

"So the thin gentleman, he said he had an offer on

some papers you owed that was long-gone—"

"Overdue."

"That's right. Nellie-Jo wasn't sure. And the fat Richmond gentleman, he says same with him, and they didn't know as they could hold onto 'em. The loan papers, I mean. Their people—"

"Stockholders?"

"Their people, they said, would demand they make good all them bad debts. It's all she heard while she was taking stuff off'n the tray. She come back and Mr. Fisher that runs the Winchester, he wouldn't let me peek in there to see them."

"Damn!"

Biddie looked at all of them and sighed. "Whyn't you just out and ask this Mr. Duckworth, Miss Maggi? 'Stead of beatin' 'round the mulberry bush. Just straight-out ask."

Maggilee looked up at Jonathan. "I'd like to get around this without an open challenge. You know what I mean. Get the notes settled up somehow, but not have to know who did this."

Jonathan, who valued his land and crops more than his life, said calmly, "I expect I could give mortgages on some of my acreage. I got no ready cash."

Maggilee put her hand on his. He looked at it for a long moment before taking it off and setting it back on her ledger.

"Miss Ellen's got lots of money, now she's married that Colonel Faire," Nahum said innocently.

The awful silence that followed this suggestion told him he had, somehow, made a mistake, and he looked uncomfortable until his Aunt Biddie said, "Not but what he's right, when all's said and done. S'pose'n you just skipped over Miss Ellen and asked the colonel. He's as generous as they come, Ma'm Doe says. Be kind of funny at that if you got the money from him to fight off a trick his wife hatched up. Bet you a cent he don't even know about it."

"Biddie!"

"I was always one for speakin' my mind," the old woman said complacently.

"Well, that's all," Maggilee said. "We'll close up and maybe I'll get an idea tonight."

They all left except Jonathan. Maggilee saw him standing in the hall after she had turned out the gas lights and given her beloved shop one last look before leaving.

"Wrong door," she called to Jonathan. "I've got Pansy and the buggy. I want to get home before Ellen and the colonel leave, or Varina will have them thinking she's Bill's wife and Shelley Ann's hers."

"She is, just about."

Maggilee had to conceed he had a point, and was honest enough to do it. "Funny. You get what you don't want and you have to fight like the very devil to hold onto the things most precious to you. Varina cared more about that damned house than she did about life or honor or any human being, including herself. And it belongs to me. On the other hand, there's the Gaynor Salon . . ." They reached Gamble's Livery Stable and the boy led out Pansy and the buggy. As Jonathan helped her up and got in, she said, and meant it, "I'd die if I lost that shop. It's what I've worked hardest to make and to keep. I want Shelley Ann to have it . . . make her self-reliant, popular—"

"Gaynor's isn't self-reliant. It needs you every step of the way," Jonathan said.

She frowned, gave Pansy the signal to start and said,

"I never thought of Gaynor's that way . . . Ellen's the self-reliant one . . . Since Shelley Ann's so much like me maybe she's like Gaynor's too. Maybe I do want someone to need me, like Gaynor's does."

"And Major Dalkett? Did he need you?"

In twenty years they hadn't spoken the name aloud. Her hands caught in the lines and Pansy lurched out of step, stopped and looked back.

For a moment Maggilee thought she was going to cry. Finally she managed, "We needed each other . . . Even strong men need love and caring, you know. Everyone treated him like a swamp-moccasin, and he was so fair to them. Nobody had occupation officers like Clinton. He was generous and—yes—just, too."

"And now you've got another bluecoat. Was it like Clinton Dalkett, worth all the pain this time as well?"

"Pain!" She stared at him, not understanding the comparison. "There was no pain connected with Bill. Unless you mean when Shelley Ann was born."

He said mildly, "I wasn't thinking of your pain, Maggi. But Ellen's."

"How can you be so . . . ? Ellen, thank the Lord, is sitting very pretty on top of Fairevale with a devoted, attentive husband she's always been fond of and the most dazzling wardrobe I ever saw. Pain!" She laughed. "Give me a little of her so-called pain and I can buy back all my shop loans."

"Maggi, Maggi," he said, softly, "will you never get over it? After twenty years . . ."

The hard lines appeared unexpectedly in her soft-looking face. "Twenty years ago Clinton Dalkett died. Some of me did, too."

He looked at her. He didn't answer that. And she couldn't believe she had said it, she hadn't even admitted it to herself in all those years. But now, saying it to Jonathan was somehow like locking it away again in a vault . . . "Anyhow," she went on with an abrupt laugh, "all this doesn't get me any closer to saving my babies. Either of them."

"How is the child threatened?"

"Bethulia says she's been impossibly cranky ever since Ellen left on that trip to White Sulphur Springs with the colonel the morning after our visit. I tried taking her down to the shop, keeping my two children together, you might say. But she cried and threw things and I had to scold her and then Bill came in and insisted I didn't know how to handle my own child. Shelley's going to be spoiled rotten and there's nothing I seem able to do to stop it."

"You could stay home with her."

"I've even tried that, stayed home Sunday, Monday and Tuesday for three weeks. But Shelley's being spoiled, no matter how I put my foot down. And during those three weeks they managed to lose me one of my best-paying customers. Mrs. Corrigan. You can imagine how much humble pie I had to eat to get her back . . . There she is now . . ." Maggilee looked out and called a greeting.

Mrs. Corrigan was leaning on her elbows against the wagon gate, scolding her son Timby for something or other. She stopped, waved her apron at Maggilee, and went on laying down the law to her large but thoroughly cowed son.

Timby stared after the buggy as if curious to get a look at Maggilee. He couldn't see her companion. Jonathan never rode with the two older Gaynor women, so the identity of her companion must have puzzled him.

Pansy and the buggy were nearing the path which cut off through the woods toward Gaynor Ferry when Maggilee touched her cousin's arm with one of her instinctively coaxing pleas. "I wish you'd come to dinner at the house, dear Jonathan. Just this once. You'll find after the first time it's surprisingly easy."

He was already refusing when they both heard a noise like a loud handclap and nesting birds flew out of trees in a panic around them. Jonathan pushed her head down hard in her lap. She didn't argue. Minutes went by. He looked all around. Some idiot . . . shooting rabbits or birds. He must have panicked. He's gone now."

"Timby Corrigan had a gun," she remembered.

"A shotgun. This was a rifle, I'd say. Let's get on."

"Nobody could have been aiming at us," she insisted.

"If they had been, they wouldn't shoot over Pansy's head. Either an accident or somebody's wanted to scare you or . . . me."

"What a far-fetched idea."

"I was just wondering if they thought I was your husband and wanted to put the fear of God into him."

"But why?"

He evaded this. "No reason, I guess . . . just somebody funning, probably."

"Not to me!"

He said nothing more. He rode with her uneventfully as far as the Gaynor lawn before alighting. He looked at her, said in his laconic fashion, "You'll save your shop. Somehow."

Her chin went up. "Of course I will."

"And try not to worry about the shooting—"

"I'll tell you this. She—he's not shooting at me! Get on, Pansy. We'll be late for our guests." She called back to Jonathan, "Why, I haven't any enemies. Haven't you heard? I'm loved by all," and she laughed without humor.

He shook his head, inhaled deeply the first cool hint of autumn in the air and went off into the underbrush.

Maggilee wouldn't have confessed it to her cousin, but she was more shaken up than she pretended to be. The accidental shooting was not the cause . . . she knew every fall there were similar "jokes" by youngsters who were out hunting food for supper . . . Much worse, so far as she was concerned, was the knowledge that a plan had been started to buy up her loans, her mortgages and, inevitably, the Gaynor Salon.

Her baby.

CHAPTER 9

***

*E*LLEN HAD put off the return to Fairevale as long as possible, looking around expectantly, saying, "I think I hear Maggilee now," or "What a shame we can't go up to see Shelley Ann, Captain! She's such a little charmer!" But it was only postponing the inevitable.

She had run off from Fairevale with her husband the morning after her seduction by Jem Faire, and it had taken all her newly acquired persuasive powers to get the colonel ready for a tiresome journey to White Sulphur Springs. Not unsurprisingly, he was nursing a monumental hangover and would have preferred the restful darkness of his own bedroom. But they had gone, spent as long as Ellen could persuade him to remain away so soon after their honeymoon journey, and even today she had seen to it that they were not met by Jem at the train depot. Any further delay in meeting the colonel's nephew was ridiculous, but she still had managed to have the colonel stop off at Gaynor House with his borrowed rig.

It was here that Jem and Bill arrived together. There had been much show of welcome home . . . even Varina allowed her forehead to be kissed by the colonel. Ellen was also astonished at Bill's easy, flirtatious manner with Varina, whom he greeted as "my love," and by Varina's mischievous response.

Then it was Jem's turn. He shook his uncle's hand and in answer to the colonel's question told her, "All's well. I bought the acreage along the Ironwood pasture fences. No trouble there, sir."

He moved on to Ellen. She was very much aware of the watchful eyes of Bill as Jem approached her, and she thought, I'd die if he guessed what happened that night.

"Aren't you glad to see your aunt, boy?" the colonel asked. But everyone saw that his nephew was ready. It was his wife who behaved with either coyness or reluctance as Jem held hands and kissed her cheek, and then close to her ear Ellen heard him under his breath, "When again, *Aunt?*"

She backed away abruptly, covering her action with the pettish excuse, "Oh, do mind! You'll muss my hair."

He looked at her, his black lashes shadowing his eyes, and she wanted to shiver, partly in fear, partly too from a remembering of his touch that swept over her even now, five weeks later.

To spite him, she corrected her sharp tone and gave

Bill her hand with an elaborately gracious gesture. "Your daughter becomes more delightful every day. We missed her terribly, didn't we, darling?" This to Rowdon, who put his arm around her and told Sholto, "You may kiss her too, my lad. Sure, when you're as lucky as me, you can afford to be generous."

Bill looked directly at her, giving her a message she did not want to read, and then kissed her on the lips. Gentle and experienced, she thought, recalling from what was now a year ago. She wondered how his marriage was really working out, but though she wanted to stay on here where she was safe from the danger posed by Jem and her own treacherous needs, Jem—damn him—cut the meeting short with, "Shall we be going, Uncle? There are a few matters I'd like to check with you. And I know my aunt must be anxious to get home and see Miss Eliza. She's been expecting you since noon today," he told Ellen, looking coolly at her.

The colonel sighed. "Poor Eliza. It's true. We did forget my little girl. Shall we be off with Jem now, sweetheart?"

Ellen said nothing. She felt that Jem was secretly laughing at her, wondered how serious he was in his feeling for her. One thing was certain . . . she was aware of his brooding presence no matter *whom* she spoke to. Watchful. Amused? Beneath it she felt the same passion that had come to her. What would her life be like if she had been able to recognize his attraction, and her response, more than a year ago. Would there have been more to their relationship than the physical? Jem Faire was popular. He was honest and capable in handling Fairevale, and it seemed to her now, judging from the gossip she'd heard since they got off the train, that Bill

Sholto was already in trouble with everyone in the county. What was he after?

Maybe Jem was trying to teach him some facts about getting along with one's neighbors. What other reason could there be for the two men to arrive together?

Ellen kissed her grandmother goodbye, and Varina made no response beyond saying maliciously, "I suppose you've heard. Our dashing captain has gone to court for the return of our land. I always told you those white-trash Corrigans were up to no good. We'll end up getting back every stick and stone and blade of grass those Yankees stole from us."

Sholto remarked pleasantly, "Maybe not, my love. But I'll push them so far they'll pay me what it's worth. And I could use the money."

Ellen noticed Jem had been taken by surprise. "You *are* going to sell the land to them?"

Sholto grinned. "When they've sweated enough. Every drop of sweat will be worth a few dollars more. And we can use it, can't we, Miss Varina?"

"Indeed, we can."

Jem said, "While you're waiting for them to sweat it out, you may get your head blown off." He left the room before the colonel and Ellen.

As they followed, Ellen heard Varina remark to Sholto, "That halfbreed really doesn't know how to behave in company. Imagine such vulgar talk . . . blowing off heads."

"And such a nice head, wouldn't you say, love?"

"That's as may be."

On the east porch they met a breathless Maggilee rushing in. "I left in good time," she assured them, presenting her cheek for the colonel's kiss. "But some boy was out shooting birds or something and scared poor

Pansy near to death." Fresh from the good-natured embrace of her rather ancient son-in-law, she moved to hug her daughter, who passively accepted the embrace.

"You left for the Springs so suddenly, honey," Maggilee went on, obviously trying to make up for her late arrival. "Shelley Ann missed you. Bill swears she can pronounce your name . . ."

She wants it all, Ellen thought as Maggilee bubbled on nervously . . . She wants my love and Bill's love and the baby and her shop, *and* on top of it all she still wants to be the belle of the ball forever . . . Well, that's mama . . .

Jem cut into Maggilee's chatter. "Who was the boy, Mrs. Sholto? Did you see him?"

"What boy?" Bill Sholto had come out to take her in his arms and kiss her soundly.

"What's this, sweetheart? Someone *shot* at you?"

"Good heavens, no! You've seen how boys are this time of year. Hardly a rabbit or a squirrel is safe. Much less anything that flies. Anyway, he ran away. I never actually saw him."

Jem, who had been tying his pony to the back of the buckboard, started to say something but broke off.

"Where was this, sweetheart?" Bill persisted. "Anywhere near the Corrigan house?"

"No. Around the Ferry turn-off."

Bill drew her to him again. "Darling, you might have been killed. You've got to be more careful . . ."

* * *

On the road home to Fairevale the colonel asked Jem, "Would the Corrigans go that far?"

"They wouldn't intend to. They never do. They had to fight with me when I got here. Testing me. They're testing Sholto now. Want to put a scare into him."

"I don't like it," the colonel said firmly. "Neither one of them's acting like neighbors—Sholto or the Corrigans. No sense to it. And Sholto talking about holding them up for money."

"He's sure not all he appears," Jem said cryptically—at least as far as the colonel was concerned.

Ellen said, without looking at him, "Who is?"

Confusing the colonel further, though, Jem answered, "Me, for one. I warn before I strike."

"Like a rattlesnake."

Which shocked the colonel, who was even more startled to hear Jem's quick, uncharacteristic laugh.

"Ellie-honey! That's not nice. You tell Jem you don't mean it."

"She's right, uncle," Jem cut in before Ellen could answer. "I've known a few rattlers. At least they're honest. They mind their own business and they do strike where and when they've warned you."

Ellen knew Jem's words were more true than malicious. Bill had courted her while he was getting her mother pregnant . . . Not that Maggilee was exactly an innocent victim . . . And as for Jem . . . well, maybe in his fashion he *had* warned her before he struck that night . . .

Miss Eliza was genuinely glad to see them and help Ellen unpack while the colonel and his nephew went out to inspect the new pasturage bought from their Ironwood neighbors. The spinster still mostly wore her black, but since her father's wedding she had adopted flashes of color—white, gray or mauve—to relieve her funereal wardrobe. Ellen had brought her a black moire bonnet with a white silk lining that did wonders to liven her appearance, and Eliza tried it on delightedly, tilting her head this way and that to find her most becoming profile.

She actually laughed suddenly, and the unusual sound and new expression improved her looks, gave her something of the personality, Ellen thought, that she must have had before her love, Beau Gaynor, found his red-haired "white-trash wife."

"Honey, you'll never guess who visited here several times while you and Pa were at the Springs."

"Persis Warrender?"

Eliza's head remained tilted briefly, then moved again. "Yes . . . and with the judge. They came to dinner every Sunday. I arranged the menus, I'm much better at it now . . . I've watched you, Ellen, you know. It's given me so much more confidence, seeing how you've managed."

Ellen took her hand. "This was your house before I ever came. You must be hostess every night you choose . . . So the Warrenders visited every week? You know, dear, Judge Warrender doesn't talk very much to anyone. I doubt if he came every Sunday just so his daughter could have Jem's company. There are other ways. Socials and dances . . . Eliza, I think Judge Warrender comes to see *you*."

Which brought a blush, a protest, and then a considered, "Well . . . he is splendidly preserved for his age, and as you say he does like so few people . . ."

"He likes quiet people, not chatterboxes like me and most of Tudor County."

"W-well—" But she was clearly pleased. She removed the bonnet and examined her tight, buttoned basque and bunchy skirt. "Ellie-honey, this isn't my best style, is it? Should it be so stiff? And there's something wrong with my shoes, too, isn't there?"

"It's too bad you can't show your ankles. They're so nice. Here . . . just slip into these shoes. They'll be too long for you, your feet are so nice and tiny. But try them anyway."

The compliment was even more persuasive then the suggestion. Eliza unbuttoned her shoes with shaky fingers. Ellen's low brown leather shoes had heels higher than the practical buttoned shoes worn by most country women, and Eliza teetered helplessly before she could stand up without help. But she was delighted with them.

"Can I get some in Gaynorville like these? Elliehoney, the judge is sure to be here Sunday for dinner after church, and if I could wear these—"

Ellen took her hand. "Come along to my wardrobe. "I've a pair of black silk pumps that pinch my toes. They might be easier for you to wear than these. We could pad them if they aren't. Let's try."

It turned out to be one of the happiest afternoons of Miss Eliza's life. Not only did the silk pumps with their pointed toes fit her but there was a deep purple silk afternoon dress of Ellen's that looked splendid on her and needed only a wide hem to be altogether perfect.

"And it's still a proper mourning color," she assured herself.

"Very proper. Will you wear it Sunday?"

"I surely will. And I'll wear the shoes every day until Sunday. Reckon that'll get me used to them."

She was as good as her word, wore the shoes all afternoon and even to supper that night. She turned her ankles occasionally but only gave Ellen a smile and, more surprising, a shy wink.

During the family supper occasional flashes of thunder and lightning made the indoors more cozy. The colonel ruled the conversation as usual, but Ellen had never been more relieved. Miss Eliza, wrapped in dreams of her new shoes . . . and more . . . left the table early to go and hem the skirt of the dark purple dress Ellen had pinned up.

Jem ate silently after asking once if they had enjoyed the Springs. He would look up at Ellen now and then, those direct looks which, much to her annoyance, made her heart race.

The colonel remarked, "Things will be different with us back home. Funny thing, Ellie, it was all your idea to stay there. Never saw anybody so insistent. But I don't think you know what you really wanted, sweetheart."

"Really, dear? Why?"

"Sure now, you think I don't know my own bride? And you so nervous you could fly during all those days and nights!" He addressed his nephew jokingly. "She was anxious to get home and didn't know it. That she was. She loves this rambling old place. And her trying to make me think she wanted to stay with those Big Bugs at the Springs! Her affections are right here at Fairevale, aren't they, m' darlin'?"

Ellen felt the stillness between Jem and herself. She attempted to break it by a light attempt at a brogue.

"Get along with you, man! It's askin' for compliments you are."

The colonel laughed, in great spirits. Such good spirits that he didn't need his usual stimulus of the whiskey decanter. Early in the evening, he put his arm around his wife and said, "Sweetheart, I'm feeling like a pup. A frolicsome one at that. Let's off to bed."

Jem dropped a load of firewood onto the hearth of the south parlor, and Ellen was startled enough to look up at him as they passed. She read his feeling for her in his eyes, and it made her long to touch him. What she felt for his uncle was just nothing like the ache she felt for Jem Faire. This silent admission to herself as she said "good night" to him—with its damnable attendant guilt—had the immediate effect of making her especially kind to the colonel that night.

* * *

She kept out of Jem's way for the next few days. She drove in to Gaynorville with Miss Eliza. She greeted her mother in the easy, familiar way she had adopted since the night she learned the truth about her pregnancy.

"Miss Eliza has decided she wants an entire wardrobe," Ellen explained, adding as an aside to Eliza, "though I don't see why, the way you are being pursued by your friends practically every night. Maggilee, we're hardly ever alone nowadays, thanks to Miss Eliza's popularity."

"Hardly *pursued*, Ellen. What a thing to say."

Maggilee let it pass and waved to Dora Johnson for the pattern books as she pointed out the elegant evening gowns on the two wax figures.

Ellen had acknowledged to herself that her purposes in helping Miss Eliza were not all selfless. She wanted, needed, to keep busy so that she might be less inclined to think of Jem or what had happened between them. And so she should have been enormously relieved when they reached Fairevale and saw Jem with a pair of varicolored serapes on one shoulder and what looked like all his wardrobe on the other.

"Moving out," he said, amid Miss Eliza's exclamations. He seemed pleased at Ellen's stupefied expression. As Miss Eliza went past him, saying she wanted to find out from her father what had happened, Jem held Ellen briefly by one arm. "Sorry to see me go?"

"Your blankets are falling off," she said as the serapes slowly slipped down to cover his hand on her arm. Then she managed a direct, "It's much for the best."

"You'll be seeing me," he promised softly, and Ellen felt a shiver go through her.

In the house, the colonel was disturbed at the loss of part of his family . . . "Why, that boy is like a son to me—"

"But, Papa, what reason did he give?"

Eliza's questions surprised Ellen. Surely Eliza's dislike of Jem in the household was well known.

The colonel reached for his whiskey decanter, hesitated, and felt for his pipe instead. "Some damned thing —pardon me, ladies—about wanting to entertain his own guests. Females, of course. Probably those tenant girls from below the Finch fields. Black and white, young or old. He doesn't seem to have any particular preference, from what he said."

"Did he actually say he wanted to—to do that?" Ellen asked, and then thought, Why not? Jem was human. Very human . . . All the same, the idea upset her. This was more like Bill Sholto. Somehow she didn't think Jem was the sort to . . .

The colonel put in, explaining it to himself as well as to the ladies, "I suppose I shouldn't be surprised. He's young. He's a male. Sweetheart, we have our needs. We're not so pure as you ladies."

Ellen felt her own hypocrisy too keenly to say more, but Eliza talked about it to her for the next hour while Ellen was busy arranging menus with the cook.

"Ellie, I really don't see why he can't eat with us. Heavens and earth! Do you think he expects to marry Persis Warrender? Their cook isn't very good, the judge tells me. Besides . . ."

Ellen examined the week's meals with intense dedication before she raised her eyes and said, "Wouldn't it be funny, Eliza, if you married Judge Warrender and Jem became your son-in-law?"

Eliza turned rapidly on her new high heels, pointing out the achievement to Ellen and adding with a little laugh, "Ellie, you read too many romances . . . They do look lovely, don't they?"

"They certainly do. And your new hair style is so becoming."

"It's too late now to walk around outside, but tomorrow I'm going to take the river path to the bridge and back, just for practice with these shoes."

"Make it late in the morning," Ellen suggested. "That's when a certain judicial gentleman is riding across the bridge to visit Ironwood up-river. I heard Persis tell the colonel."

"I didn't know a thing about it. Besides, I never paid any mind to it."

Ellen hugged her and sent her off, carefully maneuvering her way up the staircase without once turning her ankle.

The usual cold supper that night was reasonably pleasant and wholly uneventful, thanks to the absence of Jem. A little like a meal without salt, Ellen thought, but told herself this was the best thing that could happen. For one thing, she persuaded the colonel to talk about the War, which occupied him while she mended stockings and mentally lived with him through the bright and dark days of his campaigns. He managed to lower the contents of the decanter by half but Ellen convinced herself it might have been worse.

The next morning Miss Eliza was out on the river portico testing the result of her remodeling work with Ellen. One of her Sunday-go-to-meeting dresses had been transformed by a lavender and pink sash which trailed to the floor, and in some curious way it now flattered her short, nondescript figure, actually giving it distinction. The shoes, though, made the real difference. They had affected her opinion of herself, and that meant the most important change of all.

The colonel came out shortly after, saying he was on his way to inspect his nephew's bachelor quarters. "He'll appreciate a woman's touch, Ellie-honey. I surely wish you'd go along with me."

"No, dear. Not unless I'm asked. You come back and tell me all about it. Then, one day, we'll all go and see it. Maybe when Persis is here."

They kissed—like father and daughter—and he went off to the little red-brick building that had been the kitchen for Fairevale before the War.

Now that Miss Eliza had other things on her mind, Ellen decided that this was a good time to cut back the dark, dreary magnolia trees which shrouded the house in gloom. With any luck she might make another try at lighting the long parlor without upsetting Eliza's sensibilities. So, in a faded challis gardening dress she went to work. The ground beneath was covered with fallen leaves, but she had brought out a stool and reached up, cutting away recklessly, with one eye on the windowed reflection of the Ooscanoto River and the path ten feet above the shore, where Eliza strolled along with great aplomb, much more interested in the distant bridge than in Fairevale behind her.

Ellen had whacked off a branch when she was startled by a series of shrieks that tore through the quiet air. For a couple of seconds she thought it was a bird somewhere along the wooded shore south of Fairevale, but then she saw that Eliza had disappeared from the path.

Quickly jumping from the stool, Ellen called Ma'm

Doe to get help and ran for the river path. She heard the old woman lumbering as fast as she could to the cookhouse. Praying to find Eliza only shaken up, Ellen kept telling herself, It's all my fault, those cursed shoes—

Eliza had vanished. She must have lost her balance and fallen over the edge of the bank. It was only ten feet down, but the river bank was precipitous during lowwater season and anything might have happened to her. One of the high-heeled silk shoes lay there on its side.

CHAPTER 10

* * *

By THE time Ellen reached the dusty silk shoe and got a good look over the edge of the bank where the bluff had broken away, Colonel Faire and Jem were out of the cookhouse and running along the bank.

Ellen, flat on the ground by this time, spied Eliza floundering in the river a dozen feet below. She tried vainly to reach her, stretching one arm at a time, grateful to see that at least Eliza could move her arms and legs. Apparently, she hadn't struck any of the jutting rocks of the river bank on the way down as she went over the edge into the water, but in early autumn the river was about eight feet deep, enough to panic a heavily dressed woman like Eliza who never swam.

Ellen now started down the steep river bank but heard Jem shout to her, "Stay where you are." At the same time the colonel reached Ellen, grabbed her by her skirt and one arm and held her up against his wildly beating heart. When Ellen was able to turn, still held in his bearhug, she saw that Jem had dropped through the water to the pebble-strewn river bed and swum a few strokes to Eliza, whose many skirts, now watersoaked, had begun to drag her under.

With arms flailing, the woman shrieked again in panic as Jem reached her. Her mouth filled with water and she fought frantically while Jem got his arm around her waist under her breast, boosting her up so that her head was out of the water. It took him only seconds to get her close to shore but she was beyond coherent thought. The muddy green water terrified her and she struggled wildly, fingers tearing at Jem's hands. He got her as far as the river bank.

The colonel and Ellen both knelt over the bank, holding out their arms as Jem lifted up the water-soaked, hysterical woman to within reach of her father. The colonel had a tight grip around her wrists and with Ellen's help was drawing her up when a male voice called out, "Good Lord, Faire! What's happened?"

It was Judge Warrender, who had seen the episode from the Ooscanoto Bridge and hurried along the path toward them. Everybody was too busy to answer him except Eliza. The unfortunate woman, now safe, sputtered in fury as she tried to hide herself from her admirer. "Let me go. You—let me go!"

Jem pushed her up into her father's arms, trying at

the same time to duck his head out of the way of her wildly kicking feet. The judge reached her. She gave one last, furious kick, catching Jem across the temple, and he lost his grip on the rocky outcropping of the bank. The soil, soaked by the recent storm, gave him no purchase and Ellen's groping fingers touched his just as he slipped down, hoping to drop clear into the safety of the water. But he had been pressed too close against the bank and as he fell the jagged rocks and stones imbedded in the earth wall tore at his body and the side of his face.

With Ellen's cry ringing in his ears, Jem sank into the churned and muddy waters. He managed to float with the current a few yards downstream, trying to make the shore. Ellen got to her feet and ran along parallel to his course. His left temple and cheek had been torn open but the water washed away the first spurting blood from a very deep cut above his sodden collar.

Eliza had stumbled, sobbing, into the house with Ma'm Doe, and the two men hurried after Ellen to a side channel of the river, where Jem had dragged himself, face down in the pebbled channel. Anxiously, Ellen started to raise his head.

"Don't touch him," the colonel ordered her with the authority of old army days. Puffing, he explained, "I've seen it in battle. If there's anything broken around the neck here and you move him, you can paralyze a man."

. . . Please God, no, she prayed. It horrified her to see him lying here defenseless, his eyes closed, the blood from the cut on his temple now trailing down over his eyelid and his dark lashes. With a gentle finger she wiped the blood from his eye, but the head wound bled on inexorably. She caressed his hair while his uncle examined him and Judge Warrender leaned over them.

"Swam to this spot, didn't he?" the judge said. "Good

sign. But that bleeding. Ah! Mrs. Faire, quite right."

Ellen had borrowed her husband's handkerchief and applied it to Jem's neck at the point of his jawline. The bright blood soaked the linen held against the cut, but to their intense relief the bleeding began to slow afterward. At the same time the colonel agreed with his old friend, the judge. "He's all right. No broken bones, far as I can see. Ellie, is he coming around?"

"He looks so—" Her broken voice shocked her. She wondered if the two men thought her concern too great, but they were sufficiently old-fashioned so that it seemed perfectly natural to them that ladies, those delicate flowers, should go to pieces emotionally in the presence of flowing blood. She tried again. ". . . looks so pale." Actually Jem didn't look pale at all . . . that dark, weathered skin of his looked almost yellow, dreadfully unlike him . . .

"Bad business over his forehead there," the judge said. "Doesn't bleed much but it's more serious, or I miss my guess." He began to roll up the sleeves of his old-fashioned black riding coat. "As long as no bones seem broken, let's get him somewhere more comfortable."

"He's been sleeping in the cookhouse. That's nearest. I'll get Ma'm Doe's son to bring a stretcher. Some old boards would do."

The judge objected. "Shouldn't he be in the house where it's more comfortable?"

At that point, much to everyone's relief, Jem opened his right eye, winced, and muttered something.

"Yes, boy. What is it?" the judge asked as the colonel climbed up the river path waving to the two black workers in the west cornfields.

Jem opened the other eye. He even grinned faintly. "Cookhouse . . . more pri—"

"What's he saying?" the judge asked.

Ellen smiled. "I think he means—more privacy."

"What the devil does he want privacy for?" The judge stopped, thought and actually blushed. "I beg pardon, I'm sure." With a jovial camaraderie that set oddly on his sober, bearded face, he added, "We won't say anything about that to my Persis. I was a young fellow once myself, you know."

Ellen hardly heard him. She was studying every feature of Jem's face, thinking, He might have died, I might have lost him, and then, recovering her self-awareness, reminded herself that Jem Faire's life certainly didn't belong to her. If there was anyone who had his affections in future it was Miss Persis Warrender.

"Where does it hurt most?" she asked him.

Jem's fingers curved, beckoning her close. She leaned over his mouth, wondering if he was feeling worse. His whisper was low, only half-articulated, but she understood:

"Where only you could help me."

She backed off, relieved and distinctly not shocked. And when the judge asked her what Jem had said, she could only assure him, "He'll live. I'm sure of that . . ."

"Good. Sounds encouraging. Here comes Rowdy. And what is it that those boys are carrying? I do believe it's a door." He added to Ellen, shyly as a boy himself, "I wonder if I'll be needed any longer here, as long as this young man seems to be on the mend, I'd like to pay my respects to Miss Eliza."

Ellen encouraged him, knowing what his interest would mean to Eliza, who must believe by now that he despised the unfortunate, water-soaked victim of high heels and crumbling river banks. While the judge went on his way to the main house, the colonel arrived with the two young field workers. They carried an old wooden door, apparently once painted green. Even the hinges had disappeared, but it served its purpose.

At the sight of his two fellow workers, Jem rose up on his elbows, but fell back with a jar that Ellen felt. The head wound, slight and scarcely bleeding, caused him the most trouble. For a couple of minutes, as he was lifted onto the wooden slats of the door, he lost consciousness.

Ellen glanced uneasily at her husband. "Will he be all right?"

He put his arm around her comfortingly. "Ellie-honey, I saw a hundred worse wounds. Pay no mind ... Come on, Jem. You-all have a pretty girl looking to see those eyes of yours. Open 'em up." Ellen stiffened self-consciously but her husband went on, "If I'm not mistaken, the judge will have that pretty Persis of his over here to cheer you up in no time."

Ellen relaxed, but not with relief. She looked down at Jem. "Shouldn't we send for the doctor?"

"Joshua Kemp is riding into Gaynorville for Dr. Nickels. Not that he's really needed, but he can give Eliza a dose of something to calm her. In fact, a dose of laudanum wouldn't hurt Jem here."

"Not for me," Jem insisted, painfully opening his right eye. His teeth were clenched and though he sweated profusely, his flesh was cold when Ellen touched his forehead.

Jem saw their anxious faces and tried to reassure them. "I've had harder knocks than this on a rough night in Santa Fe."

He raised a hand to the colonel, who was firm but gentle. "That will do, lad. No exertions. You've got a hard head but no need to prove it."

Jem tried to smile but the effort made him groan and

he reached for Ellen's hand. "Ah! That's better. Leave it on my forehead. It helps the pain."

"Good girl," the colonel told his wife. "I'll get Ma'm Doe to bring you cold compresses, or whatever is needed. You don't mind staying with him until old Nickels gets here?"

Ellen caught the look in Jem's good eye and knew that, sick as he was, he had clearly begun to enjoy this little game he was playing with her.

Feeling increasingly guilty, Ellen said, "Not if you think I should stay."

"Oh, I think so," Jem put in, still with that look in his slanting green eyes, which saw so much more than she meant him to see.

To her husband's surprise she snapped, "I wasn't addressing you!"

"Now, now, dear, be charitable. The poor fellow has a head injury. You must make allowances if he says anything that offends you."

She gave up and kept her hand on Jem's head until he got inside the old whitewashed cookhouse and onto the cot in one corner. Though he was obviously in pain, he'd recovered considerably by the time Ellen brought him a dipper of water from the bucket by the door. He put his hand on hers, holding the dipper steady while he drank from it. There was no weakness in that hand.

Ellen let the colonel go on to the big house without her, then bustled around like an efficient housekeeper, insisting that sick people were known to die because of the filth of their surroundings. The one-room cabin had been dusted and swept in a slipshod way, probably by Jem himself when he moved in. One window above his cot looked as if it had been scrubbed and polished. It sparkled in the sunlight. The opposite window, on the right side of the big dark hearth, had a clean circle in the middle where Jem had obviously looked up at the main house.

"Why didn't you wash all of this window?" she wanted to know.

"I like to see, not be seen."

"Well, before I get out of here I'm going to have this place so clean you and your—visitors will have no privacy whatever."

He watched her. It seemed to lift his spirits to joke. Before he'd seemed very serious about their feelings for each other. Now he deliberately tried to make her jealous. "Just as long as the judge doesn't see Miss Persis." And when this didn't ruffle her at all . . . at least outwardly . . . he went on, watching her with a cat-and-mouse intensity. "Maybe you could be chaperone for us."

Busy wiping the window, she assured him she would, "with pleasure."

She thought his head was giving him more trouble when he closed his eyes, but the minute he opened them again she knew he was leading her on to dangerous territory.

"Do you know, I think you're lying,"—she caught her breath as he went on—"does it really give you pleasure to see me sparking Miss Persis?"

"You're a bachelor. Spark anyone you please."

She was relieved—and disappointed—to have to tell him then, "Joshua must have met Dr. Nickels on the road. He's coming now."

Dr. Nickels came along the path at a fast trot, followed breathlessly by the colonel. The doctor ordered Ellen out at once. "Women only get in the way."

Ellen said, "Good luck," to the scowling Jem and went outside while Jem was still insisting that he didn't need a doctor and his "bruises" would heal much faster if no pill-peddler ever touched them.

Ellen asked the colonel how Miss Eliza was.

"Fine. She and Warrender are buried in a discussion of Bullard and Lytton."

"Good heavens! What's a Bullard and Lytton?"

"Some English novel about ancient volcanoes. Old as the hills, but the judge has been reading it aloud in the evenings to Persis and the servants." He laughed. "Not quite that young lady's favorite reading, I'll be bound. Speaking of Persis, we may be seeing considerably more of her right soon. What with Bullard and Lytton being read to her, and now Jem. If I didn't know better, I'd think that nephew of mine deliberately cracked his head to attract Persis. Very romantic to ladies, that sort of injury."

Ellen ignored that last, but she was pleased that anything had brought Eliza and the judge together, even Bulwer-Lytton. She took his arm.

"Dearest, let's go back and sit down somewhere. You've been running all over the grounds."

He wiped his forehead, tacitly admitting she was right. She looked around the open doorway and asked Dr. Nickels, "How is the patient doing?"

The doctor did not turn around. He was examining the cut over Jem's eye.

"What do you say, Doctor?" the colonel asked, and this time the doctor deigned to reply.

"A cracked head, to all intents and purposes. But this nephew of yours seems too tough to let it bother him. The less activity around this cabin the better, though, for the next few days."

CHAPTER 11

***

THE COLONEL had surely been right about Miss Eliza. There was still a flush on her face but the tearful eyes now sparkled with vivacity and her still-wet hair had been swept into an oddly becoming chignon. Two ridiculous but charming curls fell onto her high, narrow forehead. She was bundled into a deep blue wrapper just short enough to reveal a pair of slim ankles peeking out below the wrapper's hem. She leaned forward, her whole face and body alive with enthusiasm as she argued with an equally enthused Judge Warrender.

"But Nydia *is* the heroine of the novel. Didn't Mr. Bulwer-Lytton say the idea came to him when he realized a blind person would be less handicapped in that volcanic dust?"

"All the same, Miss Eliza, I confess I find Ione charming. And you, of course, were in love with that handsome Greek fellow?"

Ellen whispered to the colonel, "Let's not interrupt. I'd be hopelessly lost in that conversation, anyway."

The colonel nodded and took her arm. "Never was bookish. I don't know where Eliza gets it. I swear I don't."

Eliza and Judge Warrender were still deep in conversation when the colonel rode out to examine the newly acquired Ironwood field, and Ellen finished pruning the magnolias. She was about to go inside the house when the afternoon sunlight, glimmering on the windows of Gaynor House across the river, attracted her. She noted movement on the lawn, which spread downward to the river path along the east bank. Bill Sholto had lifted his little daughter high in the air, then kissed her and returned her to Bethulia's waiting arms. Several minutes later he was on the back of old Oglala and riding toward town.

On impulse, and because she did not want to think about Jem Faire, Ellen went in, changed to a walking dress and, with parasol in hand, set off along the path to the Ooscanoto Bridge that had brought near-disaster—and apparent romance—to Miss Eliza.

Anxious to have a visit with Shelley Ann before Bethulia took her inside, Ellen passed Wychfield's riverfront without a thought for those who lived there and was surprised when she heard her name called. She turned to see Gavin McCrae dismount from his thoroughbred Kentucky mare and walk toward her.

Ellen watched him cross the faintly browning lawn and wondered again that this dull young man could have "broken her heart" so long ago.

"Good afternoon, Miss—I mean Mrs. Faire," Gavin greeted her eagerly. "Going to see the baby, I reckon."

"Of course." She whirled the parasol, looked out at him and asked, with her newly acquired art of flirtation, "How is dear Daisy? And how do you like life at Wychfield?"

"A trifle overpowering," he murmured after a look over his shoulder. She was about to ask if that was the answer to both questions when he started along the path with her, obviously intending to confide some secret.

"Miss Ellen, you were always my trusted confidante when I wanted so badly to . . . to make your mother my wife. I haven't forgotten how you urged me on to make my declaration."

Was he really that naïve?

"Well?"

"And although I am extremely attached to my dear Daisy, I can't help being concerned for Miss Maggilee's welfare."

What on earth was this all about? "Is she sick? I haven't heard."

"Nothing like that. But"—he lowered his voice, although no one more than a yard away could have heard him—"it's my father-in-law . . . Major Wychfield had a dinner guest last night. A banker named Gimmerton. The major is on the board of Mr. Gimmerton's bank."

Suddenly interested, Ellen took a deep breath. "Norfolk and Peninsula Bank."

He was surprised. "Did you know anything about this offer to buy the Gaynor Salon? Does she really want to sell?"

"It's the last thing in the world Maggilee would sell. I suspect if it came to a choice, she'd sell her child before she'd sell Gaynor's."

"I knew it. They were damned secretive"—he was so upset he didn't even apologize for the "violence" of his language—"but the bank will only act as go-between. The way I understand it, they will receive a percentage if they find a buyer. But who will he buy from?"

It seemed clear to Ellen. "The person who is paying up her loans. Not Maggilee, she keeps putting the profits back into the shop."

"Does she know anything about this, do you think?"

"I doubt it, but I have a very good idea who is doing this." Ellen astonished herself by her own anger. Why should she care? Her mother had hurt her and Eliza and who knew how many other women. She might even be said to have hurt her husband, and Shelley Ann, by neglecting them. But she *had* put her heart into Gaynor's Salon ... she deserved to keep that, at any rate. Whoever was back of this underhanded attempt was despicable. Difficult as it was to prove, Ellen strongly suspected Bill Sholto ... Apparently he'd go to such extreme lengths to make sure of the full-time wife and mother they all knew he wanted.

She sighed. "I'll have to warn her"—she looked at Gavin McCrae—"though I confess I don't particularly want to, especially to let her know who ... But she's got to know, in case it happens again."

"Then you do know who's behind it. But, Ellen, who would hate her that much?"

She thought that over. "Maybe it's not hate. Maybe it's somebody who loves her that much."

She started away, along the path to Gaynor House, twirling her parasol, trying to put a trivial look on the whole matter. She had come to trust few people in her life, and even the sober-faced, honorable Gavin was not an exception to that. He'd be easily swayed by his strong wife and even stronger father-in-law. After all, he'd betrayed her once . . .

Gavin showed half-hearted signs of following her, then stopped and called to her instead, "You will do what you said? Warn her?"

Ellen dismissed him with contempt, knowing he was too afraid to tell Maggilee himself, and wishing she didn't have to. Maybe there was some other way to let her know. A hint. A suggestion that Maggilee should investigate and find out the truth from Major Wychfield or Tom Gimmerton of the Norfolk bank. But this was cowardly, too, begging the issue. It had to be faced.

When she reached Gaynor House her grandmother was out on the river porch tatting with some difficulty, stopping after a few movements of the shuttles to massage the fingers of one hand with those of the other. Of all things, Shelley Ann's cradle was beside her with the baby gabbling to herself and playing with her toes while Varina reached out once in a while to rock the cradle.

"Why, Gran! You actually like the baby, don't you?" Ellen challenged her and kissed her cheek.

"Don't sneak up on a body like that!" was Varina's typical response. "As children go, she's a trifle above the ordinary." And to make sure her usual jab went home, she said, "You were dreadfully ordinary, my dear. If memory serves me, you didn't cry as much as this one does, but you certainly didn't do much else either."

Ellen pretended to ignore the remark. "When will Maggilee be home? Did Bill go after her?"

There was something in the way Varina's cold, blue-gray eyes avoided hers as she casually asked, "Where else would he go in town?"

She knows, Ellen thought. She probably put him up

to it . . . She then pursued a subject that Varina wanted to change. "Does he have many friends here? He almost got Maggilee shot the other day by one of the *friends* he is making."

"If you mean those wretched Corrigans, he's only teasing them so they'll raise their offer on the creek bottomlands."

"Why does he need so much money now?"

Varina said sharply, "For the Gaynor Plantation. Anyone but an idiot would see that. He wants to make it what it was before the War. For little Shelley Ann. It certainly makes him a better parent than the mother with her precious store."

"Who do you think supported us for twenty years, Grandmother? Mother and her store."

"She'd never have had that store if she hadn't used—" Varina sniffed, recovered herself and rocked the cradle too hard. The baby started to cry.

Ellen had not thought the old familiar comments would still have such power to wound . . . "Well, it seems that the baby does cry more than I did, even if she is prettier." But she was wondering what Varina meant by that accusation hastily broken off . . . "It was borrowed money Maggilee used to start the store, wasn't it?"

Before Varina could answer they heard footsteps in the hall, and Maggilee and Bill came out to greet their visitor, Bill with his arm around his wife's slim waist, drawing her closer to him. He was his handsome self, all confident, while Maggilee looked tired and curiously upset at the sight of Ellen . . . No doubt she thinks I'm trying to steal her husband, Ellen thought with irony.

The first amenities at least gave Ellen a breathing spell. There was a great deal of attention paid to Shelley, Bill lifting his daughter as he had earlier in the day, playful and adoring. "Look at her laugh. You're just the prettiest girl in the County. You surely are. Ever see such a smile, Ellen?"

Ellen said she never had. She was surprised to find she felt pain at this moment, seeing in the child her father's too-winning manner, the child who might have been her own—

Ceci Hone brought out the tea set but Ellen, dreading what she had to tell her mother, wanted to get it over and done. When Maggilee said, "If you will excuse me, I'll go and change," Ellen asked, "May I go with you?" With an effort she smiled at Sholto. "Woman talk, you know."

Everyone supposed by this that she was about to confide some peccadillo of her husband's, so Sholto didn't seem the least suspicious. Varina, however, frowned and looked after the two women as they left the porch.

The house looked much the same. Edward Hone welcomed Ellen in his quiet way, and yet Ellen felt herself a stranger here. Had the break been so irreconcilable that there could never be a return to the time before the great lover Captain Sholto came, literally, riding out of the west and into their lives? Ellen smiled silently at her own pose. Actually the three Gaynor women had always been at odds. In truth, never was there the closeness she'd been wistfully mourning.

At the door of Maggilee and Bill's room, a newly refurnished large room facing the estate drive, Maggilee remarked with surprising abruptness, "I can't imagine what you want to say to me in private. Anything you have to say can be heard by my husband, you know."

Ellen replied in kind. "Anything? I don't think so. You be the judge."

Maggilee went into the big room, obviously furnished according to Bill's tastes. She left the door open but began changing her dress without inviting her daughter to come any further. Ellen stepped into the room and closed the door.

"Secrets?" Maggilee asked too brightly. "You may have had secrets but this will be the first time you've shared them with me. After what you've done, it's a little late for this daughterly concern."

"After what *I've* done?" Maggilee couldn't know about the night Jem made love to her . . . Besides, what could that have to do with her?

Maggilee waved to her impatiently. "Do go on. I hate cat-and-mouse games. You've succeeded in your little plan, thanks to your fine husband, no doubt, and now you want to make me suffer a little. Well, Ellie, I'm not about to beg you. I never begged the others." She laughed. "I gave the orders once. I like to remember that. I suppose I did what you're about to do now. Like mother, like daughter . . . blackmail."

Completely bewildered, Ellen was of half a mind to give up and go home, but she'd gone this far in her warning, she might as well finish . . . "I happen to know your shop is in danger. It may be sold out from under you—"

Maggilee continued to confuse her by saying calmly, "First the threat, then the offer, I presume. What's the price I'm to pay? Leave Bill?"

"How do I know what price you pay?" Ellen said angrily. "Ask the Norfolk and Peninsula Bank. Ask your precious husband."

Maggilee stared at her. Finally, in a tight, flat voice, she said, "Do I understand you are accusing Bill of this?"

"But—who else—what else did you think I meant?"

"You, my sainted, sweet firstborn! My husband used all his money on the land here. You didn't know that, did you, when you decided to accuse him of what you've done? You're the only one with access to that kind of money. You did this unspeakable thing to get some kind of revenge on me because Bill loves me. Yes, difficult as it may be for you to believe, he really does. I've known for days that you were doing this—"

"What!"

"But that wasn't bad enough . . . Now you try to turn me against him by this shabby lie. Well, you've failed, so go, darlin' daughter, and do your *damnedest.*"

Ellen's shaking hand found the doorknob. She had a terrible fear she would cry in front of this fury. She didn't dare say a word. She remembered another time when she saw the gulf between her mother and herself, a time when she'd truly hated Maggilee. She didn't hate her now . . . The truth hurt, and she could understand that. But could either of them ever forget what had been said here today?

Ellen straightened up, left the room and went down the stairs to the front door, avoiding the porch where the others were. She heard the door of Maggilee's room slam hard behind her.

As Hone opened the front door for her, he said, "Miss Ellen, your mother is quick. But you mustn't mind. I'm sure she will apologize next time you come."

Ellen looked back through the house. "No. I don't think so. I've probably seen this house for the last time. Too bad. I used to love it very much."

She went out onto the drive and started walking toward the Ooscanoto Bridge road.

CHAPTER 12

***

AT THE colonel's suggestion, Judge Warrender, seconded too quickly by Ellen, sent Joshua Kempt to bring his lovely daughter over to Fairevale for an early autumn supper and to "cheer up that poor young devil with his cracked skull."

Though she didn't contradict anyone about Jem's condition, Ellen had reason to suspect that things weren't quite so grim as Jem painted them. The wound on his left temple was certainly real. The cut on his neck had bled freely. But he was a tough, healthy man and no one knew better than Ellen how strong he was.

That afternoon she had found new signs of it when she was returning to Fairevale, still depressed over what appeared to be the end of her always precarious relationship with her mother. Crossing through the Wychfield grass from the main road to the river path, Ellen looked across the river toward Fairevale. The sun was setting behind the Fairevale woods. And behind the whitewashed brick cookhouse, which interested her more.

"That devil!" she thought, seeing Jem outside the cookhouse, looking more Indian than Irish with the white bandage around his black hair. He leaned on one of the pasture fences under a crepe-myrtle tree. He was staring moodily at the river and absently tearing up leaves he had picked off the tree. Watching him, she had a flash of memory . . . his arms imprisoning her on the bed, his strong thighs, his body giving her an excruciating pleasure she'd never known was even possible. In some ways the experience was a disaster . . . From that night on she knew too well what had been missing in her life. It was far worse than the loss of Bill Sholto in that respect.

Feeling her body come alive with the heat of desire, Ellen walked on, forcing herself not to look at him across the bright sunset waters. But she was not able to avoid wondering what he was thinking about so intently.

She'd gone on home to Fairevale, to have her husband suggest, "Sweetheart, we've been thinking of some way to cheer up poor old Jem. I thought if we sent for Miss Persis, she might at least eat her supper with him."

"Properly chaperoned, you understand," Judge Warrender put in.

The colonel, looking guilty, gave his wife a kiss and a hug. "With poor Eliza not up to snuff, my dear, do you mind very much playing chaperone?"

She did and, of course, she didn't.

He went on in his most persuasive way. "Sweetheart, the poor fellow needs company. His spirits are down. Not that he'd admit it, but I saw him hobbling around outside a few minutes ago. Made him go back to that cot of his. He refuses to come back to the house, so we'll have to go to his. He's proud, is all."

"But couldn't one of the servants be there? Persis' maid, for instance?"

"She will be, I expect, but the judge, here, and I want to discuss this business of the Corrigan boys and Captain Sholto. Eliza tells me she will be retiring early, so we can have our talk."

"And you don't need me," Ellen finished for him. "Well, I'll go down there when Persis arrives." . . . Jem wasn't the only one who felt "down."

When the colonel went upstairs with her to change for their late country supper she fussed over him, teasing and tickling, helping him out of his old homespun shirt, admiring his thick, still-powerful shoulders. He understood, of course, that she was asking him to make love to her. With his newly laundered white shirt half buttoned he stopped, embarrassed, and looked into her face. He had been drinking with the judge all afternoon but he was reasonably sober when he reminded her, "Ellie-honey, we've got guests in the house. It wouldn't be proper."

She moved away from him, her face briefly flaming at his refusal. It was not the first time. She said cooly, "I'd forgotten. You're right. I'll go and play the chaperone."

As they continued to change, she asked him, openly curious, "Aren't you ever jealous?"

He playfully brushed her nose with his coat sleeve. "Not of you, though I dare say I might feel different if I'd been foolish enough to marry—say—Miss Maggilee. No offense meant, honey."

You couldn't offend me on that subject tonight, Ellen assured him silently, though she could almost pity Maggilee, knowing her mother faced a terrible awakening to her husband's schemes.

When they were leaving the room together, he seemed to feel a little further explanation was necessary. "Sweetheart, I guess I surprise . . . or disappoint . . . you sometimes. Not being a prancing stallion, exactly. Maybe it's something to do with how I feel about you. In some ways you'll always be that rather lost little girl I took to my heart years ago. But you're a woman now, too, I know that . . ."

"I know, dear."

They went down, arm in arm, Ellen reflecting as she had time and again before how fortunate she was to be married to a man who *wasn't* a prancing stallion . . . and shut out the vision of Jem Faire that had suddenly intruded itself.

The colonel patted her arm. "You keep Jem talking down there, or encourage him to rest. I don't want him listening in on the judge and me until we settle what's to be done."

"About what?"

"How much the Corrigans should pay for that Gaynor bottomland. I'd like to persuade them to make the offer. They're pretty hot-tempered and Sholto's refusal to take their first offer didn't help matters. But Jem's mighty friendly with the Corrigans. I'd as soon he didn't interfere."

Ellen told him, "I'm sure Persis is attractive enough to hold Jem there if it isn't too long. She's a respectable young lady, and he's a rather impatient person, wouldn't you say?"

He lowered his voice. "If we're lucky, Sam Corrigan

himself will ride over. He's a man of peace, even if his sons are a mite lively."

Ellen decided to make *certain* she left neither herself nor Jem open to temptation. Downstairs she met Eliza, who had changed for supper and was looking pleasantly animated as she waited for Judge Warrender to join her.

"Eliza, when Persis arrives we're going to bring a kind of picnic supper to Jem. Rowdon and the judge want to talk over some business while we're gone. Won't you come with us?"

Eliza waved away the invitation, explaining with just a trace of smugness, "But you see, that's just it. I'll be the only lady at the table here. The men do have to eat, after all."

"Eliza, you are a wicked coquette!"

"I *hope* so."

When Persis arrived, she quickly said that she thought the idea of having a picnic supper with Jem was "just the most fun! Amabel Corrigan is so jealous, Ellen, you-all can't believe how *nasty* she's been to me. Wanted Jem herself, like as not. As if he ever looked at those horrid yellow curls!"

While Ellen combed and rearranged the girl's lovely black hair, which had become slightly disheveled during the ride to Fairevale, Persis told her, "The very idea of my marrying Jem didn't pleasure Papa the least little bit, at first. But now he speaks right well of Jem."

"What brought him around?"

"Oh, that's the best part! That dear Colonel Faire of yours told him in strictest secrecy—you mustn't tell a soul, honey—that he's leaving half the Fairevale acreage to Jem and Jem is to keep managing the other half of the estate if he chooses, though the profits go to you and Miss Eliza. You are to pay him a percentage. Or something. Of course"—Persis gave it some thought—"if Miss Eliza should die before the colonel, I reckon Jem would get her quarter as well."

"Let's hope Miss Eliza doesn't die then. Think of all the problems you would inherit! I mean, if you marry Jem."

Persis gave her a look. "I'm sure I wish her well, but really, at her age, what more can she expect out of life? It isn't as if any man ever looked at her."

"From all I hear, my father did before he met Maggilee. Tell me something, Persis. Would you marry Jem if he were poor?"

"I surely would! I don't even mind him having Indian blood." With her hand on the comb she stopped Ellen's work and confided in a low tone, "You can't imagine, Ellie, how it feels when he touches you, lifts you up or down. Once I looked at him with my eyes closed. Well—I didn't look, but I stood there—" She demonstrated. "And I was *very* pitiful. I said something flew into my eye. He didn't bother to get it out. He kissed me. I thought I'd die. He just pressed my mouth—oh, God, Ellie . . . it was—"

"I can imagine," Ellen said, feeling as if she were a hundred and five. She knew very well how those kisses felt.

By a few quick twists she got Persis' hair in order and then went down with her to get the picnic supper in its napkin-lined basket. Along with Persis' apparently disinterested maid Delia, the two young women then walked down to the cookhouse with their mouth-watering basket of food. As Ellen had expected, Jem was very much up and about, throwing an impressive armful of wood beside the huge hearth that had once prepared meals for more than a dozen people in the main house. But contrary to his uncle's prediction, Jem didn't look overjoyed at the sight of the three females.

"Whose idea was this?" Jem asked Ellen while the other two were sorting out fresh-baked bread, delicious slices of ham, fried chicken, a bowl of rapidly cooling snap-beans and a bowl of buttered corn carefully scraped off the cobs.

"Not mine," she said in a tone to match his. Actually she rather sympathized with his mood . . . It wasn't likely that he felt like listening to all their chatter tonight, but on the other hand Persis and Delia *were* doing their best to make him more comfortable.

He managed to keep his voice low as he demanded, "What are they supposed to be? Your chaperones? I wanted to see you. I thought you'd be coming down here. I'm not exactly in the mood to seduce you, if that's what you're afraid of."

"On the contrary, I am the chaperone. The judge and your uncle felt it wasn't proper for Persis to share your dinner alone."

"They're both quite safe, I give you my word."

Persis worried Ellen by overhearing this. "Oh, I know that, Jem. It's just Papa who's such an old silly. Come and eat before it gets cold."

In his mood Jem didn't look as if he'd be very good company. They all drew up stools, a chair, and in Jem's case a heavy log placed on end, and sampled the picnic fare. Nobody but Jem drank the coffee he had boiled in a pot over the low-burning fire in the big fireplace, and between them, Persis and Ellen handled most of the conversation.

Persis tried sympathy with Jem, offered to re-bandage his head wound, asked several times to hear the particulars of his "heroic rescue" of Miss Eliza, but even her friendly overtures came to an end when her maid murmured, "He ain't hearin' you, ma'm."

Entering the breach, Ellen explained, "We've all had a long day. Maybe we'd better not stay too long. I know I, for one, feel exhausted, and I didn't do a thing but run up and down yelling for help."

"If there's anything I can't stand, it's false modesty," Jem announced out of nowhere, handing back the bowl of snap-beans without taking any.

Ellen and Persis looked at each other, then Persis set the snap-beans down near the edge of the table and, agreeing with Ellen, said, "Reckon we had better get on our way, everybody being in such a bad mood and all."

She got up then, and what remained of the snap-beans in the bowl, including their buttery juice, dropped upside down in the lap of her tucked-muslin dress. She screamed, burst into tears and began to scrub madly with the napkin, while Ellen and the maid told her not to touch the stain. Jem went to get a towel, soaked it in water and offered it, but Ellen waved him away.

"Persis, don't worry. Ma'm Doe will know how to remove the stains." She put her arm around the girl, trying to lead her out of the cookhouse.

"It's my Sunday dress," Persis wailed. "Papa won't let me have a new one made for—for ages. Delia, hold something in front of me. I don't want anybody to see."

"I should clean up, ma'm. It's all over the floor and Mister Jem's rug."

Jem waved her off. "Never mind. It's nothing ... And thanks for the picnic, Miss Persis. It was kind of you ... very kind." He dropped the towel and went to the door after the women. As they were leaving, he told Ellen so all could hear, "I'll have it cleaned up by the time you come back for the basket, Ellen."

Ellen started. She had not given a thought to the picnic basket, but Persis interrupted with understandable petulance, "Oh, do what he wants. He's been horrid tonight."

Ellen shrugged and without giving him any more attention went up to the house with the two girls.

Made much over by her father and the colonel, Persis was soon her own pleasant self again, her pretty dress cleaned and pressed while she enjoyed all the attention formerly lavished on Miss Eliza.

Ellen decided not to wait until after dark to return to Jem's cabin for the basket, and to help him clean up. The sooner the better. She slipped on her oldest, faded challis work dress, buttoned up the tight basque, and with her hair wrapped in a head-rag borrowed from the cook's helper, she went down to the cookhouse. She was armed with mops and rags and in her opinion, as well as that of the shocked gentlemen present, she couldn't have looked less appetizing.

As it happened, they were mistaken. Jem stared at her, looked her up and down, and then began to laugh. "Tell me one thing," he said.

"One thing." She passed him going into the cookhouse.

He followed her. "Is this scrubwoman look for my benefit?"

"No. It's for scrubbing." She took up the rug, started to carry it outside, but he took it away from her.

"If you examine it, you'll find it's clean. Just needs drying. Leave it on the hearth."

She began to put things into the basket. At least he hadn't washed up the remains of the abortive picnic. This gave her something to do, although his presence behind her made her nervous. He poked at the fire and set the poker back with a crash that made her turn around.

"I meant it," he said with an angry abruptness that was as startling as the noise he made with the poker.

"Meant what?"

He raised his hand to the head wound, lowered his hand quickly. "You act as if I was going to leap onto you any minute."

She bundled dishes, napkins and half-eaten food into the basket. Her hands shook. "I don't act or think anything. I just want to finish and go."

He moved toward the table, stretched out his arm, blocking her way, took the basket and set it down.

"Do you really want to go? Or are you just plain afraid of me?"

She tried to make a joke of it. "Both."

"All right! I only want to get rid of that damn head-rag."

She raised her hands but he brushed them aside. He pulled off the brightly colored cloth and her pale hair tumbled down around her face and shoulders. She felt his touch, the hint of leashed violence as his fingers combed through her hair from her scalp to the ends.

"Why? *Why?*"

His question baffled her. She wanted him to keep on caressing her hair. His effect on her was overwhelming, as always. She thought of her husband up at the house, trusting her. She tried to get the picnic basket between them but he wouldn't let her touch it.

"Why what?" Her breath was coming now in short gasps.

"Why do you have to belong to the one man in the world who—" His fingers stopped their movement close to her throat. His thumbs pushed aside the high, forbidding neckline of the old challis dress until they pressed into her warm flesh. She wanted to say, I don't belong to him or to anyone. Her lips formed the beginning of the protest. Maybe he understood without the words being spoken out loud. It didn't matter. It was too late.

He began to unbutton her bodice. She put her hands up again, pulling at his wrists, but she knew from previous experience that she was no match for him. And worse, she also knew she didn't want to be. Her bodice was open now, the camisole torn so that one breast was bare.

He lifted her as if she were a rag doll, with her fingers imprisoned in one of his powerful hands. She was on his cot. Moments later she felt his body press hard on hers, and she gave herself up to the terrifying ecstasy that had haunted her dreams for so many nights.

This time there was a difference. His penetration was strong and hard-driven, like himself. But the violent anger was gone. Even while she joined him in that unbelievable, ecstatic climax, she sensed the difference in his lovemaking. When they finally lay calm on the ancient cot, his hand on her bare breast threatening to rouse himself and her again, she touched the bandage around his head, then his coarse, strong hair. She whispered, "I think I loved you that first time you kissed me. But I didn't know . . ."

His lips brushed hers. "You were so damn afraid. I wanted to break you out of that shell. If I'd handled you better then—"

"If I'd been ready for you . . ."

The present was impinging again. She couldn't escape it and she suspected he couldn't either. In his fashion, he loved Rowdon Faire as much as she did. She moved in his arms. His hand had covered her breast once more as she started to move away. Her fingers touched his hand.

"I can't be alone with you again. You know that."

His fingers closed around one breast as if to hold it ... her ... prisoner. When she winced, he stirred and let her go. Watching her, he said with a bleak smile, "Now you know why I left the house to live here."

She looked down at him. "To get away from me. My love, I know that."

"To get away from the temptation of you. But it wasn't far enough, was it?"

Outside in the quiet Virginia night it was dark. Ellen hurriedly buttoned her dress. He was on his feet now, touching the padded bandage on his neck. A faint rim of blood had seeped through. Ellen saw it. "Oh, Jem, you're bleeding—"

He laughed easily. "Just too much exertion," but she couldn't feel easy. She knew she couldn't trust herself to see him alone again, and when he stopped laughing and just looked at her, she went into his arms once more and kissed him with all the passion she'd kept in for too many years. His own kiss was bruising, as hard as his body, but there was also a surprising gentleness in him afterward.

"I'll have to leave. It's the only way," he told her as he held her hands in his. She had known it from the moment she'd returned to the cookhouse tonight. She couldn't bring herself to agree, but without speaking she raised his knuckles to her lips. They were still bruised by his fall earlier in the day.

"Dear God," she whispered, "I never knew love was like this, hurting so much to say goodbye . . ." And a painful thought intruded, which she tried to make light of. "Have you said goodbye to many women?"

He smiled, not happily, but still with that unexpected, gentle teasing quality. "Not to any I loved. There's only been one. I tried to make you see that a year ago." He kissed the top of her head. No beautiful phrases. No "sweethearts" or "darlings," cheaply found and cheaply said. Direct, honest. Like Jem himself.

There would be all the rest of her life to pay for her mistake of not listening to him a year ago . . .

CHAPTER 13

***

AGAINST EVERY inclination in her nature, Maggilee Sholto transformed herself into the sweet simpleton so attractive to Harleigh Duckworth. Pushed and nudged by Biddie, and because she was desperate, she had stripped the newest fall sample out of the display window, buttoned herself into it, and with the blessing of Dora Johnson and Biddie, walked carefully downstairs to meet the Richmond banker.

She felt ridiculous in pale blue with frilled cuffs and a dust ruffle, not to mention her modest and virginal hair style, with sweet little red curls nestling in front of her ears. But ridiculous or not, the two women's efforts had worked their desired effect. Duckworth raised her hand and gallantly brought it to his lips.

"Upon my word, Miss Maggilee, you get prettier every day. You surely do."

"So kind, sir. But then, you always were. A lady knows instinctively that she may look to you for protection." (Oh, God . . .)

He had his red cardboard packet of business papers tied with red cord. They had been laid out beside him on the circular plush seat in the middle of the Salon. It was plain that in spite of all his gallantry, he meant to get his money.

"Indeed you can, Miss Maggilee. You just name the man who dares to insult you, and I'll—" He hesitated. "I'll see him severely dealt with."

"You are kindness itself. I'll ring for Isaah to bring you a glass of Madeira." As he seemed about to refuse, she added, "It's the brand my former father-in-law used to order. You gentlemen have always found it more than adequate."

His hand, which had been creeping toward the red packet of papers, now retreated to his lap.

"Indeed, yes. I know the Gaynor Madeira well. Now, how have you been since your marriage, Miss—or should I say Mrs. Sholto?"

"Between old friends, I hope it will always be Maggilee and . . . dear Harleigh."

Her fingers, curled up in her palm, lay near his. His stubby thumb brushed her hand. But he didn't look down. In fact, his eyes avoided hers. Maggilee began to feel a sick dread. He was not acting normally.

"Quite true forever, I hope, Ma'm." Was there something in his voice, a hesitation? Something he didn't want to say?

She had never before felt so terrified about the future. Not even long ago, when Clinton died. She tried again. "How is your daughter? Lina, isn't it?"

"Short for Carolina. Her mother was born near Charleston, you know. A Rutledge on the female side."

"Really? I had no idea." Who *cared?* . . . Please, God, let him extend my loan. Just a little while. Don't let them take Gaynor's. It isn't fair. I'll give you anything. My life. But let Gaynor's go on. It's a part of me. The best part . . .

"As a matter of fact, Miss Maggilee, it's partly on Lina's account that I—this is mighty painful, Ma'm. You see, Lina is about to be married. A nice boy. His grandfather was a member of the House of Burgesses, saw the Virginia Colony become a state."

She laughed and made a little joke, knowing she only put off the moment when the blow would come. "But surely, then, your daughter's engagement wasn't 'mighty painful.' "

He moved his hand furtively in his lap, as if fighting the desire to touch her. But he was unwilling to use her attraction when he couldn't make the payment she expected. He seemed to make a decision and like many kind people forced to an unkind action, he brought it out brutally.

"My daughter needs a secure future. Her fiancé's family expects it. And you do know, Mrs. Sholto, we've carried the larger of your more recent loans for almost two years."

"A year and a half." She hadn't meant to come out with it in that hard-voiced way, but things were bad enough without his exaggerating her crime.

"Yes. I meant to say—for nineteen months."

"And I paid the interest each due date on—almost on time. You must admit that."

He was emphatic. "I do. But I have others I must answer to. I am not the only bank officer."

Maggilee got up and walked around the plush seat. He watched her hips and the dust ruffles. But she was too nervous, too anxious, and it showed in her rigid movements. "I understand, but if I could pay part on the loan. Not just the August interest, which I admit is a trifle overdue, but part of the loan itself. What then?"

Bill, she thought. I'll go down on my knees to him if I have to. I'll beg him. He can help me with a few hundred dollars, at least. And there's Irene Wychfield. And the Cavanaugh women. If they pay me what they owe—yes. And there's Daisy McCrae's new fall outfit. I can do it!

"Harleigh . . . Mr. Duckworth, I need just a few days more. Less than a week. Several of my wealthy patrons will be paying me . . ."

"It's this way, Mrs. Sholto. I have my orders. Your interest payment is overdue by ten days. And the loan itself—I surely hate to tell you blunt-out like this—but it's been called in. It won't be renewed."

"There are other banks," she reminded him, trying her best to keep up her sweet facade.

"Dear Maggilee, don't count on the Norfolk and Peninsula. On the advice of Ferris Wychfield, one of their officers, I checked with them. They're calling in two separate notes they hold on the building and its contents." He looked around the Salon and overhead. Then, shamefaced, he shrugged. "Believe me, I'm sorry. Well, I think that's about all. Please don't bother about the Madeira . . . I have several calls to make."

He moved across the Salon, his boots sinking into the

carpet. Maggilee had no doubt he was sorry. It was business, something she understood very well. It wasn't Harleigh Duckworth who had become her enemy and hated her enough to take away the one thing she truly cared about.

It *was* logical that Ellen should be behind this. She was so like Varina, Maggilee reminded herself. And she'd never been a real mother to Ellen. I was too busy being a mother to Gaynor's . . .

Maggilee also knew she had never loved Ellen the way she loved Shelley-Ann. She pictured Gaynor's Salon belonging to Shelley long after its original owner was dead and gone. But poor Ellen . . . she'd been all Dunmore and Gaynor, so little, really, of her mother in her. Yes, it must be Ellen . . . Bill and I hurt her deeply, and in spite of her brilliant marriage she still wants her revenge. How like the Gaynors and the Dunmores!

In the reception hall Duckworth took her hand again. She let him. She wasn't defeated yet and she might need his help if she could persuade Ferris Wychfield to give her a little more time. She said goodbye to the banker, closed the door and stood there leaning back against the door. Her whole body ached. She couldn't wait to get out of this fancy Gaynor Salon outfit. Meanwhile, though, it was still necessary to make the visit to Wychfield Hall.

"If I only had a little laudanum. Just to get through this." But she had given her word to Bill and she didn't dare do anything that would hurt that relationship. For the first time since Clinton Dalkett's death, she had known peace at night, a man she loved and who loved her. She could forgive him much, even his possessiveness with Shelley Ann, because it further indicated how strongly he'd settled into his unaccustomed role of husband and father . . . All right, darling, if anything happens that the

Wychfields fail me, you still have a few hundred dollars you didn't put into that damned Gaynor land . . . I'll find ways to persuade you to loan it to me. Just a few hundred, along with what everyone owes me, and I know I can save the Salon . . . Hadn't she always wheedled her creditors into giving her more time? And often more money.

"I must be getting old," she told Dora and Biddie with an easy laugh. "Anyway, he's not the last banker in Virginia . . . What appointments do we have this morning before the customers arrive?"

Dora consulted the red plush engagement book. "A fitting for Miss Bertha-Winn. Reckon I should say Mrs. Wilbur Carroll. It's been over six months now."

"She's in the family way," Biddie said.

This was good news, indeed, Maggilee thought, and said so.

"Yes, she should be a fine mother," Dora said, and Maggilee looked startled, recovered with a "Yes, of course, that's what I meant," though actually she'd been thinking about an entire Gaynor wardrobe that would be needed by the expectant mother.

Shortly after, Miss Eliza arrived for a final fitting on her own new fall wardrobe and complaining that she had seen one of the Corrigan boys throw a handful of pebbles at a side window of the shop. "As a warning to Captain Sholto to accept a fair deal," she said, rather thrilled to be the bearer of dramatic news.

But Maggilee paid no attention to the Corrigans. Their quarrel with her husband had nothing to do with her. Besides, Miss Eliza was giving trouble of her own. She astonished the women at Gaynor's by hinting that two of her outfits were a trifle depressing . . . "Almost funereal," she pointed out.

Then, apparently concerned they would mention her

own inconsistent behavior, she said to Dora, rather pointedly ignoring Maggilee, "My father's wife, that dear Ellen, has been like a sister to me. And what with more visitors at Fairevale, well, I feel I owe them a pleasant, cheerful look."

"How is Miss Ellen?" Dora asked, lowering her voice. It was obvious, the way Maggilee turned away so abruptly, that she was pretending not to be interested in the answer.

"Just fine, Dora. She's so popular with everyone. The gentlemen all adore her." She raised her voice. "And yet, she remains a lady at all times. Such an important trait. That's how one can always tell good blood . . ."

Maggilee heard and understood, but took a deep breath and brought out Eliza's new walking dress, asking her to *kindly* step up on the velvet-covered stool, then stood off, studying the hemline.

"I think it should be a mite shorter," Eliza stated flatly.

Dora started to go down on her knees but Eliza stopped her. "No. *You* do it, Maggilee. You'll know exactly the right length."

Maggilee knew something else, as well. Eliza had been perfectly satisfied with the length a week ago, but she relished the idea of Maggilee kneeling at her feet. Maggilee obliged, all the while figuring what she would charge the "new Eliza."

* * *

It was late afternoon before Maggilee was able to get away from the shop. She had planned on spending all evening with Shelley Ann and Bill but the Wychfield business had to be cleared out of the way first. There would be no peace for her until she knew that Gaynor's was saved.

"Some day Shelley will thank me for it," she assured herself as she stopped a moment to stare across the Ooscanoto at the imposing bulk of Fairevale against the westerly woods and fading sun. She recalled how shocked Ellen had *seemed* at her accusation . . . If she weren't so like Beau's people I'd never believe she could have done such a thing to me. If we only *could* be friends. After all, Ellen was happy, she had everything she could possibly want—or did she . . . ? Who should know better than I how deceptive outward appearances can be . . . ? If only it had been someone else, someone like Eliza, or Varina herself . . . Oh, God, what if Ellen weren't guilty . . . ? She would never forgive me—But if not Ellen, *who* . . . ? No, it had to be her . . .

She was welcomed into Wychfield Hall by Daisy McCrae.

"It's ridiculous, Miss Maggilee, imagine Bertha being a mother before me! I tease her that it's hardly decent. She'll be a mother before she's married a year. She and Wilbur will probably spoil the child until she's worse than your Shelley. Not that little Shelley isn't adorable. And I realize you're too busy to spoil her. But the others—that husband of yours makes a perfect fool of himself over her—"

"Daisy, for heaven's sake! Have you no discretion?" Irene Wychfield demanded, trying to laugh off the girl's appalling frankness. "Maggilee, you mustn't pay any attention to my stepdaughter. She just says the first thing that comes into her mind. I mean—" She stopped in confusion and this time Maggilee laughed, too.

"I know. And she's right. But I intend to spend more time with Shelley just as soon as I get everything settled about the Salon."

"My dear"—Irene Wychfield took her hands and

squeezed them—"I can't tell you how pleased I am to hear you say that. It will be the making of your marriage. Exactly what you've always needed. To be rid of those dreadful business worries and be able to spend more time to your husband and that dear baby."

Alarm bells went off in Maggilee's head. The woman was jumping to a great many conclusions. Maggilee looked around, saw Major Wychfield coming in from the river veranda and said hurriedly, "I really came for just a word with the major, if I may. About business, I'm afraid."

With ever so slight an air of hauteur at being cut out, Mrs. Wychfield said, "By all means, my dear . . . Ferris, Maggilee wants to see you privately. On a *business* matter, I believe."

Maggilee noted the abrupt change in his expression. "Mrs. Sholto, good to see you. Do you mind if we discuss this in my study? I've no doubt it's about your bank loans. And let me reassure you, dear ma'm, everything will be taken care of. You've nothing to worry about. Nothing whatever."

They were in his study, a room in which she couldn't find a single note of color beyond the brown leather of the furniture, the black bindings of a shelf of books, and the depressing, almost puce-colored walls. There was even a bust of General Thomas Stonewall Jackson, and this too was of some blackish metallic material that might have been lava, for all she knew. The place was perfect for bad news, she thought.

"Major, I know you are a man of business, and I don't propose to waste your time. Your bank is about to call in two loans you hold on the Beauford Street ground and on the Gaynor Salon itself."

He looked uncomfortable and began to walk up and down.

"Mrs. Sholto, I'm afraid we have been talking at cross-purposes. The loans have been called in. You received notification."

She skipped that last. "But I've always paid the interest. Or most of it. You must know that. Mr. Gimmerton would tell you."

She couldn't seem to get around him. Her manner had gotten his back up. "Very true, Mrs. Sholto. But as I'm sure you are aware we—that is, the bank—have carried these loans for some years now and no payment has been made on the principal. In short, it was impossible to obtain a renewal for you."

"I see. Someone wants to purchase Gaynor's."

"I beg your pardon." He seemed surprised. "I thought you were concerned with our selling it, after the loans and the accrued interest were paid off."

Maggilee thought it was just like him to be so evasive. He had always liked Ellen, thought she was a "sensible" young woman. He had never liked her but she was too desperate to care a damn about it now. Even her pride was gone. She moved after him, tried to stop his pacing as she took his arm.

"Major, your wife owes me money for her own wardrobe. Mrs. Wilbur Carroll and Mrs. McCrae—both your daughters are in my debt. Mrs. Cavanaugh of Ironwood Plantation will pay me any day. So will Miss Eliza Faire. Within a week I should have it all. It will easily cover the interest on all my loans and still leave room to bring down the principal. Seven days, major. *That's all I ask.*"

"I am sorry my family is involved in this," he told her stiffly. "It makes the matter awkward. Naturally, you will be paid tomorrow. But you see, the process cannot be reversed. I don't think you quite understood me. When you failed to pay those loans after more than ten days' grace, they were automatically made null and void."

"But I wasn't informed!"

"That, ma'm, cannot be so. I myself posted the notices to you."

It was a lie, she decided. He simply had had a good offer for the shop, he or Duckworth, and they couldn't afford to let her pay off loans and interest.

"Does Colonel Faire know about this?" she demanded. "He would never let this happen. Ellen's simply not telling him. Does he *know*, sir?"

Major Wychfield hesitated. "I am not at liberty to discuss the matter. Perhaps your husband can help you."

Her fingers slipped off his arm. "I need someone with money," she said in a hard tone that, coming from a female, offended him. "If you won't tell me, perhaps the colonel will."

"A word of warning, ma'm. The colonel has been far too busy going over the Fairevale Estate accounts and interviewing new overseers to have much time for your affairs—"

"You mean his nephew is leaving? But isn't he one of the colonel's heirs?"

Major Wychfield went to the study door and held it open. "I am not party to the contents of my old friend's will. But I understand young Faire wants to return to Santa Fe in the New Mexico Territory. He comes from there, you know. I daresay he was homesick. At any rate, he leaves tomorrow."

No use to try to see Rowdon tonight, then. Tomorrow, after Jem had gone, she would confront the colonel with what his wife had done. At least he might be able to persuade Ellen not to go through with her scheme to get control of Gaynor's . . . On her walk home she decided not to discuss her problem with Bill . . . he'd only be relieved by her loss. He always thought of Gaynor's as his rival.

She looked across the river. Lamps were burning all over Fairevale. There seemed to be some festivity going on. A horse and buggy was being led away and another had arrived. It must be a party of some kind.

Curious, though. Everything had looked so quiet there on her way to Wychfield, only a short while ago.

CHAPTER 14

***

*T*HERE WERE moments when Ellen told herself she was glad Jem would soon be gone. Or at least should be. Anyway, it would no longer be possible to look out of the big dark room she shared with her husband and see the brick cookhouse below the grassy slope, her guilty imagination investing that little one-room cabin with all the sensuous power of Jem's love. After a while, she told herself, a few months at the most, she would forget what she had found with Jem. Forget?

At least she'd never blamed anybody but herself for

her missed chance. She'd been a silly, dreaming girl, waiting to live out fairy tales, mistaking Bill Sholto for a white knight . . . mistaking Jem for a savage of some sort . . . resisting honest earthy pleasure to be different from her supposedly wicked mother . . . And in Jem's case she knew she'd missed even more—a solid worth as great as his uncle's, and richest of all, an understanding of her as a woman.

All discovered too late. Jem was leaving Virginia tomorrow, and with this thought constantly in front of her, she found it hard, to say the least, to pay even polite attention to the dinner chatter between Eliza, describing her new wardrobe in detail, and, red-faced and still breathing hard after a day's heavy exertions, the colonel, lamenting over and over how he would ever run the huge Fairevale properties without Jem . . .

"He says he'll be back one day, but I don't know. Why else would he have been working so hard, helping me interview and trying to teach these ignorant Yankee drifters our ways?"

"But why did he decide so suddenly?" Eliza asked, and then, getting no answer, quickly returned to the subject of her clothes. "Ellen, do you think I dare wear just a tiny ribbon binding of pink on my new navy church dress?" She lowered her voice. "It's the judge's favorite color."

"I think it would be a lovely idea. And I must say, Eliza, you do wear pink beautifully. I thought so when I saw you the other night with the pink buttons you'd put on your black alpaca."

Miss Eliza blushed becomingly.

Was it only a year ago that *I* was like that? Ellen asked herself . . . anything to make the captain fall in love with me . . .

Never see him again? She felt sick.

"You know," the colonel discovered brightly, "I've been so busy all day I haven't taken more than an eye-opener of whiskey today."

With an effort Ellen flashed a big smile, encouraging him. "That's wonderful, dear."

He mopped his heavily flushed face. "Well, I don't know about that. But it's so, anyway."

After dinner, Ellen gave instructions to the cook, and the colonel stayed by her while Eliza entertained Judge Warrender and Mr. Corrigan in the river parlor at sunset.

The colonel got in an aside to Ellen . . . "I feel like a young buck tonight. And with no liquor to slow me down, I just might prove it to you. Be ready for me, honey."

"Yes, dear." She hated herself for her false brightness.

"I have this business of the Corrigans' final offer to go over with the judge and Corrigan . . . the Lord knows what Captain Sholto wants. The land is good when it's not flooded, but he's demanding they buy the whole passel of River Land, even the adjoining fields given to the Corrigans by the Federals after the War."

"Then to twenty dollars an acre," Mr. Corrigan announced as they came in to join the two men and Miss Eliza. "Sure, there's none can say Corrigan ain't a reasonable man when all's fair. But this spalpeen, he's got us Corrigans mixed with the Morgans and the Astors. And there'll be the swampy land. That's to be paid for at the rate of the good fields. Man, I say no. We Corrigans have made our last offer. It's all we can do, the missus and myself, to hold back our boys. They're rampant to fight this precious Captain Sholto. Why, he's got in mind a thousand dollars in gold. We're up to some-ut under five hundred and that's squeezing more than the land is worth." Mr. Corrigan was a quiet man, not a fine, bearded gentleman like the judge, but equally a man of integrity, and Ellen knew that the whole County respected him and his hard-working sons, in spite of their taste for a knockabout now and then.

"A thousand!" the colonel said. "That's just talk. He'll settle. He'll have to."

"I wonder why he needs it."—Eliza put in, not too interested—"he hinted, or I *thought* he hinted, that it had something to do with getting rid of Maggilee's shop, but why he needed money in order to sell is a mystery to me."

The colonel told her roughly, "I don't want to hear of you lending money to any male. It's indecent." His irritation at the thought made him cough, and Ellen looked at him anxiously but he waved away her concern.

"Quite improper," the judge agreed to Eliza, for which she thanked him modestly.

Recovering, the colonel pressed his palm against his chest and added with an apparent calm that relieved Ellen, "Not but what he's got a right good notion, getting Miss Maggilee out of that shop. It was bad enough when she hadn't a man to look out for her. But now, with a husband and that little charmer of a daughter, she has no call working like a field hand."

Mr. Corrigan said thoughtfully, "My boys figure if anything happened to that shop, Sholto would have to sell quick enough, not having the shop income, as you might say."

Eliza changed the subject, which had become far too businesslike for her tastes. "I'd think Jem might at least have come to dinner with you, Papa. After all, it is the last time. I still think his sudden going away is mighty peculiar . . . giving you less than a month's notice."

"He said he was homesick," Ellen put in.

The colonel nodded and sighed. "The desert country.

All those magnificent sunsets and sunrises. Hester used to go into raptures about them. I reckon she'd rather have had that blasted rock and desert than all this that we have here in what I'm proud to say is the most beautiful state in the Union." He grinned at his daughter's shocked face. "Say what you will, we did lose the War, honey. This is still part of the Union."

"All the same, I find the word distasteful. And it doesn't explain why he couldn't eat dinner with us."

Ellen knew the colonel was trying hard not to show how hurt he was at the desertion of a nephew he'd done so much for and who had become as close as a natural son. "Well, now, he isn't going away forever, you know. He'll get tired of that desert and all those foreign ways in Santa Fe. He's down now at old Taffy's grave. Paying his last respects. He was mighty fond of that old dog." He sighed again, then patted Ellen's hand and whispered loudly, "Never you mind Jem," and as Eliza and the two men began to compare notes on the beauties of the state, he took this opportunity to whisper to Ellen, "You get yourself up in one of those honeymoon things, you know what I mean . . . that silky-lacy one with the ribbons—"

"That got torn."

"Oh. Well, one of them. Nothing but the best for your husband tonight."

She nodded, then turned quickly to Eliza. "Shall we leave the gentlemen to their Madeira?"

Reluctantly, Eliza got up, but she moved across the floor, aware of the gentlemen watching her, with a grace that new confidence gave her, and Ellen was as proud as if she were her own daughter instead of the colonel's.

The judge called after her, "I hope we'll have the pleasure of bidding you good night, Miss Eliza." Then, as an afterthought, "And you, Mrs. Faire."

When the two women were alone in the hall Ellen pointed out to Eliza, "He doesn't give a rap whether or not I'm there to say good night, but he surely does want to see you."

"Oh, Ellie-honey, you're funning," but she hugged herself with pleasure at the thought and said, "I believe I'll just linger in the south room and read a little . . . the judge and I are well into *Ben-Hur* now. He might want to discuss it."

"Fine. I'll go on up and get my embroidery, if I must chaperone you."

The older woman giggled and waved her away. "You do that, honey."

Ellen stopped in the upstairs hall and stared for a long moment at the door of the room she and Jem had first fought, and loved in—

The door opened. It was as if the past and the present had come together. She stood rigid.

And she watched Jem start out of the room, looking back. In the doorway he turned, saw her and after an awkward few moments said, "I don't look the sentimental type, do I? Still, I wanted to say goodbye to that room."

She smiled. "That's where you said you despised me. In that room."

"It seems a long while ago." He closed the door behind him. "I wasn't going to say goodbye."

She found herself watching his eyes, reading what he felt for her in their green depths.

"I know," she whispered. "I didn't expect you to."

He moved along the hall with her to the master bedroom, opened the door for her and stood aside. She passed him and went into the room. An endless time passed in the two moments. Now that she was in the room, she couldn't think . . . accept . . . what she was doing here. She looked back at the door. Jem had not gone. He remained there, watching her. Unlike the violence of his mood in that scene months ago, he remained quiet now, but as she looked at him he held out his arms, and she went into them.

She felt drunk, her senses disordered as they kissed and, violent with a shared hunger, kissed again.

This is the last time, she thought . . . It is all I will ever have—

A sound roused them from their feverish, desperate embrace. The door had been pushed open.

The colonel stood there, breathing hard, flushed. His mouth had literally fallen open. His eyes were wide, bloodshot.

"Two of you been . . . all this time?" he whispered hoarsely, unable to get the words out.

She wanted to run to him, knew it would only infuriate him more. He was, after all, no fool. He wouldn't be patronized or pitied. She detached herself from Jem, spoke directly to her husband.

"No, Rowdon. When we discovered it in ourselves, we knew Jem had to leave. I kissed him just now because it was for the last time . . ."

Jem pulled a chair forward but the older man furiously swept it away. "Eliza warned me from the first about him. A damned redskin bastard—"

Ellen said firmly, "You don't mean that. Why do you think Jem was leaving? If he'd *stayed* it would be a betrayal."

But he wasn't listening, only reacting . . . "And I thought Eliza was jealous, a crazy old maid . . . Eliza! Where is she? . . . Damn him"—he couldn't look at Jem or refer to him directly—"took from me, then took my wife—"

"He gave you his hard work, too, he saved Fairevale . . . You've told me that often enough—"

The colonel began to cough. "—want to make things right with Eliza. I want Eliza!"

Though he shook off Ellen's attentions, he wasn't strong enough to fight both of them and Jem managed to get him onto the bed as Ellen pushed pillows behind him, then untied his tie and began to chafe his hands.

"Some water from that carafe by the bed," she told Jem, who brought the water and put it to the colonel's lips. She saw Jem's face. It was granite-hard, expressionless. The colonel pushed the water away. Ellen took it, and the colonel drank. His shaking fingers covered hers on the glass.

"I'll find Eliza," Jem said, "and then fetch Dr. Nickels."

When she looked around, he had gone.

"My . . . daughter?" the colonel was saying. "Please . . ." His face was fiery, and Ellen moistened it with water on her fingers from the drinking glass.

"She's coming, Rowdon."

His eyes, always tender before when he looked at her, seemed to bulge now from the pressures within him. He stammered, trying to make her understand. "—I want Eliza . . . Fairevale to Eliza, she never lied . . ." And then, unexpectedly, his terrible anger softened, he tried to raise one clumsy thumb to her face . . . "Don't cry . . . you cried when you were little . . . broke my heart. It wasn't only . . . the money, was it?"

"You've been the dearest person in my whole life, Rowdon. From the time I was a child. *That's* why I married you."

The water, or perhaps her words, seemed to help him. He even managed a faint grin. "Wasn't your fault . . . Mine."

"*No.*"

"Mine, honey. Rotten business, age. Only, I trusted—"

"I know. But it wasn't his fault, either, dearest . . . Please listen, don't turn away. He thought I married you for your money, and he hated me for it. And when he found out I hadn't, and how he felt, he was going away. I told you, what you saw was only goodbye . . . Please believe that . . ."

"It's—head. Hurts." He strained, actually writhed in her arms. Oh God—it hurts!"

With his rough gray head against her breast she tried frantically to soothe him . . . "Eliza is coming, I hear her now . . . Dearest, the doctor will be here . . . *Rowdon?*"

From the doorway Eliza screamed when she saw him, her voice knifing repeatedly through the room.

By the time Ellen's own head had recovered from the assault of those screams, Colonel Rowdon Faire was dead in her arms.

CHAPTER 15

***

*J*UDGE WARRENDER shook his head ponderously before he addressed the three women—weeping Eliza, a stoically cool Ellen, and his daughter Persis.

"I hadn't intended to speak of business matters on the very day of the—" He hesitated, added "funeral" and went on stentorially. "My remark to you about your heavy responsibilities, Mrs. Faire, was meant to remind you that you may count upon me for any . . . advice, and I think I may say Ferris Wychfield, as your late husband's other executor, would join me in that assurance. I had no notion about this latest development. If I may say so, it is almost unheard of."

Eliza, nearest the judge by his design, wiped her eyes, blew her nose. "I don't know what it all means. He couldn't have wanted to leave everything to me. He hardly knew I existed . . ."

"However," the judge went on, seeing from Ellen's tight, pallid face that she meant what she said about giving up her own inheritance, "If Mrs. Faire believes this to have been my dear friend's dying wish—"

"It was." Ellen closed her eyes briefly but could not blot out the look on her husband's dying, convulsed face.

Until this morning she and Jem hadn't spoken together alone since the colonel's death. Then, as she saw her husband's coffin enter the Gaynorville Community Church for the funeral later in the day, her knees suddenly weakened and she sank into one of the side pews of the darkened church, a black lace handkerchief wadded in her hands.

It was in this church that she had made her vows to Rowdon Faire less than a year ago. Here, too, in front of the flower-bordered altar, Jem Faire had slipped her husband's ring on her finger and moments later she'd felt his kiss . . . She had touched her lips with her handkerchief, had seen the black mourning lace, and began to sob noiselessly.

Jem's hand had closed on her shoulder at that moment and she saw the hard, high-boned face, dearer to her than ever because of the now insuperable barrier between them. He too had been suffering. She saw it in his sombre sea-green eyes and the tight restraint about his mouth. "He forgave you. Try to think of that," he said. "Not the other."

"He forgave us both," she murmured, her eyes filling.

His hands moved from her shoulder to her chin. "Maybe he always knew what I felt for you. If so, he knew it would never change. Don't be afraid. And don't look around. No one is here but you and me—and him up there in his coffin. But I won't lie to him. Or to you. That was how my mother loved my father. And that's how it is with me."

"Jem—"

"I'll stay until you and Eliza get a decent foreman. But I can see it in your face. After this, Rowdon Faire would always come between us." . . .

Two hours later she was at Fairevale when Judge Warrender and Persis arrived to escort the Faires to the church services, and it was then that she'd made the flat statement which so upset the judge, and about which Persis now put in with barely suppressed excitement, "But Papa, it would remain in the family . . . I mean, it's terribly generous of Ellen, but Jem and Miss Eliza would see that Ellen wanted for nothing, wouldn't you, ma'm?" She turned to Eliza, who shook her head, her voice muffled in her handkerchief.

"No . . . I mean—I don't really understand any of it except"—she raised her reddened eyes—"I always thought he despised me . . . But Ellie, he must have really loved me, after all."

Ellen assured her, "He did, indeed. He asked for *you*. Only *you*. You must never forget that."

"Of course," Persis put in.

"You see, my dear, Mrs. Faire heard him," the judge added. Then, with Eliza's hand enfolded in his, he cleared his throat, coughed and addressed Ellen. "Ma'm, this places me in a most awkward position. You see, before my friend's passing I'd intended to ask for his daughter's hand, as we used to say in my youth."

Eliza looked down at their intertwined hands. Even her tear-filled eyes couldn't completely obscure the glow this announcement brought to them.

"Nothing would have made my husband happier," Ellen told the judge. "Surely, after a suitable period of mourning, it will be most proper. The whole County will be happy for you."

"But the problem, ma'm . . ."

Ellen was baffled. "What problem?"

"I cannot condone the idea of turning over the entire Fairevale estate to the lady I hope to marry. It would be totally unethical."

Which disturbed Persis. "But, Papa, it isn't all of Fairevale. Jem inherits a part, doesn't he?"

Ellen raised her head. She sensed something of what was coming. Shocked, the judge told his daughter, "How can you possibly know that? I have never discussed such matters with you."

Persis looked uneasy. "Well . . . your file was there on your desk, Papa. All the notes you took. Not the real will, Papa. Just your notes."

He shook his head, gave the two Faire women an apologetic shrug. "In any case, my daughter happens to be wrong. We discussed young Faire's rights and the colonel told me he wanted to offer young Faire a third right in the estate but that Jem refused. He said Fairevale would sink into tenant land like the Finch Plantation if it were divided. It seems Jem suggested that the profits on the estate should go half to Miss Eliza and half to Mrs. Faire. Jem saw himself as overseer and no more. Now, of course, he tells me he will be returning to his home somewhere in Indian country."

"What! But, Papa, that's only for a visit. He wouldn't go away forever without telling—"

Her father cut Persis off sharply. "I'm afraid it is true. We must remember, this young man . . . well, he's different . . . no one can expect him to settle down forever among us . . . I did think for a time—that is, the colonel assured me—but it apparently was not to be."

The fact that Jem was not now an heir would seem to have affected the judge's opinion of him.

"But Papa! I think we ought to persuade Jem—" She got no further. Her father held up his hand with magisterial dignity, she subsided, and he then reverted to the matter of Colonel Faire's intentions which might or might not supersede his duly witnessed will.

"Mrs. Faire, it is your understanding that your husband wanted the entire estate to revert to his daughter?"

Tight-lipped, she remembered suddenly how the colonel in his bitterness denied what Jem had done for the estate. She felt deeply how that must have affected Jem. Aloud, she said firmly, "The quote, as I recall it, was 'I want Fairevale to Eliza.' He said it after repeatedly calling for her. Jem had gone downstairs to get her."

Miss Eliza began to cry softly. With his hand patting hers in consolation, the judge said judiciously, "Still, it's very little to go on. Within the law, you have the right to deed over your interest in the estate to Miss Eliza. I suggest, however, that you get in touch with some well-qualified lawyer outside Tudor County. He may dissuade you from this—if I may say so—over-scrupulous regard for a dying man's delirium. I'm sure I speak for Miss Eliza as well."

"I don't want it," Eliza sobbed. "I could never live here alone."

"Oh," Persis reminded her, "but you'll have Papa when you are married."

Which earned her such a stern frown from the white-bearded patriarch that she subsided, murmuring, "I was only trying to cheer her up."

Ellen arose from the stiff chair. "I think we are expected at the church, Judge. I expect some of my husband's friends will be returning to Fairevale from the cemetery."

Judge Warrender inclined his head. "One of your neighbors will be unable to attend. Mrs. Sholto tells me her husband is in Portsmouth on business. However, Gavin McCraw saw Captain Sholto on the road two days ago while Miss Maggilee was visiting the Wychfields, so it's possible he may have returned in time."

Ellen, indifferent to this, said, "I will be leaving in a few minutes. Eliza, are you going to the church with me?"

Eliza looked at the judge before removing her fingers from his grip. "Of course. But will we see you there, too, sir?"

* * *

Captain William Sholto was pleased with the world in nearly every way except one. He worried about how Maggilee would behave when she knew the truth. In so many ways he and Maggilee were perfectly suited. Of the many women he had known, none, he long ago decided, could compare with Maggilee. If it hadn't been for that store . . . but that would soon be changed. No more complaints of business problems, of how tired she was, how her richest customers waited longest to pay their bills, of their arrogance and rudeness to her. She might be upset, but, damn it, it was for her own good . . . for *all* their good . . .

He leaned forward, patted Oglala. "Been lonesome,

old scout? But that Ashby stable fed you well anyway, and you couldn't have taken me clear to Richmond, you know. You're no youngster."

Oglala galloped smartly ahead to prove him wrong, and they reached Gaynorville by three in the afternoon. Everywhere in the wooded sections around the town the stands of maple stood out among the less dramatic growth, ablaze with late fall colors among the more prosaic green, yellow and crisp brown. He saw Gaynor's as he entered Beauford Street and the sight of the store again gave him a brief twinge of apprehension.

Maggilee, for sure, would kick up her heels and scream a little. She would scratch and be a hellion in bed for a few days, but in the end she must see that he had done this to bring her home where she belonged with her husband and her baby. Varina had warned him he would have trouble with Maggilee, but that was hardly news, and Varina certainly had backed him in restoring the Gaynor lands.

Surprisingly few people were in the normally filled street. Most surprising, Gaynor's Salon was closed, though the shutters remained open as if business would be resumed presently.

There were a dozen buggies tethered near the Confederate Cemetery and up Church Street. Obviously, some old relic of the CSA had gone to his reward. Bill wondered which of them it could be. He got on well with most of the County's citizens and even liked a few—Jonathan Gaynor, for instance. The Corrigans hated him, but that would fade quickly enough when he accepted their offer tomorrow. He'd kept them on tenterhooks long enough.

Sholto pulled up at the hitching post before the Gaynor shop and walked toward the Community Church.

Disembodied hands opened the doors for him. He stepped inside. The interior had the usual gloomy aura, dominated by the preponderance of black on both males and females and the sweet, sickening odor of flowers everywhere.

The Reverend Archibald Sheering was droning a prayer, but Bill ignored him. He saw the long, elegant, brass-handled coffin. Someone rich, probably male. Trying to make himself inconspicuous, he stepped to one side, trying to find his wife. Maggilee seldom wore bonnets or hats except to protect her skin against the summer sun, or at funerals, but the church was crowded and he couldn't make out the ugly little black bonnet that took all the life out of Maggilee's fly-away red hair. He couldn't mistake Varina Gaynor, however. Her tall, rigid back was visible on the aisle, her regal white head crowned by an elegant black hat with a black feather and lace trim.

"Leave it to Varina to queen it even at a funeral," he thought, and at that minute Varina turned and looked back. He was surprised to note tears glistening in those sharp, frosty eyes. She shook her head, turned to the front again.

Bewildered, he looked beyond her toward the altar, squinting to identify the two heavily veiled mourners. Beside them he recognized the very dark young man whom he'd always instinctively disliked—Jem Faire . . .

So it was Rowdon Faire who was dead!

And now Ellen and that Irish–Indian could buy up the whole County.

But where was Maggilee?

He began to understand why Varina had shaken her head. Maggilee wasn't here. Of course! She was home with Shelley Ann. That would make it easier when he told her about the shop. With Shelley Ann nearby her mother's instinct must become dominant. With relief he left the church and started toward the hitching post, where Oglala had begun to stamp impatiently.

The church doors opened and the Reverend Sheering escorted out Ellen and Miss Eliza, closely followed by Judge Warrender and Persis. Jem Faire was nowhere around, and Bill wondered why he had made himself scarce. Not that it mattered. Ellen and the others were talking with the minister, and Bill took a few strides to meet Ellen. She had been crying but still appeared very much in command of herself. Miss Eliza was crying silently behind her veil, and the judge supported her with a solicitude duly noted by the other women leaving the church.

Bill went over to Ellen and respectfully removed his wide-brimmed cavalry hat.

"May I offer all my sympathy, Mrs. Faire? I only just arrived back from Richmond and—"

"I thought it was Portsmouth," Ellen said as coldly as Varina might have spoken.

"Portsmouth?"

"Isn't that what you told your wife and others? To see about shipping produce? But the bankers you're dealing with aren't in Portsmouth, are they?"

Varina Gaynor had come out and Ellen turned her back to him. While Sholto stared, shaken, he saw Ellen go into Varina's open arms.

"Now, now, child, we were all lucky to have known Rowdon every day he lived."

CHAPTER 16

***

BETHULIA said for the twentieth time that day, "'Scuse me, Miss Maggilee, best let baby crawl just where she had a mind to. She's the sweetest little thing in nature, but she's mighty set on doin' it her way."

Maggilee tried to follow instructions from the authority on the subject, but couldn't help thinking that her child had had just about everything she wanted every day of her life . . . not such a very good preparation for her later years . . . She began to talk to her daughter, confiding some of her own dreams, mostly, of course, to herself.

"And your later years will see Gaynor's Salon for your very own, maybe even with branches in Richmond and Atlanta and Charlotte ... Who knows? Just as soon as your daddy gets back we'll find a way to get the money and save Gaynor's ... all for you, and you'll love it ... yes, you will, sweetheart. I'm going to show it to you, very soon. Maybe on your first birthday ... Bethulia, what time is it?"

"Funeral's pret-near over by now. Miss Varina'll be coming home."

Maggilee went on playing with Shelley Ann, who crawled toward her over the rag rugs on the river porch. Mention of the funeral, of course, reminded Maggilee of her other daughter.

She glanced across the river toward Fairevale. "I wonder how Ellen is taking it. She truly seemed quite happy with the colonel. They always got on well together even when Ellen was a child ... It's really a shame ..."

"Sure is, ma'm. Miss Ellen is a kind lady. Don't say much, but she's there if you need her."

"Ha!"

Maggilee was about to announce Ellen's treachery over the loans when Edward Hone appeared in the doorway. He looked surprised.

"Mister Gaynor's here, Mrs. Sholto."

"Jonathan? Here?" Maggilee got up, lifted Shelley and pointed out the tall, gaunt man as he came out to the porch behind Edward Hone. He looked strange in the black suit he must have had since shortly after the War. Maggilee said, "See, Shelley? This is your Second-Cousin Jonathan. He's going to be your good friend, just as he's been to your sister Ellen ... aren't you, Jonathan?"

He took Shelley's small fist in his palm. "My pleasure, ma'm. I only hope we'll be as good friends as your sister and me."

Jonathan looked about but, discreet as ever, Edward Hone had disappeared and Bethulia backed away into the hall to follow him. Jonathan said in his low voice, "I surely hoped to see you at the funeral."

"Varina was there to hold high the Gaynor banner."

"It's not pretty, Maggie, you being flippant and all. That was a mighty good man in that coffin."

She felt as if she had been slapped. "And do *you* know what darling Ellen is trying to do to my shop? And it has to be with Rowdon Faire's money. Now, God knows how far she can go, with all his fortune. And here we are, working our heads off just to stay in front of those damned bankers. Me at the Salon, and Bill rushing off to Portsmouth to contract for the Gaynor spring crops."

Jonathan straddled a chair and played with the baby's hands as Shelley grinned, giggled and kicked her feet. "I've been up Williamsburg way. Just got back this morning. Met one of the Finch tenants on Richmond Road."

Maggilee raised her head, sensing that he was ready with another verbal slap, only no doubt harder this time. "Well? Since when are the Finch tenants news?"

He played with Shelley and spoke without looking at Maggilee. "Since one of them met Bill Sholto in the capital."

She looked at him, fighting a sudden, horrible, impossible suspicion. "Bill was nowhere near Richmond. He went to Portsmouth about—about vegetables."

"Honey"—this time he reached over Shelley's light wisps of hair and closed his hand on Maggilee's—"I made a side trip back to the County. Stopped off in Norfolk. I knew Tom Gimmerton back in old times. We enlisted the same day. He wouldn't tell me anything. Don't blame him. A matter of business honor, I reckon. But honey, your husband went to Richmond."

"He did so lie. Why are you so sure he didn't?"

"Because he'd no way of knowing what it meant when he said Bill Sholto was coming out of a bank."

... "The Richmond Dominion Bank?"

He nodded. "Whatever's gone on already, it's going to be hard fighting it. I offered to put up my winter and my spring crops to hold the loans but Tom said it was too late."

"Of course, Bill could have made the same offer to the Richmond Dominion Bank." But she didn't believe it. She got hold of herself, stood breathing hard, and then leaned over him and kissed his head. "You tried. For the second time you tried to help me. Dearest Jonathan, I should have loved you in the very beginning."

He was matter of fact as always. "No need. I loved you. It was enough."

Varina's voice in the front hall broke in. She was speaking to Bill Sholto, and they sounded on the best of terms.

Maggilee was shaken. She wanted time before she had to face this.

Jonathan got up. "You've never been a coward, Maggilee. You don't need me to tell you what to do. Just be calm, find out why he did it. Maybe there was a good reason." While she took Shelley from him, he added, "There's an excuse for almost every act... Nobody knows that better than you and me."

She shivered.

By this time Bill was hurrying out onto the porch, so delighted to see her and the baby... but a little nervous too...?

"How are my two sweethearts? Missed me, I hope."

He tried to hug them both at once without squeezing Shelley Ann, and offered his hand to Jonathan, who looked beyond him to Maggilee. "You want me to stay?" he asked her.

She shook her head, unable to bring herself to speak when she really wanted to explode. While Bill was taking Shelley out of her arms and making a fuss over the child, Maggilee watched Jonathan step down from the porch to the grass below, feeling as if the best part of her had gone.

Varina came out as Jonathan left and called to him, "Running away from us again, boy?"

He didn't look back. For Varina, as with most such situations, the behavior she disapproved was an indication of bad manners, no more. Indeed Maggilee often thought Varina would have been ideally suited to adorn a tumbrel on its way to the guillotine. She would feel that the worst thing about the whole business was the company one was forced to keep.

But now Maggilee felt there was something suspicious about Varina's too friendly chatter, as if she knew all about Bill's business and approved it . . . "Captain, tell your wife about your successes around Hampton Roads and the James."

Maggilee could hardly contain herself at this enhancing of the lie, but managed to say, drily, "Yes, do tell me all about Portsmouth and the crops and the vegetables. All of that."

Sholto was grateful when Bethulia came in and interrupted to insist that they bring the baby in . . . "It's past sundown, Cap'n. These warm days, they fool a body."

He gave her his best grin and obediently followed her into the river parlor, where the maid took Shelley Ann from him, insisting it was the baby's bedtime.

Maggilee watched it all, aware of her own tension, torn by fears, and hopes that there might be a good excuse, that he had gone to Richmond to help her, maybe to get an extension before the foreclosure.

Her feelings weren't helped by the presence of Varina, who remarked as she passed Bill, "Funerals depress me. Especially those of my contemporaries. I'll have beat-biscuits and tea in my room . . . And—Captain, why don't you tell your wife about your trip? She will undoubtedly be interested in the details. With this ominous coda she walked firmly up the stairs, and at least had the decency not to look back and watch Maggilee's reaction to her provocative hints.

"I reckon that's what some around here call class," Maggilee remarked icily.

Bill's answer was to reach for her, pull her roughly into his arms. "Sweetheart, do you know it's been three long nights? The longest we've ever been separated—"

"So long as you got your vegetables sold . . . or *whatever* it was."

He'd begun to kiss her in the hall, starting with her unruly red hair that always excited him, and which he took in one hand and held aside so that his lips on her warm neck deliciously tickled her, even now.

Mentally fighting its effect, she coaxed him further into his labyrinth. "Did you cross the James, darling, while you were going around selling next spring's potatoes?"

"Umm . . . damn little rowboats they call ferries. You're so sweet, I love every inch, I'd like to—"

"Always traffic going north," she cut in, gritting her teeth to keep herself from sharing his enjoyment.

"Traffic? Not till Williamsburg cut-off. Sweetheart, let's put off supper."

She did love his arm around her, warm and strong, comforting . . . His other hand moved over her stomach and thighs. She could feel his heat through her challis dress . . . "Richmond is so changed, it's too citified nowadays . . ." Keeping her mind on *her* subject at hand was becoming near-impossible.

"Not like Atlanta and New Orleans, but it's easy enough when you know where you're going . . . Maggi-darlin', must you keep chattering?" Then, belatedly, he began to take in the possible meaning of her words . . . Anxiety insinuated itself into his caresses . . .

She felt the nervous stiffening of his hands and body . . . "Yes, darling? Tell me all about Richmond."

His hold on her now was slack. "Maggie . . . I . . . wanted it to be a surprise. A really grand surprise, a way to take care of you and Shelley Ann long after I'm gone."

For a moment she was unsure again . . . Could he possibly have gone to Richmond to persuade the bank to renew her loans? She felt that her whole life depended on his answer.

"Bill . . . about my loans . . ."

She saw his expression, and her brief hope faded, to be replaced by an anger wilder, stronger, than she'd ever known. She pushed her way out of his arms and said in a voice that chilled him, "It *was* you. Not Ellen. You, my gallant lover. My *husband*. You also managed to destroy any remnant of affection there might have been between Ellen and me—"

"Now, look here, Maggie . . . Damn it, there's a very good explanation. Sweetheart—" He reached for her, and she backed away from him. *"Listen* to me, just listen a minute. You're wearing yourself out down at that damned shop. You come home tired to death. Those old hags never pay you. You should be home with Shelley Ann. And *me*. What about me? I need you here too—"

"You . . . you don't understand me at all. Gaynor's is me, my other self. Gaynor's was created out of blood, the

blood of the finest man I've ever known. You've taken it from me. Killed it. Don't talk to me about home and housewives. You knew what I was when you made love to me. When you said you wanted the baby so much—and I did too because it was a part of you—you knew then what the shop meant to me." The more she talked, the more she felt the truth sink in, like stab wounds. Gaynor's had been destroyed, and by the man she loved, had married . . . And worst of all, most hopeless of all, she realized, even in her anger at him, that the full meaning of her despair completely eluded him, and would continue to.

"Maggilee, I don't intend that Shelley Ann grow up like you and me, in war and poverty and—"

"Gaynor's belongs to Shelley!"

"No, honey. Gaynor's is something that's always about to go broke. But there *is* something here that deserves to be saved for her. I'm talking about what used to be the Gaynor Plantation before the War. You've lived twenty years surrounded by starved, hungry land. Acre after acre has been wasted, lost or stolen by renegades from both north and south. And you never once really looked at it—"

"I knew I could plant the fields when I paid off the shop loans—"

"And when would that be? You always poured the profits right back into your merchandise. Tomorrow I'm going to accept the Corrigans' offer. There's no way of working that bottomland anyway, we'd have to plough through the Corrigans' legitimate fields. But I've got some hard workers out there now. With the Corrigans' money along with what the banks are paying me for our rights in the shop, the land is going to come back, it's already showing promise—"

"And all this with the money you got from Gaynor's."

He had sold her life work to save some dead brown earth that belonged to the damned Dunmores and Gaynors, never to her . . .

"I've done this for our daughter," he said, growing hoarse with the effort. "Can't you see that? You act as if the shop was a person, or something. It's just a damned relic from the War days that you filled with a parcel of dresses for a bunch of silly, fluttering females who never pay their bills. It'd be better if you'd never seen the damned place—"

In one blazing instant she saw the years torn away, the beginnings, what it had meant to keep her child and the old woman and herself from begging and half starving like the other Virginia widows. Gaynor's, and Gaynor's alone, had kept them alive, with some self-respect . . . She brought her hand around and slapped him hard as she could across the face, and when he reached for her she slapped him again with the other hand. As she swung around the newel post and ran up the stairs she was sure she'd made him so angry he was about to hit her in return. Well, it no longer mattered. Nothing did except herself and her child.

She rushed into the room she and Bill shared to discover Varina and Bethulia both talking to a wide-eyed Shelley Ann . . . like two damned witches huddled over the baby with their incantations, Maggilee thought. "Get out. *Both* of you."

The black woman straightened up, appeared undecided for a moment and then, bowing her head ever so slightly to Maggilee, she left the room. Varina also stood up to her impressive height. "Your manners, as usual, are impeccable, Maggilee. I see you haven't changed from the trash my son brought home in '64."

"All right, you've had your say, now kindly leave . . . leave us *alone*."

Varina shrugged, walked to the door, then stopped with her hand on the doorknob. When she spoke, her voice was surprisingly soft. "My dear girl, have you thought—"

Maggilee cut in, dying to be rid of her and everyone before she broke down. "I've been too busy working to see what was under my nose. I've done a passel of thinking tonight, I can tell you! Please close the door tightly."

Varina, shaking her head, went out without another word.

Maggilee had held out as long as she could. She picked Shelley Ann out of her cradle and held her close. "You understand, sweetheart, don't you? You look at Mama with those big eyes as if you could read her mind . . . Gaynor's is going to be yours in spite of them all, I promise you. I'll do it somehow. Wait till you see it . . . Oh, you're going to be prideful, yes, you are, sweetheart . . ."

Except why wait any longer? I can never trust him again, I can't go to bed with him tonight . . . maybe never again . . . She looked out the open window. Nobody had drawn the drapes. It was a warm autumn night. Too late in the season for fireflies, but the autumn-scented air invigorated her.

Why wait?

She felt dizzy and the room tilted, then righted itself. It was like being drunk, she thought, except that she knew exactly what she was doing. She and Shelley would sleep in the shop tonight and the baby would get her first taste of the marvels of Gaynor's.

What do I need for her? A bottle of warm milk and a change of diapers and lots of warm blankets. And knitted booties and a cap.

Everything was at hand. Bethulia had evidently brought the bottle just before Maggilee arrived.

In five minutes Maggilee had her old mantle on and, carrying her carpetbag over her arm, picked up the baby, blankets and all. No one was in sight. As she went carefully down the stairs she heard Bill talking to Edward Hone in the dining room. Her husband was making some sort of excuse about putting off supper. Luckily neither man faced the hall doorway. She hurried past and went out over the gravel carriage road to rouse the stableboy.

"I'm going to visit Wychfield Hall," she told him, choosing the opposite direction from town.

With Shelley Ann sleepily wrapped in a cocoon of blankets beside her, Maggilee took the buggy reins and Pansy obediently trotted off. Her thoughts seesawed between hope, plans to save Gaynor's, and despair as she ruled out each possibility. She suspected now that her marriage to Bill had a lot to do with Harleigh Duckworth's rejection of her last plea . . . I should have gotten him to marry me. I could have kept Bill, too . . . And she thought of how Gaynor's had been born in the midst of turmoil very like this, but at least that hadn't brought her the awful disillusionment she felt now.

She was surprised to find herself in Gaynorville so soon. Instead of leaving Pansy and the buggy at Gamble's she took them to the livery stable on Ashby Road near the Winchester Coffee House. Then, with Shelley and the carpetbag, she walked the length of quiet, gaslit Beauford Street to Gaynor's. No one bothered her. In the black section of town the few people on the street eyed her with curiosity but luckily no one she met was familiar with her or her husband. She knew that the Johnsons and Isaah and even Biddie's nephew Nahum wouldn't approve of her wandering around town at night unescorted and with a tiny baby. Time, and even her actions, had no direct meaning for her. She looked down, thought how odd it was to see one's feet walking of their own volition, as though not part of the rest of her . . . And then she was inside Gaynor's, carefully closing and locking the door behind her as she held the now sleepy baby up before her.

"Shelley, sweetheart, look around. Isn't it beautiful?"

Shelley Ann quickly became wide-eyed. Maggilee laid the baby on the round plush settee and lighted one oil lamp. The night crowded in at one of the open south windows directly opposite the lamp, which cast a flattering pink light through its globe. She started across the room to close the window, which she or someone had forgotten, but Shelley Ann began to cry and she quickly came back. Shelley didn't want her milk and her bottom was dry, so Maggilee took her out of the blankets and let her crawl around the settee.

It was a delight to see her hands dig into the rich crimson plush and to hear her sobs turn to giggles. Maggilee unwrapped the yards of wedding veil that had been laid on the table beside the lamp. "Isn't this nice, sweetheart? One day you'll have a lovely wedding veil made of this and you'll look like an angel." But Shelley was far too busy prowling around the settee, sinking her fingers into the soft plush. "That's my girl," Maggilee encouraged her, "you and Mama love Gaynor's, even if nobody else does. Now, shall we see all the other wonderful things?"

She lifted Shelley, this time in her blanket, and was pleased when the baby fought to stay on the settee, her hands clinging to the plush. Maggilee released each of her fingers and then kissed them. "You can come back here later and play." In her state it seemed to her that Shelley understood everything she said. The child began to peer over the blanket as she was taken up the stairs to the second floor. "Here's where we keep the lengths of material until we show them downstairs." Shelves filled with bolts of cloth lined the big room. One straight chair was the only furniture.

With Shelley in one arm, she carried a glass-chimneyed candle in the other. She set the candle on the chair and carried the baby over to the shelves filled with bolts of satin and moire, crepe de chine and gauze, and to her delight Shelley grabbed at the gold satin as if she would cover herself with it.

"Yes, sweetheart, you have the right idea but the wrong color. It washes you out. How about this pretty green gauze?"

To which Shelley wrinkled her nose—probably because the gauze was rough and tickled her—but Maggilee laughed. "All right, darling, have what you want. Anything—"

Shouts and laughter from the street two stories below. Local young fellows with a little too much hard cider, or maybe that strong stuff brought down from the mountain counties. Someone fired a heavy pistol. The sound reverberated near the house so loudly it sounded as if it were in the room with her.

She quickly left the second floor, went up the narrow third flight . . . "Here under the roof is where we do all the sewing and altering, darling. It's not such a *nice* place but it's terribly important—"

Shelley sneezed and Maggilee looked around and sighed. "You're right, it's awfully dusty up here."

She set Shelley on an old cushion on the floor where Biddie had rested her feet as she sewed in the rocking chair. "Stay right there." Shelley dug her hands into the cushion while Maggilee set the candle on a shelf and went to the window. It was stuck and hard to raise. She pressed and hammered but it wouldn't budge. Finally she got Biddie's shears and pried the window up.

Almost immediately she heard a voice on the street two and a half stories below. "What the hell did you do, Timby? Where'd you get Pa's pistol?"

The boy speaking must be Sean Corrigan. The reckless shot was his older brother's, big, swaggering Timby Corrigan. Both were clearly pretty much under the weather.

"Li'l target practice. Case we see Sholto."

"What d'you want to do, kill somebody?"

"Jus' li'l scare, is all."

"Well, come away from there." Sean's voice got louder. "What in tarnation were you doing at that window?"

Maggilee started nervously and looked out the open window. "Sean? Timby!"

Timby must be around the side of the house by the open window on the ground floor . . . She couldn't see him, but she made out brown-eyed Sean in the moonlight looking up at her, his dark hair tousled by the night breeze and whiskey.

" 'Evening, Miss Maggilee. You shouldn't be up there all alone."

"I'll be all right. You boys been having a little fun?"

Sean sounded embarrassed. "Timby doesn't mean any harm. He just got kind of carried away. Can't you do anything with that captain of yours? We're just about done arguing."

Timby came running up to join his brother. Maggilee called down, "He'll be taking your deal tomorrow, boys, don't worry."

Timby waved this aside. "Ma'm, I think—"

Sean looked off into the darkness beside the house. "I smell smoke."

Timby began again. ". . . gotta get water from Gamble's. You got a li'l fire going downstairs. Guess when I shot that lamp a yours the oil caught fire on some white stuff. Veils or something." He hurried off toward the back street to Gamble's Hay, Grain and Feed.

While Sean was rushing to the open window on the first floor, Maggilee had no time to feel anything except fear for her daughter. She swung around to pick up Shelley, to get her out of the building and then put out the fire. With three flights of stairs to negotiate, there weren't even seconds to spare.

But Shelley wasn't there.

CHAPTER 17

* * *

MAGGILEE'S PANIC was a seizure. She frantically began to call. "Sweetheart, where are you? Cry out. Make a noise. *Anything.*" She ran around the dimly lighted room under the low, slanting roof, pushing furniture out of the way, knocking over Irene Wychfield's specially created wax model of her figure. The shelves? Nothing but wrapped packages and bits and pieces of trimming, spools of thread, beads, needle cases, odds and ends.

She looked at the door. She had left it open. Could

Shelley have crawled down the stairs? Shelley had crawled the length of the long river veranda a few hours ago, but that hadn't involved a steep flight of badly carpeted stairs. She rushed down the stairs, hearing a great noise of thumping and pounding on the street floor. Sean was obviously fighting to smother the fire. Worse. Now smoke had begun to seep upward to the second floor. She coughed as she threw bolts of yardage everywhere around the room, all the while calling out, "Shelley? . . . Where are you, sweetheart? Don't play tricks on Mama . . ."

Sean called from downstairs in a strained voice, "Miss Maggilee, get out quick! It's caught the drapes."

She dropped the bolt of gold satin and it spilled over the floor behind her as she went to the staircase leading up from the Salon. She screamed, "Sean, my baby's gone. Shelley's lost. Please, *please help me* . . ."

She caught herself in the midst of this horror, took a breath and looked all around again carefully, even behind the door. She heard herself calling for Shelley over and over, and worried that her voice sounded so shrill it might frighten the baby to remain hidden. She began again, overturning everything in the second-floor room before it occurred to her that Shelley might have crawled into the adjoining storeroom. With a shaking hand she carried the candle into the storeroom, heard faint sounds . . . went through every box and every shelf. Shelley was not in here.

A shadow crossed the doorway. She turned, hoping against hope—one of the Corrigan boys, Sean it was, staring around terrified, his thick brown hair all disheveled and his right jacket sleeve smoking.

"You're on fire!" she cried out.

He beat it out with his other hand while he swung out

onto the stair landing, looked into the other room and returned to her in a leap. "We've got to find her and get out. The men from Gamble's are downstairs with a bucket brigade at the back of the house but my God, Miss Maggi, everything in this building could feed that fire. It's all so dry and dusty. And all that thin, gauzy stuff . . ."

She could hardly get the words out. "Oh, Sean, I've looked everywhere." Then she screamed. "Shelley! *Answer me!*"

He caught her hand. "Didn't you hear that?"

She listened, trying not to breathe the acrid smoke that now rolled up the stairs, blotting out all view of the ground floor.

"But I've looked. Each floor. Everywhere. See?" She tore away boxes, broken furniture, flammable materials, scattering them over the floor. "Look. Even behind the door!" She ran past him to the other room. "Behind this door too!"

At the same time she and the boy both looked up at the low-ceilinged sewing room. She stared up at that door which had closed behind her as she ran down the steep attic stairs. The smoke was now so thick she could feel the heat from the flames below. In minutes the fire would be climbing the stairs to the second floor. She and Sean Corrigan were coughing so much they couldn't hear each other, but he started up the attic stairs two at a time, pushed open the door with Maggilee close behind him.

There was no mistaking the howl that went up this time. Left in darkness and in panic the baby had pressed against the door where her mother and the precious light had disappeared. Sean pushed the door open against her.

As Maggilee picked her up, smothering her with kisses, she saw that Shelley had dragged the blanket with her, and this had acted as a cushion when the door was pushed open against her. She was more scared than hurt. Maggilee turned around with the baby loosely covered by the blanket, and started back down the stairs after Sean. But it was too late. The fire had reached the second floor, which was now invisible behind the clouds of deadly smoke.

"No!" Sean began to back up the stairs, holding an arm out to bar Maggilee, who stumbled backward on the stairs above him. In the attic he slammed the door, ignoring Maggilee's frantic protest that they'd all be trapped.

He elbowed her aside, got to the open window and pushed it up as high as it would go. By now the night was broken by the yells and cries of the anxious and the curious, along with a bucket brigade of local merchants working to stem the flames that had leaped from the bolts of fabric to the wall of the hundred-year-old wooden house.

A woman screamed as the crowd saw Maggilee rush to the window with Shelley Ann.

"There's people—there's a baby up there!"

"I'll get a ladder from Gamble's," one of the men called, and ran off, but smoke was already seeping under the door.

Sean said, "We'll have to get out the window."

Shaking, Maggilee protested it was three stories. "I'll get down by the rain-spout. Somehow. Then you throw down the baby."

"No!"

"And then I'll get you down." He saw the desperate indecision in her face and said quietly, "I swear it. We did it, us Corrigans. And we'll get you out."

Young as he was, she had to believe him. She watched him climb out and, gripping the windowsill, feel with his feet for the old water-spout. It looked terribly weak, and he had no sooner started to shinny down than everyone heard the warning crack of the spout tearing loose from the house.

In the street below, Stonewall Gamble and Jem Faire had come on the run from the livery stable, Jem still in the dark funeral clothes he had worn in the afternoon. Maggilee heard him order someone to get a stout blanket. Sean Corrigan tried to get down a few yards closer to the street before letting go but the rusted water-spout now pulled away entirely and in the midst of screams and shouts from those watching, he had to drop free. He fell to the dirt street with one foot cruelly twisted under him. An instant later he was on one foot, dragging the other, and hobbling back to try to reach Maggilee. Neighbors and bystanders stopped him. Maggilee watched him being carried away, and knew she dared not risk her baby in such a fall.

While Gamble stood with his legs apart, rooted to the street, Jem put one foot in Gamble's heavy, cupped hands, and climbed up to the window frame above the first floor. Tongues of fire licked at the wax mannequin in the window, but the frame and the glass were not yet burning. With one hand grasping at the window frame and Gamble's body trembling slightly beneath him, Jem called out to Maggilee.

"Now. The baby!"

"I can't. I can't!"

Maggilee glanced quickly over her shoulder. The roar of the flames was so close she knew the attic stairs must be gone. She still dared not drop the baby alone, what had happened to Sean could happen to Shelley. Desperate, a caged animal, she swung around, trying to find another way to safety for the baby.

"It's only a few feet. Do it!" Jem ordered her.

She pulled the blanket tighter around Shelley, whose

eyes peered up at her. She stretched her body over the windowsill and reached down as far as she could with the bundled child. Jem's arm reached up. She could almost touch his hand. She let the baby go. He caught the bundle as a sigh swept over the crowd below. He held it against his body, and after measuring the distance to the ground, let go of the window frame and dropped lightly.

One of the women took the baby and called up to Maggilee, "She's right as a trivet. All safe, Miss Maggilee."

Maggilee felt the heat and the smoke searing her lungs as she tried to breathe in fresh night air, but found it tainted with specks of flying debris and dust and smoke. She saw Timby Corrigan making his way through the crowd with a stepladder, much too short.

Coughing incessantly, trying now to breathe with her face pressed against her dress sleeve, she instructed herself not to worry. Shelley was safe on the ground. "All safe," someone had called to her. Wearily, she let herself lean against the windowsill. Death must be like this, a buzzing in the head, and the dark night world all full of red cartwheels like the Fourth of July.

Somewhere a male voice—Stonewall Gamble?—insisted, "I'll get her, I got more meat on me. Don't want to drop her."

Her lungs and throat were raw. Still, she couldn't stop coughing. Heavy hands pulled her off the windowsill.

She screamed once, and then the buzzing in her head stopped.

. . . Isn't as bad as I thought, she told herself . . . Death is peace . . .

* * *

Ellen had ordered dinner served late, just before sunset, so that their closest friends and neighbors could come directly from the cemetery to Fairevale. During the meal, the guests, who included the Judge and Persis Warrender as well as Major and Irene Wychfield, Eliza was considerably cheered by the judge's solicitude for her feelings. Ellen also managed to appear more cheerful as she heard the reminiscences about her husband's past, but her thoughts, in spite of herself, returned to Jem. She knew he had remained in town after the burial in the Confederate Cemetery. His absence both relieved and troubled her now. She needn't keep pretending the indifference that was necessary when she and Jem were together, but a part of her, not at all sensible, wanted desperately to catch a glimpse of him again, to have him near her, even if they had to keep to the rigid rules she had laid down.

Shortly after dark the guests left. Eliza and Ellen were left alone in the large river parlor, which seemed even emptier without the big, warm personality of Rowdon Faire to fill it.

It was Eliza who broke the painful silence. "Ellie, you don't think I'm wicked, do you?"

Ellen, whose own conscience was none too clear, shook her head vigorously. "That's the silliest thing I've ever heard from you. No, Eliza. You certainly aren't wicked . . ."

"You know, Ellen," she went on, "I'm so *proud* to be loved by a man like the judge . . . Why, he's one of the most distinguished men in Virginia. I heard Major Wychfield say the judge puts him in mind of General Lee. In looks and all. Papa would understand my being happy, don't you think?"

"I *know* he would. He told me so," and she repeated his last words about what he wanted for his daughter.

Finally, when Eliza had gone to bed to dream of future happiness, reinforced by Ellen's assurances that her father would approve, Ellen could wander through the big house, feel her husband's presence in every room. She looked forward to seeing Eliza married and settled with the judge. She herself had given some thought to getting a job at a shop in Richmond. She felt she could offer experience in the yard goods or alterations departments. She wasn't very fond of cities, but she reckoned a person could get used to almost anything, if she had to . . .

Just before turning in she walked along the portico looking out at the river, at Wychfield Hall and further along the east bank at Gaynor House, the house of her other life. She thought of her old rivalries with her mother . . . Maggilee, she called her, in an unnatural attempt to compete . . . a situation that had on both their sides made it so difficult for them to be like other mothers and daughters . . . And yet, they *were* family, there *was* a tie of blood that had been finally—or so it surely seemed—sundered when that damned Sholto came riding in—

Suddenly her attention was caught by a glow on the dark eastern horizon . . . A fire in town. The idea sickened her . . . Gaynorville was small, largely wooden, anything could happen . . . She pulled her shawl tighter around her shoulders and watched anxiously. Smoke rolled up, first white, then black, full of specks and bits of debris hardly visible at this distance, but presently to her great relief all the light died down except vagrant puffs of smoke.

The air off the river was chilly and damp. She went inside, but the worry about that fire in town hung over her while she bathed in the big tin tub brought up for the purpose. At least her concern over this fresh worry kept her from reliving the day's burial. She glanced out the window afterward, but the town on the far horizon looked quiet and dark.

Thank heaven for that!

She got into the ancient bed and lay there, wide

awake, her mind now cluttered with images of the day's events. There actually had been two good moments . . . one when Judge Warrender had proposed publicly to Miss Eliza, the other the secret moment in the church when Jem had told her that he would always love her . . .

She was still lying sleepless, intimidated by the remembered presence of the man who had shared the bed, when someone knocked sharply on the bedroom door.

She sat up. "Yes? Who is it?"

Jem opened the door and came in.

"Jem, what is it? Something's happened—"

"There was a fire. They need you."

"I knew it!" She looked up at him. But why would anyone need her? Cold with fear, she asked, "Who needs me?"

His hands were gentle on her shoulders, above the neckline of her nightgown. "Gaynor's burned tonight, Ellen . . . an accident . . . Your mother and the baby were there but—"

"Oh, God!" She broke away, got out of bed and began to rummage through the wardrobe for her clothes, afraid to ask how they were.

He followed her. "The baby is fine—"

"And—Mama?"

"It was the smoke mostly, made her unconscious until we got her home. The younger Corrigan boy was badly crippled trying to save her. She's been what they call delirious since then . . . rambling . . . Miss Varina insists it doesn't make sense but Sholto told me you might know. She kept saying some name . . . Clinton, Kinton?"

Eliza called from the hall. "What is it? Why is everybody up?"

Jem went out to explain, and for the first time Ellen noticed that his black suit was torn, burned. His straight black hair hung lank around his face. There were bloodstains on the left side of his temple where he'd reopened the cut he'd suffered weeks earlier.

While Ellen hurriedly dressed, Eliza went along to Ellen's room, found her trying to fasten the buttons on her dress with cold, nervous fingers, and finished the job for her. "Well, she is your mother, after all, and I respect your daughterly feelings." Ellen distractedly hugged her, then hurried off with Jem, who had left word for a Fairevale horse and old-fashioned gig to be ready.

As they rattled across the Ooscanoto Bridge and down the other side, Ellen said, "I don't know any Kinton, or Clinton, although the name does sound familiar. Kinton something . . . Might have been someone who worked at Gaynor . . ." The connection continued to elude her until they were passing the Wychfield turnoff and she thought of Major Wychfield.

Jem felt her catch her breath and put out one arm to bring her close to him.

"Cold?"

"No. Jem, I think I remember! It was *Major* Clinton something. During—no . . . right after the War . . ."

He looked at her. "Don't tell me you remember 'right after the War?'"

"I just remember his name mentioned once or twice when I was a child. I was playing with Daisy and Bertha-Winn over at Wychfield. Seems to me Mrs. Wychfield made a sign for her to be quiet. It was all very mysterious."

They soon were within sight of the rooftops of Gaynor House. She sat up nervously, as if she could still hear her grandmother's stern admonition, "Straight back, my girl!"

Jem's arm remained around her. "Are you still of a

mind to let me go off to Santa Fe alone?"

She looked at him. "I don't know. I don't know what's right any more. You going one way, me another."

"You and I belonged together two years ago. That's what's right. Unless—" His hesitation made her look up quickly. "Unless you, too, think you might mistake me for a damned redskin-bastard—"

She could only stare at him, remembering that final intemperate—if perhaps understandable—outburst of the colonel . . . At the time Jem had seemed to take it in stride . . . Was it possible that he now actually could believe her capable of thinking of him as . . . ? Fury overcame the shock as she shook off his arm. "Jem, if you believe such a vile thing, you can't possibly want me, much less love me."

He made no direct answer, merely nodded as he pulled up in front of Gaynor House and she got out before he could lift her down. They went in together, very conscious of each other, their bodies with little but a pulse-beat between them, and yet they did not speak.

As they went through the lower hall behind Edward Hone, Ellen kept remembering all the times when her mother's charm had overwhelmed her, covering any resentment, loneliness or bitterness she might feel. "Delirium" had a dreadful sound. Medical conditions, which had improved so much as a result of the War, still couldn't conquer strange things like mental illness, or that perennial disease, galloping consumption. It would be terrible to think of her dying when they hadn't made up their quarrel . . . her mother never knowing that she wasn't responsible for the sale of her precious shop . . . The shop! Jem had said it was destroyed . . . Ironic. Bill needn't have bothered with all his conniving to take it from her . . .

Hone, always known for his devotion to Maggilee,

was telling Ellen, "She asked for you, Miss Ellen. Dr. Nickels is with her now. She coughed so much he's had to coat her throat with an essence that should soothe the pain. She refused laudanum until the captain persuaded her." He ignored Jem, confided to Ellen, "She calls Captain Sholto 'Clinton.' He is very upset . . . He hoped you might help clear up her confusion."

"May I see her now?"

Jem made no move to go with her, nor did Hone show any sign of inviting him. Ellen looked back and called to Jem, who was turning away, "Please wait for me." He didn't seem to hear her. She leaned over the banister. "Please, Jem."

Finally, he looked up and smiled. Ellen thanked God for that and followed the butler. To her surprise he took her past her mother's room to the big river-corner room, which had belonged to Varina as long as Ellen could remember.

Varina herself stood in the hall looking as if she didn't know where to go, or what to do. Ellen reached out to her and kissed her cheek before going into the bedroom where Maggilee had been taken. Varina did not return the kiss but hesitatingly touched Ellen's shoulder. When Ellen went in to see her mother, Varina remained in the hall, still looking uncharacteristically lost. Could the prospect of Maggilee's death upset her so much . . .?

Jonathan was in the room, silent as usual. Dr. Nickels and Bill Sholto were on either side of the bed, Bill holding Maggilee's limp hand, the doctor bent close over her, raising one of her eyelids. She was breathing heavily, with effort.

The doctor looked around as Ellen came to the bedside. "Good. Mrs. Sholto called for you several times, Mrs. Faire."

"How is she?" Ellen asked, taking up her mother's other hand in hers.

Dr. Nickels shook his head. "I don't like the sound of her breathing. But when she regains consciousness, we may begin to hope. She seems to have sustained prolonged shock—"

"No wonder," Bill reminded them all in a broken voice. "Trying to get the baby out. Not knowing if they would both—"

Maggilee's eyelids flickered. Everyone crowded closer. The doctor waved them all back.

"Yes, Mrs. Sholto?"

"B-baby?" she managed to whisper.

"Safe and sound, sweetheart," her husband cut in.

A smile flickered around her mouth. "Ellie?"

"I'm here, Mama." Ellen pressed her hand.

"Sorry, honey . . . made—mistake."

"It's all right . . ." Ellen didn't bother to look at Bill. He clearly was suffering enough.

Dr. Nickels, showing relief, said, "Hush, now. Don't lacerate that throat more."

Her eyes closed tiredly, she seemed asleep . . . Suddenly she spoke a name aloud, her voice hoarse but distinct.

"Clinton . . ."

Bill caressed her hand. Ellen had never seen him so unnerved. "Sweetheart, it's Bill. It's Bill—"

The doctor interrupted then. "You are disturbing my patient, I'll have to ask you to leave, all of you."

Bill was so reluctant to go Dr. Nickels agreed that he might remain, providing he promised not to speak to Maggilee again until given permission. He nodded, but did not let go of his wife's hand.

Ellen went out with Jonathan. As the door closed

behind them and they stood in the hall, Ellen said firmly to her cousin, "You know all about Major Clinton, don't you?"

Jonathan hesitated. Ellen looked over her shoulder, but they were alone in the hall.

"I want to know, Jonathan. God knows, it's past time."

He opened the next door, which was the master bedroom, and drew her in. "The secret belongs to some others. It's not all mine, but, all right, I'll tell you about Major Clinton Dalkett. Then I want you to give me your word you will never mention it to them that's concerned."

She went before him into the lamplit room, hugging her arms. She felt cold, more apprehensive than ever. "All right. Who was he? I know Mama loves Bill . . . so why does she keep calling for Major Clinton?"

"There's reasons, Ellen. I'm sorry anybody else has to know. We'd all be the better for it if we could forget."

CHAPTER 18

* * *

IT WAS a blurred version of a room associated with exquisite happiness. The man war-torn Tudor County called "The Bluecoat Major" must be holding one of her hands . . . She felt the familiar gentle pressure of his thumb along her palm.

What a curious dream. She closed her eyes tightly, her free hand wandering across the counterpane to the right post of the bed. She felt the smooth, rounded shape of the mahogany. Yes. This was the bed she had come to on her wedding night with the handsome, fair-haired Beau Gaynor.

And yes, she'd known the facts of life on her wedding day, but none of the pain and pleasures of it, which during the brief time of her marriage she began to feel novelists had highly overrated. Beau was a lover who satisfied himself, then rolled over and went to sleep, apparently proud of having done his duty. When she'd tried to enjoy herself by initiating overtures with his body, he was annoyed and warned her not to be common . . . "It's what I took you away from, Maggilee . . . You don't want Ma to hear the springs rattling and creaking, do you?" He'd laughed then. "How Ma hated giving up this room! But it's the master room and when I heard the news about Pa, first thing I told her was the big river-corner bedroom was mine now." . . . And how Varina had disliked her new daughter-in-law. Well, she'd made up her mind at once that she'd rather be hated than despised . . . She never let Varina get away with a thing, made her take second place, while her precious son Beau was alive, anyway . . .

Then she was pregnant, which she resented because Beau had no interest whatever in being a father, promptly left Gaynor Plantation in the hands of the women and their field workers under a dishonest overseer who'd managed to wheedle his way into Beau's high regard . . . The carefully tended, cultivated fields, the produce with its proud Gaynor name, began to fail. After Ellen was born, even Varina couldn't make unwilling slaves work, or an overseer show honest accounts, and Beau . . . Beau Gaynor was careful not to return home to such troubles. No . . . dashing Beau formed attachments in northern Virginia, and died by a sniper's bullet while returning to bivouac from a visit to his latest young lady.

Maggilee's fingers rubbed the bedpost, reliving a time over twenty years in the past, a part of her consciousness still in the present, hearing Dr. Nickels' voice as though from far away . . . "She seems delirious again, it's probably the pain and, of course, the shock . . ."

No, she thought, hearing someone cough, I'm not delirious, not at all . . . It's 1865, I know the year so well, never forget . . . Soon I'm going to meet an officer from the Federal troops occupying Tudor County. He's going to be tall, a powerful man with close-cropped, curly gray hair and an air of command that will impress even Varina . . . Odd how I know all these things before they happen . . .

He will come riding up to Gaynor House in his dusty blue uniform with his troops behind him, and the house servants who still remain will stand on the east porch with me, proud but not making a show. Not like Varina, who will sweep imperiously to the only good chair in the river parlor. She will wait there for Major Clinton Dalkett and his lieutenant and a bullying sergeant. Varina, a queen who refuses to be deposed . . .

She sighed, tried to hug her body with anticipation, but someone was holding one of her hands. It couldn't be Major Dalkett. She hadn't met him yet. She moved on, reliving those strange, wonderful days that followed the turning of Virginia Commonwealth into a Federal District policed by Union troops and ravaged by carpetbagging politicians. Gaynor House became the headquarters for the major and his officers because at the more imposing Wychfield Hall Mrs. Wychfield was in labor with a boy who died at birth. She remembered how kind she thought the Bluecoat major was to leave the sick woman and her family in their own home. She and her family were moved out to the Ferry House with her infant Shelley Ann . . . no, it was Ellen, of course, yes . . . Major Clinton Dalkett was resented by everybody except her . . . She understood how much he hated the orders he had to give, and tried in special ways to make things easier, always sending the Gaynors foods they hadn't seen nor eaten during the whole last year of the War, not to mention blankets and firewood in the fall, and when Varina had a bad sciatica attack he asked that the family be moved back to greater comfort in the main house, but his colonel refused to permit it . . . Of course all of this went clear over Varina's head. She loathed the military intruders and every time she met Major Dalkett on the grounds she called him "my son's murderer," even though the major had been nowhere near McLean when Beau Gaynor died . . . Then one day the major sent down a whole baked ham, with vegetables and a pan of spoon bread, and Varina managed to tip the elegant china platter upside down all over the young lieutenant who delivered the food, saying, "It was ours to begin with, and as long as that—that murderer sleeps in the room in which my son was born—the bedroom my husband and I shared for twenty-five years—I shall continue to refuse his charity." . . .

That was how it began. She had walked up toward Gaynor House, met the major in the woods by the river and apologized to him, which led to a lovely, quiet chat that lasted over two hours. The remote Union major turned out to be a very lonely man, not easy to know, but to a girl widowed only months after marriage, alone and lonely, with a new child and a hateful mother-in-law, he was a man to respond to, to be drawn to and appreciate.

The first meeting led to others, which she told herself were "accidental." She ached to be loved by him. His reticence, in spite of what she sensed as a desire for her, made him even more appealing to her. Inevitably their meetings led to the master bedroom in Gaynor House, and it was there that she—and perhaps the major, too—learned how much joy the body could give, and receive.

Together she and Clinton Dalkett were supremely happy. They would like there, naked in the summer nights, entwined in a unity that neither had ever believed possible, her body within his arms, his body sheathed within hers, and sometimes they would talk of the future, how they would marry someday, it didn't matter when. Yes, he was married, but his feeling for her overwhelmed anything else. He'd gone home to Illinois for a brief reconciliation attempt with his wife, testing, even trying to forget what he felt for the red-haired rebel beauty in Virginia. It was his last visit. Nothing could take her place and his wife acknowledged it too. In fact, she made it clear she was relieved her interests and his had grown years apart. When he came back his marriage was over, and his life had begun.

And for me, too, she thought.

"I never knew anyone like you," he had said, and though she had heard more than one man say as much to her, she *believed* Clinton. It was as if the old cliché became new on his lips. She loved his lips. They were the betrayal of the feelings he held so carefully in check, feelings that reminded her of . . .

"Bill Sholto . . ."

She heard herself saying the name aloud. Her hand was grasped more tightly, and she felt a drop of water fall on her cheek . . . no, it was tears . . . Someone was crying over her . . .

"You see, Captain, she is coming around," Dr. Nickels was saying.

She objected silently. She didn't want these intruders to take her away from her memories, from her wonderful, loving nights with Clinton Dalkett . . .

Usually Varina and Jonathan and the baby Ellen had appeared to be asleep when she returned to the Ferry in the late hours of the night. During the day Varina sat staring at Gaynor House, and especially at the master bedroom, which had been the birthplace of eight generations of Gaynors and Dunmores . . . "Do those devils use my son's bedroom?" she asked young Jonathan repeatedly. The boy, still limping from the thigh wound gotten while scouting Union forces on the Peninsula, would say in his quiet way, "No, ma'm. Major sleeps in the little room behind it."

"Well," Varina contradicted him, relentless as a cottonmouth, *"I know what I heard.* Biddie says there's talk among his men about him having a woman in the house. Some creature he's brought in from Ashby, I reckon. But the Lord pity him if he ever profanes my son's room."

They were all pretty much afraid of Varina, and Jonathan was careful to hide from her the shotgun he used to shoot game for food during these hard days. . . .

Varina considered this bed sacred, Maggilee reflected as the palm of her free hand moved gently over the counterpane. "You were right, Varina. It was sacred to us—"

Suddenly her dream was disturbed. Was it possible she had been wrong about this bed, that it was somehow horrible? A nightmare? She screamed, the sound wrenched from her smoke-lacerated throat. She tried to sit up but was restrained, forced back.

"No, no, you don't *understand,"* she cried out. *"It's all covered with blood!"*

Her eyes opened. She looked around, dazed, and saw Bill Sholto. Alive. The bloody memories were gone. Whatever Bill had done to her no longer mattered as much as his presence, the anxious love in his eyes. She studied him with surprise. "You mustn't cry over me," she told him hoarsely. "Just kiss me."

* * *

"They became lovers," Ellen prompted Jonathan. "I can see how it might be, knowing how Mama has always needed men."

Jonathan went on wearily . . . "About that room, the one you always thought of as your grandmother's bedroom, Major Dalkett didn't sleep there. Reckon he had taste enough to know it wouldn't set well with the ladies in the County. It was real fancy, the bed curtains, the tester and all. But when he and Maggilee got involved, it just seemed the furtherest away from his men who were in and out of the lower floor, and that corner room was always locked, to keep out any light-fingered men in his company."

Ellen pressed her fingers, hard as she could, against each other to relive some of the tension that had built up with her cousin's remarkable story. There were moments in it when she'd thought of her mother with near-disgust, but Jonathan, with his rare understanding, put it in decent perspective . . . "I saw them in the woods now and then," he told her. "I believe it was real, honest love. I never saw Maggie so beautiful as during those days."

"And then, there was her daughter Ellen," Ellen said ironically. But she heard the self-pity in her comment and winced. "I'm sorry, I know this somehow was a tragedy for Mama . . . Tell me."

Jonathan's long strides took him to the door as though retreating. Ellen reached out and touched his arm.

"You love her very much, don't you, Cousin?"

He turned away from the door. "I surely did."

"Did? Jonathan, don't say that. When did you change?"

He slapped one fist into the other palm. "I don't rightly know if I ever did. But maybe it started when Aunt

Varina began scouting around Gaynor House. I told her to stay away. It mightn't be safe. Nope. She said there was hussies up there in the bed where all the Gaynors was born and she meant to order them out. Scare 'em, she said. I kept my shotgun hid when I wasn't using it, but that's not the only kind of guns that's around an army headquarters."

Ellen held her breath, sensed what was coming.

Jonathan shrugged. "There was a race going on over the Wychfield Estate road. The house was empty. Aunt Varina went over there as usual. Or so Biddie told me. I got concerned and went after her. She must've seen something move in that bedroom. The curtain. Or a shadow. She walked right in. Major Dalkett usually had an aide or somebody downstairs. The lad had sneaked out with the servants to watch the horses come by the Gaynor turnoff. Aunt Varina walked right up the stairs. The door was locked, but she had her own key. Major Dalkett's belt was hanging on the hall-tree near the door. She reached in as nice as you please and pulled out his own gun."

Ellen closed her eyes. "Cold-blooded murder."

"Hot-blooded. The idea just hit her. The weapon was to hand and she fired point blank at Dalkett on the bed. Got him right in the chest. He died in Maggilee's arms. Matter of seconds, I'd say. That's how I came on them."

Ellen reminded herself that Jonathan had been a boy of seventeen . . . "Dear Jonathan—"

And he surprised her, this so undemonstrative man. He let her put her arms around him. His rough hand caressed her hair.

His voice he managed to keep steady as he went on . . . "Maggilee looked like one of those women in the old Greek books. Her hair was every which way. She wasn't wearing—she had on her petticoat. It was all covered with blood. She pointed at Aunt Varina and kept saying over and over, 'I'll see you hanged for it. They'll hang you . . .' Aunt Varina looked kind of dazed, like the whole thing was a big surprise to her and she didn't know how she got mixed in with such people. She still had that heavy pistol in her hand . . . Well, I explained the facts to them. There'd be a long trial and all about Maggilee and the major would come out and you, an innocent child, would be ruined for life, and then everybody'd line up and watch 'em put the black hood on Aunt Varina's head, and after she was on the scaffold they'd tie her skirts around her like a bale of hay so's not to shock anybody by seeing her limbs when the trap fell—"

"Jonathan . . . *don't.*"

"That's how it was with Mary Surratt, you know. And they weren't even sure about her guilt in the Lincoln conspiracy. So that's when I did the thing. The thing that I wish to God I never had to do."

"But you had to save Grandma . . . all of us."

"I'll say one thing, once she caught on to what we had to do, Maggilee had gumption. We cleared up all the sheets and her petticoat and wrapped the major in them. Then we got him out the back stairs and into the wagon. I drove him the long way to Gaynorville and waited till dark. Then I left him beside that tavern near Winchester House. I spilled moonshine over him. So much was going on those days they all jumped to the notion he'd gotten in a drunken fight over a girl. His men scoured the countryside but it got to be common gossip about how he died. Anybody with a good word for him got nothing but laughs . . . You know, I wouldn't have minded so much if he'd been bad. Drinking and wenching and all. But him being so decent, that's the rotten thing—"

"And those two women have lived together all these years with that secret . . ."

It surely explained a great deal, and Jonathan provided even more. "Maggilee went to work in town, first at Slagel's Hardware and then at a yard-goods store in Ashby. She managed to keep you and Varina and me till I got on my feet and then she lent me money to get my own fields planted. And pretty soon she was putting down a payment to buy that old house for Gaynor's Salon."

And now it's gone, Ellen thought. "But how did Mama get the money?"

'Blackmail. She made Aunt Varina give her the Gaynor pearls, all that silver, even the old tureen and the big, ugly silver thing that set in the middle of the dining-room table before the War. Every valuable we'd all buried in the woods in '64 when the Yankees were prowling around the James. She took it all and sold it to Yankees and God knows where else. But it kept us alive and it saved Varina from losing her beloved Gaynor House. And it put Maggie in business."

The cousins stood there together in silence. Out in the hall there were voices and someone called Ellen's name. Jonathan opened the door.

Doc Nickels said, "I thought you would want to know, Mrs. Faire. Your mother is conscious now. It looks as though she's going to be just fine, given a decent rest."

Ellen looked at Jonathan. The same thought was in both their minds. Would Maggilee ever be "just fine" again? With the memories of that old love, and his awful death? . . . "May we go in?"

The doctor nodded. As Ellen passed him, going into the bedroom which had seen the birth of so many Gaynors and the murder of one Major Clinton Dalkett, she glanced into the dark corner of the hall and was startled to see Varina still standing where she had been when Ellen and Jem arrived. It seemed a lifetime ago, though it must have been no more than an hour. Varina gave Jonathan a searching look, moved forward, straight-backed as always. Her usually proud face, though, looked shockingly crumpled and old.

"Ellen, child, he told you?"

Ellen nodded, thinking of all the pain Varina had brought—and suffered—the scars that her mother and Jonathan would carry to their graves. She found she couldn't speak, not even to give her grandmother the forgiveness her eyes obviously pleaded for. Her thoughts had switched to Jem. Would he turn away from her because she hadn't given him the answer that would mean real happiness to them both? Long ago her mother had been truly happy, perhaps for the only time in her life. Ellen wondered if she now was about to lose her chance at real happiness—with Jem.

"Ellie?" her mother was calling hoarsely. Ellen looked back, wanting to call to Jem, to ask him to wait for her, but she went into the big corner bedroom.

Maggilee looked somewhat better. Her hair had been combed and brushed and lay like flames against the pillows. Little Shelley Ann, cradled in her father's arms, was sound asleep, having apparently forgotten the disaster which almost destroyed her and her mother. Maggilee had her hand on the baby's blanket, but her gaze was fixed on her husband. Whatever memories had been stirred up by her experience in the fire and the truth about the sale of Gaynor's, everything seemed forgiven now.

Ellen felt hugely relieved. She understood so many things now. And most of all she understood her greatest desire—that she would have given a hundred shops and great houses, including the Gaynor and Fairevale land, to know she could be Jem Faire's wife . . .

Maggilee asked, with some flash of her old charm, "Can you forgive me for my old foolishness, honey?"

Ellen held out her hand, and her mother took it in her free hand. Tired as she was, her eyes sparkled. "Now I have all I love, right in my hands."

Bill leaned across the bed to Ellen. "This lady is going to have her shop back. A new one. We'll see to it."

"Is anything left of the old building?" Ellen asked, hoping he hadn't lied to Maggilee again.

He shook his head. "Nothing but a shell. Doesn't matter, though. We'll mortgage the land. Do something. She'll get her shop."

Ellen smiled. "Seems you have quite a bit to live for, Mama, so get well quickly."

"I will, honey. I promise. We're a family now, Bill and Shelley Ann and me. And Ellie dear, I hope you'll find your own happiness one day." She tried to sit up, then, and when everyone stopped her she waved them away. "Ellen, darling, if there's one thing I hope you've learned from what happened to me, hold onto your happiness. Enjoy it while you can. As I assure you I intend to."

"She's absolutely right," Bill said.

Lord, Ellen thought . . . he's been crying . . . She kissed her mother on the cheek, wished her well, and smiled at Bill.

Out in the hall, Varina was waiting. She stood directly in Ellen's way. She had even recovered some of her old imperious look. Her voice was gruff as usual. "My girl, are you going to leave without even a word for me?"

Ellen stared at her, seeing flicker across that haughty facade a shadow of the pain . . . perhaps even shame . . . that she'd carried since the night she'd shot a man to death, an act that had all but shattered the lives of three generations of Gaynor women.

Varina's feet seemed rooted to the spot, as if to wear down Ellen's resistance. No need for that. Ellen reached out and embraced her . . . not the murderess of so long ago, but the indomitable spirit of the woman today.

She left Varina then, ran down to Edward Hone, who came out of the dining room.

"Where is he? Is he still here?"

The butler shook his head, and as Ellen in panic started to the door, he said after her, "Mister Jem harnessed the gig and the horse for you. He said to tell you one thing."

Ellen had the door open. She stopped. "What was it?"

"He said the Gaynors would always have you, that you could never escape them."

"Thank you, Hone."

Ellen went out into the moonlight. The stableboy had the gig ready. She got in. The boy let the fretting horse go, and she signaled over the reins. In seconds he was trotting along the estate road.

Jem Faire's lean figure stood out against the moonlit white road. He was striding along at a fast pace. She called to him but he made no response. It took a few minutes of fast work to reach him. He looked up as she drew alongside him. The moonlight appeared to gleam in his eyes. It was almost like that first ride he had given her, when his honest emotion had scared the silly innocent that she was.

"Can I give you a ride, Mister Jem?"

"To where?"

"To wherever in the world you want to go, if I can go with you."

"No games, Ellen."

"Why not? What of the game you played with me almost two years ago?" She shook her head, added sadly,

"But I can see you've no memory of it." She allowed a smile and added, "Oh, by the way, you're wrong. I've escaped the Gaynors. Forever . . ."

He reached up, pulled her out of the gig with the reins dragging and the horse fidgeting.

She started to speak, but he'd clearly had enough of that. His mouth silenced her.

COPPER KINGDOM
by Iris Gower

The Llewelyns lived in Copperman's Row — a small backstreet where the women fought a constant battle against the copper dust from the smelting works. When Mali's mam died there were just the two of them left, Malia and her father, sacked from the works for taking time off to nurse his wife. Mali felt she would never hate anyone as much as she hated Sterling Richardson, the young master of the Welsh copper town.

But Sterling had his own problems — bad ones — and not least was the memory of the young green-eyed girl who had spat hatred at him on the day of her mother's death.

Copper Kingdom is the first in a sequence of novels set in the South Wales copper industry at the turn of the century.

0 552 12387 0 £1.95

LAST YEAR'S NIGHTINGALE
by Claire Lorrimer

Clementine Foster was young, unbelievably innocent and wildly in love with a man who didn't even know of her existence. When, one golden summer night, she stepped in front of his horse, he took her with all the drunken arrogance of a young aristocrat used to having whatever he wanted. The repercussions of that night were to forge bonds of hate, love, and tragedy in both their lives.

For the child that was born to Clementine ultimately appeared to be the only legitimate heir to the Grayshot inheritance. And, according to the law of the times, she had no right to keep her child if Deveril wanted him.

But Clementine was determined to recover her son, no matter what the cost, no matter what she had to do.

0 552 12565 2 £2.95

THE CHATELAINE
by Claire Lorrimer

Seventeen-year-old Willow, newly married to Rowell, Lord Rochford, believed she held not only the keys to a multitude of rooms, but also to her own happiness . . .

'The book, *Chatelaine*, is not actually a sweeping romance. Instead the characters build and build becoming more real on every page. The plot which features hidden babies, a beautiful girl marrying the wrong man and a corrupted doctor, zings along packed not only with action but with information. Miss Lorrimer has done her research and the book is not just a good read; it is a slice of life'
George Thaw, Daily Mirror

0 552 11959 8 £2.50

THE SUMMER OF THE BARSHINSKEYS
by Diane Pearson

'Engrossing saga . . . characters who compel . . . vividly alive'
Barbara Taylor Bradford

"Although the story of the Barshinskeys, which became our story too, stretched over many summers and winters, that golden time of 1902 was when our strange involved relationship began, when our youthful longing for the exotic took a solid and restless hold upon us . . ."

It is at this enchanted moment that *The Summer of the Barshinskeys* begins. A beautifully told, compelling story that moves from a small Kentish village to London, and from war-torn St Petersburg to a Quaker relief unit in the Volga provinces. It is the unforgettable story of two families, one English, the other Russian, who form a lifetime pattern of friendship, passion, hatred and love.

'A lovely, rich plum of a novel. Read it and enjoy'
Jacqueline Briskin

'The Russian section is reminiscent of Pasternak's *Doctor Zhivago*, horrifying yet hauntingly beautiful'
New York Tribune

'Something about the beginning of this book caught at me and I read it, then had to read it through more or less in one fell gulp. It comes across with the genuiness of a *Lark Rise to Candleford* . . . a compelling story and a splendid read'
Mary Stewart

0 552 126411   £2.95

A SCATTERING OF DAISIES
by Susan Sallis

Will Rising had dragged himself from humble beginnings to his own small tailoring business in Gloucester — and on the way he'd fallen violently in love with Florence, refined, delicate, and wanting something better for her children.

March was the eldest girl, the least loved, the plain, unattractive one who, as the family grew, became more and more the household drudge. But March, a strange, intelligent, unhappy child, had inherited some of her mother's dreams. March Rising was determined to break out of the round of poverty and hard work, to find wealth, and love, and happiness.

0 552 12375 7 £1.95

TAMARISK
by Claire Lorrimer

Tamarisk, daughter of a French Vicomte and the exquisite Mavreen, had inherited her mother's beauty — and her reckless, sensuous nature . . . All too soon she developed a passionate attachment to Sir Peregrine, Mavreen's former lover, who treated her as a child. Rejected and humiliated, Tamarisk offered herself to the most notorious poet in Europe . . . Throughout the disgrace and degradations that followed, her love still burned for Peregrine, the man whose dangerous secret she had uncovered — the secret she shared with her rival Mavreen . . .

THE RIVALRY OF TWO PASSIONATE WOMEN — MOTHER AND DAUGHTER — FOR THE LOVE OF THE SAME MAN.

112070 £2.95

THE HOUSE TRILOGY
by Norah Lofts

The Town House
The House at Old Vine
The House at Sunset

Norah Lofts's famous House trilogy spans five centuries of dramatic event told through the lives of the people who lived in the House . . .

Martin Reed — a serf whose resentment of the autocratic rule of his feudal lord finally flared into open defiance. Encouraged by the woman he loved, Martin began a new life — a life which was to culminate in the building of the House, and the founding of the dynasty who were to live there.

Josiana Greenwood — the illegitimate descendant of Martin Reed: through her, the family of the House was to be continued, living through England's most turbulent period — the Tudors, the Stuarts, the violence of Cromwell's wars.

Felicity Hatton — chance sent her to the House, first as a pauper, then as its mistress — a strange, eccentric mistress whose choice of husband was as unorthodox as her manner of living.

"The old house in Suffolk is both the link and a source of colour for . . . the people who inhabit it . . . English history finds reflection in these cameos of life and feeling"
The Scotsman

The Town House	0 552 08185 X	£1.75
The House at Old Vine	0 552 08186 8	£1.75
The House at Sunset	0 552 08187 6	£1.75

OTHER FINE NOVELS AVAILABLE FROM CORGI BOOKS

While every effort is made to keep prices low, it is sometimes necessary to increase prices at short notice. Corgi Books reserve the right to show new retail prices on covers which may differ from those previously advertised in the text or elsewhere.

The prices shown below were correct at the time of going to press.

☐	12637 3	**PROUD MARY**	*Iris Gower* £2.50
☐	12387 0	**COPPER KINGDOM**	*Iris Gower* £1.95
☐	12565 2	**LAST YEAR'S NIGHTINGALE**	*Claire Lorrimer* £2.95
☐	12182 7	**THE WILDERING**	*Claire Lorrimer* £2.50
☐	11959 8	**THE CHATELAINE**	*Claire Lorrimer* £2.50
☐	08185 X	**THE TOWN HOUSE**	*Norah Lofts* £1.75
☐	08186 8	**THE HOUSE AT OLD VINE**	*Norah Lofts* £1.75
☐	08187 6	**THE HOUSE AT SUNSET**	*Norah Lofts* £1.75
☐	12503 2	**THREE GIRLS**	*Frances Paige* £1.95
☐	12641 1	**THE SUMMER OF THE BARSHINSKEYS**	*Diane Pearson* £2.95
☐	10375 6	**CSARDAS**	*Diane Pearson* £2.95
☐	09140 5	**SARAH WHITMAN**	*Diane Pearson* £1.95
☐	10271 7	**THE MARIGOLD FIELD**	*Diane Pearson* £1.95
☐	10249 0	**BRIDE OF TANCRED**	*Diane Pearson* £1.75
☐	12607 1	**DOCTOR ROSE**	*Elvi Rhodes* £1.95
☐	12367 6	**OPAL**	*Elvi Rhodes* £1.75
☐	12579 2	**THE DAFFODILS OF NEWENT**	*Susan Sallis* £1.75
☐	12375 7	**A SCATTERING OF DAISIES**	*Susan Sallis* £1.95

ORDER FORM

All these books are available at your book shop or newsagent, or can be ordered direct from the publisher. Just tick the titles you want and fill in the form below.

CORGI BOOKS, Cash Sales Department, P.O. Box 11, Falmouth, Cornwall.

Please send cheque or postal order, no currency.

Please allow cost of book(s) plus the following for postage and packing:

U.K. Customers — Allow 55p for the first book, 22p for the second book and 14p for each additional book ordered, to a maximum charge of £1.75.

B.F.P.O. and Eire — Allow 55p for the first book, 22p for the second book plus 14p per copy for the next seven books, thereafter 8p per book.

Overseas Customers — Allow £1.00 for the first book and 25p per copy for each additional book.

NAME (Block Letters) ....

ADDRESS ....

....